THE CRIMSON SHIELD

A Medieval Romance
Part of the Executioner Knights Series

By Kathryn Le Veque

Trade Paperback Edition
Text by Kathryn Le Veque
Cover by Kim Killion

WWW.KATHRYNLEVEQUE.COM

ARE YOU SIGNED UP FOR KATHRYN'S BLOG?

You'll get the latest news and information on exclusive giveaways, exclusive excerpts, coming releases, sales, free books, cover reveals and more.

Kathryn's blog followers get it all first. No spam, no junk.

Get the latest info from the reigning Queen of English Medieval Romance!

Sign Up Here

kathrynleveque.com

He's an Executioner Knight with a royal secret that could blow England apart.

She's the last of the bloodlines from the High Kings of Ireland.

Between the two of them, they have more royal blood in them than anyone alive, but royal blood can be far more of a curse and far less of a privilege when dealing with secrets that could bring down a kingdom.

And destroy a love that was never supposed to happen.

Tristan de Royans was raised by the House of de Royans, but de Royans blood does not flow through his veins. As the secret love child of Alys of France and Henry II, Tristan has been kept hidden since the day of his birth. Aware of his true parentage, he bears the shield of the royal house in the course of his duties, hating that he bears the crimson shield of his real family.

A family that wants to kill him.

William Marshal has kept Tristan protected all these years. Having fostered in the best homes, Tristan is a knight's knight—a warrior beyond compare. The Marshal has need of Tristan's strength in Wales, protecting properties belonging to Ajax de Velt, but before Tristan can assume his post, a chance meeting changes the course of his life.

Enter Andromeda "Andie" de Coursey.

Andie is as unique as Tristan is. Her maternal grandfather is the last Norse-Gaelic King of Dublin, Ascall mac Ragnaill, and much like for Tristan, royal blood was a curse. Pursued by her grandfather's enemies, she was sent into hiding a long time ago with an Irish-Norman family who changed her name. As it turned out, King John wanted to use her as a bargaining chip when the time was right, but when he died, his ambition to utilize her died with him. Now, Andie is little more than a servant in a Norman house, hidden from the world. Her future seems bleak.

Until she meets Tristan.

The hardened Plantagenet warrior is immediately smitten with the beautiful woman with the pale blue eyes. With her bloodlines, and his, they could effectively rule nations if they were to join forces, but in their case, the relationship they form is born of love… not conquest.

But there are those who seek to use Andie in just that manner. *Conquest.*

Join Tristan and Andie in an adventure of a lifetime, where a love that was never meant to be suddenly becomes the very air they breathe. As factions endeavor to tear them apart, a love for the ages refuses to die. Tristan must bring out the king in him to survive.

And Andromeda must bring out the queen.

Love, as they discover, is the strongest force on earth.

Executioner Knights Motto

Milites umbrae et immani

Knights of Shadow and Savage

LIST OF EXECUTIONER KNIGHTS/SPIES FOR WILLIAM MARSHAL

As of 1215 A.D.

(Note: some later Executioner Knight tales take place years later, but as of 1215 A.D., this is where these knights serve and/or are in command of. Also note that while some Executioner Knights may be mentioned, not all appear in this story.)

William Marshal – Earl of Pembroke, Pembroke Castle and Farrington House

Christopher de Lohr – Earl of Hereford and Worcester, Lioncross Abbey Castle

David de Lohr – Earl of Canterbury, Canterbury Castle, Bellham Place

Peter de Lohr – Lioncross Abbey Castle, Lord Pembridge/commander Ludlow Castle

Gart Forbes – Dunster Castle, Devon

Caius d'Avignon – Richmond Castle, North Yorkshire – also Hawkstone Castle

Maxton of Loxbeare – Chalford Hill Castle, Gloucester

Kress de Rhydian – Seton Castle, Scotland

Achilles de Dere – Caversham Manor, Berkshire

Susanna de Tiegh de Dere – a Blackchurch-trained knight, wife of Achilles

Alexander de Sherrington (Christin de Lohr) – Lioncross Abbey Castle/commander, Wigmore Castle

Bric MacRohan – Narborough Castle, Norwich Castle, Norfolk

Dashiell du Reims – Ramsbury Castle, Wiltshire – also Thunderbey Castle, East Anglia.

Sean de Lara – King John's personal bodyguard

Kevin de Lara – Canterbury Castle (in the service of David de Lohr) – also Hyssington, Caradoc, and Trelystan Castles – Welsh Marches

Cullen de Nerra – Rockingham Castle, Northamptonshire

Cole de Velt – formerly William the Lion's personal guard, now at Berwick Castle, Baron Blackadder at the death of his father

Addax al-Kort – service to Christopher de Lohr and William Marshal

Essien al-Kort – service to Christopher de Lohr and William Marshal

Morgan de Wolfe – in service to Caius d'Avignon, Richmond Castle

Gareth de Llion – in service to William Marshal

Rhys du Bois – service to Christopher de Lohr/after 1201 living in France under an assumed name

Keller de Poyer – in service to William Marshal at Pembroke Castle/Nether Castle (Keller is more of a knight for William Marshal than he's actually a spy)

Garran le Mon – technically, he's believed to be dead after 1201 A.D.

Marcus Burton – Lord Somerhill and Dunnington, Somerhill Castle

Ashton de Royans – serves Ajax de Velt

Beau de Russe – serves Ajax de Velt

Tristan de Royans – serves Juston de Royans, Ajax de Velt, William Marshal. Garrison commander, Wrexham Castle

Juston de Royans *(Lord of Winter)* – an original Executioner Knight. Too old to be active at this time, but has trained most of the men listed

AUTHOR'S NOTE

Well, I finally figured it out—because I'm embarrassed to admit that I've lost track—but this is my 152nd published novel. That count doesn't include the novels I've written and lost over the years (the infamous hard drive crash about thirty years ago), so it's not "just" the 152nd novel I've written. It's the 152nd novel I have published. And I've got a dozen more half-written stories in my files I haven't finished, plus enough outlines and plots to keep me busy, releasing eight to ten novels a year, for the next ten years at least. At least seventy-five more novels to come (yes, I counted). All this to say that I really hope you like my books, because they're going to be coming for years! LOL

And with that—welcome to the thirteenth Executioner Knights story!

Even though the books aren't in any particular order (other than the first three—*By the Unholy Hand*, *The Mountain Dark*, and *Starless*, which make the most sense if they're read in that order), this is the thirteenth in the series that I've written. This is an interesting one—with an incredible premise.

What if Henry II and Alys of France (who was meant for Richard the Lionheart) had an illegitimate son? It's true that they had an affair. She was meant for Richard, but Henry had an eye for her. If you've seen the play or the movie *The Lion in Winter*, then you have seen a glimpse of their relationship.

Using the premise that they had a son (at least in my Medieval world), we met that child in *Lord of Winter*. That's the first place he popped up. Then he was mentioned in *The Dark Angel*. He's been around, but never the focus. It has been intimated that he's very, VERY much like his father in demeanor—I think it was said somewhere that he was "mean." He has the auburn hair of Henry and the Plantagenet temper.

As I mentioned, Tristan's first appearance was in *Lord of Winter* as a nine-year-old who had no idea of his true parentage. His full name is Philip Alexander Tristan, by the way. Juston de Royans, the hero of *Lord of Winter*, makes it very clear in the epilogue of the book that he has no intention of telling Tristan who he really is. In fact, Juston adopted him and stated in the book that Tristan would grow up to be a great knight because Juston himself would train him. If you know anything about *Lord of Winter*, then you know that Juston de Royans was the mentor to many of my greatest heroes—Christopher de Lohr, David de Lohr, and Marcus Burton, to name a few.

Shifting subjects, I want to address something I've had a few questions on, so hopefully this will clear it up—Berwick Castle. I did an author's note for it in the back of the novel *The Dark Spawn*, but I'll make mention of it here also. If you've read the de Velt and de Wolfe series, then you know Berwick has belonged to both of them. The House of de Velt took control over Berwick in 1210 when they took it back from the Scots, who were preparing to let the Vikings use it to launch some mutually beneficial raids. Therefore, Berwick was with de Velt until at least 1267, when Patrick de Wolfe took command of it. How or why did that happen? We don't know because I haven't written about it yet, but the castle has passed from one house to the other. Then, by 1333, the Scots have it again because it passes to a third Le Veque hero, Stephen of Pembury (Dragonblade series). How did de Wolfe "lose" it? I have no idea, but I'm sure we'll find out one day. The truth is that Berwick was probably the most contested castle on the border—for real—so the flip-flopping of owners isn't unusual to that castle's history.

And speaking of de Wolfe Pack, guess who has a major secondary role in this novel? None other than William de Wolfe himself. We actually get to see William as a non-leading character along with Paris de Norville and Kieran Hage (two of his best friends). Keep in mind they are *very* young in this—William and Paris are eighteen years of age to Kieran's seventeen years of age, but they've already made a reputation for themselves—or, at least, they're trying to. What fun it was to write about "young" William. As always, a huge favorite of mine—and yours, too, I hope.

Lastly, this book has a pretty intense battle scene in it, so be forewarned. It's the Executioner Knights, after all, and they tend to get a little graphic. But all in all, there's such a lovely romance in this book that everything else is just icing on the cake—even a battle!

The usual pronunciation guide:
We're dealing with some Irish names, which are difficult to pronounce for those of us not well versed in Gaelic, so we have a few of them:

Andromeda – not Gaelic, but the pronunciation is ann-DROM-uh-duh.

Alecia – Alicia/Alisha, basically. Just a different spelling.

Ceara – see-ARE-uh

Wrexham – Wrec-sum

And with that, I hope you enjoy Tristan and Andromeda's complex and romantic tale!

Hugs,

Kathryn

PROLOGUE

Year of Our Lord 1215
London
The Pox tavern

HE DIDN'T LIKE the look of him.

In fact, he'd seen him before, and although he couldn't immediately place the slovenly man with the enormous scar across his chin, he knew one thing—wherever that man appeared, death happened.

Then it occurred to him.

They had to get out of there.

But it was easier said than done, unfortunately. The Pox, perhaps the most notorious tavern in all of England, was full on this night because several merchant cogs had rolled down the Thames and anchored near the tavern, which sat right on the smelly, littered banks of the dirty river. The clientele in the tavern looked as if God himself had put all of mankind's rejects into one establishment, and they commiserated in their similar filth. But it wasn't simply the dregs of society that came to The Pox.

Kings had come there, too.

So had earls and nobles.

That was because The Pox was notorious for its wealth of gambling opportunities. Men could gamble on literally anything, and there was good money to be made and excitement to be had. The food was also good, strangely enough, and the alcohol was some of the best around. Shipments came straight off the cogs that anchored along the Thames and straight into the storerooms of The Pox.

That made it quite popular.

But it had also been known to have murderers and thieves within the old walls. That gave the place a real element of danger, so when Alexander de Sherrington realized that he was seeing one of the deadlier assassins from King John's arsenal lingering in the shadows and pretending not to notice who was coming and going, he knew there was going to be trouble.

Where there was one assassin, there were usually others.

"Come," he said, urging his companions toward the door. "The Marshal has sent Tristan and I to fetch your filthy hides, and you will do as you are told. Get out now or you will pay the price."

Since no one moved immediately, he grabbed a younger knight by the neck and practically lifted him out of his chair, but the companion he'd mentioned, Sir Tristan de Royans, wasn't so subtle. He wasn't a tall man, but he was quite muscular and built like a bull. He was also mean. So very mean. He was a knight's knight, born and bred to fight, and it was never more evident on anyone than it was on Tristan. That meant he didn't disobey orders, including the one just given by Alexander, whom he considered his superior officer even though they were technically equal in rank. He grabbed the nearest knights, yanking them up by anything he could grab.

Heads.

Hair.

Anything.

"Out with you, lads," he said, still holding on to the hapless young knights, who happened to be new additions to William Marshal's household guard. "The Marshal told you not to come here, but you did not listen. You thought you knew better than the Earl of Pembroke. That was not wise on your part."

With that, he shoved them through the entry door, out onto the dirt walkway. Unfortunately for them, the walkway was about six feet wide before it started sloping down to the river itself, so one of them was propelled across the walkway and began stumbling down the slope. Only quick thinking from his companion stopped him from ending up in the river.

Tristan stood at the entry door, ham-sized fists resting on his narrow hips, shaking his head at the clumsy young knights. But Alexander was chuckling.

"You do not know your own strength, Pat," he said, a glimmer of mirth in his eyes. "I think they could have walked out under their own power. They did not need to be tossed."

Pat. That was an affectionate nickname Tristan had earned over the years because his birth name was Philip Alexander Tristan—P.A.T. His close friends called him that, but his commanders and subordinates called him by the name he'd always gone by—Sir Tristan or just plain Tristan. He was quite formal, even with men who had commanded him for years.

No one grew close to Tristan de Royans.

It was rare when he let anyone in.

But he'd let Alexander in years ago. Sherry, as he was called, was married to the Earl of Hereford and Worcester's daughter, and they had a growing brood. Hereford, a man also known as

Christopher de Lohr, was in town this night, in fact, and in residence at Farringdon House, William Marshal's townhome. Christopher and the Marshal worked closely together, both of them commanding great armies and strongly allied in the fight of the welfare of England. No one knew why Christopher had come to London on this particular night, but that wasn't unusual. He came and went sometimes and no one really knew why, but the Marshal did. In fact, he was recalling his knights to Farringdon House, having sent Alexander and Tristan, among others, to trawl the city for the younger knights who had fanned out to enjoy a brief respite.

But it was a respite no more.

Something was in the air.

Having collected their four knights from The Pox, Tristan eyed Alexander as they headed back the way they'd come.

"I've never known a man yet at The Pox who would willingly leave under his own power, you included," he said. "It's better the young knights know we mean business. They'll be quicker to obey an order next time."

"Or avoid The Pox altogether."

"I doubt that is going to happen. *We* do not even avoid The Pox."

They looked at each other, smirking. "That is true," Alexander said. "But I will admit that my wife does not like me to visit. I will not let her go, so she says that I cannot go, either."

Tristan snorted. "Your wife is a unique woman," he said. "Married only a year, is it?"

Alexander nodded. "A year," he said. "One glorious year."

"I heard you saved her from the king's lust last year."

Alexander shook his head. "Nay," he said. "She saved herself. Trust me on this. But you were not with us last year, were you?"

"I was at Bowes Castle, with my father," Tristan said. "Pembroke recalled me to London about six months ago, if you recall. He and my father decided that I would evidently make a good spy, so here I am."

Alexander grinned. William Marshal was the commander of a group of seasoned warriors known as the Executioner Knights, a collection of some of the deadliest and most talented men in the known world. They were spies, as Tristan said, but they were so much more. Assassins, bodyguards, and any number of roles that they were skilled enough to assume. They worked in secret, and usually had a cover story that was quite plausible, but the truth was that the Marshal used them to suit his own agenda, which was almost always along the lines of ensuring England's survival.

To be an Executioner Knight meant a man was the very best at what he did.

Even Tristan knew that.

"You performed flawlessly with the matter at Westminster a few months ago," Alexander said. "Were it not for your sword, we might not have been successful."

Tristan lifted a wry eyebrow. "I am a knight, Sherry," he said. "If anything involves a sword, I will be successful. But the Executioner Knights… it involves things I am not particularly familiar with."

"Like what?"

"Like being sly and secretive," he said, almost agitated in manner. "I am a forthright man. If I have something to say, I will say it. If there is something I must do, I will do it. I will not sneak around."

Alexander was starting to chuckle. "That is true," he said.

"I've never met a man as brutally honest and forthright as you are."

"It is a gift."

Tristan said it with a smile, as if it was the sweetest virtue he had. That brought more laughter from Alexander.

"I believe that it is," he said. "I also think you frighten the hell out of people because you are genuinely fearless in everything you do. There could be a thousand men with a thousand daggers running right at you and you would stand there and challenge them."

"Another gift."

Alexander conceded the point. "Very true," he said. "But the Marshal thinks those gifts would be extraordinarily valuable to the Executioner Knights. You will make a great one."

For the first time, Tristan's air of confidence wavered a little. He wasn't entirely sure he was cut out for life as a spy, but his father wanted it for him, and it was a great honor. The knight's knight would add something more to his arsenal of skills.

He would become an agent for the Executioner Knights.

"Mayhap," he said quietly, watching the four young knights walking ahead of them, just out of earshot. "I… I simply do not wish to disappoint anyone, least of all myself."

"You will not."

Alexander said it with confidence as they entered one of the darker avenues leading north, a street lined with brothels that were still lively even at this time of night. They could hear the laughter and music as the ladies entertained their clientele. The avenue was lit by flames from great iron bowls, fueled with peat, on stone pedestals. Those fires would light up the streets until midnight, when half would be doused. On this particular street, the bowls of flaming peat were well kept, paid for by the brothels to light the way for those last-minute customers.

But Alexander and Tristan weren't paying attention to the buildings or even the fires along the street. They were watching for any threats from the shadows, the mode of hunter versus prey, which was completely normal for them. Given their line of work, one didn't live long if one wasn't vigilant, so they maintained their awareness even though Farringdon House wasn't far away.

They still had to make it there through the darkened streets of London.

While Tristan was looking for normal threats, Alexander kept thinking of the man he'd seen back at The Pox. He was guilty of patronizing The Pox as much as any of the other Executioner Knights, even though the Marshal told them to stay well clear of it, and so did his wife, but the man he'd seen wasn't part of the normal rabble. He'd never seen him there before. He wasn't particularly concerned, but he was curious. Knowing that the king kept his own stable of murderers and assassins, he was always curious when he saw a king's man.

It made him wonder what the man was up to.

Unfortunately, he was about to find out.

The first sign of trouble was when they came through the street of brothels and made the turn west onto the wide avenue of Trinity Road. The boulevard ran east to west in London, one of the larger avenues, and they could hear something behind them. By the time Tristan and Alexander turned around, a lone man appeared, shuffling his feet as he walked.

The very man Alexander had been pondering.

Somewhat shocked to see the man behind them, he didn't say anything. He simply turned around and kept walking, which encouraged Tristan to do the same. But the man behind them had other ideas.

"I've not seen the prince for many years," he said in a heavy Occitan accent. "I was not sure it was him, but the fact that he looks so much like his father tells me it is true."

No one knew whom he was talking to or talking about because he was alone, several feet behind them, and talking into the air. There was no one around, so they were starting to think he was simply mad.

But Alexander knew better.

God help him.

"Keep walking," he told Tristan when the man turned around to look at the fool behind them. "Pay no attention to a madman unless he produces a sword."

Tristan did as Alexander suggested. He kept walking as the four knights in front of them slowed their pace, eyeing the lone man with curiosity and concern. Alexander motioned to them to continue walking, and they did, but the man trailing after them didn't shut his mouth.

"We've been looking for you, prince," he said. "We heard rumor that you were in the north and then on the marches. Someone then told us that you were in the retinue of the Earl of Pembroke. I was not expecting to see you in London, but here you are. What a mighty stroke of fortune."

Tristan started to turn around again, but Alexander thumped him on the chest, silently indicating he continue walking. They were all walking, heading for the junction of Trinity Road and Bread Street, which would take them up to the main thoroughfare where Farringdon House was located.

"Given that this encounter is most fortuitous, I must insist that you come with me," the man said. "Someone wants to speak with you. Do you not hear me? I would be grateful if you would accompany me to Westminster. Your brother wishes to see you. He longs to know you."

Alexander finally came to a halt, and his men with him. Slowly, he turned around.

"Crawl back into that bottle that clearly has you in its grip," he said. "No one knows what you are speaking of."

The man snorted. "I think you do," he said. "In fact, I *know* you do. You know that your companion is the most prized man in England and France. Royal bloodlines on both sides makes him quite… special. Do you hear me? His brother, the king, wishes to speak with him. Prince Philip? Do you comprehend me?"

Alexander was shaking his head, as if the situation was ridiculous, but Tristan didn't react one way or the other. He had no idea whom the man was addressing or what he was talking about, but it occurred to him that his first name was Philip. A common enough name, that was true, so he didn't give it further thought.

Now, he was simply annoyed.

"Leave us or you'll feel my wrath," he growled loudly. "We've no time for your madness."

The man grinned, his teeth glimmering in the moonlight. "You sound just like your father," he said. "You favor him a little, although you are much larger than he ever was. Henry never had the size and strength you clearly have."

Tristan looked at Alexander and rolled his eyes. "When we get to Farringdon House, we'll turn the dogs on him," he said.

He began walking away, with Alexander and the young knights moving with him. "Agreed," Alexander replied. "But the truth is that there's aways one madman roaming the streets of London on any given night."

"True enough," Tristan said. "And he had to find us."

"Exactly."

Tristan continued their walk, his focus on the darkened street around them. "Have you heard why de Lohr has come?" he asked.

The subject was shifting, and Alexander was glad for it. Their follower had him edgy because the man clearly knew things he shouldn't, things that only a select few people knew, and the more they put distance between them, the better.

"I'm not entirely sure," he said. "I've been away from home for about a month, much to my wife's distress, so it could be that something new has come up."

"A new mission?"

"Possibly."

"Prince Philip!" The man following them would not be ignored. "My lord, there is no need pretending that you are not Prince Philip. I know who you are. I have seen you over the years, though the Marshal has kept you well hidden. He and Richard and Eleanor protected you ably over the years, but Richard and Eleanor are gone. They've been gone for many years. John has permitted you to live in obscurity, but no more. He wishes a word with you, and you *will* come with me."

Alexander didn't respond, though the man was becoming more detailed in his conversation. He'd already addressed Tristan twice by the name *Prince Philip*, which thankfully hadn't brought a reaction from Tristan. Not yet, anyway.

He didn't recognize it.

And that had been the plan from the start.

Before Alexander could turn around and threaten the man, however, Tristan came to a halt and spoke to him.

"I've no tolerance for fools," he said. "You're drunk and mistaking me for someone else, so be on your way. I'm not Philip."

The man following them came to a halt as well. "You are Philip Alexander Tristan."

"Enough," Alexander roared, unsheathing his sword. He had to take a stand now or this would get out of hand, if it hadn't already. He had to stop the momentum. "Get out of here, you bastard, before I remove something you treasure."

The man shifted his gaze to Alexander, regarding him coolly. "De Sherrington," he said in a tone that sounded as if he was visiting with an old friend. "Are you his protector now?"

"Still your tongue or I will cut it out."

"Did you truly think you could hide him forever?"

"I will not warn you again."

That seemed to end the conversation, and the man following them didn't hesitate to react to the threat. He unsheathed his own weapon and, suddenly, several men emerged from the shadows. It was clear that he hadn't been alone the entire time. Tristan's sword came out, but of the four younger knights they'd shepherded away from The Pox, only three had broadswords, while the fourth had apparently lost his earlier in the evening in a gambling game. But those who had swords unsheathed them to the shrill sound of metal as they came free from their leather casings, and the clash was on.

It was nasty from the start.

From what Tristan and Alexander could see, there were at least six to eight men on the attack, all of them armed, all of them seemingly heading straight for Tristan. In fact, Alexander was preparing to take one swordsman on when the man veered around him and ran at Tristan. That had Alexander and the four younger knights jumping in to help.

Fists, as well as swords, began to fly.

It was dark on this avenue, unfortunately, and fighting in close quarters, as they were, was inherently dangerous. The younger knight with the dagger was making short work of some of the men, grabbing them only to stab them in the kidneys or slit the tendons behind their knees. Three of the men fell away with wounds that wouldn't kill them, but would cripple them, as the knight with the dagger went on the attack.

More struggling, more fighting. Tristan was in a sword battle with the man who had been following them, but his size and superior skill quickly had the man retreating. The others had disengaged, grabbing their wounded comrades and dragging them back into the shadows. But the man who had started it all, the one who had been following, refused to leave.

"This is not the end," he said, still holding his sword but about twenty feet away. "John knows you are here, Philip. He knows where you are. He would much rather have his brother as an ally than an enemy. Leave Pembroke and come with me. I will take you to your destiny."

The younger knight with the dagger hurled it at the man, clipping him in the shoulder. It didn't lodge, but rather clattered to the dirty road, but the man took off after his comrades anyway. He'd survived a battle with Pembroke knights.

He was fortunate, and he knew it.

The homes within earshot of the fighting began to stir. Dogs barked and candles began to glow as people opened their windows to peer into the darkness and see what the commotion was about. That had Alexander grabbing Tristan by the arm hurriedly.

"Come," he said. "Quickly, Pat. *Move*."

Tristan did, rushing down the road, following Alexander and the other knights.

They ran all the way back to Farringdon House.

The London townhome of William Marshal was an enormous, four-storied monstrosity that was built to withstand any onslaught. The walls were of stone, not wattle and daub, and there was one fortified entrance on the bottom floor that opened up into a courtyard in the middle of the house. The sentries on duty admitted the six knights, shutting the heavy oak and iron gates behind them. As the younger knights headed back to their quarters, Tristan grasped Alexander by the arm and stopped him from going any further.

"What just happened?" he asked.

Alexander was trying to pretend it wasn't anything of consequence. "Who knows?" he said. "A drunkard? A madman? London is full of them. I would not take it so seriously."

He started to walk away, but Tristan's voice stopped him.

"He called me by my full name," Tristan said. "He called you by your name. He knew us, Sherry."

"So we are famous. What of it?"

Tristan didn't seem amused. "What did he mean by your being my protector?" he said. "And what is that 'Prince Philip' nonsense?"

Alexander shook his head. "I cannot tell you any more than I already have."

Tristan stared at him a moment before closing the gap between them. "I am going to ask you one more question," he said. "You will not lie to me."

"I never have and I never will."

"Do you know what he was talking about?"

That brought Alexander pause. Nay, he couldn't lie to him. He'd already said he wouldn't. But Tristan was asking a question about something only a handful of people knew, and those that did know had been sworn to secrecy. It wasn't Alexander's truth to reveal, but he could see by the look on Tristan's face that the damage had been done.

There would be no avoiding this one.

Faintly, he signed.

"I do," he said. "But before you ask me another question, you must speak with Pembroke. I cannot tell you any more than I already have."

"You said that."

"It is true."

"Then you *do* know more."

"Aye."

"You simply cannot tell me."

Alexander nodded. "If I could, I would, but this is something you must ask Pembroke," he said quietly. "Only he can give you the answers you seek."

Tristan continued to look at him, puzzlement rippling across his face. "God's Bones," he finally muttered. "Then there truly *are* answers to what just happened out there?"

Alexander could only point to the entry door that faced onto the courtyard. Tristan understood the meaning, but he wasn't ready to go yet. He just stood there, feeling increasingly bewildered and having no idea why he felt that way. But the feelings weren't unfamiliar; he hadn't felt that way since he'd been a very young boy.

Feelings of bewilderment he'd pushed out of his mind.

Until now.

"That's not the first time that has happened, you know," he

finally muttered.

Alexander cocked his head. "What do you mean?"

Tristan lifted his shoulders. "That," he said. "Someone mistaking me for someone else. Someone calling me by another name. It has happened before."

"Oh?" Alexander said. "What have you been called?"

Tristan scratched his head. "Names," he said after a moment. "Names I'd forgotten because they didn't mean anything. It has been happening my entire life. I grew up in a poor household until I was about six years of age, you know. On the Welsh marches. Then, one day, I was taken away by a knight and I never saw that place again."

"You told me. Erik de Russe?"

Tristan nodded. "Aye," he said. "Sir Erik de Russe took me away, and I spent about two years with him at Pembroke Castle until I was taken to Bowes Castle and left with Juston de Royans and his wife. It was the first time I really knew a family life, you know. Ashton and Wynter and Brenton and the rest of them. They treated me like part of the family, and they were my brothers and sisters. That is why I bear the de Royans name."

Alexander nodded. "I know," he said. "You were trained by the best knights in the world at that point, my friends among them. I know your story, Pat."

Tristan looked at him. "I haven't thought of it in years," he admitted. "But tonight… that man following us, calling me Prince Philip… it made me remember something."

"What's that?"

"The fact that I never questioned why a lad from a poor household should end up training as a knight."

"You never asked?"

He nodded. "I did, once," he said. "I asked Sir Erik. He told me that my father had been a great knight."

"And the family?"

"Paid to take me in."

Alexander bobbed his head in understanding. "That is not unusual, you know," he said. "Especially when the child is a foundling."

"Or a bastard." Tristan shrugged. "I do not really care if I am or not. That does not define me, but I will admit that my obscure lineage has concerned me from time to time."

Alexander cracked a smile. "Why should it concern you?" he said. "You've made your way in life. You're a powerful, seasoned knight who serves the Earl of Pembroke. That is nothing to be ashamed over."

Tristan shook his head. "I did not mean that," he said. "I meant it has cost me a wife. Her family was not interested in a knight with no familial background, and I doubt anyone else will be, either. That's why when something like this happens, with the man who thought I was someone else, I wonder if the man might not be wrong. If he might know who my father was. He said I looked just like him."

Alexander wasn't sure how to answer. "I think we should go inside now," he said. "Come along, lad. Pembroke awaits."

Tristan didn't ask any further questions, knowing Alexander wouldn't answer. The man had made that clear. But that didn't mean his curiosity was sated. Quite the contrary, in fact. As they headed indoors, his interest was growing. Odd how something he'd simply pushed into the recesses of his mind for many of his thirty-seven years upon the earth was now at the forefront because of a skirmish in the street.

But the man who had spoken so strangely had called him by his full name.

Philip Alexander Tristan.

Very few people knew that was his full name, but a stranger had.

Perhaps it was time for some answers.

☙

"SPEAK UP. I did not hear what you said."

"The Pox, my lord. He found us at The Pox."

It was one of the younger knights speaking, part of the group that Tristan and Alexander had chased out of the notorious tavern that had just been named. The young knight, the spokesman for the group of very contrite-looking warriors, had been forced to confess their location to their liege.

And William Marshal didn't look happy.

A tall man with white hair, enormous hands, and brown eyes that had yellowed over the years, he eyed the collection of strong, young men from good families most disapprovingly. They were in the first-floor solar of Farringdon House, a chamber that covered nearly half of the floor, and it was a very big floor. There was easily room for fifty or more men in the chamber with its great stone hearth, exposed beams overhead, and painted walls. The floor was made from wide slats of wood, thick, but pocked from the heavy boots of men who had walked upon it with their spurs. But the truth was that it was a spectacular room, meant for men of greatness, and the old walls had seen much of that over the years, including the man who was sitting by the hearth.

Christopher de Lohr, Earl of Hereford and Worcester, was listening to everything.

The Marshal knew that. And he knew that de Lohr was silently laughing at him. It wasn't any secret that he forbade his knights to go to The Pox, and it wasn't any secret that they disobeyed those orders. Regularly. The Marshal didn't really care with some of the more seasoned veterans, but the young knights needed the fear of God put into them from time to time.

And he was just the man to do it.

"I see," he said with abnormal calm. "Then you disobeyed a direct command, du Reims?"

The young knight who had handled the dagger so ably was also a big man, with blond hair and intense, dark eyes. "We saw no harm in it, my lord," he replied. "The other taverns were quite busy for the evening, and—"

"And you picked one that was also quite busy, the exact one I have told you repeatedly to stay out of," William finished for him. He frowned, a gesture that was designed to terrorize. "You are related to the Earl of East Anglia, du Reims. The man is your uncle. You are also related to Hereford, the very man in this chamber, who is your cousin. And your companions—d'Vant, de Bretagne, and de Leybourne—are all from some of the finest families in England. Your pedigrees are impeccable. Yet you disobey a direct order from me. A man who controls England. I simply want to be clear about this."

Sir Lukas du Reims had no recourse. He had nowhere to turn and no one to blame but himself. With a sigh, he nodded his head.

"We did, my lord."

"Was it worth it?"

Du Reims shook his head. "It was not, my lord," he said. "I lost my broadsword to a swindler. It was an extremely expensive lesson."

The way he said it had the Marshal fighting off a grin because his words were like a verbal punch to the head—his own. As if he was the biggest fool on the planet. He glanced at Christopher, who was facing the flames of the hearth, and he could see the smirk on the man's lips. That nearly did him in. Clearing his throat loudly, he turned away from the four remorseful knights.

"Get out," he said. "Get out before I lose my temper. Go to your quarters and do not leave until I send for you. If you do not obey me, I will send de Sherrington and de Royans after you, and that is something you do not want. Do I make myself clear?"

"Aye, my lord."

"Get out of my sight."

The knights fled, but as they were hastily leaving, Tristan and Alexander were entering. They very nearly knocked the pair down, who were forced to stand aside to allow for the stampede. When the young knights fled down the stairs, Alexander came into the chamber, his eyebrows raised.

"What did you say to them to make them run like that?" he said. "If there is a closed door between here and their destination, that door will be no more. They won't even stop to open it."

In his chair, Christopher burst into soft laughter, and even the Marshal cracked a smile. "They received nothing less than they deserved," he said. "What must I do to keep you men out of The Pox?"

"Burn it down," Alexander said, his eyes twinkling with mirth. "That is your only hope."

That brought a snort from the Marshal. "I shall consider it," he said. "But until I can get down to the river's edge with a flint and stone, I suppose I shall continue to have nights like this. In any case, you are the first ones to return. Did you see anyone else while you were out?"

Alexander shook his head. "Nay," he said. "Beau and Addax were heading to the north side of the city. Tristan and I headed towards the south."

He was referring to the other two senior knights who had gone off to find the errant younger knights Beau de Russe and Addax al-Kort. Beau was part of the prestigious de Russe family, a powerful knight who, despite his near-deafness, was quite competent and able, and Essien was a knight of great talent who was born in a land far to the east. Both of them would probably not be as kind to the younger knights as Alexander and Tristan had been, and the Marshal knew it.

With a sigh, he scratched his head.

"Did you pass through the street of the brothels?" he asked.

"Aye, but we did not see anyone we knew," Alexander replied.

"None of my men were there?"

"That we could see."

The Marshal finally nodded, turning away from Alexander and Tristan and moving to the hearth to warm his hands. "Sherry, send a servant for food and drink," he said. "We may as well be comfortable. Chris has a good deal to tell us when everyone arrives."

Alexander's gaze moved to Christopher. "Is it serious?"

Christopher looked over his shoulder at his son-in-law, who was married to his eldest daughter, Christin. "There is a buildup on the northern marches that the marcher lords in the area are quite worried about," he said. "We may have some trouble."

Alexander puffed out his cheeks at the news, blowing out a heavy sigh. "We've been hearing word of it for over a year now," he said. "The Welsh have been building up near Chirk Castle for just that long. Are they finally moving forward?"

Christopher half shrugged, half nodded. He didn't want to speak any further on a subject he would simply have to repeat when the others joined them. Therefore, he stood up, stretching himself out in front of the fire, as Alexander went to the chamber door and summoned a servant for the food and drink the Marshal had requested. As Christopher began to throw more peat on the fire, Tristan came out of the shadows.

"Before the others come, my lord, I wonder if I may address a… situation," he said. "I have a question. Sherry said that you would have the answer."

Over by the chamber door, Alexander turned sharply to see Tristan addressing the Marshal, who was preparing to take a seat next to the hearth. Before he could say anything, because he didn't want the Marshal to think he'd put Tristan up to it, William pulled out a stool and plunked a booted foot on it.

"What situation is this?" he asked.

Alexander moved toward Tristan. "When we were at The Pox, I saw Odilo Nivard," he said, hoping to explain a little before Tristan blindsided him with a rather serious question. "You know of whom I speak, my lord?"

The Marshal didn't hesitate. He nodded as his gaze moved to Alexander. "I know the man," he said. "In The Pox, you say? A rare occurrence, I should think. He does not stray from John's side."

"My thoughts exactly," Alexander said. "He was sitting there, alone, as we herded the knights out of the place. I did not even think he saw me, but I was mistaken. When we were by the street of the brothels, he appeared. He followed us."

"He brought men with him," Tristan said, taking over the

story that Alexander was telling. "We were attacked, though it was a brief fight. However, before we were attacked, there was a conversation of sorts."

"Oh?"

Tristan was trying to find the right words, feeling foolish even as he spoke, thinking that perhaps he'd only been paranoid. But he knew that wasn't the case. He looked at Alexander, who was gazing back at him steadily. There was encouragement in that expression, something that gave Tristan courage.

"The man called me by my full name," he said after a moment. "He called me Philip Alexander Tristan. He also called me Prince Philip. He told me that I looked like my father. I would not give the man any credence, of course, but he did call me by my full name. He also knew Sherry's name. He spoke as if he knew us, my lord."

By this time, the Marshal was watching him curiously. He also had the attention of Christopher, who had stopped putting peat in the fire and was now simply watching the situation. Without Tristan even noticing, Alexander went over to the chamber door to shut it. He also bolted it. As he leaned against the door to prevent anyone from coming in at this particular moment, a crucial moment in the evolution of Tristan de Royans, the Marshal spoke.

"Go on," he said steadily. "What is your question, Pat?"

Tristan took a long, deep breath. "I asked Sherry if there was any truth to what the man said," he said. "He would not tell me. He said that I must ask you."

There it was. The question that had been waiting thirty-seven years to be asked. A question that the Marshal knew he would be facing at some point. He wasn't exactly sure how much to tell Tristan, or even how to answer him, because he'd spent nearly all of his association with Tristan poisoning him against the very family he was biologically part of.

That great secret he'd always kept from him.

Now, the doorway to that secret was threatening to open.

It wasn't that the Marshal was caught off guard with the query. In truth, he'd been expecting it for years. But perhaps he hadn't been expecting it tonight. Not on this night when they were dealing with other important issues. Frankly, he wasn't sure how Tristan was going to handle the truth, but the older he became and the more people who knew his identity, as John's dirty assassin clearly had, the more he would be in danger if he didn't know the truth and was unprepared to defend himself.

Nivard wouldn't be the only one coming for him.

There would be others.

"What, exactly, did Nivard say?" William finally asked.

Tristan thought a moment. "He called me Prince Philip several times," he said. "He told me that you and Richard and Eleanor had protected me over the years, but that John wished to know his brother. He told me that John wished to be an ally and not an enemy."

The Marshal looked at Christopher as if startled by what he heard, but Christopher met his gaze evenly. After a moment, however, he nodded vaguely, silently giving the Marshal the encouragement he needed to address the situation. They could all feel the tension in the chamber, the strain of a secret they'd all sworn to keep. A secret that was now on the verge of being exposed to the one man it could truly affect.

A man more valuable, and more royal, than he could ever possibly imagine.

"Sit down," the Marshal said after a moment, waving his

hand in a lowering gesture. "Sit and be comfortable. If you truly wish to know the answers to your questions, then you had better be seated. This will take some time."

Tristan wasn't expecting that request. He looked at Alexander, standing over by the chamber door, who nodded his head. That had Tristan seeking the nearest chair as the Marshal headed in his direction.

"You want to know what the truth is," William said thoughtfully. "Truthfully, I have spent your lifetime avoiding telling you, but if Nivard knows, then others know. It would be dangerous for you not to know the truth at this point, so I will tell you. But understand that nothing coming forth from my lips is a fabrication. Do I make myself clear?"

Tristan gazed up at the man, nodding once. "Very clear, my lord."

The Marshal drew in a long, pensive breath. "Before I begin, tell me what you remember from your childhood."

Tristan cocked his head, thinking back to those carefree days, now more dreamlike to him than reality, as most long-distant memories were.

"I remember chasing a pig," he said. "That is my first real memory. Of chasing a speckled pig with children I thought were my brothers and sisters until I was about six years of age and Sir Erik came for me. I remember my mother weeping when I left. She hugged me and told me she loved me. I remember clinging to her, not wanting to go, but Sir Erik insisted. So I went."

"What else?"

Tristan shrugged. "What most men remember, I suppose," he said. "I ended up at Bowes Castle, where I remained for a few years, with Lady Andromeda and Lord Juston. They became my parents. I became part of their family as I assumed their name. But I went to Kenilworth and Bamburgh before returning to Bowes. When Sir Erik went to the Levant, I remained in England. Is there something specific you would have me remember, my lord?"

The Marshal was watching him closely. "Nay," he said. "But did you not think it strange to have been raised as a farmer's child only to be turned over to the cloister for an education? But not just any cloister—Canterbury. Then an elite knight took you away and you ended up with a noble family. Did you not think any of this odd?"

"I did."

"Did you ever ask Erik?"

Tristan nodded. "I did," he said. "He said that he was following orders."

"No more than that?"

"No more."

"But surely you suspected over the years that there might have been more."

"Aye," Tristan said. "I was just saying that very thing to Sherry tonight. Over the years, men have mistaken me for someone else. Or they have looked at me as if they know me. I have long suspected there was more to my background, that I wasn't simply a foundling, as I had been told."

The Marshal pulled up a chair and sat opposite Tristan, who was sitting rather stiffly upright. He was usually a man in control of his emotions, but at the moment, he had a rather anxious look on his face. All of those years of wondering, of imagining, were about to come to a head, and he wasn't sure how he felt about it. Tristan had always thought those moments of men knowing him were only in his imagination.

It was a little frightening to realize those moments had been real.

"You are the product of two royal households," the Marshal said. "Your father was Henry Curthose, the father of Richard and John and the rest of that royal brood. Your mother is Princess Alys, sister to King Philip of France. Surely you know that Alys was betrothed to Richard the Lionheart, but Henry took her for his mistress. There have always been rumors that she bore Henry a child when, in fact, she did. *You* are that child, Tristan. Your father was the King of England and your mother is a princess of France."

Tristan stared at him, looking for any hint that he might be wrong or jesting or mistaken, but there was no gesture forthcoming. As the news began to sink in, his eyes widened.

"He… *Henry*?" he repeated in shock. "My father was Henry?"

William nodded. "Indeed," he said. "The moment you were born, your mother asked me to take you away, and I did. I gave you over to a trusted servant, who took you to her sister to raise. The sister was married to a farmer, and that is where we hid you. Among the peasants. Again and again, we hid you—with Canterbury, with an elite knight, and finally with de Royans. We did it to save your life, lad. Had your birth been discovered, it would have been quite… dangerous."

Tristan was filled with disbelief. He leaned away from the Marshal, so much so that he leaned right out of the chair and ended up on his feet, pacing away from the man, feeling a need to run yet also a need to stay. He couldn't decide what he needed to do. He stood there in horror, absorbing everything, before he could even speak again.

"Then what that man said was true," he said, sounding

oddly hollow. "He referred to John as my brother… and he is."

William nodded. "He is your half-brother," he said. "Richard was also your half-brother. You, Philip Alexander Tristan, are the son of a king on your father's side and the nephew of a king on your mother's. You could not be more royal if you tried, and, by all rights, you are far more high-bred than anyone in this chamber. You are a prince. De Lohr and I should be genuflecting to you, in fact. You wanted to know the truth, and now you have it."

Tristan digested that statement, word for word. In fact, the words kept rolling around in his head. He was unable to stop them. For a man who had lived rather simply his entire life, it was too much to take. He was being told that he was a member of the ruling class, but he'd never had ambitions. He followed orders. He didn't give them, not really. He was happy carrying out difficult tasks, working himself to the bone for the common good, and considering himself fortunate for his position in life as a trusted and highly trained knight. But he wasn't merely a knight.

He was far more than that.

God help him… so much more.

"Tell me what that means," he said, struggling with his emotions. "What, exactly, does that mean for me?"

The Marshal stood up. "It means that you have a claim to the throne of England and also to the throne of France," he said. "It means you have a claim to the Vexin, the Aquitaine, and several other French provinces. It means you are a rare individual, Tristan, more than you realize. But with this uniqueness comes danger. Knowing you have a claim to two thrones, it means that your brother, John, will destroy you if he can. No matter what Nivard said, he does not want to ally with you. He wants to kill you, to reduce the threat against his own claim. His son, Henry, will want you dead also. With you alive, there will always be that threat, and they know it. The same is said for the King of France, your uncle. You are his sister's son, the son of the King of England. Even if you do not realize how much power that gives you, Richard and Eleanor did."

"Eleanor?" Tristan said, looking at him sharply. He was starting to turn red in the face. "God's Bones, she killed Arthur, Geoffrey's son. She also went after Elizabeau, Arthur's half-sister, because she was declared Arthur's successor. I remember this because de Lohr and his men were involved in spiriting Lady Elizabeau away. The woman was nearly executed, but one of de Lohr's men helped her escape. Why did Eleanor not try to kill me, too?"

The Marshal could see that he was becoming agitated. "Because you were more valuable to her," he said. "You were her husband's bastard with a princess. Arthur and Elizabeau were merely children of a royal offspring. With you, she could bargain with the French because you were Alys' son. She practically raised Alys, you know. She was also present at your birth. She watched as I took you away, but if you must know, I did not trust her. I never have. She asked me once, when you were about six years of age, where you had been taken, and I would not tell her."

The light of understanding went on in Tristan's eyes. "That is when Sir Erik came to fetch me."

"Exactly," William said. "I needed you protected by knights, not hidden away with a farmer where you had no protection if you were found."

"Surely your history with her told you that she was not to be trusted when it came to the welfare of a child."

William lifted his eyebrows. "My history with her told me many things, not the least of which is the royal family can change their minds at a whim," he said. "I did not wish for you to be a whim."

So much was becoming clear to Tristan now. As shocking as it was, as horrifying as it was, he realized that he wasn't entirely surprised. Those years of strange things happening, like men who thought they knew him, were starting to make some sense. Living with a farmer and then being taken to Canterbury Cathedral before being adopted by a noble family. If he thought hard about it, perhaps he'd always known that his identity would be something catastrophic. But a full-blooded royal prince, linking two countries who were both family and enemy to one another? He'd never imagined that, not in his wildest dreams. Tristan had been around nobles and royals and politics long enough to know what bloodlines like his meant. There wasn't anyone like him in the entire world that he knew of, not like this. Even as that reality saturated every recess in his brain, he could still hardly believe it.

"How many people know this?" he finally asked.

The Marshal looked at Christopher and Alexander. "Everyone in this room," he said. "A few others, men I trust, like Juston de Royans. Several of the Executioner Knights know, but they were in on the secret from the beginning. They will take it to their grave. And you may need them someday, Tristan. You want men like that to know so they can help you if you need it."

That was probably true, but Tristan wasn't sure how he felt about any of it. His shock was turning into numbness, and the numbness into distaste. He wandered over to one of the lancet windows facing south. In the distance, lit up with torches against the night sky, he could see Westminster Palace. *I am the son of a king,* he thought.

God, that left such a bad taste in his mouth.

"Don't think this makes me happy," he muttered. "Don't think that anything you told me makes me proud or happy. I've grown up hating Richard and John and Henry, that greedy and immoral trio, so nothing you have told me gives me any sense of gratification. I wish with all my heart that it was untrue."

"I know," William said solemnly. "But it *is* true, and you must know the truth because if John is trying to find you, to make contact, he will not stop. You must protect yourself, Tristan. In this case, knowledge is power. For your own safety, you must stay away from John. He only means to harm you."

Tristan looked at him. "If he tries, I will kill him," he said frankly. "I know your goal for the Executioner Knights is to protect the Crown, to protect England, but I am telling you at this moment that if John tries to get close to me, I will kill him, and then you will have young Henry on the throne. If he sends men after me, I will kill them, too, and then I will kill the boy. I'll kill anyone who tries to harm me. I have every right to defend myself."

William put up a hand to ease him. "There is no need for that," he said. "I think it is safe to say that you can continue with your duties, as you always have without any disruption, but simply stay vigilant. I will send you to the marches with de Lohr, and you can serve with him for a while."

Tristan shook his head. "I do not want to go to the marches," he said, still agitated. "Forgive me, my lord, but where de Lohr is, John is. It is well known that John has been trying for twenty years to kill or disable de Lohr. The man is a target for the king, and I do not want to be in his service."

The Marshal looked at Christopher, who couldn't disagree

with Tristan. He came away from the fire, moving toward the knight who had just found out he was a prince.

"I do not blame you," Christopher said. "It's my suggestion that you go north, to Pelinom with Jax de Velt. Your brother, Ashton, is already there, and the two of you can serve together. It is well known that as much as John is attracted to me, he is terrified of Jax. Everyone is. You will be safe there, and Jax could use your sword."

He was speaking of Ajax de Velt, a warlord known throughout England as the Dark Lord. Twenty-five years ago, Jax had been a ruthless and merciless barbarian who tore through the Scottish marches on a conquest campaign, using vicious and horrifying tactics on his enemies. King Henry, at the time, had been so fearful of him that he'd paid the man a tribute not to attack royal properties. Even though marriage to a good woman and a family had calmed Jax's bloodlust, he was still quite feared. What Christopher suggested was sound, and Tristan knew it.

"Please know that I mean no offense towards you, my lord," he said to Christopher. "But you are a favorite of John's, and not in a good way."

Christopher smiled without humor. "How fortunate for me," he said with irony. "And I was not offended. But I think you would be best served far to the north, under Jax's command. At least for now."

He looked at the Marshal, who nodded. "If Tristan would like to," he said. "He can learn a great deal from Jax, and he would be serving where he is needed."

"Does Lord de Velt know my… origins?" Tristan asked.

The Marshal nodded again. "He does," he said. "He understands your worth. And the danger."

Tristan took a long, deep breath, struggling to reconcile himself to the sharp turn his life, and future, had just taken. Things were to be different from now on, he knew that. And he hated it.

Little did he realize just *how* different his life was to be.

Destiny was upon Philip Alexander Tristan.

CHAPTER ONE

Year of our Lord 1218
The Siege of Wrexham Castle

IT WAS A glorious sight.

Mighty Wrexham Castle, one of the largest structures between Windsor and Edinburgh, had finally fallen to the English after almost two months of a horrible and deadly siege. Victory was in the air for the English armies, and relief rippled through the ranks.

The end was in sight.

No one was more relieved than Tristan.

He'd been with it from the start, and it had been an enormous undertaking. The Welsh, who had enjoyed a somewhat peaceful existence during the reign of King John, had decided upon his demise that they would resume their usual belligerence when it came to English rule. Led by Prince Llywelyn, the rebellion went in surges, and this was just one more surge in a country with a history of them. In this case, their target had been the northern end of the Welsh marches and the well-fortified castles that lined the border.

Because Christopher de Lohr and his allies held the southern to the mid marches, the weak point was the northern marches between Chirk Castle and Liverpool. It was true that there were several castles on the northern end, including Shrewsbury, but those castles hadn't seen the activity that the castles toward the south had seen. Since major English properties were in the southern part of Wales, that always seemed to be the flashpoint for most of the rebellions, and the warlords there were forearmed.

But not in the north.

Since John's passing and the ascension of his nine-year-old son, Henry, the Welsh seemed to think a child on the throne was the perfect time to assert themselves. About a year after John's death, they started moving against smaller outposts along the northern marches, a tactic that English warlords soon realized meant they were testing the waters, so to speak. They were systematically testing the outposts and the reaction of the allies when one of them was attacked to see where the strengths and weaknesses were.

William Marshal, whose major property of Pembroke Castle was deep inside Welsh territory, kept a particularly close eye on what they were doing. The Welsh usually left Pembroke alone simply because William Marshal could summon thousands of men to crush any manner of attack, so they had learned long ago that Pembroke was not an easy target. However, there were several outposts along the marches that did make fairly easy targets, and they made a habit of harassing them on a regular basis. More than two and a half years after John's death, the Welsh became aggressive on the northern marches, and two months ago, they finally made the big push for the biggest prize.

Wrexham Castle.

Wrexham wasn't merely impressive. It was positively sublime. It had been built by a subject of William the Conqueror two hundred years earlier with the purpose of containing the northern marches, protecting Liverpool and Cumbria, and controlling the roads that headed into Anglesey. There were other castles in the area with similar objectives, but none so mighty as Wrexham.

And the Welsh wanted it.

The Lord of Wrexham was a descendant of the man who built it. Rufus de Gresford was the last surviving male of the family line, and he'd gotten married late in life to a Welsh warlord's daughter, Nessa. Nessa had been very young, and pretty, and Rufus had put great faith in his new wife and her father, who served Llywelyn. Nessa and her father made a good show of being loyal to de Gresford when the reality was much different.

Llywelyn wanted Wrexham.

The unfortunate necessity was that de Gresford was part of that plan. The marriage with Nessa had been carefully cultivated, and once she was in Rufus' bed, the real siege of Wrexham began. Her father, along with Llywelyn, sent Welsh warriors into the castle disguised as servants, all of them settling in and earning trust, just as Nessa was earning her husband's trust. Lonely Rufus wanted to make his wife happy, so he allowed her to bring her kinsfolk to live at Wrexham, allowing an influx of Welsh into his castle.

He never even saw it coming.

One night, Nessa slit her husband's throat, and a rebellion was staged from within the castle. The de Gresford soldiers were caught off guard, and half of them were dead before they realized what had happened. Those that remained fought back, but by that time, the gates were open and the castle was overrun. Some de Gresford soldiers managed to flee, and word soon reached Christopher de Lohr and other marcher lords of what had happened. William Marshal wasted no time in sending an army to reclaim what was inarguably the largest castle on the northern marches, something he most definitely didn't want the Welsh to have.

That had been two months ago. Wrexham Castle had been designed by a genius, with enormous curtain walls surrounding what was essentially an island set within a massive moat. The walls themselves were twenty feet high and several feet thick, built of the gray granite that was so prevalent along the marches. Rising from within the curtain walls was a keep several stories high, with a parapet on the roof that allowed for skilled Welsh archers to fire the enemy. The gatehouse was half the size of the keep but still utterly enormous, four stories in height. Set within that gatehouse were dual portcullises, massive grates of wood that were sheathed in iron so they were nearly impossible to burn.

This was the castle that the Marshal's army faced.

The siege of Wrexham Castle had been no easy feat from the start. The moat was so vast and the walls so strategically placed that it made the approach of any army incredibly difficult. There was no possibility to gain the advantage of surprise, so the Marshal didn't try. He had five allied houses with him and an army of close to ten thousand men, including a thousand archers and eighteen siege engines. The only thing they could do was wheel the engines up to the edge of the moat and anchor them into position.

It made for an awesome sight.

When the siege actually began, Tristan was put in command of those massive war machines. They began their bombardment, slinging boulders at the walls, trying to break them down. The archers on the top of the keep and on the wall walk fired at the enemy soldiers, trying to keep them away from the machines, but they weren't entirely successful. Although it made the men manning the machines move slower because they had to continually protect themselves, it didn't stop the siege engines. Huge boulders were dug up from the rocky hills near the River Clywedog and brought to the siege engines on wagons pulled by oxen. Those boulders were then loaded into siege engines and slung into the walls.

The first area to be destroyed were the archer positions.

The truth was that the English wanted the castle back but they didn't want to completely demolish it, so after three days of bombarding the walls and knocking holes into them, they started another tactic. They began coating smaller boulders with flammable liquid, like fish oil and pig's grease, lighting them on fire and then tossing them up over the walls. The purpose of that was to burn anything in the interior of the castle that was worth burning and, hopefully, destroy the food supply. They weren't beyond burning the Welsh out.

But the Welsh weren't easily burned.

The flaming siege engines went on for a couple of weeks before the English returned to simply hurling boulders into the walls. But what the Welsh didn't realize was that it was a diversionary tactic, because while the boulders were flying, there were fleets of men in the trees to the west building pontoon bridges with which to cross the moat. Since the only real access in and out of Wrexham was the gatehouse, they had to get to it before they could actually get into the castle.

Since it was such a large-scale attack, the Marshal had

summoned several of his Executioner Knights and the armies who served them. Most of his senior agents had outposts or garrisons, men with responsibilities other than being an Executioner Knight, and he used that to his advantage. De Lohr from Lioncross Abbey Castle had come, leaving Alexander behind in command of the castle, while Christopher's eldest son, Peter, came from his garrison of Ludlow Castle. From the south, Gart Forbes from Dunstan Castle had brought his army, and Caius d'Avignon from Hawkstone Castle had come also.

But there were more.

From nearby Cloryn Castle, Bretton de Llion and his son, Gareth, had brought a rather compact but heavily armed army. Gareth, in fact, was an Executioner Knight, but he'd returned to Cloryn to serve his elderly father in the last years of Bretton's life. But the last two armies, and big ones that that, were that of the House of de Winter, with Bric MacRohan in command and Maxton of Loxbeare from Chalford Hill Castle. These were older men, with decades of battle experience, and they had to tap into everything they knew in order to breach Wrexham. It took two months, but it could have easily taken two years with less experienced men. On the dawn of the sixty-second day of battle, it was Tristan and his men who finally managed to break through the damaged portcullises.

That was when the fall of Wrexham began.

Now, it was evening on the sixty-second day, and Tristan was on a portion of the battlements that hadn't been destroyed by his siege engines, watching the sunset in the west. He was fairly certain that it was the first time since the siege began, other than intermittent sleeping, that he'd come to a full stop. All of the past two months had seen him on the move, except for this very moment.

He was able to pause.

He could breathe.

The sunset was spectacular. A storm had rolled over the land earlier in the day, clearing away to leave a soggy landscape and a brilliant sky. He could smell the rain and the damp. Down below, in the bailey, the English armies had moved in, and the smell of cooking fires was heavy on the air. The hall, with a mostly smashed roof, was habitable nonetheless. Men were already gathering and the hearth was burning steadily. They would definitely eat well tonight.

He could already taste it.

"Here you are."

A heavy Irish accent came from behind, and Tristan turned to see one of the veteran Executioner Knights picking his way across the damaged parapet. Bric MacRohan, who commanded the mighty armies of de Winter, was an Irish legacy knight, sworn to the English but Irish to the bone. He also happened to be Tristan's friend. Behind him came a pair of Irish knights who had come from the Marshal's properties in Ireland.

Carr MacMurda and his comrade, Dermot MacEdan, couldn't be more Irish if they tried. They were fiercely loyal to their homeland, but also quite loyal to the Marshal, which made for some strange dynamics at times. They loved the English knights and harassed them with great humor, but tended to become sullen if they were harassed in return. They could dish out insults all day long, but they couldn't take them. It had been a hilarious situation at times during the course of the siege, but Tristan could see that Carr and Dermot already had cups of something in both of their hands.

Ale, he suspected.

The celebration, for the Irish, had begun early.

"Aye, here I am," Tristan said.

"What are you doing?"

"Thinking."

Bric, a massive man with pale blue eyes and white-blond hair, cocked his head. "What about?" he asked. "The difficult thinking is finished now that the battle is over. You should only have victory on your mind, Pat. Our glory has come."

Tristan smiled faintly as he leaned forward on the parapet, looking at the ground below and the men moving about busily. "It was a hard-fought battle, to be sure," he said. "These are the battles about which poets write sonnets that men weep over. I was thinking of the words to describe a night like this."

Bric glanced at Carr and Dermot, both of whom rolled their eyes. It was well known that Tristan liked to write poetry, but it was only poetry in the literal sense. It wasn't lovely or moving, but quite frankly some of the worst poetry anyone had ever heard. Beneath that serious, sometimes gruff knight was a man with the heart of a warrior, the soul of a poet, and the ability of a drudge. No one ever told him so, of course, because the poetry clearly meant something to him, but Bric should have supposed—they *all* should have supposed—that Tristan might try to compose a tribute to victory on this night.

And they meant to prevent it.

There wasn't one man among them who hadn't been present for some of Tristan's recitations. He wasn't afraid to recite his poetry among the knights, but he wouldn't do it in front of men he didn't know, and he never did it in front of the armies. He didn't recite his compositions with any regularity, but he did it enough that his friends tried to avoid it if they could.

But they were too late.

"While flaming rocks muster up their resolve," Tristan

murmured as he created what was undoubtedly a masterpiece in his own mind. "Much of the path feels 'bout with peace. Sometimes we lose ourselves *in* ourselves."

The knights were waiting for more to the epic poem, but none was forthcoming. Tristan seemed satisfied with the words he'd spoken, which made no sense at all. Dermot even shook his head quickly as if perhaps he hadn't heard correctly. He shook his head to clear up his hearing. Or his brain. He looked for clarification to Carr, who shrugged rather lamely because he had no idea what the poem meant either.

It was up to Bric to divert the subject.

"Your words speak of truth," he said stoically. "But let us speak on the current situation, looking to the future and not to the battle of the past. The Welsh have fled. Maxton and his army have chased them back to the border and beyond, so we won't be seeing that lot anytime soon. They'll think twice before returning."

Tristan nodded as he looked toward the castle, surveying the damage. "But they *will* return," he said quietly.

Bric nodded. "They will, have no doubt."

Tristan didn't doubt it in the least, but he was hoping there would at least be some respite before any counterattack came. "They took the castle through subterfuge, but they could not hold it," he said. "Whatever the Marshal does, he is going to have to keep a thousand men here or more. A place like this demands a huge army. That's where de Gresford made the mistake."

Bric took one of the cups that Carr was holding and handed it to Tristan. "True," he said. "But you will not."

"What won't I do?"

Bric's pale eyes were glimmering. "Make a mistake," he said.

"I've heard rumor that Pembroke plans to make you the garrison commander of Wrexham. Congratulations, lad. Next to de Lohr, you will have the biggest castle on the marches."

Tristan frowned. "Me?" he said. "Where did you hear such madness?"

Bric shrugged. "I heard talk."

"*Who*?"

"Christ's bloody bones, MacRohan, tell the man," Carr said with exasperation as he focused on Tristan. "Someone heard the Marshal and de Lohr speaking of it. All the men are talking about it down in the hall. The general consensus is that you'll do a fine job. We're proud of you, Pat."

"Aye, lad," Dermot chimed in, his green eyes twinkling. "Very proud. Well done."

Tristan's frown turned to disbelief. "Pembroke has had me stationed at Pembroke Castle," he said. "I've served for three years there. And now he's moving me to…?"

Carr nodded with delight. "Wrexham," he said. "Think about it—who else can he put in command that doesn't already have one? You have been the right hand of the Marshal for some time, Tristan. You've performed flawlessly. I can see that, even if you *are* a bloody Englishman. This is your reward for service, lad. I couldn't be happier for you."

"Nor I," Bric said. He threw a thumb at Carr. "And I suspect this foolish whelp of a man will serve with you. The two of you seem to make an excellent team."

"And why not?" Carr said, thumping Bric on the chest. "My lineage dictates greatness. 'Tis all I'm capable of."

Bric cocked an eyebrow. He tolerated Carr because the man was from Ireland, like he was, but he thought Carr was a bit of a fool at times. He didn't have the moody seriousness that he had.

Or Tristan had. Yet, somehow, their dynamics worked.

At least they weren't trying to kill one another.

At the moment, anyway.

"He thinks because he's descended from Irish kings that he has come claim to importance," Bric muttered. "Royal blood doesn't dictate competence, and in the case of Irish royal blood, sometimes it dictates rage over reason. I ought to know."

Carr frowned. "I'll not let you disparage my bloodlines, MacRohan," he said. "Though, to be truthful, I'm not the one with the important royal lines. That would be my wife, Brigid. Her maternal grandfather was the last King of Dublin, Ascall mac Ragnaill, and she's the daughter of his only child. That makes our daughter the lass with the most royal blood of all."

Bric rolled his eyes. "I've heard it all before."

Carr's eyes narrowed. "And this is the respect you show me?"

Before they could get into a verbal brawl, which they'd done before when discussing their mutual proud Irish heritage, Tristan intervened.

"Andie?" he said to Carr. "Isn't that your daughter?"

Carr nodded firmly. "Aye," he said. "Andromeda will make a fine ruler, someday. But I've not seen her in many a year. She's remained in Dublin with an English family while the Marshal and I have had our time together."

Tristan wasn't particularly interested in Carr's daughter, but he knew that the fact that the man was related to the last King of Dublin, and had royal lines himself, was the very reason he was in the Marshal's service. William Marshal wasn't stupid when it came to royal blood or hereditary heirs—it was better to keep them close than to let them run amuck or serve others. In fact, Tristan knew that was why he, personally, was in the

Marshal's service.

So William could keep an eye on him.

Aye, he'd learned that over the past three years, ever since his true identity had been revealed on that dark night in London. It seemed so long ago. In fact, those three years had been a time of understanding and of reconciliation for Tristan—understanding who, exactly, he was and resigning himself to the fact that he was in a very unusual and sometimes precarious position. The death of King John had somewhat eliminated any real threat against him, and the Marshal had become one of young King Henry's regents, so there was more harmony than there had been. At least Tristan didn't feel as hunted or nervous as he had when John was alive.

But he knew that William Marshal was keeping him close for a reason.

He was a man who could effectively challenge two thrones.

Not that Tristan had a mind to. If the past three years had taught him anything, it was that rule wasn't his ambition. He didn't care if he was the son of one king and the nephew of another. He simply didn't have a greedy or ambitious bone in his body, but he did have pride. He was very proud of what he'd achieved in his life, and his body of work as a knight. His friends and fellow Executioner Knights all knew who he was, and the fact that he was more nobly bred than all of them, but no one treated him any differently. He was still the same Pat that he was before he'd learned the truth, and for that, he was grateful.

But news of command of Wrexham was something else. He'd never asked for a command, and he'd never lusted for one, but if what Bric said was true, then he was going to have a positively glorious command in Wrexham Castle. He could still hardly believe it. But in the same breath, he was ready.

Ready to take the next step in his career as a knight.

"Speaking of time with the Marshal," Tristan said after a moment. "I should find him and see if this rumor is true. If I'm to take command of this behemoth, then I'd better prepare myself."

Bric moved aside slightly as Tristan walked past him, toward one of the damaged towers that held the stairs leading down to the bailey below.

"I'll go with you," Bric said, falling in behind him. "If the rumors are true, you've got your work cut out for you. Prince Llywelyn may have lost Wrexham tonight, but you'll need to plan for his return."

Tristan paused before heading down the stairs, his gaze toward the west and the dark, shadowed mountains of Wales. "Unlike de Gresford, I won't marry any Welsh nobleman's daughter," he said. "The Welsh cannot saddle me with a traitor for a wife."

"Alliances are made in such ways."

"And you see what happened to de Gresford."

That was true. Tristan glanced at Bric, who simply waggled his eyebrows. They both knew this wasn't the last they'd see of the Welsh, but meanwhile, Tristan was evidently to be put in command of a castle that everyone seemed to want.

It would be his job to hold it.

Truth be told, Bric didn't envy him that task in the least.

CHAPTER TWO

"MY HEARTIEST PRAYERS for success, Pat."

Tristan had walked into an ambush.

A friendly ambush, anyway. He'd just entered the damaged great hall of Wrexham, which was full of men as the damp evening turned into a cold night, and there were men all around congratulating him for his new command of Wrexham Castle before he'd even officially been told of it by the Marshal himself.

If the rumors weren't true, he was in for a big disappointment.

Men were shaking his hand and clapping him on the shoulder. He walked headlong into Caius d'Avignon and Gart Forbes, men who didn't normally show much emotion, but men who were smiling at him. He almost found it off-putting. Caius was enormous, with dark hair and eyes, and a terrifying man if there ever was one. But Gart was even worse—big and muscular and bald, with piercing eyes and hands the size of trenchers, his bad humor and fierceness in battle was legendary. But here he was… smiling. Or at least as close as Gart could get to the gesture. It looked like a grimace. The fact remained that the men Tristan served with weren't a smiling bunch, but when he thought about it, this was indeed a cause for celebration. One of their own was being elevated in the ranks, no longer a follower but now a leader, and that was most definitely a celebratory event.

Tristan didn't even realize how much he'd coveted a position like this until he had it.

Now… it felt good.

"Thank you," Tristan said, cocking an eyebrow. "I think. I've not heard anything officially, so time will tell if the rumors are true."

Gart put a ham-sized hand on Tristan's shoulder. "I heard it from the Marshal himself," he said. "The command is yours. You have nothing to worry over."

Beside him, Caius snorted. "Nothing?" he said, incredulous. "He has the Welsh to worry over. *I* have the Welsh to worry over because my holdings aren't far from here. You do not understand that, Forbes, living in the south as you do. All you have to worry over are wild animals and pirates."

Gart's castle was on the coast of Devon, so what Caius said was true, but Gart didn't like the insinuation that he led an easy life.

"You should be so lucky that the Welsh are all you have to worry over," he said, pointing a finger at both Caius and Tristan. "If you want real trouble, I'll send the pirates your way. Men by the name of Kraken and Malcolm One-Hand. That one hand can do a good deal of damage, I assure you."

Caius was trying not to laugh at him. "And you think the pirates do more damage than the Welsh?"

Gart lifted an eyebrow at him. "Careful, Viper," he said, referring to the nickname Caius earned in the Levant as the Britannia Viper. "I must pass your holdings on my way home. If

I'm feeling petulant enough, I might harass your castle, and your wife might even weep in terror at the mere sight of me."

Caius burst out laughing. "My darling wife will take a club to you," he said. "No one tries to frighten Emelisse and lives to tell the tale."

"Then she has saved you this time, but insult me no more or I will be forced to challenge her to get to you."

Even Tristan was grinning by now. "And these are the allies I have to look forward to?" he muttered. "I'll take my chances with the Welsh."

He clapped Caius on the shoulder as he pushed past the bickering pair, trying to make his way to the dais to find the Marshal, whom he'd caught a glimpse of upon entering the hall. But through the smoke and broken furniture and clutter of men relaxing after a long battle, he was having difficulty pushing his way through the masses. That went double when he was suddenly cornered by Gareth de Llion and Bric.

"Why you should be given command of Wrexham and not me is appalling," Gareth said with feigned outrage. He threw a thumb into his own chest. "*I* am the one who was born and raised on the marches. *I* am the one who knows everyone and everything on the marches. Why on earth they put a knight from Northumberland in command of Wrexham is a mystery."

Tristan genuinely liked Gareth. A grandson of Ajax de Velt through his eldest daughter, he had the de Velt size and talent. He also had the pride and arrogance that his uncles, Jax's sons, had.

Tristan cocked an eyebrow.

"I do not think I like your tone, Gareth," he said. "Are you intimating that I am unworthy for such a post? Be cautious when you answer, because you know I have served your grandfather. Much of my training comes from him. If you insult me, you insult him, and I shall make sure your uncles know of this."

Gareth turned his nose up at him. "They do not frighten me," he said, though it was a lie. The sons of Jax de Velt frightened everybody if they had any sense. "Tell them what you must. But I suppose you are better than some of the other fools around here because you are de Velt trained."

"How generous of you."

Gareth couldn't keep a straight face any longer. "I know," he said, reaching out to take Tristan's hand. "If you must know, I think it is marvelous. My grandfather would have been very proud of you."

Since Jax had been killed in battle against King John a few years earlier, it was a bittersweet moment between two men who had loved him. Worse still, Tristan had been involved in the battle on that terrible day, and it still resonated with him. As Jax's family went into mourning, in the middle of the battle, it had been Tristan and his younger brother, Ashton, who had kept John from taking Jax's castle. Echoes of that awful day would probably always be with him.

"Thank you," Tristan said with uncharacteristic softness in his voice. "I am equally sure he would have had a great deal of advice on how to handle the Welsh. He has six castles along the marches, doesn't he?"

"Four," Gareth said. "He gave Cloryn and Rhayder to my father, but his men still command the others. At some point, my Uncle Cole will probably give them over to my father because he has no real interest in maintaining a presence on the Welsh marches."

They were speaking of Jax's eldest son, Cole de Velt, also

Baron Blackadder, who was now the head of the de Velt empire. Tristan knew Cole quite well, and knew the man's inclinations on the Welsh marches. "He has his hands full with the properties on the Scots border," he said. "He is more concerned with the two main castle de Velt castles, Pelinom and Berwick, than the four smaller ones in the wilds of Wales."

"Very true."

Abruptly, there were cups of ale being shoved at them, courtesy of Bric, who had grabbed them from a serving wench's tray. "Drink," Bric commanded. "No more talk of Welsh castles. Let us drink to Tristan's new post and to Jax de Velt, whose absence is sorely felt."

That was much appreciated by both Gareth and Tristan, who lifted their cups in salute before downing the entire contents. Tristan, who oddly enough didn't have much of a tolerance for strong drink, ended up sputtering as he handed the cup back to Bric.

"Good God," he said hoarsely, clutching his throat. "What is that swill?"

Bric grinned. "That swill is what we found in the vault of Wrexham," he said. "It all belongs to you. I wish you luck drinking down that rancid liquid."

"If I am dead in a week, you shall know why."

Bric and Gareth started to laugh, but another presence joined their group. The Marshal had made an appearance, reaching out to grasp Tristan by the arm. He pulled the man away from his colleagues with a manner that seemed both firm and irritated.

Tristan would quickly find out why.

"I had hoped to tell you of my decision for Wrexham personally," the Marshal said. "But I know that you've already been told by men who keep secrets that forge nations, yet cannot keep their mouths shut when it comes to one of their own."

Tristan found himself fighting off a grin at the Marshal's disgruntled statement.

"I do not know much, truthfully," he said. "Only rumors and drunken cheers."

"Good," the Marshal said as he continued to pull Tristan through the crowd of knights and soldiers so he could get the man alone. "Since you already know of my plans, let me elaborate on my decision. Wrexham is a very important and strategic castle, Pat. You know this. You have spent two months trying to wrest it back from the Welsh, and we were able to do that, in large part, due to your strategies with the siege engines. But it is not only that—you have served me flawlessly for many years. You served Jax de Velt flawlessly, as well, and your father, though understandably biased, has only praise for you."

Tristan was modest. "I have only been doing my duty, my lord."

The Marshal nodded. "I realize that," he said. "And you are not the ambitious sort. I've seen too many of those over the years. You would not step on one man to achieve your end, and that is an admirable trait, especially for a Plantagenet. It is shocking, truthfully."

Tristan didn't like being reminded of his true bloodlines. They'd all discovered that over the past few years when Tristan would stiffen up the moment the subject was introduced. He did it even now, his jaw twitching faintly, as William watched him carefully.

In his opinion, it was an understandable reaction.

"I knew your father and brothers as well as anyone," the Marshal said, lowering his voice. "I knew that they were capable of. I've seen the evidence firsthand. But you… you do not have that unethical trait. You do not have their blind ambition, which leads me to believe it was a learned characteristic on their part and not an inherent one. In any case, the command of Wrexham is yours. I believe you will make a fine commander, Pat. It is no less than you deserve. In fact, if there were any justice in the world, you'd have a few earldoms and lands in Ireland in your possession and we would all be taking orders from you. But, alas, that is not the case. Wrexham now belongs to me, and I put you in command. You have my permission to fly your crimson shield from the battlements alongside my scarlet lion. Let the world know who is now in command of Wrexham."

The crimson shield. Tristan's adoptive father, Juston de Royans, flew a blue shield on his standard, and when Tristan was given command of one of Juston's outposts, Ravensworth Castle, Juston had commissioned a crimson shield for Tristan to signify his command. It flew alongside Juston's blue shield, and now it would fly alongside the standard of William Marshal.

It was a great honor, and Tristan knew it.

"Thank you, my lord," he said sincerely. "You humble me."

"I know you will not fail."

Tristan drew in a long, slow breath, digesting his new assignment and everything it entailed. "Nay, my lord, I will not," he said. "But I have been thinking, and I know that I will need help. I have a very big task ahead of me."

The Marshal's yellowed eyes twinkled. "You came to that conclusion by yourself, did you?" he said, jesting. But the twinkle soon faded. "Bigger than you know. Llywelyn will not take this loss well. He will be back."

"I know. I was just saying that to MacRohan."

William looked around him, seeing Bric and Carr and Dermot standing with Caius and Gart several feet away. There were others around, as well—Peter de Lohr, a bright, powerful young knight and commander of Ludlow Castle, a Crown property, went to Bric, putting his hand on the man's shoulder in greeting. Christopher was sitting on the dais, in conversation with a couple of the Marshal's advisors, but standing behind Christopher, surveying the room, was a very big knight at the exceedingly young age of seventeen years. But he was standing there for a reason, and the twinkle came back into the Marshal's eyes.

He had an idea.

"I am sending the Irish with you," he said to Tristan. "Carr and Dermot are strong warriors, cunning, and they hate the Welsh more than we do."

Tristan nodded. "Thank you, I think," he said, watching the Marshal snort. "I would also like to request Addax. He has been serving de Lohr, but I need him, my lord. I would feel better with his sword."

"Agreed," the Marshal said. "I will send him up from Lioncross. But there is one more sword I'm giving you, and he is a powerful one. The question is whether or not you can control him."

"Who?"

The Marshal tipped his head in the direction of the dais. "See the knight standing behind de Lohr?"

Tristan turned around, spying the subject. "De Wolfe?"

The Marshal nodded slowly. "Aye," he said. "William de Wolfe. He's seventeen years of age and has already been knighted by the Earl of Teviot. I've never seen such raw talent in my life. The man has the makings of a legend."

Tristan's gaze was lingering on the very young, but very big, knight. He was a few inches over six feet and built like a stallion—big arms, big chest, big neck, and enormous hands. He was also excruciatingly handsome, and even Tristan had heard rumors now and again about the de Wolfe squire that no one could seem to control or contain, men and women alike.

William de Wolfe was in a league all his own.

"I've seen him over the past couple of months," Tristan said, eyeing the young knight in the shadows. "Though I've not really spoken to him. He was with Hereford, and I had my own men to command. Why would you give him over to me? Will Hereford be willing to part with him if he is so good?"

The Marshal snorted. "Let me tell you a little something about William de Wolfe," he said. "He is a genius. I do not use that word often, but in his case, it is true. He is the youngest son of Edward de Wolfe, Earl of Wolverhampton, and the lad has something of a shadowed past."

Tristan looked at him, a smile on his lips. "At his age?"

"At his age," the Marshal confirmed. "Surely you've heard of him."

Tristan shrugged. "A little," he admitted. "Not all of it flattering."

The Marshal cocked an eyebrow. "No doubt," he said. "He's been an experienced gambler since he was a small lad, and he's probably richer than you are. He fostered at Kenilworth, but even the master knights couldn't beat the scoundrel out of him, so his father sent him to Northwood Castle on the Scots border, hoping the action in the north would tame him."

"It didn't?"

The Marshal shook his head. "Hardly," he said. "He nearly

took over Northwood Castle. He and his comrades, other squires who were in league with him. That young man had a gambling ring organized, and he was bleeding the soldiers into poverty. The only reason the Earl of Teviot didn't send him away immediately was because the lad is hell with a sword and he has a mind for tactics and warfare. He's so good, in fact, that he was knighted quite early. From what I heard, he won several skirmishes for Teviot against the Scots."

"But he's no longer there," Tristan said, pointing out the obvious. "Why not?"

The Marshal sighed. "Because Teviot was afraid that William might actually try to overthrow him and take over his castle," he said. "Not seriously, of course, but William is a force to be reckoned with. He is bright, experienced, and cunning. Teviot could not handle him and finally sent him back to his father, but his father sent him to Hereford. William is not allowed to move away from Hereford's side, hence the way he is standing behind the man. But did you not see him when the gatehouse was breached?"

Tristan thought about that. "I think so," he said. "I seem to remember he was one of the first men through the breach."

"He was," the Marshal said. "There is something both immortal and irreverent about de Wolfe, something I intend to harness. And that is why I will leave him with you. We've all had a go at him, and we've failed. I want to put him under your command against the rebellion Welsh because he was brilliant against the Scots. I think he can help you if you do not end up throwing him in the vault first."

Tristan wasn't quite sure what he could say to that. He was to have two feisty Irishmen and one uncontrollable squire. It didn't sound like a recipe for success to him, but it did sound like an interesting one. It seemed that nothing about this command was going to be simple.

"Very well," he said. "But may I make a request?"

"What is it?"

Tristan looked at him. "I want free rein with de Wolfe," he said. "If you truly want to put him under my command, there will be no following his progress or his father inquiring about his welfare. I will not send him back to his father. If I fail with him, I will throw him to the Welsh."

The Marshal almost chuckled but thought better of it because Tristan was serious. It was true that they'd all had a try with young de Wolfe, but he was, as his father so kindly put it, incorrigible. But he was so brilliant that no one was willing to cast him aside. If Tristan thought he could finally take the wild wolf in de Wolfe, then William was willing to let him try.

Even if he did think Tristan was being unrealistic.

"Do what you must," he said. "But remember he is a valued knight and the son of the Earl of Wolverhampton. Unless you want real trouble on your hands with Edward de Wolfe, you will treat his son accordingly. And that is all I will say about it."

Tristan simply nodded, his gaze lingering on de Wolfe for a few moments longer before he turned back to the Marshal.

"Is there anything else I should know or be aware of with Wrexham?" he asked.

The Marshal shrugged. "I have two old soldiers who served de Gresford and know the politics of the area, men who will tell you everything you need to know," he said. "One of them is gravely injured and may not survive, but the other one should do well enough. I would learn all I can, Pat. You have quite a task ahead of you, and you want to be as well informed as you can be."

Tristan was aware of that. He tried to look at the situation as any other task he'd been entrusted with, but he hadn't been as excited about any of those. For this particular task… he was excited.

As excited as he could be, at any rate.

"I will educate myself on everything I can that has to do with Wrexham and the surrounding area," he said. "My life depends on it. I will not fail you, my lord. And I am grateful… very grateful… to have your trust."

The Marshal smiled weakly. "It is I who is grateful," he said. "I know you do not like to speak of your origins, so I will say one more thing and let the subject rest. As I mentioned, I knew your father and brothers. I knew them very well. I know you do not want to hear this, but I will say it anyway—I have a feeling you would have made a magnificent king, Pat. You have all the makings for it. But I also think you would not have survived, because you have character when others do not. You trust me when you should not. And that is the advice I will give you for this command—be careful of whom you trust. Assume a man is untrustworthy until he proves to you that he is. Be cautious, be wise, be vigilant. Will you do this?"

Tristan nodded smartly. "I will, my lord."

"Good," the Marshal said. "Now, you will go back to your friends and drink the night away. And if I were you, I would have a word with de Wolfe and establish your position."

Tristan's gaze moved to the tall, powerful knight still standing ramrod straight behind Christopher. "Does he know he is to remain here with me?" he asked.

The Marshal nodded. "He does," he said. "I told him."

"He is displeased?"

"On the contrary," the Marshal said. "He is very happy to

serve at a highly contested castle. I think he is also glad to be away from de Lohr's tight grasp."

Tristan nodded faintly, his gaze still on de Wolfe. "I do not think he is going to like my tight grasp any better."

The Marshal snorted, heading back toward Christopher as Tristan stood there, watching the dais a moment before turning his attention to the room. It was a vast hall, with half of the roof missing, and he honestly couldn't relax when he knew how much work he had facing him. The entire castle was compromised, and the armies that had claimed it wouldn't remain forever. They'd all be leaving in the next few days, which meant he had to utilize their manpower to repair the castle before they left.

He had plans to make.

"Well?"

Peter de Lohr appeared at his side, a younger version of his father. Peter was positively splendid as a knight and as a spy, and Tristan had heard stories of what, exactly, Peter had accomplished. The rumors were truly staggering. But one would never know the depths of darkness Peter had sunk to simply by looking at him. He was blond and handsome, looking every inch the shining and noble knight.

"Well, *what*?" Tristan asked.

Peter grinned, looking up at the ceiling because Tristan was. "I heard the news," he said. "Did the Marshal officially give you command?"

Tristan was looking at a beam that had been broken in half by the projectiles he'd sent over the walls. "He did," he said calmly, as if he wasn't at all delighted by it. "He is leaving Carr and Dermot with me and sending Addax al-Kort up from Lioncross."

"Excellent."

"He is also leaving de Wolfe with me."

Peter's gaze moved from the ceiling to the dais where de Wolfe was standing behind de Lohr and now the Marshal. "God help you," he muttered. "The knight everyone wants, but no one can control. I wonder if he knows what the seasoned men think of him?"

It really wasn't a question, but more of a comment. Tristan thought on the statement before answering.

"Pembroke called him brilliant," he said. "Given that assessment, I suspect he knows what others think. I further suspect he does not care. Have you been around him to any great extent?"

Peter shrugged. "I've known him since he was born," he said. "Our fathers are close friends. I know his older brothers, too—Jonathan and Robert. They're good men, but William is the warrior in the family. There has always been something about him that speaks of intelligence and cunning. As if he's already three steps ahead of you. I think part of the problem is he makes other men feel stupid because he's so bright, and that is a blow to any man's pride, including Pembroke. Why do you ask?"

Tristan began to look around the room again. "Because he seems like a man who operates alone," he said. "He seems… solitary."

Peter shook his head. "He is not solitary, I assure you," he said. "Haven't you heard that he has two cohorts, men he fostered with, men who are always in on his schemes? That's why he was sent back from Northwood—alone. The Earl of Teviot sought to separate him from those friends he's always with."

"Do you know them?"

Peter cocked his head thoughtfully. "A little," he said. "Paris de Norville and Kieran Hage are also stunning examples of young knights, but they have the same devious streak that William does. Truthfully, I think gossip has them behaving worse than they actually do. But the Marshal is correct—de Wolfe is brilliant, but so are his friends. When they mature, they are going to be quite formidable. My father says they are in a league of their own, and he is right, but in order to tame de Wolfe, they have separated him from his pack. I'm not entirely sure how he will function without them."

Tristan glanced over his shoulder at the young knight. "I am about to find out," he said. "But I wonder… has anyone tried to come to know him? Take him under their wing? All I've heard is of his unsavory behavior and the knights looking down their noses at him. And even now, he's standing behind Hereford, alone. He *looks* alone."

"What's your point?"

Tristan shook his head. "I do not know," he said. "But I do know that de Wolfe and I are going to come to know one another very well in the coming days and months. And if I do not like what I see…"

Peter looked at him. "What will you do?"

Tristan simply shrugged because he really didn't have an answer. They weren't speaking of a foolish squire anymore. They were speaking of a powerful knight, someone who couldn't simply be cast aside. Without another word, Tristan headed off toward the dais, leaving Peter standing there, wondering if Tristan's new command had already been set up to fail by adding an uncontrollable young knight to the situation. Tristan was made of stone and was a solid commander, but even stones could crack.

Peter hoped de Wolfe wasn't the hammer to do it.

Life at Wrexham Castle from this point forward was going to prove… interesting.

CHAPTER THREE

Rockbrook Castle, South of Dublin
Demesne of the de Courcy Family

"YOU CANNOT GO back to retrieve anything. We must go. *Now.*"

The woman who had raised her was yanking her along a dark corridor. She was in a sleeping shift and robe, heavy against the cold night air, and someone was trying to put a cloak on her shoulders. She could hear others running behind her, down a narrow corridor that was dark and smelled of the damp, with the only light being the lamp in the hand of the woman who was pulling on her and urging her to run.

And she did.

Truthfully, she wasn't entirely oblivious to what was going on. There had been rumors of it for months, enemies of her grandfather who had wanted a marriage between her and a man of their choosing. They wanted to breed her into a rival line and meld his bloodlines with theirs, hoping to breed out his entire lineage.

She was the last of her kind.

Andromeda Ní Murda de Courcy was running for her life.

"My mother?" she asked, trying to keep the terror from her voice. "What of my mother? Have they gone for her as well?"

The woman with the lamp in her hand was focused and businesslike. "I do not know, lass," she said. "I've not heard of her fate, but it's you they want, not her. Everyone knows who Brigid's father is, and they know you are the daughter of two kingdoms. They want you and they do not want her. There is no time to waste."

Andromeda was trying very hard not to break into tears. She was worried about her mother, someone she'd been kept from her entire life over safety concerns, but someone she loved very much. Her entire life had been one of hiding and secrets, of pretending to be someone she wasn't. Even the name Andromeda wasn't the name she'd been given at birth. When she'd come to Lord and Lady de Courcy as a toddler, they changed her name from Morrigan, after the Irish war goddess, to Andromeda, after the most beautiful woman in the ancient world. Andromeda was all she'd ever known. But Morrigan was who they wanted.

They were coming for her.

"They do not only want me for a marriage," she muttered after a moment, following the woman down a slippery stairwell that was as dark as the night outside. "They want to use me as an example. They want to shame me and my bloodline. Hiding me from them and changing my name… it was futile. The truth has found me."

The woman pulling her along didn't reply immediately. She kept the lamp up, held high, so they could see where they were going and focused on the path ahead. As a practical woman, there was no time for regrets.

"It will be futile if we do not get you to safety," she said steadily. "We knew this day might come, and we have planned for it."

She sounded so… cold. No emotion, only duty. Andromeda couldn't help it—the tears began to come. She was rushing through the ground floor of the home she grew up in and knew exactly where she was—in the kitchens. The chambers were small, so there were several rooms used by the kitchens. She could smell the smoke from the great cooking hearth and the yeast for the morning's bread. It was, in fact, close to morning, and the woman pulling her along was none other than the lady of the castle herself, Lady de Courcy. Andromeda had little doubt that the people behind her were trusted servants, including the woman who had been a nurse to all of the de Courcy children. She could hear old Breeda sniffling and huffing as they ran.

But Andromeda had no idea where, exactly, they were running to.

"But why must I leave?" she wanted to know. "Can you tell me why I must go? I have lived here much of my life. My sisters and I have…"

"You mean my daughters," Lady de Courcy corrected her softly. "They are *my* daughters, Andie. I know you were raised together, but they are my daughters, and I must protect them."

"But—!"

"You do not wish for Ceara and Alecia to be in danger, do you?"

She didn't. Of course she didn't. But Andromeda still didn't understand why she was being forced to flee in the middle of the night.

"*How* are they in danger?" she said, suddenly digging in her heels and forcing everyone to come to a halt. "I do not understand why I cannot stay. Will these old walls no longer keep out those who wish to do me harm? Can you please explain? Rockbrook is the sturdiest castle in Ireland. Are you telling me that it cannot withstand whatever we are running from?"

Lady de Courcy wasn't trying to be cruel. But she did have a task to complete and a family to protect, so she faced Andromeda with as much patience as she could.

"Because you are the last of your kind, my dear," she said softly, putting a hand on Andromeda's cheek. "My husband and William Marshal had a plan for you when you were born. You are of royal Irish blood on both sides, with your mother being the last King of Dublin's only daughter and your father of the royal Uí Faelaín house. Your grandfather was murdered by his rival, and now, that rival faction is coming for you. They have always known of your existence. When they discovered we had taken you in, the marriage offers began. We have refused them for years, but no longer. They are at the gate, demanding you be given over to them, and my husband is refusing them entry. But they will not accept that. They will bring more men. Unless we want the castle razed, we must open the gates and let them in to search for you. But you must not be here."

Andromeda understood all of that. She'd come to live with Lord and Lady de Courcy at an extremely young age, and ever since her thirteenth birthday, when they revealed her true identity to her, she'd known of her unique bloodlines. The woman she thought was a cousin was actually her mother. Her own father had gone to England to serve William Marshal because the Earl of Pembroke had lands in Ireland and a treaty with her father's family, but more than that, King John had plans for the granddaughter of mac Ragnaill, plans that died out when it did. It was all quite complex and confusing, but that moment she never hoped would come was here.

"Where am I going?" she asked, sounding scared.

Lady de Courcy began to walk again, pulling her along behind. "Lord de Courcy has trusted men to take you to Wales," she said. "You must go to your father at Pembroke Castle. Only he will be able to protect you from those who wish to force you into a hellish marriage."

Andromeda was once again trying not to panic. "How long must I stay?"

They had reached the kitchen door, the one that opened out into the kitchen yard with the postern gate beyond. Rockbrook Castle was so fortified that even the postern gate had a portcullis built into a small gatehouse that was low and squat, dug deep into the ground. As soon as Lady de Courcy opened the gates, there were four heavily armed soldiers waiting. Andromeda was startled by the sight, coming to an unsteady halt in the doorway.

"My lady?" she said fearfully, eyeing the man. "Must I—?"

"You must." Lady de Courcy had to yank her out of the doorway and into the yard. She faced the soldiers that were laden with weapons and bags, clearly meant for travel. "You will take the lady and follow the plan laid out by his lordship. There is a boat waiting at the river to take you to the coast, where one of Lord de Courcy's ships is waiting for you. Hurry, now; there is no time to waste."

Old Breeda had managed to fasten the cloak around Andromeda, pulling the hood over her head as another servant tied sturdy leather shoes to her feet. Lady de Courcy turned to her, kissing her on the cheek and embracing her, fighting off her own tears now that she and Andromeda were soon to be parted.

"I am sorry it must be this way, my dear," she whispered in

Andromeda's ear. "The kingdoms in Ireland are many, and the hatred between them is great. But know that we love you and we shall pray for you. *Go!*"

Andromeda wept softly as one of the soldiers reached out and took her by the arm, pulling her toward the postern gate where several de Courcy men were standing, protecting the entry from the angry Irish clan of mac Lochlainn, who were at the main gatehouse. As Lady de Courcy said, they hadn't brought their army yet, but they would when they realized that Liam de Courcy, Earl of Kilternan, wasn't going to let them in. When they realized they were being denied Ascall's granddaughter for the last time. Right now, Liam was trying to buy Andromeda time to leave.

Time to get clear of the Irish who wanted to take her.

And Andromeda knew it. She knew all about her grandfather, Ascall mac Ragnaill, and how he'd been murdered. Now, another kinsman ruled in his stead, but there were so many factions vying for the throne of Dublin that it was difficult to know who was friend and who was foe.

It was better to get Andromeda out of Ireland altogether.

For good.

Out into the dark night Andromeda and her soldiers went, down to the River Dodder, to a small cog that took them out toward the sea. Beyond that, only uncertainty and fear awaited.

And a new, unexpected life that Andromeda was terrified to face.

Alone.

CHAPTER FOUR

Year of Our Lord 1219
Wales

THE WEATHER WAS typically Welsh.

At least, that was the way Tristan felt. He'd been in command of Wrexham Castle for twelve months and, to his recollection, it had rained every one of those days. Every damn one.

He was sick of it.

But he wasn't sick of Wrexham, or his garrison, or anything that had to do with it. Frankly, he was in his element. He'd taken to commanding one of the largest castles on the marches with shocking ease. As if he'd been born to it, which, of course, he had. It was in his blood. As a man who had spent the majority of his career following the orders of others, and doing it efficiently, to finally have a command was something that fulfilled him more than he realized it could have.

And it showed.

Ever diligent and focused, Tristan had put everyone to work within a day of taking command of Wrexham. He'd utilized the armies that had remained for a few days before heading home, using the manpower to repair walls and fix roofs. Though the Marshal headed back to Pembroke Castle almost immediately, leaving about two thousand men with Tristan, and Bretton de Llion headed back to Cloryn Castle with Gareth, the other armies weren't so quick to depart. They lingered, helping repair the castle.

When Bric and Christopher and Peter wanted to return home, however, Tristan asked for a few more days so their soldiers could help with the workload. With thousands of men working on the grounds, the repairs were being completed quite quickly, but the few more days that Tristan had asked for turned into more days, and then weeks, and finally Christopher and Bric had to sneak out before dawn one rainy morning, unable to stomach more of Tristan's begging. Tristan had stood on the battlements and shouted insults at them as they passed through the gates.

Cowards was a word used frequently.

Bric had laughed at him; Christopher had ignored him.

Gart, Maxton, Peter, and Caius were the last remaining men with armies, which ended up being a good thing, because a month after the Welsh had been chased away, a small buildup was reported off to the southwest, near a village called Ruabon. Maxton and Gart took their soldiers into the village, destroying the countryside as they went, and the small force of Welsh scattered. That led the English to believe it had been an isolated incident of rebels, nothing organized by Llywelyn.

And that had been the last gathering they'd seen.

So far.

But eventually, the English warlords had to return home. Gart, Maxton, and Peter all departed, leaving Caius as the last man. Caius was closer, geographically, than almost anyone else, so he could make it home in just a few days. When Addax al-Kort finally arrived from Lioncross Abbey, Caius went home, leaving Tristan with his men to manage Wrexham Castle. It was nearly fully repaired by the time Caius departed—there were still a few things that needed to be fixed, but most of the major work had been done, including the great hall ceiling and the gatehouse with its twisted portcullis.

These days, not quite a year after the siege that saw Wrexham return to the English, everything was quiet, for the most part. Tristan was learning to put his senior knights in charge of things like patrols and duty assignments for the men, but it was difficult for him. He was used to doing those things, and to stay out of a patrol… well, he was struggling with it. The man who had always been the obedient knight was still adjusting to delegating.

Sometimes, he simply gave up.

Like today.

Wrexham had six patrols out at any given time, and today, simply because he couldn't stay out of it, Tristan was riding patrol with Addax and de Wolfe, leaving Carr in command of Wrexham as Dermot took a patrol to the north. Tristan, Addax, and William headed west, sweeping south throughout the day, and ending up in the village of Ruabon.

Tristan hadn't been to the village in a few months, but his patrols made a regular habit of sweeping through it because this was the last place they'd seen any manner of rebel activity. The land was gently rolling here, rather bland in appearance, with trees that were barren from a particularly cold winter. Even though it was spring, it was still cold, and although the knights were dressed accordingly, a six-hour patrol had seen the iciness seep into their hands and face. Moving into the town, the first business they came across was a tavern with a great amount of smoke pouring from the chimney.

"They must have quite a blaze going," William said. "That means a big fire. Much heat. Flame. Warmth. Comfort."

Addax, who positively hated icy temperatures, glanced over at the young knight. "Are you trying to tell us something, de Wolfe?"

William gestured to the gray-stoned tavern with the heavily thatched roof. "Unless you are dead, you should understand me," he said. "I can no longer feel my fingers. A warm fire and some warmed wine would save my life at this point."

Tristan was cold as well, but he frowned at the dark-haired knight. "You spent all of that time in the north where it is well known to be cold much of the year?" he said. "How did you survive?"

William flashed a brilliant smile. "I can survive anything," he said. "But even us immortals need a fire and hot wine. In fact, I will pay for it if you will let us stop for a while."

That was an offer Tristan couldn't pass up. He looked at Addax, and they shrugged at one another, which was an approval as far as William was concerned. He immediately reined his horse toward the tavern, moving down an alley on his way to the livery behind it. The others followed because no one wanted to leave their horse out in such cold weather, so once the horses were settled in a warm stable with plenty of oats, the knights and soldiers headed into the tavern from the rear entrance.

Opening the door, the stale warmth hit them in the face like a slap. It was a big tavern, two stories, with rented rooms on the top floor and a big common room on the ground floor. It was half-full at this time of day, not terribly busy, but as William had guessed, there was an enormous fire spitting heat and clouds of smoke into the common room. The eight men immediately headed for the hearth, with the knights taking the table closest to it while the five soldiers were left to drag another table over to it. The knights sat down at their table, the soldiers at theirs, and the call for drink went out.

Those back in the kitchens began to scramble.

"I think this is the first time I've seen de Wolfe spend his money on something other than horses and more games," Addax said as he removed his helm. "This is something of an event. I think I want something to eat, also."

Tristan removed his gloves, but it was taking some effort because his hands were chilled. "As do I," he said. "We've been on patrol for several hours. We deserve something to eat at de Wolfe's expense."

William's lips twisted wryly. "I said I'd pay for drink," he said. "I never said I'd pay for a meal."

Addax turned his head, shouting over his shoulder for food, as he peeled back the damp linen hood he wore beneath his helm to protect his head. "It is the least you can do," he said. "I've had to pay the last two times you and I have been to a tavern, so it's your turn."

"You've had to pay because I won our wager."

"What wager?" Tristan said, finally able to remove his right glove and going to work on the left. "Christ, Addax, don't tell me you've been gambling with him. What have I told you about that?"

"I have not been gambling with him," Addax said. "Except to see who will pay for drink. That is *not* gambling."

Tristan looked at William, who lifted his hands in surrender. "When you assumed command at Wrexham, I made you a promise that I would not gamble with the soldiers," he said. "I have kept that promise. You never said anything about the knights."

That was true. Tristan remembered that conversation well, one of the first real conversations he'd ever had with William. He grunted at the recollection.

"You are correct," he said. "I said nothing about the knights because they have sense enough not to engage with you. But what else did I say?"

William took his helm and gloves, which had been on the table, and put them on a chair as serving wenches began setting steaming pitchers on the tables. He waited until the women walked away before replying.

"I remember everything you said," he said, reaching for a pitcher and a cup. "There is no need to repeat it."

Tristan was rather surprised that William gave him the first cup he poured. He took it, sipping at the hot and spicy wine, before speaking.

"I told you that great men lead by example," he said. "I told you that you would never truly be great until you could set an example for men to follow."

William passed another cup to Addax. "You did."

"I told you that all eyes are turned to you," Tristan continued. "I told you that you were failing the expectations of everyone—the Marshal, de Lohr… everyone, because you set a terrible example by gambling with the soldiers and taking their hard-earned wages. Noble knights do not behave in such a fashion."

It was clear that William didn't want to be lectured yet again. "I know," he said. "Do we have to talk about this now?"

"We do," Tristan said. "The Earl of Teviot knighted you

four years before you should have been knighted because he saw greatness in you. He also thought that by giving you such responsibility, it would settle you down. But he was wrong. Even your father had enough of you. The Marshal gave you to me because I was the last hope you had for a respectable position. No one else wanted you, de Wolfe, but here you are."

William's jaw pulsed as he looked away. "Aye, here I am."

"One of the best knights I have ever seen."

The corner of William's mouth twitched with a smile. "Of course I am."

"But I'm better."

William looked at him, outraged. "You were not better than I am at my age," he said. "No man has ever existed who was better than me at my age."

Tristan was trying hard not to grin at the young knight who had every reason to be arrogant, but he couldn't miss the chance to knock him down. Only humility would help William mature just a little. Not that he wasn't responsible and flawless in his decision making as a knight, but there was still work to do with him. Every man needed a dose of humility to keep him grateful and grounded. That was something de Wolfe lacked at his age.

"Let me tell you something, William," Tristan said, thumping on the table to make a point. "There will always be someone better than you. There will always be someone with a better sword, or better equipment, or a better horse, or even better breeding. You are an earl's son, and on your mother's side, you descend from Saracen warriors, and that is excellent breeding, indeed."

William nodded in agreement. "Of course it is," he said. "My bloodlines are impeccable."

Tristan lifted an eyebrow. "But mine are better," he said. "I have the blood of kings in me. My father was a king, my mother was a princess, and my uncle is the King of France. If the situation had been different, it would be me ruling England, not my nephew. So keep that in mind the next time you think you're so great. You have the privilege of serving someone who is truly greater than yourself, and that is a difficult thing to come by in your case."

William cast a long glance at him, shaking his head as if thinking the entire conversation was ridiculous, before breaking into a grin.

"If you were king, would you have me serve you?" he asked.

It was a cheeky question, and Tristan frowned. "God, no," he said. "I'd have you shoveling shite from the royal stables."

Addax burst into soft laughter. "Knowing de Wolfe, he would find a way to light it on fire and burn down your castle," he said. "Or he'd use the pitchfork to incite a riot."

Tristan chuckled as William drained his cup and moved to pour himself more.

"Do not make me out to be so rebellious," he said, on the defense. "I would make an excellent royal champion."

"You would," Tristan agreed. He regarded William for a moment, knowing he'd teased the man enough. "To be truthful, I will take this opportunity to tell you that I'm proud of your growth over the past year. When the Marshal left you with me last year, I truly wasn't certain how the situation would go. I'm happy to say that you have done well, William."

William took a big swallow from his cup. "I had little choice," he said. "You told me on the very night that Pembroke gave you command of Wrexham that if I did not give up gambling with the soldiers and behave myself, you would throw me in the vault and tell everyone I ran away with a caravan destined for the Levant."

"And you believed me."

"Clearly, I did."

"Did you really?"

William's lips were twitching with a smile as he settled back in his chair, toying with his cup. "Probably not," he said. "But it was something you said to me on that night, something that stayed with me."

"Don't keep me in suspense," Tristan said. "What is it?"

William thought back to that dark night in a great hall with only half a roof, crowded with victorious English. "You told me that you needed the best of me, something we'd not yet seen," he said. "I think you were right."

"And that made you settle down and stop gambling?"

"Nay, the threat of locking me in the vault did, but the thought of greatness not yet achieved was intriguing," he said, his hazel eyes glimmering. "I thought I should at least give that a try first before we started wrestling for the vault key."

Addax started laughing again. "Cheeky bastard," he said. "You're so full of yourself sometimes that I'd like to poke a hole in you and watch all of that swollen cheese you have for brains spill right out of you."

William snorted in spite of himself, taking another drink of ale just another wench brought a heavy tray laden with food. In fact, William found himself helping the girl set it on the table because she was in danger of dropping it. She thanked him quietly, in an accent that wasn't English and wasn't Welsh, and he glanced at her as she turned away and scurried back toward the kitchens. She was petite, wearing clothing that didn't fit her correctly, and he caught a glimpse of a pleasing profile and long, nearly white hair that was tightly braided. He might have even been interested in her if she wasn't so dirty.

The lass had dirt all over her.

But he didn't give her a second thought as he began to inspect the tray of food she'd brought. Tristan and Addax were inspecting it, too, all of them grabbing for the contents as they began to eat. William had just put a huge piece of buttered bread in his mouth when something hit him from behind. Liquid began dripping down his arms and over one shoulder. Chewing, and quite displeased, he looked over his shoulder to see a man wrestling with the dirty serving wench.

He had evidently grabbed her by the wrist when she'd been carrying a pitcher of warmed wine, causing the wine to fly through the air and hit de Wolfe between the shoulder blades. The man was quite insistent with the wench, demanding she sit on his lap. The girl, clearly upset, was begging him to let her go. The man ignored her, kissing her hand, trying to reach out to fondle her, and she yelped, slapping his hand away. When the man yanked on her, pulling her against him, she threw a fist into his face.

After that, the fight was on.

"William," Tristan muttered. When de Wolfe looked up from his food, Tristan tipped his head in the direction of the assault. "Go."

William took the hint. As knights, they simply couldn't sit around while a woman was threatened, and since William was the junior knight amongst them, he would be sent on the duty. With a sigh, William stood up and, still chewing, went over to the tussling couple and grabbed the woman, pulling her away from the man who was pawing at her. When the man took offense at that, William shoved him back by the chest, sending him crashing onto the floor. Utterly insulted, the man unsheathed a long dagger that had been at his waistband.

William shook his head as if the gesture was completely ridiculous. “Do you truly wish to engage me in a fight?” he said. “You will lose.”

The man, older and round, was struggling to his feet. “You are about to learn a lesson, knight,” he growled. “It’s foolish to interfere in another man’s business.”

William unsheathed his enormous broadsword, the one with the wolf’s head and eyes of topaz. His father had given it to him some time ago. Even at his age, the sword had claimed many victims, so he was ready with it as the man finally got to his feet.

“You made this my business when you threw the wine into my back,” he said. “Leave the girl alone and go on your way and nothing will come of this. But continue on your path and you will not live to see the end of this day.”

The man hesitated because he was studying William closely. He may have been young, but there was no disputing his size and obvious strength. He wasn’t timid in the least, either, which gave the man concern.

“How old are you, boy?” he asked.

“Old enough to kill you,” William replied steadily.

That was true. Seeing this was a situation he couldn’t win, the man took another tactic. “Where is your father?” he said. “I demand to speak with him.”

William’s eyes narrowed dangerously. “My father is the Earl of Wolverhampton,” he said. “If you wish to speak to him, you must go and find him. Otherwise, this is a matter between you and me, and I am growing weary of your cowardice. If you are going to charge with that dagger, then do it. If not, then stop wasting my time."

By this time, Addax had stood up, unsheathing a spectacular broadsword that caught the light, flashing wickedly. The man may have been a fool, but he wasn't stupid. He knew he couldn't survive two heavily armed knights with the dagger he had. Therefore, he sheathed the dagger, kicked over the table he'd been sitting at so that the food scattered all over the ground, and charged from the common room and out into the rain beyond.

And with that, he was gone.

With a triumphant smirk, William sheathed his sword and was preparing to turn back to his table when he caught sight of the serving wench standing several feet away. She was pale with terror, and he paused, looking over her slovenly form for a moment before crooking his finger at her.

She scurried over to him.

"My apologies, my lord," she said, her voice trembling. "I did not mean to involve you. The wine was an accident."

He held up his hand to let her know he wasn't angry at her. "It was not your fault," he said. "Did he hurt you?"

She shook her head. "Nay, my lord," she said. "You have my gratitude. I am sorry to have troubled you. Usually, a finger in the eye or a fist to the throat will stop them."

"I take it that this isn't the first time it has happened?"

The young woman shook her head regretfully. "It is not," she said. "It happens more than you know. That is why I've taken to smearing mud on myself, to deter them, but in this case it did not work."

That explained her filthy appearance, and William completely understood. He was also not unsympathetic. He was old enough to know what women went through in life, for he'd seen it himself. The fairer sex had their share of trouble. Before he could reply, however, the tavern keeper came out of the kitchens to survey the damage. He saw the upended table and food all over the floor before looking accusingly at the wench.

"What did you do?" he boomed.

The girl didn't shrink at the tone. "I was only doing my duties," she said. "The man grabbed me, and—"

He cut her off. "And you caused this?" he said, outraged as he pointed to the upended table. "You sent away a paying customer?"

"She did not cause it," William said in his deep, steady voice. "The man was quite bold with her and would have hurt her had I not intervened. Where were *you* when this happened? Do you not protect the women who work for you?"

The accusations were now on the tavern keep, who didn't like it one bit. Ignoring the knight, he looked at the young woman, his features alight with fury.

"I told you to behave yourself," he said. "You came to me, begging for a job, but you do not have the sense of an alley cat. I told you not to strike the customers or insult them, but you do not listen to me. You cause trouble!"

The young woman wasn't in the mood to be scolded for defending herself. Her cheeks turned red as the tavern keep shouted at her.

"If I do nothing, they are allowed to touch me at will, and I have told you that I will not permit that to happen," she countered. "But if I tell you what has happened, you reward them. You ply them with drink so they will not be insulted that we did not respond to their pinching and slapping and probing hands."

The tavern keep wasn't used to being spoken to in such a

manner, and most especially not by a woman. Taken aback that she should have the gall to point out his way of handling drunk patrons who fondled his wenches, he waved his hands at her and turned away.

"Take your things and go," he said. "I do not want to see your face again. You are too much trouble."

He stormed off, back to the kitchen, shouting at his staff as he went. The young woman stood there, mouth agape. When she realized that she no longer had a position, she looked as if she was about to weep, but held herself in check. She had already made enough of a spectacle. She looked at William to see what his reaction was, but he was already turning away from her. She presumed he was returning to his business. Blinking away the tears that were threatening, the young woman quickly turned away, but William grasped her by the arm.

"Not so fast," he said, somewhat quietly. "Come here and sit down."

Her head was down and she was resisting him somewhat. "I cannot, my lord," she said. "I must quickly gather my things before he steals them."

"Why would he steal them?"

"I do not know," she said as she began to lose her composure. "If he does not like the way we speak to a customer, he will not pay us a full wage, or if he feels as if we eat too much one day, he'll not feed us the next day. When I was ill not long ago and could not work, he took my only cloak. He said it was payment for my lodgings, since I was not working."

He looked her over, so dirty and with the ill-fitting clothing. At closer inspection, she had perfect facial features, and he suspected that underneath all of that dirt, she was a beautiful woman. But there was something about her that seemed so...

lost.

He was intrigued.

"When was the last time you ate?" he asked.

She didn't seem comfortable telling him but knew she couldn't refuse. "Yesterday," she said. "In the morning."

"And you have not eaten since?"

She shook her head, averting her gaze, and William was displeased with her answer. With a sharp sigh, one of exasperation, he tugged her over to an empty table not far from where Tristan and Addax were still sitting.

"Sit down," he commanded quietly. "I will return."

The young woman did, but she was perched on the edge of the chair as if prepared to run at a moment's notice. William had gone into the kitchen, and she could hear voices, but not what was being said. There was a bang and a crash somewhere in the middle of it. Very shortly, William emerged, followed by a serving wench bearing food and drink. He silently pointed to the table where the young woman was sitting, and the wench set everything down before darting off nervously.

William sat down opposite the young woman.

"Eat," he said. "My meal was interrupted by your foolish suitor, so you will eat with me."

The young woman wasn't sure how to respond. She was looking at the food as if overwhelmed by it all, but there was also fear in her eyes. She had no idea what was happening, or why the knight wanted her to eat. She only knew what she had to do.

She had to get out.

"I really must gather my possessions," she said. "If he steals anything from me, I will not have the money to replace it."

"He will not steal anything from you," William said, pouring her a cup of warmed wine and putting it in front of her. "Drink this."

"How do you know he will not steal anything from me?" she said, not moving to take the cup. "I told you that—"

He cut her off. "He will not steal anything from you because I told him that if he did, I would cut his hand off," he said steadily. "Drink the wine before it cools."

She stared at him a moment before looking toward the kitchens in confusion. Was it possible that this knight actually defended her to the horrible tavern keeper? Was it possible she actually had a few moments of reprieve from him? When she began to realize she might actually have a champion in the bold young knight, her gaze returned to the table, and she hesitantly picked up the cup. One small sip led to two large gulps. She was very thirsty.

William handed her a knife.

"Butter your bread," he said. "It is good bread."

She took the knife, timidly reaching for the butter as he tore off a hunk of bread and handed it to her.

"He uses good flour," she said. "At least, for the better-paying customers."

"Like me."

"Aye," she said, torn between buttering the bread and looking at his face. "And just who *are* you, my lord?"

"My name is de Wolfe," he said, mouth full. He gestured toward the table about ten feet away. "Those are my comrades. We are from Wrexham Castle. Where are you from?"

She took a bite of the bread, chewing before she answered. "Far away," she said, sounding sad. "Too far away."

"What are you doing here?"

"I came to find my father."

"Where is he?"

"Pembroke Castle."

William cocked his head. "Pembroke?" he repeated. "That is several days' ride from this place. What are you doing *here*, anyway?"

The young woman took another bite of bread, a very big bite because she was so hungry. She chewed a few times, swallowing, before she could answer.

"If you must know, I was abandoned," she said. She paused, looking at him, her features awash with sorrow. "You do not really want to hear of my plight, do you? Because I should not like to burden you with it, but I would like to ask a question."

"Ask."

"Do you know of an honorable man who might escort me to Pembroke Castle?" she said. "I cannot pay much, but I will give them everything I have earned if they will only take me there."

William's brow furrowed. "Why not send for your father to come here to you?"

She sighed heavily and looked back to her food. "I did," she said quietly. "I paid a man all of the money I had to take a message to my father, only that was almost nine months ago and the man has never returned, nor has my father shown up. I fear the man has run off with the money just like my escort did. I've been working at this tavern since then, trying to earn enough money to pay for someone to escort me to Pembroke."

William stopped chewing. He sat back in the chair, studying her intently. He suspected there was far more to what she was telling him, and, being a man of compassion, he was compelled to hear it.

"I want you to start your story from the beginning," he said.

"I am getting pieces of what seems to be a terrible injustice done to you, so start from the beginning by telling me your name and where you came from. Then you will tell me how you came here."

She gazed back at him. "You are asking quite a bit."

"I know," he said. "But tell me. Please. If I can help, I will."

That seemed to prompt her. The young woman took a deep breath, brushing tendrils of her white-blonde hair from her eyes. "My name is Andromeda de Courcy," she said. "I was born in Ireland, raised by Liam de Courcy at Rockbrook Castle south of Dublin. My father serves the Earl of Pembroke, and Lord de Courcy paid six soldiers a good deal of money to escort me to Pembroke Castle. We crossed the sea to Liverpool and took a road south, but by the time we reached this village, they decided they were no longer interested in escorting me to Pembroke. I awoke one morning and they were gone, leaving me to fend for myself."

William shook his head in disgust. "And with no money, you found work here."

"I did," she said. "I was able to pay for a man to take a message to Pembroke Castle, but as I said, he never returned, and my father has yet to show his face, so I am certain the man simply ran off with my money."

"Who is your father?"

"His name is Carr mac Murda."

William's eyes widened. He opened his mouth to say something but thought better of it. Quickly, he stood up.

"Continue your meal," he said. "I… will return."

He was moving across the floor before she could respond. At the table next to the hearth, Tristan and Addax were finishing up the meal that had been brought to them. Tristan happened to look up, catching a glimpse of William bearing down on them.

"You're too late," he said. "The food is gone. The wine is gone. My hands are warm again, so it is time we head back to Wrexham. Say farewell to your lady friend and we shall be on our way."

William held up a hand. "Wait," he said. "Pat, that woman over there has just told me something astonishing."

"What is that?"

"Her name is Andromeda de Courcy and her father is Carr mac Murda."

Tristan's eyes widened just as William's had. "She's *what*?" he said, peering around William to see that filthy, poorly dressed woman as she stuffed her mouth with boiled mutton and gravy. "She told you that she's mac Murda's daughter?"

"She did."

Tristan was caught off guard by the news. "But that's impossible," he said. "Mac Murda's daughter lives in Ireland."

"No longer, evidently."

Tristan frowned, unwilling to believe this. "She must be lying," he said. "That simply isn't possible."

"I do not believe he's lying, Pat."

"Then what in the hell is she doing here?"

William's eyebrows lifted. "I asked her," he said seriously. "She told me that she was sent here with six soldiers, paid by de Courcy to escort her to Pembroke Castle, to her father. Evidently, the escorts ran off with the money and abandoned her at this place. She says she has been trying to earn money to pay for another escort to Pembroke."

That made a little more sense to Tristan. Perhaps it was indeed Carr's daughter, come to visit her father after all these years, and she'd run into an unscrupulous escort. That was quite shocking if it was the truth. Given what Tristan knew about Carr's daughter, she should be protected by an army at the very least. But here she was, alone…

Working as a serving wench.

Passing a shocked expression to Addax, who was equally surprised, Tristan stood up and brushed his hands off. He was going to get to the bottom of this. He made his way over to the table where Andromeda was sitting with William on his heels. When Andromeda saw them both approaching, she appeared rather startled. Possibly frightened.

But she didn't run.

Tristan walked up to her.

"My name is Sir Tristan de Royans," he said. "I am the garrison commander at Wrexham Castle, but I also serve the Earl of Pembroke. William has informed me of what you told him. Carr mac Murda is your father?"

Andromeda nodded. "He is," she said, some excitement in her voice for the first time. "Do you know him?"

Tristan nodded. "Indeed, I do," he said. "He serves me at Wrexham Castle."

The hope in her eyes faded. "Wrexham," she repeated. "Sweet Mary… he's not at Pembroke Castle?"

"Nay, my lady."

"Is Wrexham far away? Farther than Pembroke?"

Tristan shook his head. "Nay, lady," he said. "It is only a few hours' ride to the north."

The hope was back in her expression. Andromeda stood up, her manner both eager and nervous. "I will pay you everything I have if you will take me to him," she said. "Please, my lord. I promise I will not be any trouble."

Tristan could see that she was verging on tears, terrified he was going to deny her. Simply by her reaction, he was coming to think that he'd been mistaken when he accused her of lying. He was a fairly good judge of character, and of liars, and he simply didn't sense that from her. All he sensed was desperation.

"That is not necessary, my lady," he said. "It would be our pleasure to escort you to your father."

Andromeda's eyes widened as if she were shocked by his polite response. Shocked that she suddenly wasn't directionless and destitute. She had a destination, a place to go, where her father was. He would take care of her. She was shocked that the hell she had endured over the past year was evidently coming to an end. Perhaps she shouldn't trust these knights, but the man who called himself de Wolfe had saved her. She'd seen enough lascivious men to know he didn't seem the type, so perhaps it was really true. A year of turmoil and despair was over.

She was so desperate that she was willing to take the chance.

Tears filled her eyes, spilling down her cheeks as she struggled desperately to stop them.

"Thank you," she breathed. "I cannot thank you enough, my lord, truly. I will gather my things and be ready to depart in just a moment."

Tristan nodded, watching her scurry off, wiping the tears that wouldn't stop falling. He shook his head with disbelief when she disappeared from sight.

"*That* is mac Murda's daughter?" he muttered. "She looks as if she has been living in the gutter."

William nodded. "I know," he said. "She told me that she smeared herself with mud to discourage the customers with less-than-honorable intentions, so it seems to be a disguise of sorts."

Tristan lifted his eyebrows. "God's Bones, let's hope so," he said, turning back for their table. "Go across to the livery and see if they have a palfrey we can borrow for her. If so, pay them a few coins for it. I do not want that filthy woman riding with me, and I doubt you do either, so get her a horse."

William nodded, collecting his helm and gloves before heading out the rear of the tavern. Tristan took more of his time to collect his things as Addax stood up, belched, and began to fix his linen hood.

"So?" he said. "Is it mac Murda's daughter?"

Tristan shrugged. "We shall find out soon enough," he said. "The only one who can tell us for certain is mac Murda. She seems to think she is."

"As you said, we shall find out soon enough."

That was the truth. With nothing more to say about it, they replaced the equipment they'd taken off when they arrived, and Addax went to pay the tavern keep for the meal. That left Tristan waiting for the lady, who appeared quickly with a small, torn satchel in her hand but nothing else. No cloak or cover. Considering they were traveling in cold weather, she would quickly become chilled.

Tristan gestured at her.

"Where is your travelling attire, my lady?" he asked.

Andromeda looked down at herself, in the terribly fitting dress that she'd purchased off another wench. "This is all I have, my lord," she said.

He frowned. "Where is your cloak?"

She appeared uncomfortable, averting her gaze. "As I told de Wolfe, the tavern keep saw fit to steal it from me one day when I was ill and could not work," she said. "He told me it was compensation for not working."

Tristan's frown deepened before he looked off toward the kitchens, the last place he saw the tavern keep. "He did that, did he?" he asked.

Andromeda nodded. "He did, my lord."

Tristan's gaze moved back to her. She had the bluest eyes he'd ever seen, wide-set and big. When she blinked, he could see a heavy fringe of dusky lashes. They were lovely eyes, to be truthful, but it was difficult to tell with the rest of her because she was covered with so much filth.

"And those clothes you are wearing," he said. "Is that all you have?"

"Aye, my lord."

"What happened to the clothing you brought from Ireland?"

She looked up at him again. "I never had any," she said. "I left rather… quickly."

"Why?"

She was starting to look uncomfortable again. "Because men were out to kill me," she said. "I left in the middle of the night, with only the clothing I was wearing. I had nothing else."

Tristan waggled his eyebrows, but it was a sympathetic expression. He didn't want to get into why men were out to kill her because, frankly, it was none of his business. That was between the lady and Carr. If, indeed, Carr was her father. He was starting to think so, however, because she had her father's eye color, that very pale blue.

"Then is there anything we can procure for you before we reach Wrexham?" he asked. "Anything you need?"

She looked as if the question itself baffled her. She looked at her little satchel, at her clothing, and simply shrugged her shoulders. When their eyes met, she smiled weakly, and Tristan could see what a stupid question it was. The woman had nothing. She needed everything.

But the first thing she needed was her cloak.

Addax was heading back in their direction, having just paid the tavern keep for the meal, but Tristan stopped him.

"Wait," he said, a hand on the man's chest to prevent him from going any further. "I want you to return to the tavern keep and ask him to return the lady's cloak. He evidently stole it from her by unethical means, so you will get it back. Put the fear of God into him if you must, but get it back."

Addax's dark eyebrows lifted as he looked between Tristan and the lady, but then he grinned, pleased at the prospect of scaring the devil out of the worthless tavern keeper. Given his size and manner, Addax was perhaps one of the most intimidating men around, and he loved to display that. Rubbing his hands together gleefully, he headed back to the kitchen.

Predictably, the cloak was returned in less than ten minutes, and shortly, they were on their way to Wrexham.

And to destiny.

CHAPTER FIVE

"I HAVE NOT seen my child in fifteen years," Carr said, perturbed. "I do not know what to do with her. Should I send her to a convent? Is she too old to send to foster in another household?"

It was nearing sunset on the day Andromeda de Courcy had been reunited with her father, who was more than surprised to see her. At first, he didn't recognize her. She was a filthy little urchin, and the last time he saw her had been when she was a child. He still wasn't sure he recognized her, or at least that was what he told others, but the truth was that he did recognize her almost immediately. She looked like his wife.

Another woman he hadn't seen in fifteen years.

Rather than being pleased to see his only child, he was irritated that she had come. Quite irritated. Tristan had seen that from the start, so instead of letting the pair make a scene for all to witness, he had sent the lady off with a couple of female servants for a bath and food while Carr became used to the idea that his daughter had come to him. While the lady was bathing and eating, Tristan learned a great deal about Carr that he'd never known before.

The man didn't like his womenfolk around him.

Simply put, Carr was a selfish man. He'd come to England to serve the Marshal, and he'd been very happy with the freedom. No family, no wife, nothing to bind him. He was free to pursue any affair of his choosing, which in Carr's case was with both married and unmarried women. He wasn't particular so long as she had a pretty face and was willing. Tristan had never involved himself in Carr's affairs because it wasn't any of his business. Carr acted like a man with no attachments, and that was the way he liked it.

But the appearance of Carr's daughter had the selfish side of the man showing up, as if Andromeda had appeared simply to annoy him. Tristan watched Carr rage in the solar of Wrexham, a vast chamber with a vaulted ceiling and the luxuries left behind by de Gresford. There were hides on the floor and on the walls alongside deer antlers because de Gresford had been quite a huntsman. There were deer antlers in the solar, the entry, and the great hall. They were everywhere. Tristan found himself looking at those antlers, pondering the surprising depths of Carr's selfishness, as the man ranted and raved around him.

Tristan finally put a stop to it.

"It's not as if she planned this," he said. "I do not know the details, but it sounds as if she was in great danger and de Courcy sent her here for her own safety. The least you could do is ask her."

"I will ask her," Carr said angrily. "And then I will send her on her way."

"Send her where?"

"Back where she came from!"

Tristan shook his head at the man's stubborn nature, casting a long glance at Addax, who was leaning against the enormous table in the chamber that contained maps and other things. Addax, too, had had enough of Carr's selfish nature.

"She told de Wolfe that men were coming to kill her," Addax pointed out. "You would send her back to her death?"

Carr came to a halt, looking at Addax. "Nay," he said, frustrated that he couldn't do it. "I… I do not know what I shall do if I cannot send her back. Mayhap I *will* send her to a convent."

"Why a convent?"

"Because I do not want her here!"

Tristan scratched his ear. "She's here and she is going to stay," he said, becoming increasingly exasperated at Carr's attitude. "At least for a while. The woman isn't even my daughter, and even I can see that she has suffered greatly since her flight from Ireland. It would be the kind thing to allow her to remain until she has recovered herself."

Carr sighed sharply. "She was supposed to remain in Ireland," he said. "You know the woman has royal blood. I have told you that before. She is the only descendant from the last King of Dublin, and there are many men who would see her returned to the throne. What I never told you is that King John knew of her birth, and he was the one who arranged, through William Marshal, to have her raised by Liam de Courcy. He didn't want an Irish princess raised by the Irish, so it was out of my hands when she was born."

"And you never fought for her?"

"Why?" Carr said. "John wanted to marry her to the right man. Her destiny through the king would be greater than anything I could do for her."

Tristan could see the bigger picture. The fact that King John had sent the child to live with an English family, so she could learn English ways, made perfect sense. Then he would make an advantageous marriage for her. It was his way of controlling Ireland and the destiny of those bound to the throne. Carr had never mentioned John until this moment, so the situation was making more sense. John had wanted to use her, once, but with his death, the ambition had clearly died. But that didn't stop the Irish from wanting her back.

Clearly, they did.

"John is no longer here to determine her destiny," Tristan finally said. "But she is here now because something has occurred. Don't you think you should talk to her before blaming her for something that may have been beyond her control?"

Carr wasn't so apt to agree. "De Courcy did this," he said. "He sent her on to me and shirked his duty."

"Shirked his duty for what?" Tristan nearly demanded. "He didn't shirk anything—he did his duty and sent her to safety. If we're being honest about this, you're the one shirking your duty, Carr."

Carr's eyes narrowed. "What do you mean?"

"I mean that you are her father," Tristan said. "She's your duty, yet you are acting as if you want nothing to do with her. That is not a pleasant attribute in a man I would trust my life with. If you refuse to help your very own daughter, what will you do with men you are not related to who might be dependent on you in the heat of battle?"

Carr almost snapped back at him but thought better of it. It never did any good to snap at Tristan, because if the man was riled, the results would not be pleasant. Truthfully, Carr didn't know why he was angry with Andromeda's appearance, only that he was. He'd gotten along fine for fifteen years without his wife or daughter around, and he didn't want to change that arrangement. Though there was more to his resistance, deep down, that was something he didn't want to entertain. It was something he'd put to the back of his mind many years ago, and that was where it was going to stay.

Simply put, he was a man set in his ways, and that didn't include Andromeda.

"It's only that I am surprised to see her," he said, trying to calm himself because he realized that he was starting to look like an unreliable hypocrite. "The intention was for her to remain in Ireland. She was never to come to England."

"Yet here she is," Tristan said. "I cannot believe Addax and I are the only ones accepting of your daughter's arrival. Christ, Carr, you could show a little more compassion. Your daughter seemed deeply troubled by her journey here, and now she has to face a father that wants nothing to do with her. Don't you see how cruel that is?"

Carr did. Not that it changed anything, but he knew he was being cruel. Unwilling to answer for his behavior, he simply shook his head and headed for the solar door.

"I have duties to attend to," he muttered. "I will talk to her later, when I've had the opportunity to recover my composure."

Tristan didn't stop him. He let the man go, looking at Addax as Carr's footfalls faded away. "Now what?" he said. "It never occurred to me that Carr did not wish to see his own daughter."

Addax lifted his big shoulders. "He is a stubborn man," he said. "He leads the life he wishes to lead, without the hindrance of a wife and child, and now that child is on his doorstep and he does not want her to interfere with his life and how he leads it."

"She's a grown woman," Tristan said. "She is not interfering."

"She is if he must now find a husband for her," Addax said. "Or worse, provide a dowry for her. And what about that convent he was talking about? He would need to make arrangements for it. And what's this about de Courcy shirking his duties? The woman is *not* de Courcy's daughter."

Tristan shook his head. "She is not, but she has fostered with the family for many years," he said. "You know as well as I do how that makes one part of a family even if they are not related by blood. Truthfully, I did not even know why she lives with de Courcy until Carr just told us. But the truth is that I do not know anything more about that situation, and I do not care because it does not involve me—but now the daughter is here, at my garrison, and that *does* involve me. Unless Carr decides to take charge of her, I cannot simply let her sit in a chamber and rot."

"What will you do?"

"What can I do? I will have to assign her duties, I suppose."

Addax looked at him strangely. "You intend to make her work?"

"Not work," Tristan said. "But she is a woman of noble birth. That means she has fostered in a fine home and has been trained in the aspects of running a household."

"Ah," Addax said, coming to understand. "Managing servants, managing stores and inventory, things of that nature."

"Exactly," Tristan said. "I have no chatelaine here, and it shows. Mayhap for her duration at Wrexham, she will fill the role. At least it will keep her occupied and make her less of a burden to me or to Carr, who seems to think that's the only reason she has come."

Addax rolled his eyes. "Incredibly selfish of him."

Tristan wasn't hard-pressed to agree. Standing up from the chair he'd been planted on, he ran his fingers through his thick hair. "I will find the woman and see if she has everything she needs," he said. "I will see you at sup."

He left Addax in the solar as he headed up into the labyrinth that constituted the upper floors of Wrexham's keep. Even if Carr refused to see to his daughter's welfare, that didn't mean Tristan wasn't going to be a polite host. But he had to admit that seeing Carr's reaction to his daughter's arrival had changed his opinion of the man. He'd never known him to be one to shirk his duty, but in this case, Carr seemed to have little inclination toward his own daughter.

With a sigh, he took the steps toward the upper floors.

☙

IT WAS ENORMOUS.

Wrexham Castle was the biggest castle Andromeda had ever seen, with enormous stone walls and a keep that seemed to stretch right up to the sky. Planted right in the middle of the eight-man escort, she was riding a little gray palfrey, one that plodded over the lowered drawbridge and through the gatehouse as hundreds of men parted way to welcome the escort. Gates opened, portcullises lifted, and men shouted around her as these things were accomplished. Through the gatehouse she went, following her escort into a bailey that was as large as a small village.

All of it awe-inspiring.

William brought the escort to a halt, bellowing orders to the mounted men, who began to dismount and hand their horses over to the grooms in wait. De Wolfe and the knight she'd been introduced to as Addax Al-Kort split off, leaving Tristan, the garrison commander, to take charge of her.

Not that she was sorry about that.

She'd gotten a good look at him back at the tavern, and he'd been riding off to her right as they'd headed to Wrexham, so she'd been able to steal glances at him now and again. He wasn't particularly tall, but he was very well built from what she could see, with a handsome face buried beneath a reddish beard that had been neatly trimmed. His hair was red—dark red, glistening around the temples as if preparing to turn silver in that very spot. He kept it short, but not so short that she couldn't see the curl in it.

And his eyes… They were a soft shade of brown, a common enough color, but somehow his was more intense. As if he could see right through her. He had a bit of a big jaw, square and masculine, and the one time she saw him smile, all she could see were big white teeth. She thought him quite handsome, indeed.

And here she was, looking like a bit of street rubbish.

Perhaps that was why her father looked so strangely at her when they were introduced. She recognized Carr when William brought him out of the gatehouse, and she was prepared to jump into his arms, but he looked at her as if he didn't know her in the least. She might as well have been a complete stranger for the way he reacted to her, but when he finally acknowledged their association, he seemed almost outraged at her appearance. There was no warmth there, only shock. He made no move to kiss her or touch her, though she hardly blamed him, given the way she looked. And smelled. But she had been hoping for something nicer than a polite but cold greeting.

Truthfully, it had hurt her.

They'd simply stood there in awkward silence.

Mercifully, Addax had sent for a couple of the kitchen maids, women who worked solely in the keep, and they had appeared about the time the silence truly became uncomfortable. It was Addax, the knight with the long, dark braids against his skull who had suggested that she retreat into the keep to bathe and eat, giving both father and daughter the opportunity to become reconciled to each other's presence. Addax muttered something to the maids, who appeared the least bit uncertain at first, but soon realized they had a charge to take care of. In a castle full of men, there simply wasn't anyone else to do it. Andromeda was led away by the two kitchen maids, straight into the keep. And that was the last she'd seen of her father.

Forgetting about him for the moment, she could see very quickly that the keep itself was positively enormous, and there were many corridors and chambers. It had a musty, dusty smell, like a tomb. She followed the servants up the stairs, and they were tight and narrow steps, ending up on a landing that had a low ceiling and limited natural light. Branching off either side of the landing were two small corridors with three doors each.

The servants were moving quickly, whispering and hissing to one another, as they took Andromeda to the very last chamber on the right. It was then that she noticed that it was one large chamber that had two doors, a second door she had mistaken for an additional single chamber. However, once inside the chamber, she could see almost immediately that they were faced with a problem.

The chamber was empty.

Puzzled, she turned to the servants.

"If you wish for me to sleep on the floor, I would at least like a blanket," she said, turning to look at the chamber once more. "It seems quite… empty."

The servants seemed nervous. "It *is* empty, my lady," one woman, with very rosy cheeks, said. "We must find a bed for you from the leavings of the previous lord."

Andromeda cocked her head curiously. "What leavings?"

"After the battle, my lady," the other servant said. She was tall, with bad teeth. "There was a great battle here a year ago. The Welsh took the castle from Lord de Gresford, and then the English took it back from the Welsh. There are many things left from that time, so we're sure we can find you a mattress if my lady will give us time. We would have had it ready had we known you were coming."

So the place had a history. Andromeda looked around the room, noting pieces of wood here and there, a broken stool near the hearth, but little else. As she'd first observed, it was quite empty. And almost… sad.

"Where is the chatelaine?" she asked. "Sir Tristan told me that he is the garrison commander. What of his wife? Does she not manage the keep?"

The servants shook their heads. "He's not married, my lady," the rosy-cheeked servant said. "He and his knights sleep in the keep and have use of the solar, but that is all. No one else does anything in the keep, so the rooms they do not use are dusty and empty. There are only men at this place, and men do not care what condition the keep is in so long as they can sleep in it."

That explained quite a bit, at least enough that Andromeda was starting to get a picture of her situation. She'd never been one to sit around and lament her situation, as evidenced by the fact that she'd found a position in a tavern to earn money after her escort abandoned her. Lady de Courcy would not allow her or her daughters to be idle or lazy, so being productive was what Andromeda knew. Looking around the room, she saw a need, and the servants seemed to want direction. They seemed upset and confused. If she was going to have something to sleep on this night, perhaps she needed to contribute to her own comfort.

"Very well," she said, looking between the servants. "What are your names?"

"Flora, my lady," the rosy-cheeked servant said. Then she indicated her companion. "This is Aldis."

Andromeda nodded. "We have work to do, do we not?" she said. "Can you show me where the things are that were left behind? Mayhap we can find something salvageable in them."

Flora and Aldis were more than willing to show her. They went back into the corridor, taking her to a smaller stairwell that led to the floor below. That was where they found a room of yesterday's treasures.

And what a trove it was.

Everything left behind by the English and subsequently the Welsh had been brought to this chamber. Anything that had been scattered throughout the keep or pieces of furniture had all been piled in this room. There were buckets, stools, pieces of furniture both whole and in pieces, as well as fabric. There was a great deal of fabric, either in tapestries or cushions or even coverlets. Because it was dusty and deteriorated, it was difficult to tell what, exactly, some of the fabric pieces were part of, so Andromeda had the servants pull out some of the items that looked as if they might have been a mattress or a coverlet at some point.

Methodically, the process began.

Andromeda had something of an analytical mind. She wasn't afraid of hard work, and she had been well trained. It looked as if some of the furniture was kept relatively intact, so they were able to find a bedframe and a mattress quickly. There was an enormous wardrobe back against the wall, a fine piece of furniture that was painted and polished, a surprising thing in such a dingy place. For some reason, that wardrobe caught Andromeda's eye, and she had the servants pull away the junk that was blocking it. Once they were able to clear away stuff from in front of one of the doors, they were able to open it up.

What they found was quite surprising.

Everything in the wardrobe seemed to be quite fine and expensive. There were folded silk scarfs, and tucked into protective bags were carefully rolled garments made from silk and brocade and damask. It was an incredible amount of finery, clearly meant for a wealthy woman, and Andromeda was astonished. Lady de Courcy had possessed a wardrobe like this, but she was married to a wealthy Irish lord, and that kind of adornment was expected. But to find that this kind of lavish wardrobe tucked away in a military garrison was something of a shock. As Flora and Aldis began to pull out the clothing and carefully lay it aside, Andromeda inspected it with wonder.

"Where on earth did this come from?" she wondered aloud. "These are very expensive things. Whom did they belong to?"

"If I could guess, I would say they belonged to Nessa, wife of Lord de Gresford."

The distinctly male voice came from behind, and, startled, the three women turned to see Tristan standing in the doorway. His gaze was focused on Andromeda, who felt as if she'd been caught doing something she should not be doing. He'd sent her inside as his guest and then found her rummaging around in a chamber full of expensive things.

She hastened to explain.

"My apologies, my lord," she said quickly. "It is simply that there was no bed in the chamber I was given, and the servants were kind enough to tell me that there was a chamber with unused items. I thought we might find a mattress here. I did not mean to violate any trust you might have placed in me, but it was either find a mattress or sleep on the floor. I will sleep on the floor if that is what you wish."

She was rambling on, stumbling over her words, and Tristan's lips twitched.

"Do you always talk so much when you are nervous?" he asked.

Andromeda nodded unsteadily. "I think so," she said. Then she sighed heavily. "Aye, I do. But I am very sorry if I have displeased you by wandering into this chamber."

He shook his head, though his eyes were glimmering at her. "You did not," he said. "In fact, I came to find you. I know that the chambers in the keep are relatively bare, so I was coming to see what could be done about it. I see you have already taken the initiative to do so."

Andromeda nodded with some relief. "I have, my lord," she said. "I will take the bed, and we will vacate immediately."

She quickly turned around, instructing the servants to grab hold of the old mattress, but Tristan stepped into the chamber.

"Hold," he said, heading over to where she was and noticing the fine clothing and open wardrobe. "So you've found some clothing, have you? I forgot this was here. As I said, I believe it belonged to the previous lord's wife."

Andromeda looked around at the lovely silk gowns laid out on the backs of dusty chairs. "These things are exquisite," she said. "Lord de Gresford must have been very rich."

Tristan shrugged. "Rich and stupid," he said. "He bought

the clothing for a wife who ended up killing him."

Shocked, Andromeda looked at him. "Sweet Mary," she exclaimed softly. "Even after he bought her these wonderful things?"

Tristan cracked a smile. "I'm fairly certain she wasn't in the marriage so he would buy her wonderful things."

"Why else would she marry him?"

He lifted his eyebrows. "Her father wanted the castle," he said. "She married de Gresford so she could kill her husband and turn the castle over to her father and to his liege, Llywelyn. But they did not count on William Marshal taking the castle back from them."

"And now you are here?"

"The Marshal made me the garrison commander," he said. He gestured to the goods. "I suppose that means all of this belongs to me, and since you do not have any clothing, you may have it all. I shall give it to you."

Andromeda's mouth popped open in shock. "My lord," she gasped. "You… you are too generous. But you cannot give me all of this."

"Why not?"

"Because you could sell it for a small fortune," she insisted. "Mayhap I could borrow a garment or two until my father purchases some clothing for me, but I cannot take all of it. It would be too much."

Considering Tristan had just come from Carr, he wasn't certain the man was going to do anything for his daughter. But he wouldn't tell her so because he hoped Carr would come around at some point. She was his daughter, after all. He simply couldn't abandon her.

At least, Tristan hoped not.

"I have no intention of selling anything," he said. "I haven't the time, so please take what you wish, as much as you wish. I'll send soldiers in here to take the bed and furniture up to your chamber. Which one is it?"

Andromeda had no idea. She looked to Flora and Aldis for a reply, which Flora was quick to give.

"On the floor above, my lord," she said, pointing to the ceiling. "I took the young lady to the chamber that overlooks the bailey."

Tristan shook his head. "Too noisy," he said. "Put her in the chamber that overlooks the meadows and mountains to the east. Pull everything out of that wardrobe that she can wear and anything else you come across, jewelry or belts or combs or soap—anything."

Flora and Aldis nodded quickly and rushed back to the wardrobe, leaving Andromeda standing alone with Tristan.

"Truly, my lord," she said sincerely. "I do not wish to be any trouble at all."

His gaze drifted over her dirty face. "You will not be," he said. "But I think I will also have a bath sent up to you. There's a tub around here, somewhere, and I'll have it brought up. If you do not find any soap in that wardrobe, then I'll have some of that sent up as well."

Andromeda looked down at herself, still in the ill-fitting clothing. "That would be very much appreciated, my lord," she said. "I cannot recall the last time I've been able to bathe in hot water. Usually, it was a cold stream or a lake."

Tristan could see that the servants had found something else in the wardrobe because they were hissing with delight over whatever it was. "I would not worry about that any longer," he said. "You are at Wrexham now, and we have baths and hot water and food. Clean yourself up, find a dress that fits you, and we will see you in the hall for sup. I'm sure your father is eager to become reacquainted with you."

A little lie, but he felt that he had to say something positive about a father who had clearly been uninterested to meet her. Andromeda smiled weakly.

"It has been a long time," she said quietly. "I am sure we will have much to speak of."

"Of course you will."

With that, the conversation was over, and Tristan excused himself so he could hunt down some soldiers to help move the furniture. But Andromeda's thoughts lingered on him after he was gone, the big and handsome knight with the intense eyes. He was kind, too, and had been from the start. Tristan and his knights had gone out of their way to make her feel safe. Considering she hadn't felt safe since that terrible night at Rockbrook, that was worth everything to her.

With a smile tugging at her lips, she went to help the servants pull more garments out of the wardrobe.

CHAPTER SIX

HE COULDN'T BELIEVE she was here.

He'd seen a woman coming through the gates with Tristan and Addax and William when they'd returned from patrol, and he had watched as the escort came to a halt and the woman was removed from her palfrey. It had been years since he'd seen Andromeda de Courcy and, honestly, he'd had no idea who she was until the rumor mill began to churn and the soldiers began to talk. He'd been in the gatehouse when word reached him—the woman who had been brought to Wrexham was none other than Carr mac Murda's daughter. A woman with a true Irish name beneath the English trappings.

Morrigan Nic Murda had arrived.

So many things ran through Dermot's head as he realized what it meant to him, a man who had been posing as a supporter of mac Murda and the entire Dubliner dynasty when, in fact, the truth was much different. But Dermot was clever—he came from a long line of clever men, nobles who had fought and died for the high kings of Ireland—so as much as royal blood was in the veins of Carr and his daughter, the blood of rebellion was in his.

He'd been well placed.

Well trained.

And William Marshal knew nothing about it.

Odd how the man who was so entrenched in the politics of England and was rumored to be the commander of an elite spy force should not suspect who Dermot really was. It was a tribute to his training and how he held himself, because he made sure he was affable and obedient, never a man to take charge or voice an opinion unless asked. His entire mission was to watch William Marshal and the English and relay any plans or observations back to the collection of men he'd dedicated his life to.

They called themselves *Aingil Lochlainn.*

Angels of Lochlainn.

They were devotees of the last great High King of Ireland, Muir mac Lochlainn, a man who had been decidedly at odds with the King of Dublin, Ascall mac Ragnaill. It hadn't always been like that, but the animosity had developed over the years. Though the Irish kings had allies and enemies, and there were many kings and many factions, this was the faction that Dermot was involved in. The deadly angels who supported the family they believed to have the last true High King of Ireland and the family who had known of the birth of Morrigan, renamed Andromeda, and sent to live with an English family to hide who she truly was.

The woman through whom all royal Irish blood flowed.

She was more royal than God himself.

The trouble had started years ago when Lochlainn's family had offered for the hand of Brigid, the only daughter of Ascall, and been denied. Lochlainn's family believed a marriage with Brigid could form ties to cement an alliance that would bring peace and a united Ireland, but Ascall saw it as the family trying to absorb his only daughter. Perhaps they would turn her against her father and follow suit with any subsequent children of the marriage. Ascall had, therefore, denied the suit, and the Lochlainn son, Caine, had married another lass of royal blood from the Leinster tribe, and they'd had a son, Gavan. Caine passed away years ago in battle, but Gavan was now of marriageable age. When the *Aingil Lochlainn* had made their way to Rockbrook Castle last year to discuss a possible marriage between Gavan and Ascall's granddaughter, whom they knew to be living in the House of de Courcy, they'd been chased away and the granddaughter had vanished.

But *Aingil Lochlainn* was clever.

They knew that Brigid's husband, and Andromeda's father, served William Marshal. That was why Dermot had accompanied Carr to Pembroke those years ago. Carr had served the Marshal in Ireland at his Irish properties, and Dermot had endeared himself to Carr back then, so when he moved to England, bringing Dermot along seemed natural. They were friends and colleagues and, truthfully, Dermot liked Carr. They got along well. It wasn't as if he was there to hurt Carr, but he was there to watch over him and report back to his *aingil* brethren.

About a year ago, when the marriage with Gavan had been proposed and Andromeda disappeared, Dermot had received word in a missive from his own mother explaining the situation and telling him to keep an eye out for her appearance. No one was sure if she would go to her father, whom she hadn't seen in years, but Dermot kept vigilant.

That vigilance had paid off.

Andromeda, the lass of pure royal blood, had arrived.

And with her, the keys to the Irish high kingdom.

Before the day was through, Dermot sent a missive to his mother, telling her of the damp Welsh weather, the food, his general health, and of the glorious news that a comrade's daughter had arrived at Wrexham. If the missive was intercepted by Ascall supporters, and there were plenty in and around Dublin still, it would seem like a joyful letter from a homesick Irish soldier to his mother. They more than likely wouldn't know that the comrade's daughter was none other than the lass they'd all been looking for. But Dermot's mother would.

And so would *Aingil Lochlainn.*

All Dermot had to do was wait for help to arrive.

A united high kingdom was on the horizon.

CHAPTER SEVEN

My rough beauty, how you inspire me

Let me compare you to cheerful prey

How they are too blind to see, but always dreaming about the divine in us all

Death is but a heartbeat from life

Addax looked up from the vellum he'd just read aloud. "Is… is that all?"

Tristan nodded. "She's the only woman I've seen here at Wrexham for months," he said. "I was inspired to write something about her."

Addax blinked. "I see," he said, desperately trying to find something redeemable in that horrific three-line poem. "Cheerful prey. That is an interesting choice of words."

"Is it wrong?"

Addax quickly shook his head. "Not wrong," he said. "Just interesting. I do not think I have ever heard those two words used together. Why would you compare her to prey?"

Tristan shrugged. He took the vellum back from Addax, the one that had his careful handwriting on it as he'd composed a poem in the hour before the evening's feast began. He found that was his best time to create his poetry because it was usually quiet at that time of night, the calm before the storm of the evening's feast.

He put the vellum back on the table.

"I know it's terrible," he said, giving the man a timid smirk. "You do not have to tell me. But it's something I've always done, terrible or not. So much of my life is harsh and difficult and brutal. It's the one thing that seems to calm my soul, as dreadful as it is. It just comes out of me, and I do not know why. It comes out in words like *cheerful prey*."

Addax smiled with some sympathy. "It is not dreadful," he assured him in a kind lie. "Your poetry is truth. She *is* a rough beauty. There is nothing untruthful about that."

"I doubt she would like to be called that to her face."

"Probably not," Addax said. He eyed Tristan a moment as if summoning the right words to continue. "You find her... beautiful, then?"

Tristan looked at him sharply, realizing what he was asking. "Nay," he said flatly, moving past Addax and toward the solar door. "She is not a feast for my eyes, as much as you want me to say so. She's Carr's daughter, and if I seem to show any kindness towards her, it's simply because her father is preparing to treat her abominably. That's not right."

Addax followed him to the door, clapping him on the back. "Be at ease, my friend," he said. "I did not mean to intimate you plan to marry her tomorrow. But I suspect beneath the dirt, she might be pretty."

Tristan cast him a long look before heading out of the door. "You'll shut your lips if you know what's good for you," he growled. "I am not interested."

Addax erupted into soft laughter, holding up his hands in surrender, before following Tristan from the solar and out of the keep.

The night air was cool and damp, with an enormous full moon in the sky above. The walls of the castle were so tall that they tended to block out everything but the sky, so there was nowhere to look but up. The battlements were heavily lined with sentries, men with torches and, in some cases, dogs as they walked their section of the walls, watching the countryside for any hint of danger.

Vigilance, at Wrexham, was always the order of the day… or the night.

Truth be told, Tristan was never far from the top of the wall. Much like the patrol and his inability to stay out of it and simply command, he often found himself on the wall walk as well, watching the land, making sure all was well. In recent months, he'd been thinking about summoning some of the local Welsh lords, because he was a firm believer in understanding the perspective of the enemy. Only then could one either anticipate the next move or try to resolve the differences. Addax seemed to think it was a good idea, as did William, who had spent all of that time on the Scottish border against the Scots. Understanding one's enemy was key to achieving peace.

Or at least success in battle when the Welsh surged again.

And they would.

"I smell beef," Addax suddenly said, interrupting Tristan's thoughts. "Is it possible that we might actually have something other than mutton for sup?"

Tristan nodded. "It is not only possible, it is reality," he said. "Shrewsbury sent us several of their red beasts in exchange for those small ponies we were using to haul the rocks necessary for repair."

Addax lifted his eyebrows. "Is that why the Shrewsbury knight was here last week?"

"That's why."

Addax smiled with pleasure. "Excellent."

Tristan looked at him. "Why are you so excited?" he said. "You do not traditionally eat beef."

Addax shrugged. "I know," he said. "That comes from the religion I was born into. Beef is usually avoided because cows are viewed as sacred, but since I was converted by the Christian knights who took my brother and me under their wing when we were young, I find that I have a taste for beef from time to time."

Tristan's attention returned to the great hall looming before them. "I am not entirely sure I could worship a god who did not permit a man to eat beef," he said. "Sounds unusually cruel."

Addax snorted. "It is not," he said. "It is a religion that respects all living things and promotes a diet that does not include living creatures."

"What does that leave you with?"

"Plenty of fruit and vegetables and grains," Addax said. "But I confess, I'm happier with a good beef knuckle than a bowl of turnips."

Tristan fully agreed with him. They entered the great hall at that point, the cavernous chamber with the hearth that was taller than a man. In the past, there had been a firepit in the middle of the floor, and the smoke had evacuated up through the roof, but de Gresford had built a proper hearth, so now the fire pit in the middle of the hall was simply a depression that drunk men would trip in. But the new hearth was much nicer and far less smoky.

"There's Carr," Addax muttered. "See him? At the dais?"

Tristan did. "I see him," he said evenly. "I must say, I'm curious how he is going to behave with his daughter this evening. Something tells me that I might be punching him in the mouth before the evening is through."

Addax simply waggled his eyebrows because he, too, had been wondering the same thing. As they approached, they could see Dermot sitting with Carr but no William, as the young knight had the night watch. Approaching the table, Tristan and Addax took their seats.

"I could smell the beef across the compound," Carr said. "You'll be lucky if I do not crawl inside that carcass and eat it from the inside out."

Tristan smiled weakly as a servant approached and put a cup of wine before him. "You'll have to fight Addax for the privilege," he said. "He, too, was commenting on the smell."

Carr was already into his second cup of wine and in much better spirits than he had been earlier. "In Dublin, there are herds of small black cows with sharp little horns," he said. "They make for the most delightful eating. It's one of the things I miss."

"Do you ever think you'll return?" Addax said, collecting his own cup of wine. "A man should be able to return to his homeland once in a while, I should think."

"But you have not," Carr said. "A pity. I heard that you and your brother were chased out by assassins."

It was a delicate subject he had veered onto, but Addax didn't let it bother him like it used to. His younger brother, Essien, was much quicker to temper, but Addax—the man who had been the crown prince of his country—was calm and wise in most things. It had been thirty years since they'd left their country of Kitara, and sometimes Addax felt as if that entire part of his life had only been a dream.

Sometimes the mind shut out what was too painful to deal with.

Even childhood memories.

"I shall never return," he said simply. "There is no reason to unless I want to raise an army and attempt to take back my father's throne. But Ireland is much closer than my country, and you did not leave under violent circumstances, so I was simply commenting that, if you are able, a man should have the right to return to the country of his birth."

Carr studied the dregs in his cup for a moment. "Mayhap," he said. "My grand-uncle was a king of Leinster, and today, a cousin claims the throne. There is really nothing for me there other than Irish factions who wish to fight against one another because one believes it should rule over the other. In Ireland, I spent my entire life in a bare-knuckle fight because of it. But my wife… she is a *banphrionsa*. That means princess in the Irish."

"Her lineage is stronger than yours?"

"Much."

"Surely she is beautiful."

Carr shrugged. "She looks like an Irish lass," he said. "And before you ask me anything more about her, know that I am here and she is in Ireland because I did not wish for her to come to England when the Marshal brought me here. I do not miss her."

Addax looked at Tristan, who rolled his eyes and shifted so his back was mostly to Carr. The subject of his family had come up, and already the man was being belligerent. Carr was close to irritating Tristan already, but he evidently didn't realize it because he turned to the man, unconcerned that he was mostly turned away from him.

"Have you seen my daughter since last we spoke?" he asked Tristan. "Did you tell her to join us in the hall for the meal?"

Tristan nodded, but he didn't turn to face him. "Aye," he said. "I told her. I also told her she could choose some clothing from the things that were left behind by de Gresford. She clearly needs something to wear until you have the opportunity to have clothing made for her."

Carr looked at him as if he'd just said something ridiculous. "Have clothing made for her?" he repeated. "She came here uninvited. Let her pay for whatever she needs. I will not do it."

That was the reaction Tristan had expected. He didn't say anything because whatever came out of his mouth was sure to start a fight. He'd never seen such selfishness, especially from a man he thought he knew. It was utterly shocking, as far as he was concerned.

"Why did she come, Carr?"

The question came from Dermot, who, thus far, hadn't been privy to anything said about Lady Andromeda's arrival. The man, usually so quiet in an almost introverted sort of way, had been on the walls when the lady arrived. He didn't know anything about the situation. Tristan was curious to know what Carr would tell him.

"Because de Courcy sent her to me," Carr said with disgust. "He did not want her burden any longer, so he sent her to me."

"Has she done something wrong?" Dermot asked.

"I do not know," Carr said. "Truthfully, I do not care. All I know is that she has come here to be a burden on a man who is a virtual stranger to her."

"That is not exactly true," Addax said from across the table, his dark-eyed gaze moving between Carr and Dermot. "The lady told de Wolfe that men had come to kill her, so de Courcy spirited her out of Rockbrook Castle with an escort with the intent of sending her to safety in England. If you're going to disparage your own daughter, Carr, then you should get the facts straight. And mayhap you should speak to her before you tell everyone you do not want her here. Do you think hearing that from you is going to cause men to respect her? They'll look at her as unwanted baggage, and some might even treat her that way. Is that what you want? Your daughter assaulted because you show her such disregard? An honorable man would not speak so of his own child."

Carr was red in the face by the time Addax was finished. "This is none of your affair, *coimhthíoch*," he said. "I will say what I please."

He'd called Addax an outlander, which was a term in Ireland for people who weren't born there. It mostly meant undesirables, and Addax, an intelligent man, knew enough Gaelic to know that. Before he could reply, Tristan turned to Carr.

"If you use that term with regards to Addax again, I will send you back to Ireland without hesitation," he said evenly. "You will never again show any man in my command such disrespect, because if it comes down to it, you are a *coimhthíoch* in England, bred from a warring race so barbaric that you cannot rule your own lands. You are here serving an English lord, and you take orders from him every day. You are a servant and nothing more. Shall I go on?"

Carr was taken aback by the threatening tone and harsh words. He and Tristan usually enjoyed a good relationship, so this kind of banter was not normal between them. He could see that he'd overstepped, but it was a difficult thing to swallow his pride. With a heavy sigh, he looked at Addax.

"My apologies," he said. "This situation has me unbalanced. I… I should not have spoken to you so."

Addax wasn't sure he believed the apology, but he didn't say so. He simply nodded his head briefly and looked to Tristan, who was still incensed over Carr's comment. Addax thought Tristan might even continue to verbally lash the man, but he seemed to settle down with the apology. He just was sitting back in his chair again, bringing his cup to his lips, when his gaze caught something over Addax's head, in the direction of the hall entry. The cup froze, nearly to his mouth.

Addax would remember the expression on Tristan's face for as long as he lived.

CHAPTER EIGHT

THERE HAD BEEN a bath.

Not so much in a proper tub as it had been in an enormous iron pot used to boil down bones and God only knew what else, but it was large enough for Andromeda to bathe in. She was so desperate to clean up that she would have bathed in a coffin had they brought her one.

Flora and Aldis were able to find soap among their own possessions, along with combs and other things for the lady's bath, and then the pot was half-filled with steaming water. While Flora helped Andromeda, Aldis focused on a couple of dresses they found that might be of some service. As it turned out, whoever owned the garments had been a big woman, tall and full, and Andromeda was considerably smaller. Aldis had her own sewing kit, so she collected it from her room and returned to the lady's chamber determined to make the dresses serviceable.

Before the bath could happen, however, they had to wait for the soldiers Tristan had sent to bring up a bedframe and mattress. There was a small army of them filling the chamber with a bedframe and chairs, a stool, two tables, a mattress, two dusty rugs, and a chest. They even brought up that magnificent wardrobe, up two flights of stairs, and it took eight of them to do it. But they managed to get it into the chamber and push it against the wall. It was still full of everything that had been crammed into it, which had caused the thing to be quite heavy. When all was said and done, Andromeda had the first proper bedchamber that she'd had in a year.

The mattress, however, still needed to be stuffed, but Flora told Andromeda that they would do that when she went down to supper. When the soldiers departed and a fire was burning in the hearth, Andromeda finally stripped off her ill-fitting clothing and climbed into the steaming water. Flora took her very own soap, smelling of rosemary, and a horsehair scrub brush used to clean off the kitchen tables, and went to work on her young charge. She scrubbed and scrubbed, washing off months of grime that Andromeda's limited washing opportunities hadn't been able to cleanse.

The layers of dirt began to come off.

As Andromeda sat in the pot and gripped the sides to prevent Flora from scrubbing her right under the water, Flora washed hair and arms and anything else she could get her hands on. The brush was coarse, but it was clean. It was also necessary. Flora set it aside when she soaped up Andromeda's hair, using her fingers to wash out the dirt and oils, before rinsing it in the water. Then she rinsed her hair with stale ale, letting it sit for a few minutes before rinsing it out again with clear water.

Andromeda felt weak and languid after such a scrubbing. It was like being pleasurably beaten to death. But along with something she'd once taken for granted, something as simple as a bath, sitting in that hot water had done something to her—it made her remember better days, of days at Rockbrook when she and Ceara and Alecia, women she considered her sisters, had fine beds to sleep in, good food, and regular baths. They'd had a rather pampered existence, truthfully, but it made Andromeda realize that she had lived like an animal over the past year. She had been struggling to survive, every single day, and it would have been very easy to give up. But there was nothing in her that could condone a surrender to her situation. She always believed something better was on the horizon if she could only fight for it. If she could only make it to her father.

And here she was.

She and her father were going to have to have a long talk about her future, because she couldn't go back to Ireland. She'd had time to think about his cold reception, and although she wasn't sure why he should treat her as if he didn't know her, she was going to get to the bottom of it. Perhaps it was only because he was startled to see her. In any case, she was going to make sure he understood that she intended to be obedient and productive. She didn't want to be a burden.

Perhaps that would make him more agreeable to seeing his daughter again.

When the water grew cold, Andromeda reluctantly climbed out and into a towel that Flora had warmed by the hearth. The kitchen servant dried her vigorously, wrapping her up in a stained but clean piece of cloth, before sitting her down on one of the chairs the soldiers had brought up from the storage chamber. With the chair positioned next to the hearth, the warm air was wildly comforting.

As Aldis continued to work on the dress, Flora set about combing Andromeda's hair. It was very long, and nearly white, with a wave to it. The washing and rinsing in the ale had made it very shiny, and as Flora combed, it dried rapidly in the heat of the hearth. By this time, Andromeda was growing sleepy, having a difficult time keeping her eyes open as Flora combed.

Truthfully, it had been an eventful day for Andromeda, and she was starting to feel it. Sensing this, because more than once Andromeda closed her eyes and started to tip over, Flora threw a couple of the big coverlets on the floor next to the hearth and fashioned a pallet. The moment Andromeda lay down on it, still wrapped tightly in the towel, she fell into a deep sleep.

The sun was down when next she opened her eyes to Flora's gentle shaking. Aldis had finished one of the garments for the evening meal, which was clearly underway, because the smell of roasting meat was in the air. It wafted through the open windows on the evening breeze. With a yawn, Andromeda stood up and went over to the bed, where Aldis had the altered garments laid out.

A shift went on first, one that had been too long, so Aldis had to hem up the bottom by several inches. It was roomy, with long sleeves, but it was very comfortable and well made. Over that went a very fine garment of silk in a pale shade of blue. It had silver embroidery around the neck and wrists, and ties in the back of it so one could lace it to fit. As Andromeda stood patiently, Flora and Aldis fussed over her, tightening up the ties and then loosening them again simply to make sure they had the right fit.

In truth, the dress gave Andromeda a stunning figure. She was full-breasted, with a slender waist and generous hips, so the dress emphasized those attributes. As she stood there and yawned, trying to stay awake, the servants finished with the dress and helped her put on a pair of slippers that had also been found in the wardrobe. They were a little too big, so Aldis took them off again, and while she went to put a stitch in the heel to help them stay on Andromeda's feet, Flora came around with the comb again and brushed Andromeda's hair until it gleamed. It looked like the rays of the sun, warm and soft and flowing.

She didn't look like the same woman who had entered the chamber. Combed and cleaned and in a dress that actually fit her, Andromeda looked like a goddess. Aldis finished with the slippers and helped her put them on again. They fit better than they had before, but they were still big. As Andromeda looked down at herself, smoothing over the blue dress, Flora approached her with a necklace she had found in the wardrobe.

"You look like a proper lady now," the old servant said with satisfaction. "It's astonishing what soap and water can accomplish."

Andromeda smiled weakly. "I'd forgotten what it felt like to be clean again and wearing clean clothing," she said. "I cannot thank you enough for your help. I owe you much."

Flora beamed. "It was good to be out of the kitchens and doing something I used to do in my youth," she said, holding up the necklace. "We found this in the wardrobe with other pieces of jewelry. I think it will go well with the dress, my lady."

Andromeda took it in her hands, looking it over with delight. It was a gold chain with pearls woven into the chain itself, and at the end of it was a square-shaped golden medallion with blue stone and pearls set into it.

"Sweet Mary," she whispered. "This is a magnificent piece. And you said you found it in the wardrobe?"

Flora nodded. "There are others," she said. "But that is blue. Like your eyes, my lady."

She was smiling as she said it, and Andromeda grinned bashfully, but she put the necklace on and the medallion hung right between her breasts. She didn't have a mirror, but she wished she did. She would have liked to see herself clean and properly dressed for the first time in a year.

"I suppose I should join them in the hall now," she said. "Will you show me how to find my way from this place so I do not wander for years, unable to discover the door?"

She was jesting a little, referring to the size of the place, and Flora nodded. "I will, my lady," she said. "Aldis is going to stay and finish with the other dress. She's also going to take another look at the other garments to see if there is something else she can alter to fit you. You must have proper clothing, after all."

Andromeda thought on that, fingering the medallion as she snorted softly. "I'd forgotten that," she said. "My life over the past year has been so trying that… I had forgotten what it feels like to wear something that fits, or the warmth of a bath. I've forgotten what it is like to be a lady."

Flora's gaze lingered on her with concern. "Have… have you been traveling long, my lady?"

Andromeda nodded. "Long," she murmured, remembering the hell of the last year and then thinking she should try to push it out of her mind. "Long, indeed. Now… will you show me how to find the hall?"

Flora nodded quickly, heading for the door. "This way, my lady," she said, opening the chamber door. "We'll stuff the mattress while you're eating so the bed will be ready for you when you return."

Andromeda gathered the skirt so she wouldn't step on it, as it was still a little long for her. "You have my gratitude," she said. "Thank you for your kindness."

Flora went ahead of her out of the chamber, down the narrow, steep stairs that they had taken down to the storage chamber. Because the dress was still long and she was terrified of plunging to her death down the stairs, Andromeda took her time, taking each step carefully. They went down two flights, ending up in a small corridor that opened up into the keep entry. From there, they headed out into the moonlit night.

The sky looked as if a million diamonds had been thrown against it, sticking to the black expanse, glittering down on the land below. The smell of smoke was heavy in the air, drifting on the night air, and it only served to reinforce how much better Andromeda felt. She was home, in a castle, and although it wasn't like Rockbrook, it was still a setting she was familiar with. Far better than the taverns she had lived in over the past year. She was in a place, a setting, where she felt comfortable. Her mood was lightening.

She was ready to face her father.

The door to the great hall opened wide. Flora left her to go in alone at that point, and she did, stepping into the warm, stale hall that was full of soldiers having their meal. Servants moved among the tables, and the hall was so large that there were several, but she spoke to the first servant she came across and asked where Carr mac Murda was.

The servant pointed to the opposite end of the hall.

She could see the dais through the smoke and haze, so she headed in that direction. Head held high, feeling confident for the first time in a very long while, she walked straight for the dais. She could see her father talking to another man she didn't recognize, but she did recognize Tristan and Addax, two knights she'd ridden from Ruabon with. Her first gesture when she reached the table was to thank Tristan for allowing her to use the clothing left behind, so she smiled as she drew near the table, fixed on his bearded face.

He looked slightly startled.

"My lord," she said, dipping into a curtsy. "I want to thank you for allowing me use of the clothing left behind by the previous occupants. It was very generous. And I hope you do not mind that I wore a necklace one of the servants found. It seems to go with the dress."

Tristan blinked. It was a sort of slow, odd blink, suggesting either he didn't understand what she was saying or he was in utter disbelief. Probably both. He didn't answer right away, prompting Addax, who was across the table from him and nearer to Andromeda, to answer for him.

"I am certain the garment has never looked so good, demoiselle," he said politely. "In truth, I do not think anyone at this table recognizes you. We thought an angel had walked into our midst. Didn't we, Pat?"

Tristan seemed to snap out of whatever trance he was in. "Indeed," he said. He stood up from his chair, looking at her incredulously. "It *is* you, Lady Andromeda?"

She chuckled. "I know it is difficult to believe, but it is me," she said. "Soap and water can accomplish quite a bit."

Tristan nodded, a quick, oddly nervous bob of the head. "I would say that is an understatement," he said. Then he gestured to the chair between him and Carr. "Please come and sit. I cannot remember when last we had such charming company."

Gathering her skirt, Andromeda stepped up to the dais, on a raised platform above the rest of the hall. She went straight to the chair Tristan had indicated and sat. He waited until she sat down before he took his chair again, summoning a servant for drink. Wine was placed in front of Andromeda, and as she grasped her cup, she found herself looking at her father.

She had his full attention.

"Jesus," he muttered when their eyes met. "You look like

your mother, only your mother never possessed your beauty. What I saw today… Why were you so dirty, lass? You should have come to me looking as you do now. I might have been proud to receive you."

Andromeda sensed judgment in that statement, and it put her on her guard. Truthfully, she didn't remember her father much. She had been so young the last time she saw him. He'd come to visit her at Rockbrook a couple of times in her youth, but the last time had been several years ago. Truth be told, she didn't remember him being very warm even back then.

"If I could have come to you clean and properly dressed, I would have," she said. "Since you did not permit me to tell you why I have come, allow me to do it now. I have come because Lord de Courcy sent me out of Ireland for my own safety."

Carr settled back in his chair, looking over a daughter who was a spectacular beauty. Truthfully, he was shocked. "So I have heard," he said. "What has happened that you had to come to England?"

Andromeda took a sip of the tart red wine before answering. "There is much fighting going on at home," she said honestly. "Where we live, it is the Dubliners and Leinster against Lochlainn and his allies."

"I know," Carr said. "Lochlainn and mac Amlaib, the King of the Isles. They were conspiring against us before I came to England."

"But they've grown bolder," Andromeda said. "Not long ago, they came to Lord de Courcy with an offer—it seems that the man who wanted to marry my mother, Caine mac Lochlainn, has a son named Gavan, who is of marriageable age. They wanted to discuss a marriage between me and Gavan. Lord de Courcy refused to discuss a marriage, and Lochlainn became bolder. They threatened to simply abduct me and force me into a marriage, so on a dark night about a year ago, they came to the castle and demanded entry. Lady de Courcy spirited me out of the castle as her husband held their attention, and I was given over to six soldiers who were supposed to take me to you at Pembroke Castle. We made it across the sea to Liverpool on one of de Courcy's cogs, but once we reached the village of Ruabon, they decided to simply take the money they were paid and abandon me. That is where I have been ever since."

Carr was looking at her incredulously. "They simply left you?"

"They did."

"Then why did you not send word to me?" he asked as if she were stupid. "You could have sent a messenger to Pembroke."

Andromeda took another sip of wine because repeating her story was beginning to upset her. "The soldiers took all of the money," she said. "I had nothing but the clothing on my back, and even that had been stolen off a servant because the soldiers would not spend any of the money they'd been given on me. What was meant to pay my way was used, by them, to fund their comfort. While they slept in good beds in the taverns, I was forced to sleep with the servants because they would not pay for a room. After they left me, I procured a position as a serving wench at a tavern. As soon as I earned enough money, I hired a messenger to take a missive to Pembroke, but the man took my money and never returned. I never heard from you, so I assume he simply took my money and never did what I hired him to do."

Carr was eyeing her rather ominously. "So you have been… a serving wench?"

"I was trying to earn enough money to hire an escort to take me to Pembroke."

Carr sat back in his chair again, looking at his daughter with an expression of great distress. "Jesus," he mumbled. "You have been working as a serving wench. *My* daughter."

Andromeda could see that it upset him. "It is not the life I would have chosen," she said, thinking he was speaking out of concern. "My main worry was keeping away the men who thought I was a… Well, they thought I was a woman they could pay to warm their bed. That is why I was so dirty when I came here—smearing dirt seemed to be the only way to deter some of them. It was very difficult at times, but I was able to earn money. I can honestly say that I learned things that fostering in a fine home will not teach you."

He frowned. "And you are proud of this?"

"I am proud that I survived," she said. "Aren't you?"

He began to drink again, downing the contents of his cup before answering. "You are not to tell anyone else that you were a common serving wench in a lowly tavern," he said. "No one must know."

"Why not?"

"Because it is humiliating!"

Throughout the conversation, Andromeda had thought her father was being sympathetic toward her. Perhaps even protective. But now she was coming to see that he had great disdain for what she'd done. He was embarrassed by it.

And then it occurred to her.

The cold reception when she arrived and now this. He wanted nothing to do with her. They'd never spent any time together, living in the same household, so he was viewing her as a stranger who happened to bear his name and his blood. A stranger who had worked as a common serving wench and could possibly shame him in front of his friends and colleagues. He wasn't concerned for her at all.

Only himself.

Now, she understood him.

"I see," she said quietly. "You are humiliated by the fact that I took a position to earn money. What did you call me? A common serving wench? How understanding of you, Carr. How generous."

She called him by his given name. Not Father or Papa, but Carr. When he realized she was being sarcastic and possibly disrespectful, his eyes narrowed.

"I never asked you to come here," he said. "How dare you shame me in front of men whose respect I have earned. I am disgusted at what you have done, yet you are proud of surviving. I do not call becoming a filthy servant survival."

"What do you call it?"

"Disgraceful," he hissed. "I do not want you here!"

There it was. The truth. He had no need or use of her. Stung, Andromeda didn't give in to tears of remorse or fits of begging. She could see her father for what he was, and she'd only known the man, *really* known him, for just a few short minutes. That was all the time she needed to see what kind of man he was.

Now, she was the one who was mortified.

"And I do not want to be here," she said steadily. "I especially do not want to be known as the daughter of a careless, unfeeling, selfish animal such as you. God has played a terrible joke on us both, Carr. You're not worthy of me, and I cannot stand the sight of you. I think I'll go to London and earn my living as a harlot and tell every man I take to my bed that I am the daughter of Carr mac Murda, the most appalling excuse for a man I've ever known in my life. I hope the humiliation of it drives you to an early grave."

She spat the last few words, throwing the remainder of her wine in his face and bolting up from her chair. She rushed from the dais as Carr roared, wine stinging his eyes. Tristan and Addax had been watching the entire thing and were quite pleased to see the direction it had taken. The woman had fire, and it was good to see. But it had come at great expense, at least for her. Even Tristan could see that. He gestured to Addax to keep an eye on Carr as he stood up and followed Andromeda as she rushed from the hall.

He caught up to her in the bailey.

"Wait," he said, calling after her as she headed for the keep. "My lady, please wait."

Andromeda came to an unsteady halt. As he came up behind her, he could see that she was wiping her face. Faintly, he sighed.

"I do not know why your father is behaving that way," he said quietly. "I've known him for a few years, and he never struck me as being someone who was selfish. Vain and ridiculous at times, but not selfish. Not like this. I am very sorry he has treated you so poorly."

Andromeda sniffled as she turned to him. "It is kind of you to say so," she said. "But you should not defend him."

"Definitely not," Tristan said. "He is indefensible. I must say that I am quite disgusted by it."

She sniffled again and looked up at him, forcing a smile. "You are a kind man, my lord," she said. "I am sorry my arrival has caused trouble. It never occurred to me that it would."

"You have not caused trouble," he said. Reaching out, he

gently took her elbow and turned her for the keep. “Come inside. I’ve not eaten yet, and neither have you, so let us discuss this over a meal.”

Andromeda let him lead her toward the keep. “I am not certain what we need to discuss,” she said. “My father does not want me here. I must leave.”

“Will you really go to London and become a harlot?”

She missed the fact that he’d said it with some humor because she was still entrenched in her sorrow. “Nay,” she said glumly. “I only said that to hurt him as he had hurt me. I would not know the first thing about becoming a harlot. I think I would make a terrible one.”

Tristan fought off a grin, choosing not to comment on something that could be considered bawdy. They went up the stairs and into the keep, which was dim at this hour. There were a few torches about in the interior, creating halos of light, as he took her into the solar. There were always servants in the keep, and Tristan summoned one of them, sending the man for food. Heading back into the solar, he went for the hearth, which was burning low.

He began to throw peat into it.

“I do not know if this will make any difference to you, but I think you have shown great resourcefulness in your situation,” he said, poking at the peat. “I do not know many women who would have had the presence of mind to do what you did when your escort abandoned you. That kind of initiative must be applauded.”

Andromeda was still standing because he hadn’t invited her to sit yet. “If I wanted to eat, then I had to do something,” she said. “I am in a country not my own, so it is not as if I have friends or relatives I can seek help from.”

He turned to look at her, seeing she was still standing, and indicated the chair next to the hearth. “Sit down,” he said. “I think I may have a business proposition for you if you are willing to listen.”

Andromeda sat in the chair, which was cushioned and comfortable. “Of course, my lord,” she said. “What manner of proposition?”

“A mutually beneficial one, I hope.”

“It doesn’t have anything to do with being a harlot, does it?”

He started to laugh, his beard concealing the big dimples he had in each cheek, when he realized she had understood the humor of his harlot question earlier.

“Fortunately, it does not,” he said. “But it is something I will pay handsomely for.”

With the fire beginning to blaze, he set the poker aside and took the chair opposite her. For a moment, he simply looked at her. The woman before him was not the same filthy creature that he had escorted from Ruabon. This was an elegant, graceful woman of astounding beauty.

Because her hair had been braided at the back of her head when he first met her, he had no idea that it was white-blonde and silken and beautiful. She had it parted on the side of her head, part of it over her shoulder and hanging down her torso. Her face, now scrubbed clean, was like nothing he’d ever seen before—she had wide-set eyes, but the eyes themselves were large and lovely. He could see her dusky lashes when she blinked. She had a pert nose, a round Irish face, and a smile that was nothing short of enchanting. She had a slight gap between her front teeth, but it only made her smile more endearing. It was perfect.

She was perfect.

"I was discussing your arrival with Addax earlier today," he said. "We were discussing you and your role at Wrexham if you are to stay."

"I would have a role?"

"Everyone has a role here," he said. "Everyone has duties. If you are to stay at my castle, then you must contribute to Wrexham somehow. I do not tolerate laziness, but after what I have just heard from you, I suspect you do not tolerate laziness either."

She smiled shyly, shaking her head. "Lady de Courcy was quick with a switch if any of her children were idle," she said. "I learned to be productive."

"Then I hope you will appreciate this proposition," he said. "When I came into command of Wrexham, it had been occupied by the Welsh for some time. It was as if animals lived here. You can see what an enormous keep it is."

Andromeda was listening carefully. "I have never seen such a large keep," she said. "How many rooms does it have?"

"Including the vaults in the sub-level, there are twenty-seven chambers," he said. "Some are smaller, some are larger, and there is one enormous chamber at the very top of the keep where I sleep. I think it was meant for an entire family because it is so large. In any case, this very large keep has no one to manage it. I do not have a chatelaine—I have a quartermaster who oversees the kitchens and feeds the men, but that is where it ends. I am in desperate need of a chatelaine, and that is what I would like to propose to you—I would like to offer you the position. In exchange, I will provide you with a bed, food, and twenty pounds a year. That is about fifteen shillings a day. Would you be interested in this?"

Andromeda's eyes widened. "Interested in…?"

"Would you require more money?"

She shook her head quickly. "Nay, my lord," she said, clearly overwhelmed. "That is a great deal of money you offer. All for being your chatelaine?"

"I'm assuming you know how?"

She nodded firmly. "I was well trained, my lord," she said. "I can read and write and do sums. I know how to keep inventory and how to manage money. I can determine how we can make money on our own by selling eggs or vegetables or even livestock. I was well schooled in these things."

He smiled faintly. "I believe you," he said. "Will you consider it?"

Her pale eyes glimmered. "I do not have to," she said. "If you truly need my help, then I will gladly do it. If my father does not wish for me to remain, however, it may create a problem."

Tristan lifted his eyebrows. "For him but not for me," he said. "Frankly, your arrival was fortuitous. I need a chatelaine and you need a position. I believe working here, at Wrexham, will be much better than working at the tavern."

Andromeda smiled broadly, nodding most fervently to his assertion. "It will be, my lord," she said. "But I… I think…"

She suddenly lowered her head and burst into quiet tears. Concerned, Tristan moved his chair closer.

"What is it?" he said. "Did I say something to offend you?"

Andromeda wiped her face furiously. "Nay, my lord," she said. "It's not that. It's simply that… up until this very moment, I had no hope. Not hope at all. My father does not want me here, and I did not know where I was going to go, so you have saved me. I do not think you realize that."

He was embarrassed by the praise. "And I do not think you

realize that you have helped me also," he said. "I had a great need for a chatelaine, and here you are. I am grateful."

"As I am," she said, beaming at him once again as the tears faded. "As am I. To thank you does not seem quite enough."

"You may thank me by making this a proper keep where I would be proud to have visitors," he said. "As it is, it is no better than a stable."

She nodded quickly. "I will make it so that it will directly reflect on your reputation and honor," she said. "It will be a fine place when I am finished with it."

"Good," he said. "And do not worry about your father. This is my castle, and he serves me. If I want you to remain because you fill a need, then you shall remain. He has nothing to say about it."

Her emotional outburst was fading as she fell quiet for a moment, thinking on her father and his reaction to her appearance. "We do not know each other well, my father and I," she admitted. "The truth is that we are strangers. On those occasions when he did come to Rockbrook to visit, he would only speak of the glory of my bloodlines. How I could make the whole of Dublin rise up and follow me with just a word. It seemed to me that he was always interested more in *what* I was than *who* I was. I suppose that was reinforced here today."

Tristan could easily believe that. "He has spoken of your bloodlines before," he said. "How your mother is the only daughter of the last King of Dublin, but he's never really spoken of why you went to live with de Courcy until the day you arrived. He said that King John wished it."

She smiled ironically. "He did," she said. "He, and William Marshal, decided that I must be hidden from the enemies of my grandfather, but it was more than that. I was told by Lord de

Courcy that King John wanted to marry me to an English prince, a marriage that would link England and Ireland by blood. But I knew it was because such a marriage would take me away from Ireland and water down the Irish bloodlines. When one wants to conquer a country, isn't that what happens? By destroying those with the right to rule?"

Tristan was impressed that she should understand the rules of conquest. "That is true," he said. "The Normans did it when they arrived in England centuries ago."

Andromeda nodded. "I know," she said. "I was taught English history, so I know it well. I know it better than Irish history. In fact, my birth name is not Andromeda—it is Morrigan. I was named after the Irish war goddess. But my name was changed when I was hardly old enough to speak, and I became Andromeda. Andie is what most people call me. Morrigan has not existed for a very long time."

Tristan understood something about royal bloodlines and being hidden from one's enemies. "Andie," he repeated. "I like that. May I call you Andie?"

Andromeda nodded. "I would be honored."

"Thank you," he said. "But King John and his intentions aside, somehow, your grandfather's enemies found you."

"They did."

"How long have they known about you?"

She shrugged. "It was around my thirteenth year when a servant in the de Courcy household betrayed me," she said. "At first, my grandfather's enemies came as friends. At least, they pretended to be, but it was not the truth. They wanted to watch me grow and determine what to do with me. That was when the marriage offers began to come."

"The one you told your father about?"

She nodded. “Aye,” she said. “The one to Gavan. Someone must have told them about King John’s intentions for me, to marry me to an English prince, because they were persistent and increasingly hostile.”

Tristan lifted his eyebrows. “If a servant betrayed your presence, then it is more than likely that the king’s intentions were also betrayed to the opposition,” he said. “Did anyone send word to John or William Marshal about it?”

Andromeda shook her head. “I do not think so,” she said. “But I don’t really know. I heard Lord de Courcy tell his wife that John had so many problems with his barons that marrying off an Irish princess was the least of his concerns.”

“Probably,” Tristan said. “John did, indeed, have a massive amount of problems with rebelling warlords, as did the Marshal. John’s reign was a tumultuous time for us all.”

“I was forgotten, thankfully.”

“It seems that way,” Tristan said. “But even if John forgot about you, your Irish enemies did not. It seems they wanted to marry you to Gavan before John married you to someone else.”

“Possibly,” she said. “But the night that I was finally sent away, it was a harrowing situation. They had come to the gates of Rockbrook armed for war. Lord de Courcy sent me away for my own safety. Had they gotten into the castle and captured me, there is no knowing what they would do to me. I heard Lord de Courcy say that he believed the marriage offer was a ruse. They wanted me for something else.”

“What else?”

“To be made an example of, as Ascall mac Ragnaill’s granddaughter.”

“To kill you?”

“More than likely,” she said. “My grandfather was murdered, after all."

Tristan knew enough about the dangers of enemy factions when it came to those of royal blood. He knew what Eleanor of Aquitaine had done to Arthur, the son of his half-brother, Geoffrey. With the English, there had been so many things that had to do with royal blood and eliminating the threat to the throne of England that made Irish politics look like child's play. But he was quite aware of the danger Andromeda was in. The more he thought about it, the more he wondered if she was truly safe. Surely the enemy faction would know she had escaped, and the assumption would be that she would go where she would be the most protected. That meant going to her father in England.

That would bring the Irish to his doorstep.

But he couldn't think about that now. She'd been out of Ireland for an entire year, living on her own, and no one had found her, so it was possible they thought she had died somewhere along the way. That would have been the best of all worlds, because he knew, as he looked at her, that he wasn't going to let anyone get their hands on her. He would defend her. He'd only known the woman a few short hours and, already, he knew that.

"I would say that you are safe now," he said, unsettled by the fact that he felt rather strongly about protecting her from those who meant to do her harm. "Even if your grandfather's enemies assume you've gone to your father, they know he serves the Earl of Pembroke, and that would be the first place they looked. No one knows he's at Wrexham, though it's possible that if they asked around, they might discover his location."

She tried not to look too fearful. "Do you think they will?"

He shrugged. “It is difficult to say,” he said. “If they truly want you, they might.”

“Then it’s possible they may come here.”

“I would not worry over it,” he said. “You have been living without protection for a year now. I think it’s just possible that you hid yourself very well by working as a serving wench. Even if the Irish came to Ruabon, they probably would not have recognized you. You *did* look quite different.”

His dark eyes were glimmering as he said it, and she smiled reluctantly. “It was out of necessity, I assure you,” she said, but she sobered quickly. “But if they come here, I will leave. I do not wish to cause you more trouble than I already have.”

He shook his head. “You will not leave,” he said. “I will make them wish they’d never come, so do not worry. You are part of Wrexham now, and we protect our own.”

She looked at him, shocked. “You… you would protect me?”

“I said I would.”

“But… but the fight is not yours,” she said. “You cannot assume my burden.”

“Are you not my chatelaine?”

She blinked as if startled by the question, but she answered. “Aye,” she said slowly. “I agreed to your terms.”

“Then you are part of Wrexham, and we protect our own.”

Andromeda stared at him. One moment, she was in the chair, and in the next, she was on her knees in front of him, grasping his hands.

“Thank you,” she breathed. “You cannot know how much it distresses me that you should risk your men to fight my battle, but I thank you all the same. I can never repay you, my lord, but I swear to you that you have my undying gratitude.”

Tristan was rather startled by her sudden movements. But he realized quickly that he didn't like her on the ground, and he didn't like the fact that what he considered to be a reasonable gesture had her nearly collapsing in appreciation. It made him angry, in fact, because when her father should have been the one pledging to protect her, it had to be a stranger. How in the world Carr could disregard such a sweet, delicate, but wholly strong creature was beyond him.

It was infuriating.

"Get up," he said, standing up and pulling her to her feet. "You do not need to fall to your knees and worship me like I'm some bloody priest."

She was holding his hands tightly as he helped her stand. "I know," she said. "I am very sorry, but you must know how grateful I am. I thought… I thought I was completely alone until now. A father who was supposed to protect me does not seem to have the inclination to, so you cannot know what your words mean to me. Where Carr mac Murda has failed, you have taken a stand when you did not have to. A man with such honor is a rare thing."

There was a knock on the solar door, interrupting them, and Tristan let go of her to open the panel. Servants appeared carrying trays of food and pitchers of drink, and Tristan instructed them to set it all down on the table near the hearth. He had to sweep a few things off the tabletop, mostly clutter, but soon laid out before them was a feast fit for a king.

And a queen.

Andromeda had never eaten with such gusto, and such relief, in her entire life.

Perhaps coming to Wrexham had been a godsend after all.

CHAPTER NINE

WILLIAM HAD SEEN them from his vantage point.

It had been a usual patrol out toward the Clwydian hills to the west, a place of foothills and vales and forests where the Welsh liked to gather. It was a wild and verdant land, reeking of mystery and magic. There were a couple of important warlords in the area, and Tristan liked to keep an eye on them. In fact, Lord Rhewl and Lord Gryffyn were men that Tristan wanted to send word to, to meet with them to see if they couldn't come to some kind of peaceful existence between them. The warlords were brothers by marriage, as far as Tristan had heard, and they had been part of the group that sacked the castle when de Gresford was in residence. But Tristan had also heard that the two had tried to reason with the supporters of Llywelyn and convince them to negotiate with the English, but the battle was over before that could happen.

It gave Tristan hope that the pair might be reasonable.

Even so, the patrols kept watch on them. That was prudent. And William was glad they did, because on his routine patrol earlier in the day, he'd seen hundreds of men flocking to Lord Gryffyn's fortified home, called Garth Hall, near the River Dee.

Dermot had been with him, and together, they'd hidden in the trees and watched the influx of Welsh.

That sent them rushing back to Wrexham to relay the news to Tristan, who hadn't been pleased to hear of the latest development. Even now, he stood near the windows overlooking the bailey, pondering what William had reported.

He didn't like the sound of any of it.

"Did the men look as if they were armed in any way?" he asked. "Did it look like a war council?"

William shook his head. "We were not afforded the best view of Gryffyn's home or the arrivals," he said. "But the men we did see did not look as if they were armed. It could have been a family gathering or a wedding for all we knew, but there was an absence of women that led me to believe it wasn't either of those things."

Tristan turned away from the windows, looking at William and Dermot. "There was nothing obvious to suggest an attack is imminent?"

"Nay," William said. "But prudence would dictate that we send more men out to watch the house."

"True," Tristan said. He looked to Dermot. "Tell Carr and Addax what you have seen. We will discuss this tonight at sup. Go now, and send Addax to me once you have told him."

Dermot nodded smartly, heading out of the solar and leaving William still standing there awaiting further orders. They weren't long in coming.

"We will be alert from now on," he said quietly. "That means the gatehouse is not to remain open. Gates will be closed and secured, day or night. We can have a contingent of guards outside the gate to admit people who have business here, but anyone who wants to pass through those gates must be interrogated before they are made welcome."

William nodded. "Agreed," he said. "If I may make a suggestion, I feel that we should double the patrols. If Gryffyn is hosting a gathering and it is meant as a precursor to an attack, others might be, too, unless Gryffyn plans to attack us alone."

Tristan shook his head. "I cannot imagine that he would," he said. "Did you check his brother's home?"

William nodded. "There was no activity that we could see, but that could change."

"Then organize double patrols," Tristan told them. "Have them report directly to you."

"Aye, my lord."

Tristan opened his mouth to say something else, but they could hear voices on the other side of the door. There seemed to be some commotion going on. Curious, Tristan went to the door and opened it, only to find Andromeda out in the entry with several new servants who had been hired from the nearby English town of Nantwich when she took over as chatelaine. There were buckets and mops and brooms, everything necessary to clean an entryway that was full of grime and cobwebs.

Andromeda didn't see him, however. She was bent over one of the new servants, describing to the woman how she wanted the floorboards scrubbed. William came up behind him.

"There she is again," he said, a smirk on his lips. "Do you know she had her army of militant scrubwomen clean the knights' quarters two days ago?"

Tristan grinned. "I'd heard that."

William's mouth twisted into an expression of displeasure. "God help those of us who were in the building when she arrived," he said. "She demanded all of our clothing to wash it so we would not bring grime back into her clean rooms. She scrubbed that place from top to bottom with salt and vinegar that I am still smelling. She even scrubbed the ceiling!"

He was genuinely incensed, and Tristan couldn't help but chuckle. "She is doing what I asked her to do," he said. "She has only been here a week."

"It feels like a year."

Tristan turned away from the door and headed back into the solar. "You had better get used to her," he said. "That's what I told her father."

William glanced at him. "Is he still angry that you permitted her to remain?"

Tristan shrugged. "Possibly," he said. "But that is his own issue, not mine. If he doesn't like it, he can return to Pembroke Castle. That woman in the entry has been of more value to me in seven days than Carr has been in an entire year, so if I have to make a choice, I will choose her every time."

William wandered toward him, his manner pensive. "I should probably tell you that Carr has not been quiet about his displeasure," he said. "He only voices it to me or Dermot or Addax, but I know the men have heard."

Tristan sighed heavily, thinking on a man who would treat his own daughter like an enemy. "Have you ever seen a man disregard his own child so?"

"Never."

"I do not know what to do about it," Tristan said. "Short of threatening him, I suppose he has every right to speak about his daughter any way he wishes. I cannot tell him what to say."

William pondered that, looking toward the solar door when he saw Andromeda pass in front of it as she worked.

"If the men think her own father has no respect for her,

then they are going to ask themselves why they should," he said quietly. "You had better speak to him, Pat. He is going to cause his daughter trouble if he does not shut his mouth."

That was something Addax had expressed also, leading Tristan to believe they were right. Andromeda may be Carr's daughter, but Carr simply wasn't treating her well. Even a week after her arrival, he wasn't apt to protect her or praise her or even speak to her.

And that brought up a new set of concerns.

"I've been thinking," Tristan said, watching Andromeda through the open door. "Were you aware that it was King John and William Marshal who sent her to live with the de Courcy family?"

William shook his head. "Nay," he said. "I'd not heard that."

"It's true," Tristan said. "According to Carr and to the lady, John wanted to marry her to an English lord of royal blood. Linking Ireland to England, as it were, but those plans evidently died with John."

William looked at him curiously. "What have you been thinking about, then?"

Tristan shook his head faintly. "I'm not sure," he said. "I'm thinking I should send word to the Marshal to tell him that she's here if, in fact, he was involved in sending her to live with de Courcy. He might have even been involved in the marriage plot. But, then again, he may not even care any longer."

William shrugged. "Possibly," he said. "But if she told you he was involved, then mayhap you should notify him."

Tristan wasn't sure he wanted to, but it was something he'd been thinking about over the past few days. He wasn't quite sure why he didn't want to tell the Marshal, only that he wasn't sure he wanted Andromeda out of his sight. It was possible that the Marshal would leave her at Wrexham until he could decide what to do with her, but equally possible he would send her away somewhere. Marry her off to someone of his choosing.

That was the part that Tristan didn't seem to like.

"There's something else," he said after a moment, diverting the subject. "That Irish faction that tried to abduct her from Rockbrook. She told you about that when you met her in Ruabon for the first time, did she not?"

William nodded. "She did."

"I have been thinking that if I were determined to wipe out the line of my enemy, I would not give up so easily."

"What do you mean?"

"I mean that I would not let her disappearance from Rockbrook Castle stop me," Tristan said, looking at William. "I would not give up. I would think that if she has fled Rockbrook, then the logical thing to assume would be that she would go to her father to seek protection because there is nowhere else in Ireland she could go that would be safe. England would be the most logical choice."

William was beginning to understand. "You think they have come to England?"

Tristan shrugged. "If it were me, I would not stop," he said. "I would follow the trail to its logical end—Carr mac Murda."

William cocked his head in thought. "But they've had an entire year to look for her," he said. "If they knew she was going to Carr and they knew he served Pembroke, that should have them going to Pembroke Castle."

"True," Tristan said. "They would go there and ask for him, and then they would be told that he no longer serves there. Being clever, I would assume, the Irish would probably tell a story of how they needed to get word to him or find him. Any number of stories. Depending on whom they spoke to at Pembroke, they would either be told where he is or they would be sent away without the information."

William was following that line of thinking. "What would you do if a group of Irish came looking for Carr and said they needed to find their brethren?"

"I would ask why."

"And they gave you an excuse that sounded reasonable, for example, his wife was ill or something like that."

"Then I would probably tell them that he's at Wrexham Castle."

William lifted his big shoulders. "If all of that happened as we have speculated, then they would have gone to Pembroke some time ago," he said. "They would have been to Wrexham already, and they would have asked about Carr mac Murda. No one has."

"How do you know?"

"Because Carr cannot keep his mouth shut," William said. "He would have told us. We would have known about their presence because Carr, undoubtedly, would have recognized them as an enemy faction."

"Possibly," Tristan said. "Let's say that's the case—they've come here, looking for Carr but have not contacted him. If it were me, I would stay locally so that I can watch the castle. Mayhap they're in the village, waiting for her to arrive. Just because she wasn't at Wrexham six months ago doesn't mean she isn't going to show up at some point."

William shook his head. "If that is what has happened and they are still here, Carr would quite possibly hand her over to them if he knew of their presence," he said. "The man does not want her here. It would be his chance to be rid of her for good."

Tristan waggled his brows. "Let us hope he has more compassion and good sense than that," he said. "But I would not trust him to make the right and just decision where his daughter is concerned."

"Nor I."

That hung in the air between them as they listened to Andromeda firmly but politely direct the servants. She was a master at managing them and, as Tristan had discovered, managing everything else. In the few short days she'd been at Wrexham, she had accomplished so much that it was difficult to know where to start when praising her skills as a chatelaine.

Finally, Tristan shook his head.

"Can you imagine," he muttered. "A woman like that in the hands of Irish rebels?"

"Nay," William said firmly. "I cannot. It would be a bloody shame. Which is why I think we need more knights who are not part of an Irish brigade. No offense to Carr or Dermot, but I think we need more English here, Pat."

Tristan had been thinking the same thing, unfortunately. "Addax and you are formidable," he said. "You're worth five good knights each in my opinion, but you cannot be everywhere all at once. I fear we may need men who are not emotionally invested in the arrival of an Irish princess. At the very least, their objectivity would be helpful. Has Dermot showed any outward reaction to Lady Andromeda's appearance that you are aware of?"

William shook his head. "Nay," he said. "He's been quiet about it. But, then again, he's a quiet man."

"He is," Tristan agreed. "The man barely says a word, but I'm certain he is sympathetic with Carr. They're quite close."

"They are," William said. "Dermot could very well side with

Carr in the matter of Lady Andromeda and we wouldn't know a thing about it—which brings me back to the fact that you should have more English knights at your disposal if the Welsh are indeed amassing for another round with their English enemies. Unfortunately, I do not think the Marshal has men to send you."

"What do you mean?"

"I mean I do not think he can send us a Cole de Velt or a Maxton of Loxbeare," William said. "Most of the Marshal's senior knights and agents already have a valuable post where they are needed."

Tristan conceded the point. "That is true," he said. "But I know the Marshal has young knights coming up, men he is training. What about Lukas du Reims?"

William nodded. "An excellent sword," he said. "But the last I heard, he had been sent to the garrison of Richmond Castle. Since Caius d'Avignon moved to Hawkstone Castle, Richmond was without a commander."

Tristan lifted his eyebrows. "And the French want that place badly."

"Exactly."

That brought Tristan back to where they started. "I can always send word to my father to send me a knight or two," he said. "He usually has an entire stable of young knights."

"I have a better idea."

Tristan looked at him. "What?"

William tried to sound relatively neutral. "Send the request to Northwood Castle," he said. "The Earl of Teviot has several excellent knights. Two of them are my closest friends, in fact. Paris de Norville and Kieran Hage."

Tristan stared at him a moment before his brow furrowed.

"I know those names."

"Because they are great men."

"Nay. I know them because Teviot sent you back to your father to get you away from them."

William fought off a grin. "He overreacted," he said, trying to downplay the legendary deviltries of William and his two cohorts since their days of being pages at Kenilworth Castle. "The truth is that they are two of the best knights I have ever seen. Individually, we are magnificent, but together, we are unbeatable. And that is what you need at Wrexham."

Tristan wasn't so sure. "I have enough trouble," he said. "I do not need to worry about you three."

William stopped grinning and looked at him head-on. "You will not have to worry about us," he said. "But you will need us if the Welsh attack and the Irish use the chaos to get into the castle and take their prize. You will want knights of our caliber to fend off two very strong factions who have been known to get what they want. God only knows if Carr and Dermot will help the Irish. I'd say you have bigger problems than three young and talented knights who have been known to get into trouble on occasion."

He was quite serious, which in turn made Tristan quite serious. He stared down the young knight, a young man who hadn't even seen his twentieth year, but a young knight who was ageless in his skill and wisdom. Tristan knew, as everybody did, that William de Wolfe was going to go on in life to do something great.

And he did have a point.

"And you think Hage and de Norville can help?"

"I would stake my life on it."

Tristan knew he didn't make that pledge frivolously. Perhaps the Marshal would think he was a fool for even considering William's proposal, but the truth was that he did need good swords in light of the fact that he wasn't sure how Carr and Dermot would react if a gang of Irish showed up, intent to take the lady from him. That would leave him with Addax and William to fight off the Irish, the Welsh, and anyone else who wanted to take something important from him—a castle, a lady, or both.

Perhaps he really had no choice.

"Very well," he said, his dark eyes intent. "I will accept your suggestion. But listen to me well, so there is no mistake."

"I am listening."

Tristan cocked an eyebrow. "Good," he said. "You know me well enough to know that I do not take lightly what I am about to say to you. But the truth is this—I am Plantagenet. I am also descended from the kings of the Capetian dynasty. That makes me the most royal, unique, and potentially powerful man the world has ever seen. Do you understand my lineage?"

William nodded firmly. "I do, my lord."

"Good," Tristan said. "Because understand that you serve a man who could easily be King of England or France, or both, if he had the ambition. That makes you the servant of a king. It means that I could have more power than William Marshal if I wanted it. I could call forth nations if I had a mind to do it. It also means I can destroy foolish knights who make empty promises of obedience. If you tell me you and your comrades will behave if I allow the three of you to serve together, then I will believe you. But one instance of violating that oath and I will destroy you. You will never be able to serve a reputable lord in England ever again, nor in France when I get finished with you. I've not yet thought of Scotland, but mayhap I will marry a

Scottish earl's daughter and then I can deter the Scots from you as well. All this I will do if you betray my trust. Is this in any way unclear?"

William took the threat seriously because he knew the man wasn't bluffing. The truth was that neither was he. He and his friends had been together since they were children. They'd been separated a couple of times during the years because it was a fact that when they got together, things could happen. Naughty things. William was a master gambler, and although the Executioner Knights knew it and sometimes joked about it, he was better than anyone in England at wresting money away from another man. He'd made a secondary career out of it.

But now, things were different.

William was a fully fledged knight, and he was growing up. He'd not yet seen his twentieth year, but he was as seasoned as a man who had been fighting twice as long. Up until this point, the gambling and the punishment that followed had been a game to him because he knew his worth. He knew William Marshal wouldn't discard him entirely. But now… now, as a knight, he had a reputation to establish, and he knew that childhood antics wouldn't help him. They wouldn't help Paris or Kieran, either. He knew that all men must mature and evolve, and this was his time to do just that.

But he had to prove it.

"It is clear, my lord," he said after a moment. "Perfectly clear."

Tristan's gaze lingered on him a moment before the glimmer of warmth came back to his eyes. "Excellent," he said. "Because I would hate to do that to you."

William was impressed by the way Tristan could go from deadly intimidating to warmly humorous all in the blink of an eye. "As would I," he said. "Although I think some part of you might sickly enjoy it."

Tristan started laughing. "You'll never know, hopefully," he said. "Go now and send word to Teviot and ask permission, on my behalf, for the service of your friends. If he is agreeable, tell them to come swiftly. There is no time to waste."

"Aye, my lord."

"And organize the double patrols."

"Aye, my lord."

Tristan smirked at him, and William snorted in return, making sure they both understood the situation between them. Not that William disbelieved that Tristan would do what he said he was going to do. It really had nothing to do with that. It was more that Tristan was begging him not to violate his trust in this matter. Tristan was relying on him, and they both knew it. He didn't want William to fail.

And neither did William.

As de Wolfe quit the solar and ran headlong into the small army of servants scrubbing the entryway, he caught sight of Andromeda on her knees near the door, scrubbing old wood slats furiously.

"You there," he said with authority, though there was jest in his manner. "I meant you, Lady Andromeda. Do you remember me?"

She looked at him, though there was no humor on her face. She seemed oddly detached. "Of course I remember you," she said. "Why would I not remember you?"

William wasn't sure why she was so humorless, but it didn't stop him from continuing. "*I'm* the one you stole the clothing from," he said, jabbing his thumb into his chest. "Remember that? I'll let you know that I'm hiding all of my clothing from now on. Filthy or not, you shall steal nothing."

He was referring to the incident in the knights' quarters two days before, and Andromeda forced a smile.

"Very well," she said. "But if you bring new dirt into a freshly scrubbed chamber, I'll take a stick to you."

"You'll have to catch me first."

"Are you willing to take that risk?"

William flashed a toothy smile and was gone, heading out through the entry. Andromeda watched him go before returning to her task, scrubbing a few more inches before another servant came over and took the duty from her. Standing up, she brushed her hands off, her gaze moving toward the solar entry. The door was still open.

It had been partially open when she heard everything that Tristan had said.

God, she wished she hadn't.

CHAPTER TEN

I am a Plantagenet. I am also descended from the kings of the Capetian dynasty. That makes me the most royal, unique, and potential powerful man the world has ever seen.

Those words were still rolling around in Andromeda's head. She'd been scrubbing near the doorway simply because she wanted to catch a glimpse of Tristan. It hadn't been with the intention of eavesdropping, but he had the kind of voice that resonated so that she'd heard every shocking word.

Now, she was stunned.

As he'd told de Wolfe, *that makes you the servant of a king.*

That made her the servant of a king, too.

Very quickly, she was starting to feel foolish. Foolish and unsteady and confused. But she hadn't started out that way—not at all. She'd started out this day just like every other day since her arrival at Wrexham.

She'd come to prove her worth.

Seven days after her arrival at Wrexham, Andromeda was deeply entrenched in her new duties. Never one to stand back and direct others, she was a producer. She liked hard work. That was why she'd done well as a serving wench, because hard work didn't frighten her, and cleaning up a twenty-seven-chamber keep was merely a challenge and not an intimidation.

Tristan had been appreciative from the start. A word of thanks or praise always seemed to come from him, and she thrived on it. She'd spent much of her life surrounded by kindness with Lord and Lady de Courcy, so the advent of a garrison commander who was grateful for her skills made her want to work harder. But overhearing Tristan's conversation with de Wolfe made her realize that she had been pining after a man who was royalty. Not just English, but evidently French as well. She'd heard the part about his finding the daughter of a Scots earl so he could gain more power. Or maybe not so much power, as it would simply be finding a woman of his own social station. A lady with something to give.

Not an Irish lass descended from a king who was murdered for his throne.

She had absolutely nothing to give him.

Ashamed, not to mention greatly disappointed, Andromeda stood back and supervised the servants who were scrubbing the floors with salt and vinegar. There were two male servants who had rags on the top of very long sticks, and they were dusting the cobwebs high on the walls and on the ceiling. So far, it had been a productive morning, but that all changed when a young servant girl, whom she'd been using as a runner to bring salt and vinegar and water to those who were cleaning, came rushing back with more hot water and ended up slipping on the newly scrubbed floor, and all of that water crashed into Andromeda like a tidal wave. Instantly, the entire lower portion of her garment was wet.

But that wasn't the worst part.

Because she'd come with no clothing, she'd been wearing

garments that Aldis had altered for her out of the painted wardrobe. The unfortunate fact was that none of the clothing was meant to work in, as it was all very fine silks and brocades and more, so the moment the water hit the dress of green silk that she was wearing, the dye began to drain out of the fabric.

The girl began to panic. She'd fallen heavily when she slipped, landing on her back and hitting her head, but she was just rolling to her knees when she saw what she had done. She pleaded for forgiveness and began to weep as the other servants saw what had happened. One of the older women, who had worked in other fine households in the past, came up to Andromeda and took a close look at the fabric that was dripping green onto the floor.

"It can be saved, my lady," she said as the servant girl wept. "It's not worth tears, I promise. If you soak the dress, all of the dye should come out. Then you can simply dye it another color."

Andromeda was looking down at herself with some dismay. "It was an accident," she said. "I will put it aside for now, and we will decide what's to be done with it."

The old servant picked up the edge of the silk as it dripped. "I would remove it and put the entire dress in water to wash out the dye," she said. "Then you can hang it up to dry. I can help you with it if you wish."

Andromeda forced a smile at the old woman when she really felt like weeping. It was a borrowed dress, and she didn't want Tristan to think she was careless with her things—but before she could reply, she heard his voice from behind.

"What's amiss?"

Andromeda turned to see Tristan standing in the doorway in all of his auburn, manly glory. Every time she saw him as of late, her heart skipped a beat. She was willing to give in to the familiar giddy feeling she usually had when he was around, but then she remembered what he'd said to de Wolfe. Not only had he laid bare his heritage, but he'd threatened the man with it.

Perhaps he'd do the same to her now that she'd ruined something he'd let her borrow.

"The dress was… damaged, my lord," she said, hoping to explain before he became angry. "It was not the servant's fault. She slipped on the water because the floor has not yet dried. But the garment… I have tried to be careful, I swear it, but the dresses you have permitted me to borrow are such fine garments, and they are not made to work in. I will ask the servants to help me fix it, I promise. You needn't worry."

She was speaking rather quickly by the time she was finished, and she sounded nervous. Tristan looked at her strangely because this wasn't the woman he'd come to know over the past week. A woman who could easily laugh, or was quick with her wit, or, quite frankly, was simply a pleasure to be around. He tried not to look at her too much because he didn't want any of his knights to think he had interest in her, as Addax already suspected, but he knew he hadn't been very good at keeping his attention off her.

Like now.

She was the only thing in the room, as far as he was concerned.

"I'm not worried," he said evenly. "And the garments are yours. I have given them to you. But why did you not tell me you needed more serviceable clothing?"

She looked at him in surprise. "It… it is not your burden, my lord," she said. "You pay me well, and I am saving money to purchase the fabric I need for more durable clothing. Truly, you needn't be concerned."

He looked down at the bottom of her silk dress, now streaked with green as the color drained away. "I beg to differ," he said quietly. "You are doing work that I have asked of you in clothing that is clearly not up to the task. Much as soldiers or knights cannot work well without the proper weapons or protection, you cannot work well in clothing that is not suitable. It did not occur to me that the garments left behind in the wardrobe were unsuitable."

"As I said, I am saving money for proper fabric, my lord."

He shook his head before looking to the older servant woman who had been trying to help Andromeda with the dress. "What is your name, woman?" he asked.

The woman didn't seem intimidated by him. "Leonie, my lord."

"Do you know what Lady Andromeda is attempting to accomplish here?"

The woman gave him a blank expression before looking around, seeing that all of the servants had come to a halt because the garrison commander was in their presence. After a moment, she returned her attention to Tristan and nodded.

"Aye, my lord," she said. "She's trying to clean up a nest of men."

Tristan tried not to laugh, but he couldn't quite manage it. "How true," he said. "My point of the question was to ask you if you could continue her work while I take the lady away for a few hours. Can you manage it?"

Leonie nodded. "I can, my lord," she said confidently. "I was a servant at Ruthin Castle for many a year. I know how to keep these dusty barns clean."

Tristan was still smiling as he looked at Andromeda. "I

think the task is well in hand," he said. "Will you come with me?"

Andromeda still wasn't sure what was going on or why he'd asked the old servant if she could take Andromeda's place. "Where are we going?" she asked.

He motioned to her as he headed back into the solar. Reluctantly, she followed, tracking green water as she moved. She stopped just inside the doorway.

"I must remove this garment," she said. "There will be green footsteps everywhere I walk if I do not."

He glanced at her as he went to the table that contained a clutter of things. "Then go ahead and do so," he said. "I will wait for you here."

"Where are we going?"

He had a big, heavy chest sitting on the corner of the table, and he fussed with the lock. "Into the village," he said. "There is a merchant there whom I have done business with before, and he has all manner of clothing and fabric. He should have something good enough for your purpose."

Andromeda watched him open the chest and fish for something inside. But as she watched him, her thoughts kept going back to what he'd said to de Wolfe. The big, brawny knight with the neat beard and rather thick auburn hair was no ordinary man. He could move mountains and countries according to him, and, clearly, de Wolfe had believed him.

She was feeling increasingly unnerved by it.

"When I have enough money and am ready to purchase fabric, I shall seek this merchant, my lord," she said. "But I do not have enough money for what I need. The purchase must wait."

He looked up from his chest. "I told you that I would supply you with whatever you need," he said. "Hurry, now; go and change your clothing. I'll have horses prepared."

Andromeda couldn't do it. "Please, my lord," she said, trying not to sound like she was being obstinate. "I would rather purchase it myself. I am sorry if my appearance displeases you, but I do not want you to feel obligated."

He stopped digging in the chest and looked at her. "What is the matter with you?" he asked. "You have not addressed me formally in days."

"What do you mean?"

"You haven't addressed me as 'my lord' in days. Why now?"

Andromeda was, if nothing else, a truthful woman. She wasn't one to hide things or play games. That had never been something she had been adept at, and most especially when it came to men. She'd never been fond of a man in her life, at least not one she thought was handsome and charming, so this was all quite new to her. Tristan had enchanted her with his kindness and compassion, and to discover he wasn't who she thought he was had her unnerved.

Reaching out, she shut the door so the servants couldn't hear.

"I have never wanted to work harder in my life than I have for you," she said quietly. "I thought we were establishing a pleasant and honest relationship between us, something that… I've not had many people be completely kind to me as you have, and I realized it was something… something… Oh, forgive me. I am not making much sense."

He came away from the table, looking at her with concern. "Then something *is* wrong," he said. "What is it? Have I done something?"

She shook her head quickly. Then she nodded. Then she

sighed heavily and hung her head. "I do not want you to purchase anything for me, my lord," she said. "I would rather do it myself."

"Why?"

"Because you have given me far too much," she said. "You have been far too generous."

"And that is a problem?"

She nodded, quickly, unable to look him in the eye. "Men talk," she said. "They may think there is something inappropriate between us. They may think you are buying my favor."

He was quiet for a moment. "Am I?"

"Nay, my lord."

"That's a pity."

Her head shot up, looking at him with big eyes. "What do you mean by that, my lord?"

He waved an irritated hand at her. "Stop calling me that," he said. "You haven't called me anything for days. I have been waiting for you to ask permission to call me by my name, but you haven't yet. You haven't called me anything at all, and I do not want to hear you address me formally. My name is Tristan. My close friends call me Pat. Call me either of those names and I will answer, Andie. But do not go back to addressing me formally because I do not want you to."

Her eyes were wider than before. "B-but why?" she stammered. "You are my liege. It would not be right for me to call you by your Christian name."

Now, Tristan was the one unbalanced. Little by little, the conversation had chipped away at him, and now he was feeling… odd. Disappointed, even. Lifting his shoulders, he plopped down in the nearest chair and looked at her.

"I understand," he said quietly. "There is no hope here."

"Hope for what?"

He lifted a hand in a gesture that suggested he probably shouldn't say what he was about to, but he did it anyway. "I thought…" he said, then stopped himself. But the pause was only momentary. "I think you are the most beautiful and enchanting woman I've ever met. You are bright and talented and gracious. You are a survivor. There is so much about you that intrigues me, and I was hoping… hoping you might feel the same way."

Andromeda was thrilled and bewildered. What he said sounded suspiciously as if he felt giddy when he saw her, just as she felt giddy when she saw him. It was the first hint he'd ever given her that it might be the case. But he'd spoken clumsily, so she wasn't clear on what he was trying to say to her, exactly.

And she very much wanted to be clear.

"Feel the same way?" she repeated. "About what? That I intrigue… myself?"

He chuckled softly, putting a hand over his face. "Nay," he said, muffled through his fingers. "About *me*. I was hoping you felt the same way about me."

Now, Andromeda understood everything. It was what she'd suspected all along, but she needed him to be plain about it. Stunned, she stood there for a moment, looking at him as he sat in the chair with a hand over his face. It occurred to her that it must have taken a great deal of courage to say what he'd said. It was true that they'd spent the past several days smiling at one another, speaking on many subjects during the evenings at supper, and generally having wonderful conversations. At least, she thought they were wonderful, which was why she'd felt massively disappointed by the conversation she'd overheard. A man like that couldn't possibly marry a woman like her.

But now… what he was telling her now was too good to be true.

"I think you would have to have been deaf and blind not to realize that I think you are a handsome and charming man," she said. "Aye, I feel the same way, but… but I heard what you told William. I will confess that I was scrubbing the floor near the entry to the solar, not so I could hear what was being said, but because… because I wanted to watch you if I could. But I heard you tell William that you are the son of kings."

Tristan didn't hesitate. He nodded as his hand came away from his face. "I am," he said. "So you were really scrubbing by the door simply to catch a glimpse of me?"

He was focusing on the wrong thing, and she didn't want to engage in a gentle flirt with him. The truth was that they'd not really flirted with one another since they met because other people were always around. Tristan never let the conversation become personal or too sweet, and nor had she, so there had been no flirting to speak of.

She wasn't going to let him start now, not when this moment was so crucial.

"I heard you tell de Wolfe that you were going to marry the daughter of a Scots earl," she said, lowering her gaze. "That is exactly whom you should wed, Tristan, and I will be happy for you when you do. But I will not be a flirtation or an affair before that happens. No matter how attractive I find you, I could not engage in anything scandalous. I am sorry."

She turned for the door, grabbing at the latch, but he was on his feet, rushing toward her.

"Nay," he said softy but firmly, grasping her wrists to prevent her from opening the door. "Don't go. Please. I know what you heard, but I did not mean I was definitely going to marry the daughter of a Scots earl. I was speaking of something that would never happen. It was an empty threat to de Wolfe and nothing more."

Andromeda still wouldn't look at him. "I understand," she said. "But I repeat that I cannot engage in anything improper. I must make my position clear."

"That is good, because I would never suggest anything improper."

"Then we are in agreement."

His lips twisted with disapproval. "We are *not* in agreement," he said, gently pulling her back into the chamber. "We are not in agreement at all. I am telling you that I find you alluring and enchanting. I am telling you that I would like to begin a courtship. I will ask your father, but I wanted your agreement first. Andie, I find you quite charming and kind and, frankly, more appealing to me than any woman I've ever met. Is your reluctance because you heard of my lineage? Because you're Irish and the Irish hate the English?"

Andromeda shook her head firmly. "Nay," she said. "I was raised by an English family. I feel as if I'm English more than Irish."

"Then *what* is it?"

She looked at him then. Gazing into his dark eyes was like losing a piece of her soul. Every second that passed, another piece broke off and was sucked into the vortex of his stare.

"*Who* is your father?" she finally whispered.

"King Henry," he said without hesitation. "Henry Curthose, the father of King Richard and King John. Henry carried on an affair with my mother, Princess Alys of France, and I was the result. My half-brothers were kings of England, my nephew currently sits upon the throne, and my uncle is the King of

France."

"You're a bastard?"

Tristan looked at her as if, suddenly, it all because clear to him. "Ah," he muttered, releasing her wrists. "I see what it is. I am my father's bastard. That is why you are reluctant."

Andromeda immediately shook her head. "That is not the issue at all," she said in a surprising show of strength. "Tristan, you are the son and brother and nephew of kings. And you want to court the granddaughter of the last King of Dublin?"

"Why not?"

She threw up her hands. "Because that is not nearly prestigious enough for you," she said. "Don't you understand? A man like you must have a wife to bring him wealth and lands and prestige. I can give you none of those things. My lineage is not only bereft, but I have men out to find me and destroy my family's line."

"I will kill them all."

"You cannot have a pitiful, dying breed for a wife!"

Their voices, which had been raised, were now suddenly still as they just looked at one another. The very air around them was pregnant with tension. Andromeda was coiled, trying to plead her case to a man who wouldn't listen, and Tristan was simply taking it all in. At first, he thought she was resistant to him because she didn't think he was a good enough match for the last descendant of Ascall mac Ragnaill, but now he was coming to realize that she thought that she would be sparing him for something better than her.

It was one of the more selfless things he'd ever witnessed.

After a moment, he reached out and grasped her wrist again, dragging his hand down her flesh until he came to her fingers. They were green from the dye that she had touched, and he simply stood there a moment, looking at those delicate green fingers. They were pretty and perfect, like the rest of her.

"I find myself in a very odd position," he finally murmured. "You see, I'm rather old for not having been married. I suppose my vocation as a knight has taken up all of my time. There have been women from time to time that turned my head, but no one that ever turned it as much as you have. I understand that you feel you are, as the last of your line, unworthy for marriage to someone like me. But I am a bastard, so it is not as if I am a prince. I'm nothing, really. I'm simply a knight for William Marshal. You consider yourself imperfect, and God knows that I'm imperfect, so mayhap we will be perfect *together*."

Andromeda sighed again, looking at his hand as it fondled hers. "But…"

"Please," he said quietly. "Just… think on it. I am not looking for an answer today or tomorrow. But I will ask you to think about it. Will you?"

He was battering down the walls of her resistance with his soft words and gentle touch. God, to be touched like that for the rest of her life by a man who had all of her attention would be like something out of a dream. Where she could awaken every morning to his face, see his smile, hear his deep and gentle voice. The lines of his face, the shape of his muscles, the way he held himself… he was glorious.

Would she think about it?

"I will," she murmured. "I promise, I will."

He smiled at her, the dark eyes twinkling. "Thank you," he said. "May I ask something else?"

"What is it?"

"That you change out of that horrible garment before it makes green rivers all over my solar?" he said, watching her grin. "And then let me take you into the town to the merchant I told you about. If you are worried that you do not have enough money saved, I will deduct it from future earnings. Will that be acceptable?"

Somehow, she couldn't stand turning him down yet again. He looked so hopeful and was being very polite. Reluctantly, she nodded.

"Very well," she said. "It is acceptable."

He grinned, flashing those big white teeth. "Excellent," he said. "Go and change. I will be waiting for you in the bailey."

She nodded and began to turn away, but he wasn't ready to let her hand go yet. That forced her to pause, and as she watched, he brought her green fingers to his lips and, hunting around for a spot that wasn't green, deposited a sweet, bristly kiss onto her flesh. She tasted so good that he did it again.

Andromeda very nearly stumbled out of the study on her way to change out of her wet clothes, blushing to the roots of her hair.

CHAPTER ELEVEN

"HE'S DOING IT simply to spite me."

"But why should he want to spite you?"

"Because he has an eye for her, Dermot. Are you blind?"

Carr and Dermot were on the wall of Wrexham Castle, looking southwest. There was an expanse of green fields and, in the distance, blue mountains that disappeared into the clouds. A wind was blowing in from the west, snapping the crimson shield and scarlet lion standards overhead. They had the watch together, and, inevitably, the subject of Carr's daughter had come up.

It was not a happy subject.

"She has nowhere else to go, Carr," Dermot said. "I do not think he's keeping her here to spite you. He's keeping her here because he simply cannot turn her out into the cold."

Carr knew that, theoretically, but these days, everything was starting to take on a personal connotation for him. Everything Tristan said, or Addax said, or anyone else said, when it came to his daughter, was personal to him, no matter what it was, and the fact that Tristan had made Andromeda his chatelaine infuriated Carr to his very core.

And he was determined to do something about it.

"I've made friends with English knights over the years," he said. "Serving the Marshal has given me more English friends than I need. I thought I would send word to a couple of them to see if they need a companion for their wives or daughters. Mayhap they need a nurse to take care of the children. There are two of them in particular I will send word to—Sir Beckett Ashlington and Sir Augustus Magnesson. One is a Saxon and one is a Northman, so they're inclined to be more sympathetic to a non-English lass. Augustus alone had eight children the last I heard, so surely he'd appreciate someone to tend them."

Dermot knew the two knights he spoke of, men who had once served William Marshal. "It would not be a terrible thing to find her employment in a good house."

"That is my thinking, also."

"But I think I may have a better idea."

"What is that?"

Dermot had been waiting for this moment. Ever since the night Andromeda arrived and he sent word to his brethren in Ireland, he'd been thinking the same thing:

Gavan mac Lochlainn.

Dermot knew about the attempts to marry the Lochlainn lad to Andromeda. He'd known that for years because it was something that had been going on for years. His communication with the *Aingil Lochlainn* was semi-regular, through his mother for all of these years, so no one was ever the wiser. In fact, it had been Dermot who told them about King John's plan to marry Andromeda to a lord of his choosing, which had spurred his Irish brethren into pushing their suit with young Gavan. If he could get Carr's agreement on it, then as her father, that could very well supersede William Marshal's directive when it came to the church. No doubt, the church would side with the blood father of a woman and not some powerful English lord when it came to marriage, especially in Ireland.

This was what the *Aingil Lochlainn* had wanted all along.

Dermot was going to give it to them on a silver platter.

"Your daughter needs a husband," he said after a moment. "It seems to me that it is the most logical solution to the problem. Find her a husband and she will be his burden and no longer yours."

Carr leaned against the parapet. "I have thought of that," he said. "But I was told, long ago, that it was not my responsibility to find her a husband."

Dermot looked at him strangely. "You are her father," he said. "Of course it is your responsibility."

Carr shook his head. "My marriage to her mother was arranged by our families," he said. "Henry Curthose came to Ireland during the time of my father, about the time I was born, and because of my royal blood, I was watched by the English, even as a child. But my father was wise and pledged me to mac Ragnaill's granddaughter, something that displeased the English. When we married, it displeased them more because if we had a son, he would have a very strong claim to the throne of Dublin. When Brigid became with child, all eyes were upon her, and when she delivered a daughter, the English stepped in to take control. John had just become king, I went to serve William Marshal, Brigid was sent back to her family, and our daughter was sent to be raised in an English household. I was told that John would select a suitable English husband for Andie."

Dermot knew most of this but pretended he hadn't heard it before. "Did he?"

"Nay," Carr said. "Not before he died. I am assuming Pembroke will select a husband for her, since he has been involved in the situation."

"Is that what you want?" Dermot asked. "Pembroke taking control of your own flesh and blood?"

Carr looked at him. "He is my liege."

"And he's essentially cut off your ballocks," Dermot said in surprisingly strong language for a man who was usually quite meek. "Andie is your daughter. You have every right to select a husband for her. An Irish husband."

Carr furrowed his brow curiously. "How?" he said. "I've not lived in Ireland for fifteen years. I do not know of any eligible men for her."

Dermot grinned. "But I do, lad," he said, clapping Carr on the arm. "This is what I think—since de Royans has been keeping Andie here, working her to the bone and making her supervise the servants, I suspect he's not sent word to the Marshal about her presence. Why would he do that and risk having the Marshal send her away?"

Carr cocked his head in thought. "True," he said. "He does seem to make her want to work."

Dermot clapped him on the arm. "So I send word to my mother," he said. "I've got a cousin of marriageable age. A bright lad with money. She'd make a fine Irish wife for him, and her bloodlines remain Irish. *Your* bloodlines remain Irish and not *sasanach*. She'll be married, and the Marshal will never be the wiser. Hell, if he doesn't know she's here, he's probably forgotten about her altogether. Don't you think he has more important things to worry about?"

Carr liked the idea very much. "Pembroke rules England like God rules the universe," he said. "He'll not care about a lone Irish lass who doesn't mean anything to anyone."

"My thoughts precisely."

"Do you think your cousin will marry her?"

Dermot nodded. "Probably," he said. "If he won't, there are a dozen other lads that will. Let me send Andie back to Ireland to stay with my mother. She'll keep her safe until a husband can be found."

"Do you think your mother would be willing?"

"I think she will," Dermot said. "She never had any daughters. She always wanted a lass around."

For the first time since Andromeda's arrival, Carr was feeling some hope. "Then send word to her immediately," he said. "If she's willing, I'll send Andie back to Ireland to stay."

Dermot had the missive heading for his mother before the night was out.

CHAPTER TWELVE

Six weeks later

SHE WAS LOOKING for Addax.

In a new frock made of durable brown broadcloth that Aldis and Flora had made for her from fabric she'd purchased at Tristan's merchant, Andromeda was out in the bailey of Wrexham on a day that was quite warm. Summer had arrived, and the sky was bright, the ground a little dusty, and the scent of flowers as they bloomed was in the air.

Lifting her hand to shield her eyes from the sun, Andromeda was on the hunt for Addax, as she had been for about a half-hour. Morning duties had been light for her even though she, and several servants, were in the process of cleaning out the chamber that had been stuffed with all of the relics from past inhabitants. Anything that resembled furniture had been distributed into several of the sleeping chambers, and things like pots and pottery and shoes and any other random items had been inspected and set aside to repair, use, or sell.

But it was an ongoing project.

This morning, she had just gone over the menu for the week with the cook, the burly man who was also the quartermaster but who was surprisingly good with preparing food. After that, she'd poked her head into the storage chamber to see a few servants there, trying to piece together what looked like several broken chairs. Leaving them to their task, she'd continued outside on her hunt for Addax.

There was something she needed to discuss with him.

In due time, she found him at the gatehouse, which was one of two usual posts for him. The other was the troop house where the men were run through drills. William was running them through their exercises today, and he was the one who told her where Addax would be. She sighted him on the walk above the portcullis as he spoke to Dermot, and she came to the base of the gatehouse, waiting for him to look away from the Irish knight before she waved at him. When he waved back, she motioned for him to come to her. Addax made his way down the enclosed stairs of the gatehouse, emerging into the hustle and bustle of the bailey.

"Greetings, my lady," he said politely, though Andromeda and Addax had become great friends over the past several weeks and he'd called her Andie on occasion. "How may I be of service this morning?"

Andromeda looked around, almost nervously. "Is there somewhere we can speak privately?"

Curious, Addax nodded and led her off toward the armory, which was vacant at this time of day. He took her inside the large chamber built into the wall of Wrexham but didn't close the door. He did stand by it, however, to make sure no one would eavesdrop on their conversation, and to also ensure he was a proper distance away from her.

"It must be serious," he said. "Have you been offended? Is there a knave I must punish?"

She grinned. "I think you know enough about me by now to know that I would have punished him myself."

"So I've heard."

Andromeda couldn't help the giggles, but they were short-lived. She'd come to speak on a serious, if not slightly awkward, subject.

"In truth, I do think I have a problem of sorts, and I need your wisdom on the matter," she said. "I do not feel that I can speak to Pat about this."

Pat. She'd taken to calling Tristan by his nickname over recent weeks, something he'd asked of her, and she was happy to comply. *Philip Alexander Tristan*, or Pat, as he'd explained it. She was touched that he would ask her to use it.

But, then again, she would have done anything he asked.

And Addax knew it. In fact, everyone knew it. It was no secret that Tristan thought she was something special, and she felt the same way about him. They'd developed a sweet romance over the past few weeks even though they kept it discreet. But discreet or not, the hint of it had infuriated Carr and seemed to alienate Dermot, so the two Irish knights had been the only negative in an otherwise deliriously lovely time in the lives of both Andromeda and Tristan.

Addax was coming to wonder if her problem had something to do with her father.

"I see," he said after a moment. "May I ask why you cannot discuss it with Pat?"

She sighed faintly. "Because I do not want to anger him," she said. "He will kill anyone who… well, anyone who might pay me attention."

"What kind of attention?"

She reached into the pocket of her crisp linen apron and

pulled out a slip of vellum. Handing it to him, he took it hesitantly, having no idea why she would give him a piece of vellum—until he looked at it.

Then he knew.

"Someone has been slipping those… those poems under my door," she said quietly. "It is not every day, but it is becoming more frequent. I'm terrified that Pat will discover that someone is trying to woo me. At least, I think someone is. It is difficult to tell because the poetry is quite… odd."

Addax held the slip in front of him, reading the words aloud.

And my love drowns,
Whilst brushing her hair with a great tortoise comb.
Should she refuse my love, or leave me,
I shall crawl from the wreckage and return to the womb.

He had to put his hand over his mouth to mask the smile that threatened. He'd never known Tristan to write poetry while infatuated with a woman, and, as he could see, it grew particularly strange when romance was involved.

Quite simply, it was bad.

So very bad.

"And… and you have not mentioned this to Pat?" he asked.

She shook her head. "Nay," she said. "As I said, I do not want him to become angry at whoever is writing it, so I thought I would ask you what I should do. Should I find out who it is and tell them to cease immediately?"

Addax had no choice. He had to tell her, especially since she thought someone else was sending her love poetry. Or some kind of poetry.

If it could be called that.

"Andie," he said softly, handing her back the slip. "Pat wrote this."

Andromeda's eyes widened. "He *what*?" she gasped. "*He* wrote this?"

Addax nodded. "Do not tell him that I told you," he said. "But you must not think that someone else is trying to lure you away from him. Pat has written poetry for as long as I have known him. He knows that he's not very good at it, but he writes it because it's something that means a great deal to him. He's a man of little emotion, so I believe the poetry is his way of expressing himself."

Mouth agape, she looked at the slip again, reading over the words in shock. Maybe even a little horror.

"Oh… Addax," she breathed. "He is trying to write love poems for me?"

Addax smiled, but it wasn't in a way to shame Tristan. It was in a way to honor him. "Aye," he said. "It must mean he cares a great deal for you, because he keeps this side of him rather hidden except to his friends."

As the shock wore off, Andromeda smiled timidly. "It's really rather sweet," she said. "Mayhap it is not poetry that the bards would write, but he is trying. It is the effort that makes it wonderful."

"I agree."

She looked at it again. "I'm not entirely sure I would use the word 'womb' in a love poem, however."

Addax scratched his head, trying to be tactful. "Or 'wreckage.'"

She wrinkled up her nose as her eyes flicked up to him. "It *is* terrible."

Addax closed his eyes, nodding fervently as he struggled not to laugh. “Please do not tell him that.”

“Never,” she said, pressing the slip against her heart. “It’s the most precious thing I have ever been given.”

“Good lass.”

“Where is he?”

“The stables,” Addax said. “He had two new horses brought in from a dealer in Liverpool, and he is settling them.”

“Then I will go and see him.”

She started to move past Addax, who reached out to stop her. “Remember,” he said. “Do not tell him I told you he wrote it. Let him tell you.”

She grinned and gave him a wink. “I do believe I can force a confession.”

“Nicely.”

“*Very* nicely.”

With a smirk, Addax let her go, watching her walk across the bailey as she headed toward the stables.

The truth was that Andromeda had forced a confession of sorts out of Addax, though he didn’t even realize it. She suspected it had been Tristan all along, the mystery poem writer slipping bits of vellum under her door, because very few people had access to the keep between sunset and sunrise, and Tristan was one of them. Not wanting to directly ask him, she’d thought Addax would know the truth.

And she’d been right.

Now, to wrest the confession from Tristan.

Andromeda suspected it wouldn’t be a difficult thing. They’d spent the past five weeks learning about one another, each day a discovery anew, and it was easily the most exciting time of her life. She’d never known anyone like Tristan—

handsome, brave, commanding, witty, and, at times, a man who easily succumbed to a woman's wishes. That was the sweetest thing of all, she thought. One word from her and he'd move heaven and earth to accommodate her.

The days that flew by had been like a dream.

Since that day in the solar, when she'd dripped green dye on the floor, he hadn't brought up marriage again, which was both maddening and welcome. Maddening because she wanted to marry him but welcome because she didn't want to feel pressured into an answer. He was giving her time to make her decision, and his patience was going to be rewarded. She intended to tell him that she would be honored to be his wife very soon.

But not until he told her about the poetry.

In a way, perhaps that awful poetry had convinced her.

The stable yard was full of men and animals at this time of day. Horses were out being brushed and watered, and goats roamed in packs. She expected to see Tristan somewhere in the mix, but when she didn't, one of the grooms pointed inside the stable. She followed the trail, heading into the dark, hay-smelling structure, on the lookout for a certain brawny knight.

Their encounter wasn't long in coming.

"My lady," a voice purred in her ear as a big body gently pushed her against the wall of the stable. "What could you possibly be doing here, I wonder? Were you looking for someone?"

Backed against the wall, Andromeda smiled up at the familiar face with the dark, twinkling eyes. He had a way of looking at her that made her heart burst right out of her chest. But she quickly turned her head away.

"I do not see him," she said, pretending to be uninterested

in his attentions. "He must be elsewhere."

"Will I do?"

She broke into a smile and looked at him again. "I suppose," she said softly, putting a hand to his bearded cheek. "You're handsome enough."

"Thank you, my lady."

"And you *are* rather sweet."

"Again—thank you."

"But I'm afraid I cannot give you my heart."

"Why on earth not?"

She sighed loudly and pushed away from him, digging into her pocket and pulling out the poem he'd written her.

"Because I intend to give my heart to whomever has written this poem," she said with feigned dramatics, holding the vellum up. "I am sorry to tell you that I have been wooed away from you. Someone has been writing love poems and slipping them under my door, and after the last one came this morning, I realize that I must seek out whomever has done this. Any man who writes me poetry must surely be worthy of my love."

Tristan stood there, lips twisted wryly and his big fists resting on his hips. "Is that so?"

"It is," she declared, putting her hand to her forehead, the back of it against her skin in a gesture that suggested she was about to swoon. "I am mad for this man and will not rest until I find him."

He was trying very hard not to smile. "I see," he said. "I should not wish for you to be so distressed. May I help you find him, then?"

"Aye," she said. "I was hoping you would. It is a generous offer, considering it will cost you my hand in marriage."

"I will survive."

"Then my loss must not be that great."

He put his hand to his mouth, pretending to rub at his chin when he was really covering up his grin. "It is not," he said. "But I must confess that I think I know who wrote those poems."

"Truly?" she said, pretending to be very interested. "Who is it? Tell me this instant."

He was still rubbing his face. "I think it's one of the priests in the village," he said. "You know they're not allowed to have anything to do with women, so he's trying to lure you into his lair. All he wants is to ravage you and leave your bones for the birds."

Now it was Andromeda's turn not to laugh. "Is this true?" she said. "Is he handsome, at least?"

"He thinks so."

"Rich?"

"A priest? Hardly."

"Then he must have something worthy of such talent?"

Tristan just stood there and shook his head at her. "Surely you are not so blind."

Her brow furrowed. "Me?" she said. "Blind? Do not be a poor loser, Pat. Tell me who it is this very moment."

He rolled his eyes and let the grin break through. "You silly wench," he said. "*I* wrote the poetry. Who else would dare to leave you notes like that?"

"A priest trying to lure me into improprieties."

"Do you truly believe that?"

"You *told* me so."

"If I told you the moon was blue, would you believe that?"

"I would believe anything you told me."

He snorted, but he also moved like lightning and was on her in a flash. Suddenly, she was in his arms as he carried her into the nearest stall, listening to her giggle as his mouth slanted over hers.

The giggling stopped.

The kiss was heated. He was such a big man that for Andromeda, it was like being enveloped in a powerful mound of flesh, safe and warm and delightful. She wrapped her arms around his neck, matching him kiss for kiss. When he pried her lips apart with his tongue, they feasted on one another, and Andromeda lost herself in the man. He drove bolts of excitement through her body, sensations she'd never felt before but a sensation that made her feel hot and weak.

She couldn't get enough of him.

Her reaction to him was purely instinctive. Her body responding to his, her limbs winding their way around him, arms and legs holding him close. Before she realized it, he had her pinned against the wall of the stable, her thighs parted and his big body wedged in between. His mouth left hers, sucking her neck as his hands held her knees. It was a lovemaking position, though she didn't realize it, but his pelvis was against hers, and she could feel something hard pressing against her woman's center through the fabric. As he devoured the flesh of her shoulder, she put her hand down where he was pressing against her, only to feel his rock-hard erection straining against his breeches.

The moment she touched him, he jumped, and she nearly fell to the ground.

"God," he breathed, holding her up so she wouldn't tumble. "I'm sorry, love, but don't… don't do that right now."

Andromeda was breathing heavily. "Don't do what?"

He sighed sharply. "Put your hand… down there. Against me like that."

Andromeda knew what he meant. Sort of. She looked at him seriously. “Are you in pain?”

He snorted loudly, struggling not to laugh because he could tell she really didn’t know what he was talking about. “Aye,” he said with a hint of sarcasm. “I am, so don’t touch me like that. Not now, anyway. But there will be a time when I will welcome it.”

Andromeda scratched her head, trying to put the pieces of his puzzle together. She ended up looking right at his swollen manhood, contemplating their kiss, his stiff crotch, but she still wasn’t entirely clear on the situation.

“Forgive me,” she said. “I will admit that I am rather naïve when it comes to the ways of men and women. Or, at least, I was fairly naïve until I started working at the tavern in Ruabon. I saw quite a bit there that leads me to believe your manhood is swollen because you were kissing me. I saw that at the tavern.”

Tristan wasn’t entirely comfortable talking about the subject. In fact, she was being far more logical than he had the capability of being when it came to the joining of men and women. It was a deeply private thing to him and always had been. The truth was that Tristan de Royans, a seasoned and experienced knight, was the slightest bit… prudish.

“I can only imagine,” he said. “But it is unseemly to speak on such things, so let us end the subject.”

Andromeda refused to comply. “How can I learn anything if you will not talk about it?”

He lifted his eyebrows. “That is a simple answer,” he said. “If I were your husband or your intended, it would be proper. But we are not betrothed. I cannot speak to you of such things because it simply isn’t proper.”

She frowned. “Yet you grab me and kiss me and suck the

breath out of me," she pointed out. "How is speaking on the ways of men and women any different from kissing?"

She had a point. Tristan eyed her a moment before sighing sharply. "Aye, my manhood is swollen because I was kissing you," he whispered loudly. "That is because my body is reacting to yours. It wants to join with you as a husband joins with a wife. It wants to love you, but I do not have permission to do so as of yet, so that is why you cannot touch me… there."

She knew what he meant—she hadn't yet consented to his offer of marriage, which made her smile. She went to him, pressing her body up against his as she gazed up at him.

"I think weeks of sweet kisses and flirtation have been enough of a consent," she murmured. "But since you do not think so, I will make it plain. Aye, I will marry you. I would wither away and die if I could not marry you. You are the air in my lungs and the blood in my veins, Tristan de Royans. You have my permission to love me."

A smile spread, very slowly, across his bearded lips. "Thank you," he said simply. "You have made me a very happy man."

"Have I really?"

His answer was to wrap her up in his arms and kiss her deeply again, this time with all of the lust and passion and emotion he was feeling. Andromeda gave herself over to him, willingly, feeling his hard crotch against her belly because he was much taller than she was. She reached out to touch it again, and he whispered, "Stop," with his lips still on hers. She giggled, he giggled, and all was right in the world.

All was right with them.

"Although it is only a formality, I suppose that I must ask your father for his permission," he murmured in between heated kisses. "I will ask him today."

Andromeda had her arms around his neck, holding him close to her. "I do not know why," she whispered as he kissed her chin, her neck. "He cares nothing for me. Why should a man who has never had any involvement in my life suddenly need to be consulted?"

He slowed his kisses to look at her. "At the very least, I must tell him."

"I would agree with telling him," she said. "But do not ask him. He has not earned that privilege."

He nodded, kissing her one last time before releasing her. "Then I shall find him immediately and tell him," he said. "Another person I should tell is William Marshal. Since he and John were the ones planning to marry you to someone else, I think it is only right he know that I intend to marry you. I cannot imagine he will contest it. If he wanted an English noble for you, then he shall have it in me."

Andromeda straightened out his tunic and brushed off any chaff from their encounter. "That is true," she said. "But I think we should be married sooner rather than later so he cannot have it annulled or otherwise break it. You never told him I had arrived at Wrexham?"

Tristan shook his head. "Nay," he said. "I was afraid of what he would do if he knew."

"Like what?"

"Like send you away so I would never see you again."

She smiled at him, touching his scratchy cheek. "That can never happen, my love," she said. "No matter where I was sent, I would always find my way back to you."

He grew serious, his dark eyes liquid with emotion. "Promise?"

"Promise."

He hugged her again, fiercely. There was no lust or urgency to it, only the simple joy of one human to another, feeling the power of what was developing between them. Tristan had never been a particularly eloquent man, as evidenced by his poetry, so holding her against him was the best he could do at the moment to express himself.

That and the poems.

He could feel one coming on.

"*May the sun shineth down for all eternity upon you and me,*" he whispered, feeling the words flowing to him as tribute to the moment. "*To draw upon the strength within, to smash the source of all my strife. We will eat the sweetest cheese of life, together.*"

Andromeda, who had been holding on to him with her eyes pressed tightly closed, slowly opened them. She could hear one of those odd poems in his words, spoken so reverently, but it took great effort not to smile at the sheer peculiarity of it. He tried so hard to be articulate, and she had seen, over the past few weeks, how much the poetry meant to him. Whether or not it was any good wasn't the issue.

It meant something to *him.*

Therefore, it meant something to her.

"You must write more poetry for me," she said, pulling back to look at him. "If I inspire you, then I am honored."

He smiled faintly, putting a big hand on her hair, smoothing it down. "I am the one who is honored," he said softly. "I worship at your altar, Andie. Surely you know that. As for the poetry… no one said I have talent. Even I know I do not. But the creation of it fills something in me. I'm sorry if it is awkward at times."

She shook her head firmly, standing on her toes to kiss his

cheek. "It is heartfelt," she assured him. "I would rather have one of your poems than all of the expensive gifts in the world."

He grinned modestly, returning her kiss to the cheek. As they smiled at one another, they began to hear voices outside the stables. Someone was speaking loudly, and Tristan recognized Addax's voice. He stepped out of the stall, holding Andromeda's hand, and led her out of the stable where Addax was standing near the entrance. As soon as Addax saw him, he headed in his direction.

"Ah," he said. "There you are. I wanted to inform you that de Wolfe's comrades have arrived. Paris de Norville and Kieran Hage are at the gatehouse. De Wolfe is with them. I've told him to take them into the solar."

"Excellent," Tristan said with some satisfaction. "Teviot agreed to my request, which is either flattering or concerning. Mayhap he was glad to be rid of them, eh?"

Addax chuckled. "They're big knights, Pat," he said. "These are not scrawny young men. Hage alone must be worth ten men in battle."

"We shall see," Tristan said with the lift of an eyebrow. "I will meet them in the solar. You will attend as well."

"What about Carr and Dermot?"

"Not now."

Addax nodded in understanding, heading back to the gatehouse as Tristan turned to Andromeda.

"Will you have refreshments for us, my lady?" he asked politely, kissing her hand. "And make sure there are beds in the knights' quarters for them, please."

Andromeda nodded. "Of course," she said. "But… Pat?"

"Aye?"

"Will you consider moving them into the keep?" she said.

"Addax is in the keep, and so are my father and Dermot. Don't you want all of your knights in the same place?"

That was true. William was the only knight in the knights' quarters because Addax, Carr, and Dermot refused to sleep there. They were snobs, and that was the truth. Therefore, Tristan considered her request.

"Where would you put them?" he asked.

"On the second floor, right at the mouth of the stairs," she said. "There are three good chambers there, and they could get to the bailey in a few seconds if needed. Also… also, they could guard the stairs for anyone coming up that should not be there."

He nodded. "Very well," he said. "Do as you wish."

Flashing him a radiant smile, she was gone. Tristan watched her go, her long blonde hair waving in the breeze until she disappeared from sight.

His chatelaine.

His betrothed.

His very life.

He hadn't thought it was possible to be so happy.

☙

"… AND WE ended up winning five pounds off the man." A tall, muscular blond with pale eyes and a handsome face was speaking with great animation to William. "We've been living like kings all the way from Northumberland."

He slapped the arm of a man sitting to his right, a man with impossibly wide shoulders, arms like tree branches, and fists the size of a man's head. Even so, Kieran Hage flinched when Paris de Norville slapped him. He rubbed the spot as William, listening to the exploits of the two, shook his head.

"All well and good," he said quietly. "But I must speak to you before de Royans comes in. You are to tell him none of this, do you understand? The only reason he allowed me to summon you was on the condition that there be no gambling, no games, and no outrageous behavior. If you do not listen to him, he has the power to destroy. More than Teviot or my father or even William Marshal. De Royans can end us all."

Paris, the more outspoken of the trio, frowned. "That is not possible," he said. "What has happened to you, William? Since when do you fear anyone's wrath?"

William eyed his arrogant friend. "Since you ask, I will tell you," he said. "This is something that only a few men know, so take this to your grave. If you do not, the grave will come sooner than you expect."

"We're listening," Kieran said. He was a handsome man with dark blond hair, intense brown eyes, and a square jaw. He was also quite calm in any given situation, not at all like Paris and his devil-may-care attitude. "What's so serious, William?"

"De Royans," William said, fixing on Kieran. "Do you know the man?"

Kieran shrugged, looking to Paris to see that he was shrugging also. "A little," Kieran said. "He was stationed at Pelinom Castle for a couple of years, and we saw them on occasion, but we were squires then. We did not mix socially with the knights. What about him?"

William stepped closer to them and lowered his voice. "He is the adopted son of Juston de Royans of Bowes Castle," he said. "His parentage has been kept quiet, but the truth is that he is the bastard son of Henry Curthose and Alys of France. The man is Plantagenet and Capetian, and more royal than any man on the planet, but he chooses to serve as a knight in William

Marshal's stable and conceal his true heritage. However, the fact remains that should he be wronged or disobeyed, he can ruin us. He has that power. That means we obey him in all things. Is that clear?"

By this time, Kieran and Paris were looking at William with some astonishment. "He's *Henry's* son?" Paris gasped. "God's Bones… that is astonishing."

"It is," William said. "In fact, de Royans should be on the throne right now, and were it not for his lack of ambition, he would be. He would not be a knight on the Welsh marches, but that is what he chooses, and if we want to continue to serve together, it is time for us to evolve. The boys must become men."

"I *am* a man," Paris spat. "Bring me a wench and I'll show you just how much of a man I am."

"He does not mean that," Kieran said, casting Paris an impatient look before returning his focus to William. "I know what you mean. And I do not disagree. Reputations are being built, and that means if we ever want to be trusted by prestigious lords, we must establish who we are as knights."

"As *men*," William said quietly. "We've already established reputation as knights. That is why we were knighted at such a young age. But we are no longer youths who can explain away an indiscretion because of our age. That means no more gambling. No more betting on Kieran to wrestle every man at Wrexham. No more rolling the bones and taking the money of every dense soldier at the castle. It means we behave while we are here. Do you understand?"

Kieran nodded while Paris resisted. He had the size and strength of a grown man but the mind of a fifteen-year-old boy at times. He liked to have fun. While there was nothing wrong with that, he was still having difficulty with the concept that knights didn't behave like squires, and they didn't play games of chance with the soldiers.

"Can we not discuss this?" he said. "There are over a thousand soldiers here, William. Think of the money to be made."

William shook his head. "I gave de Royans my personal guarantee that there would be no unknightly behavior," he said. "If you do something that violates that oath, I will personally send you back to Teviot. Any man—even you—who causes me to break my word is not someone I choose to associate with. Do you understand me, Paris?"

Paris did. He didn't want to make William look bad, but he also didn't like the idea of no fun and no riches for their duration at Wrexham. "I understand you," he said begrudgingly. "But *only* at the castle, correct? What we do outside of the castle is our own affair."

"As long as it doesn't get back to de Royans or affect his command, but I wouldn't go around announcing it." When Paris continued to look dubious, William pointed a finger at him. "If *I* am willing to do it, then you should be willing to do it."

It was a compromise Paris would have to make. He was just about to say so when the solar door swung open and Tristan appeared, followed by Addax. Kieran stood up as the three young knights faced the lord who had given them a last chance to serve together. Tristan made his way over to his table, eyeing the three big, strapping men.

Powerful young swords for Wrexham.

"Welcome, good knights," he said to Paris and Kieran. "I suppose William has already told you why you've been summoned?"

Kieran was the first to speak. "Not yet, my lord," he said. "We've not seen one another in quite some time, so the greetings were long."

Tristan folded his enormous arms over his chest, looking over the trio. "No doubt," he said. "Has he at least told you what my expectations are?"

"That we did manage to discuss, my lord," Kieran said. "No wrestling, no gambling at the castle."

Tristan looked at the intensely serious young knight who was, quite frankly, broader and more muscular than any man he'd ever seen in his life. "And you feel that you can uphold these requirements?"

"Aye, my lord," Kieran said. "We will do what you ask of us."

Tristan believed him. He seemed honorable enough. His gaze moved to the blond with the pale eyes and comely face. He, too, was big and muscular, but leaner muscle in his case. "And you?" he asked. "You're de Norville, aren't you?"

Paris nodded smartly. "Aye, my lord."

Tristan looked him over for a moment. "I served at Pelinom Castle for a couple of years," he said. "We saw some action with Northwood Castle, as I'm sure you know, because you were there. In one battle at the River Tweed with Clan Gordon, I seem to remember someone trying to drown an English knight, and you cut the offender's head off."

Paris nodded. "He was trying to kill my trainer, my lord," he said. "I was not going to allow that to happen."

"And you," Tristan said, turning to Kieran. "I remember a squire getting involved in the same skirmish and breaking a man's neck with his bare hands before using a severed arm to beat down his friends. That was you."

Kieran nodded without hesitation. “I was caught behind the line without a weapon, my lord,” he said. “I was forced to improvise.”

Tristan looked at Addax, who fought off a smile at the resourceful but deadly young knight. That caused Tristan to break into a grin and shake his head.

“It was bold and imaginative of you,” he said. “It was at least three years ago.”

“Five, my lord.”

“How old were you?”

“I was nearly thirteen years old, my lord.”

That caused Addax to break into a soft snort, amazed and amused by such a story. “By the looks of you, I imagine you were taken into battle as a young child, and you did quite well,” he said. “I have spent a good deal of time in the north, Hage. I know of you. I know of your companions. You are the next generation of great knights, but you lack one thing.”

Kieran turned his attention to the fearsome man. “What is that, my lord?”

“Discipline.”

“That is true,” Tristan said. “I will not pretend I have not heard of your antics, all of you. I will not pretend that I did not relay terms to de Wolfe as to the cost of reuniting you. If he had not already told you, he would have. I expect nothing but good behavior and obedience. Give me that and we shall all get along fine. Deviate and I will deal with you personally. Is that clear?”

“It is, my lord,” Kieran and Paris answered in unison.

Tristan nodded. “Excellent,” he said. “But I will also make you a pledge on my part. Since I have not been in command of you when your antics have taken place, you will start with a clean slate with me. But one wrong move, as I said, and my trust will be at an end. Fair enough?"

The three of them nodded. "It is fair, my lord," William said quietly. "We will not fail you."

Tristan looked at all three. While William and Kieran seemed resolute, de Norville looked as if he had something more to say.

In fact, he did.

"I will not fail you, either, my lord," he said. "But we are young. We are allowed some entertainment of our own choosing when our hard work is done. As long as it does not affect you or the Wrexham army, and as long as it does not occur in the castle grounds, may we at least know a moment of relaxation in a tavern and mayhap a roll or two of the bones?"

He seemed confident and a little loud—arrogant, even—but he hadn't said anything unreasonable. Tristan didn't think so, anyway, but he didn't want de Norville thinking he would be forgiving should they slip back into old behaviors.

"I do not care what you do when you are not on duty and have my permission to go into town," he said. "But one failure, one offense, and there will be no second chance. Use my words as your bible when planning your recreation and do what you feel is correct. Am I making myself clear?"

"As rain, my lord."

"That is good," he said. "Now, I am hoping we may move to a more pleasant subject. Or, at the very least, a more important one. The reason why I agreed to let de Wolfe bring you here."

"Then there *is* a reason, my lord?" Kieran asked.

Tristan nodded but was precluded from answering when there was a knock at the solar door and it swung back on its hinges. Andromeda scurried in, leading a convoy of servants who were carrying food and drink into the chamber. Tristan quickly pushed aside some of the clutter on the table so they could put down trays of warmed beef, bread, cheese, fruit, and watered wine. They were swift and efficient, and when they darted out of the chamber, Andromeda smiled politely at the men and moved to follow the servants, but Tristan stopped her.

"My lady, wait," he said, reaching out to take her by the wrist and pull her over to where the men were standing. "Good knights, allow me to introduce you to Lady Andromeda de Courcy. She will answer to Lady Andie. She is my chatelaine, and a more efficient woman you will never meet."

He let go of her wrist and smiled at her as she dipped into a curtsy for the knights. "Good men," she said. "Should you need anything, please do not hesitate to ask. When you are ready to retire, I have had your chambers prepared."

Everyone was being distantly polite to her except for Paris. He took a few steps toward her, pushing past Kieran, as he went to speak to her.

"My lady," he said in a tone that bordered on seductive. "I had no idea there was such beauty in the wilds of Wales."

Andromeda eyed him. "There is beauty everywhere, my lord, if you will only look for it."

He smiled, a rather dashing gesture. "I have," he said. "I see it now. You have made this duty far more pleasant already. Mayhap we can speak later, and you can tell me of your upbringing. I am interested in such things."

Andromeda wasn't intimidated by him, but she clearly didn't appreciate how close he'd come to her, nor the tone he used. He was brash and young and conceited. She knew how to handle men like that because there had been plenty of them in Ireland, and, being a pretty girl, she'd run into her share. Not only that, but working in the tavern in Ruabon all those months had taught her a thing or two about being assertive with bold men.

Best to establish the rules from the start.

"Further discussion between you and I will be unnecessary, my lord," she said, smiling prettily. "But I can tell you that I was raised in a fine home where we were taught manners and how to be respectful to people we have just been introduced to. I can see you did not receive the same lesson, for if you ever address me in a tone like that again, I'll ensure the next dish you eat is full of mud or horse droppings. Mayhap that will remind you not to be so bold with a woman you have just met. Do you understand me?"

Paris' eyes widened and he straightened up. "I meant no disrespect, my lady."

Andromeda continued with her lovely smile. "Surely not," she said in a manner that suggested she was mocking him. "You would never do that, would you?"

"Nay, my lady."

"And certainly not in front of the man I am betrothed to."

Paris' head snapped to Tristan, who was gazing back at him steadily. Knowing he had put himself in a very bad position, Paris threw his hands up and backed away, about as far as he could without actually going through a wall.

"My apologies, my lord," he said, eyes averted. "It will not happen again, I swear it."

The smile never left Andromeda's face. "I'm certain it won't," she said. "Now, if you will all excuse me, I have duties to attend to."

With that, she quit the chamber, leaving smirking faces and one frightened knight in her wake. Through it all, Tristan couldn't have been prouder. Paris, and the rest of the young knights, received her message loud and clear, and he hadn't had to lift a finger.

This time.

Whether there was a next time was entirely up to de Norville.

Given Paris' expression, Tristan didn't think there would be.

CHAPTER THIRTEEN

HE'D SEEN THE young English knights arrive and was well aware they'd been invited to a meeting in the solar with Tristan and Addax that neither he nor Dermot had been invited to. Somehow, over the past few weeks, the divide between English and Irish was growing. A chasm was developing.

But he didn't particularly care.

Carr had been stewing for weeks, waiting for the reply to the missive Dermot had sent to his mother the week Andromeda arrived. Somewhere, Dermot had an unwed cousin, and Carr was anticipating a marriage for his daughter with more gusto than he should have. It was his chance to be rid of his child, to send her back to Ireland and away from Wrexham. Truth be told, the wait had been frustrating because there was a certain baker's assistant in the village that he'd been unable and unwilling to see since his daughter arrived. No one special, simply a woman to bed, but that aspect of his life was paused until he could get rid of his daughter, and that delay was frustrating him more with every passing day.

He was tired of waiting.

But today had been a busy day for Wrexham in general.

Along with the English knights from Northumberland and a delivery of horses, a messenger had arrived from Liverpool. Given that one of the largest ports on the western coast of England was only forty miles to the north, it made things easy when sending missives or men to, or from, Dublin, which was directly across the sea from Liverpool. Missives could be sent to Dublin in less than a week, and replies could come just as fast because there were any number of ships crossing the rough Irish Sea on any given day.

Today, the missive had finally come from Dermot's mother.

As Tristan and Addax met with the new knights, Dermot had relayed the contents of his mother's reply, which included the information that Dermot did, indeed, have a young cousin who was looking for a bride. He was a smithy by trade and could earn a good living, according to Dermot's mother. Carr had no way of knowing that the very Irish who had tried to break in to Rockbrook Castle now knew exactly where Andromeda was, thanks to Dermot and his mother. He had no way of knowing the young cousin was none other than Gavan mac Lochlainn. Carr was trusting and never asked to see the missive as Dermot gleefully told him that an Irish husband was ready and waiting for Andromeda.

All Carr knew was that he was about to be rid of her.

But there was more that Dermot hadn't told him.

Along with the missive from his mother was a second missive describing "cousins" that had reached Wrexham some time ago because of the information Dermot had supplied. When he'd sent word of the lady's arrival on the day she'd come to Wrexham, according to his mother's missive, the "cousins," which was a code for the *Aingil Lochlainn*, had quickly acted on the information. Up until that point, according to the old lady, they'd focused their search for her in Ireland. But Dermot's information was an answer to prayer, and they had made their way over to Liverpool, with their destination being Wrexham Castle.

Everything was finally falling into place.

Dermot suspected they'd been in Wrexham for weeks, but no one had made the attempt to contact him yet, which was probably for the best. They were working through Dermot's mother because her missives were not suspect at the castle, simply a mother writing to her son, so the second missive had mentioned sending the bride home with the cousins as escort. That meant the *Aingil Lochlainn* were somewhere in Wrexham, waiting for contact with Dermot.

Waiting for the lady to be brought to them so they could take her back to Dublin.

It was smart of them, really. They could never send enough Irish over to infiltrate the castle or fight to claim the lady, so although they were in Wrexham—somewhere—they were waiting to make contact with Dermot. They were being patient. He hadn't known of their presence until he read the second missive, but now that he had, he would have to make the effort to get out into the town and look for them. Once he found them, they would make plans to whisk the lady out of Wrexham Castle.

That was where Carr came in.

Of course, the man knew nothing about the *Aingil Lochlainn* and Dermot's involvement. It was better that way, because although Carr was averse to his daughter being at Wrexham Castle, he was still technically an enemy of the *Aingil Lochlainn* because they were enemies of his wife's grandfather. Dermot wasn't entirely sure that Carr would actually allow them to take his daughter. He might suddenly find his backbone and defend her. Dermot couldn't take the chance.

So… he told Carr what he wanted to hear.

A groom was waiting.

As Dermot went off to burn the missives from his mother, Carr was armed with what he believed to be his daughter's destiny. He'd avoided her for the weeks she'd been at Wrexham Castle, but now he had something to say to her. No matter their relationship, she was still his daughter, and any decision he made for her, whether or not she liked it, would be upheld by the law and the church. That meant that whatever plans Tristan had for her would be superseded by Carr's determination to send her back to Ireland.

He was about to take charge.

His daughter was usually in the keep, the kitchen yard, or in the hall. He'd rarely seen her stray from those areas. He slept in the keep, but on the ground level, and both he and Andromeda had gone to great lengths to avoid one another. Since Tristan was meeting with the new knights in the keep, he wandered in that direction, but he didn't want Tristan to think he was trying to barge into the gathering, so he avoided going inside. Instead, he headed to the kitchen yard with the plan of asking the cook if he might know Andromeda's location.

The kitchen yard was surrounded by a tall stone wall and reinforced with a heavy iron gate that, when secured, could keep out an army. The gate was unlocked, however, and Carr went inside, shooing some chickens away from his feet and pushing aside a goat that came too close. He stood there a moment, looking for the burly, one-eyed cook, when he suddenly caught sight of his daughter coming from the stone buttery.

Immediately, he moved in her direction.

Andromeda had a half of a wheel of cheese in her hands as she headed for the open door of the kitchen, which was built into the sub-level of the keep. A door opened onto stairs that led down to the kitchens below. She wasn't paying attention to her surroundings, but rather trying to find a comfortable position to hold the cold and heavy cheese, when Carr put himself in her path.

She nearly ran into him.

"God's Bones," she muttered, nearly dropping the cheese. When she looked up and realized who it was, her manner stiffened considerably. "Do you require something, Carr? You do not usually come into the kitchen yard."

Carr. She couldn't even bring herself to call him by his name, but he didn't care. His manner, too, was hard as he faced her.

"You and I must speak," he said in a commanding tone. "Put the cheese down and come with me."

Andromeda didn't move. "Whatever you have to say, say it now," she said. "I have work to do."

She was being unfriendly, matching his mood, and he hissed at her. "I told you to come with me."

"And I told you to say what you will now. What is it?"

His jaw twitched dangerously. "Is that what years with de Courcy have taught you?" he said. "Such disrespect?"

She sighed, shifting the weight of the cheese in her arms. "I do not have time for this," he said. "*What* do you want, Carr?"

He snorted rudely. "What I want is for you not to have come to Wrexham," he said. "But, clearly, I shall have to make amends for that. I have brokered a betrothal with a cousin of Dermot's. The man is a smithy, and he is looking for a bride. I am sending you back to Ireland to marry him."

Andromeda stared at him without any discernible reaction at first. She digested his words, finally cocking her head in a curious gesture.

"You are ridiculous," she said. "I am not going back to Ireland. I am staying here, where I am needed, and if you do not like that, it is no concern of mine. That is your problem."

Carr's features were growing tenser by the moment. "You truly have no concept of how the world works, do you?" he said. "I give the orders. You will obey them."

"The only person I obey is Tristan, as the garrison commander."

Carr's lips twisted in a smirk. "I suspect that is in all aspects," he said. "How long have you been warming his bed? Since your arrival, or did it take a few days?"

Andromeda's disgust masked the fact that his words had wounded her. "I suppose you think I'm like you in that respect," she said. "I've heard you take women to your bed that are not my mother, but it is no concern of mine. If you want to rut like a bull, that is your affair. Do not try to impress your lack of morals on me, for you would be wrong."

Carr's eyes widened. "Who has told you such things?"

"It seems to be common knowledge that you are the male version of a trollop."

Enraged, he grabbed her by the arm, and the cheese ended up on the ground. "Listen to me, you little chit," he snarled. "I am your father, and you will not speak to me in such a manner. You will go to your chamber now, pack your satchel, and be prepared to ride to Liverpool at dawn."

Infuriated, not to mention somewhat frightened that he'd grabbed her, she slapped his hand away and stood back, out of range, with the fallen cheese between them like a line in the sand. She balled up her fists, waiting for him to charge her again.

"Nay," she fired back. "I will *not* listen to you. You lost that privilege years ago when you allowed the English king and William Marshal to take me away from my mother and put me in an English household for safekeeping."

"You do not understand how the world works, but you will."

"I understand that you are a feckless, irresponsible fool, and I am ashamed to be your daughter."

He reached out to grab her again, and she slugged his hand, which caused him to rush at her. Panicked, Andromeda stumbled backward, grabbing the first thing she could find, which happened to be a heavy wooden pitcher used for milk. It was sitting empty outside the buttery along with a few others. Getting a grip on it, she swung it at Carr's outstretched hand, and he yelped in pain. Terrified, she hit him three more times, beating him back. Once, she even hit him in the face. He was finally forced to retreat because she'd clipped him well with the pitcher.

"You wicked bitch," he said. "You'll be sorry for that."

"Leave me alone," she shouted. "You have no right to touch me. Go away and leave me alone or I'll bash you over the head!"

Carr rubbed his smarting cheek. "You'll do as I say," he said, jabbing a finger at her. "You're coming with me. I'll lock you in the vault until tomorrow if I have to."

"I'll kill you before I'll let you do that!"

Carr started to come after her again, and Andromeda raised the pitcher, preparing to beat him back again, but she caught movement out of the corner of her eye. A blur was coming in through the kitchen gate, and suddenly her father was on his face in the dirt. Something had hit him in the head, very hard. Shocked, Andromeda looked up to see Tristan standing there, a cocked fist at chest level.

He was as angry as she'd ever seen him.

The pitcher fell to the ground.

"Thank God," she breathed, realizing how terrified she had been. "Thank God you came when you did. He wanted to throw me in the vault and send me back to Ireland."

Addax had come in behind Tristan, and was now bent over a dazed Carr and rolling the man onto his back as Tristan lowered his fist and went to her.

"I was coming to the stables to show Addax my new horses when I heard your shouting," he said. "Did he hurt you?"

He was grasping her hands, looking for blood, as she shook her head. "Nay," she said. "But the man has gone mad, Pat."

"Why? What did he say?"

Andromeda tried to catch her breath. "He told me that he brokered a betrothal with a cousin of Dermot," she said. "He told me that he was sending me back to Ireland to marry him."

Tristan's eyebrows lifted as she mentioned Dermot. "I see," he said, rage in his dark eyes. "Then Dermot is part of this, too."

She shook her head. "I do not know," she said. "Possibly. Probably. If my father has promised that I will marry one of his cousins, then clearly he is involved."

Tristan still had her by the hands as he turned to Addax. "Find Dermot," he said. "I want him and Carr placed in the vault immediately."

Addax nodded swiftly, calling to some soldiers as he headed out of the kitchen yard. Meanwhile, Tristan could see how shaken Andromeda was, and he pulled her into his powerful embrace, kissing the top of her head as she rested against his chest.

"I fear the Irish knights have separated from the English," he muttered. "I thought that might happen. I was going to ask your father permission to marry you, but obviously, that is not going to happen."

"What will we do?"

He pulled back to look at her. "That is simple," he said. "We shall marry today. Tonight. I will send for a priest immediately, and we will be married before the day is over. Then your father cannot send you back to Ireland because you will be my wife."

She smiled weakly. "I am sorry you have been forced into this so quickly," she said. "You can still refuse. I would not blame you."

He looked at her as if she'd lost her mind. "Why would I do that?" he said. "Unless you are unclear about it. If that is the case, we will wait until you make a firm decision, but regardless, your father and Dermot go into the vault until I decide what is to be done with them. They cannot be a threat to you."

She smiled at him, putting her fingers on his lips and watching him kiss them. "I am not unclear," she said softly. "I've never been clearer about anything in my life. If you wish to marry today, then that is my wish as well."

"Are you sure?"

"Absolutely."

He was trying not to smile too much because he didn't want to look like a giddy fool, but that was certainly what he felt like. William suddenly appeared in the yard along with Kieran and a few soldiers, and they went straight to Carr, who was just starting to stir. Kieran bent over and heaved the man over his enormous shoulder as if he weighed nothing at all, hauling him out of the kitchen yard with several soldiers as escort.

William went over to Tristan and Andromeda.

"Addax told me what happened," he said, looking to Andromeda. "I hope he did not hurt you."

Andromeda shook her head. "Nay," she said. "But he tried."

William conveyed his sympathies with his expression before looking to Tristan. "It's as you suspected," he said. "The Irish are banding together."

"Where is Dermot?"

"He was on the wall, but Addax cornered him."

"Is he going peacefully?"

"Addax threatened to throw him over the wall if he caused trouble."

"That's a relief," Tristan said, looking to Andromeda. "You may now move about the castle freely without fear of your father or Dermot harassing you. It was either lock you in your chamber for your own safety or lock them in the vault, so I made the correct choice. They must be contained."

Andromeda put her hand on his arm in thanks and possibly for comfort. He seemed almost as shaken as she was about the whole thing.

"Not to worry," she said. "I am well. We are well."

Tristan nodded, taking more comfort in her words than he realized he would. But his attention shifted to William.

"I need you to do something for me," he said.

William nodded. "Anything."

Tristan took Andromeda's hand as he spoke. "I would like you to go into the town and fetch a priest," he said. "I am going to marry the lady before the night is through. Carr and Dermot seemed to have made plans for her to marry someone in Ireland, but those plans will never know fruition. The lady is mine, and I am going to make it official in the eyes of God and the law."

William smiled as he looked between the pair. "I would be honored to summon the priest," he said. "May I take Paris with me? To start acclimating him to the town?"

Tristan nodded. "You may," he said. "But do not linger. I'd like to get this settled quickly."

William smiled, looking to Andromeda before turning on his heel and quickly heading from the kitchen yard. Tristan and Andromeda watched him go before looking to one another. Tristan lifted the hand he held and kissed it.

"Go about your business," he told her. "As soon as the priest arrives, I will send for you. Be ready."

She grinned. "I am ready now."

Tristan laughed softly and bent over to kiss her tenderly on the lips. "So am I," he whispered. "But we must wait for the priest."

With a chuckle, Andromeda gave him a wink and turned back for the cheese she'd dropped on the ground, picking it up as Tristan came to help her. He held it while she brushed it off, but all the while, he was simply looking at her, realizing his life was about to take a dramatic turn that very night.

And he was not the least bit sorry for it.

CHAPTER FOURTEEN

"IT WAS A lovely wedding, William," Paris said. "I'm surprised I was invited to witness it, given the fact that I nearly had my head cut off earlier by de Royans when I tried to flirt with his intended."

William was fighting off a smile, glancing at an equally smirking Kieran. "That is *not* what was nearly cut off, if you get my meaning," he said, watching Paris grin. "All is forgiven, I am sure. But if I were you, I would stay clear of Lady de Royans from now on. De Royans is quite protective over her, and you do not want to end up on his wrong side."

"True," Paris said, gazing up at the stars, which seemed unusually bright on this cold evening. "But it seems to me that there is quite a bit going on here in the short time since we arrived. We put two seasoned knights in the vault earlier today, and all I was told is it was because they were conspiring."

"They are."

"What is *really* going on, William?"

The three of them were walking in the bailey, heading to the gatehouse to take over the night watch, something Dermot usually did. With the wedding of Tristan and Andromeda complete, the happy couple was celebrating with Addax in the great hall, while William and Paris and Kieran had charge of the castle for the night. But the day had been odd, to say the least, and Paris and Kieran wanted answers.

William didn't blame them.

It was time for total truth.

"Lady de Royans is the last of her family," William said quietly. "She is the granddaughter of the last King of Dublin, a man who was murdered by a faction who tried to abduct the lady about a year ago. That's why she's here. She was raised by Liam de Courcy, who sent her here when it was no longer safe for her to remain in Ireland."

They came to a halt in the torchlit bailey, facing one another, as Paris spoke. "But why is her father in the vault?" he said. "And what part does Dermot play in this?"

William lifted his shoulders. "I do not know about Dermot, only to say that we believe he is allied with Carr mac Murda, the lady's father," he said. "Carr has never made any secret out of not wanting his daughter here. He's been most resistant about it to the point of being violent about it. Today, he confronted his daughter, whom he has barely spoken to since her arrival, and told her that he had arranged for a marriage to one of Dermot's cousins. He intended to send her back to Ireland, a place she just fled for her own safety."

"So de Royans married her to keep her safe and out of Ireland?" Kieran asked.

"Partially," William said. "But he married her because he loves her. He has from the start of their association, so it is a love match. Carr and Dermot are in the vault because de Royans doesn't trust them. Carr wants her back in Ireland, and Dermot has supplied the man for her to marry, so draw your own conclusions. Something very strange is going on with those two."

Kieran was looking off toward the gatehouse with the door that led down into the vault as Paris frowned.

"Strange, indeed," he said. "But they're Irish. I would expect nothing less."

William shrugged. "I do not want to agree with you, but given the evidence, I will not argue," he said. "But there is more to the situation that you should be aware of. De Royans has speculated that the faction that tried to abduct Lady de Royans from her home in Ireland would not give up so easily. He has speculated that they might have suspected she would come to England and that they may have followed her here."

Paris and Kieran were listening intently. "But how would they know where she had gone?" Paris asked.

"Because they know her father serves the Marshal," William said. "It is not a secret. They know he would be at Pembroke, so logic suggests they would go to Pembroke looking for her. It's quite possible that someone at Pembroke told them that Carr mac Murda is now serving at Wrexham, so…"

"So they would come to Wrexham," Paris finished for him. His eyes were alight with the mystery afoot. "Then it is equally possible those two Irish knights know that."

"Know it and are in on the plot," Kieran added. "If mac Murda does not want her here, then he would have the perfect opportunity to send her back with the group that wants her."

William nodded. "It may be that Carr was planning to take her straight to these Irish rebels," he said. "To be quite honest, I have served with Carr and Dermot for about a year, ever since de Royans took command of Wrexham, and during that time they have been trustworthy. But the moment Carr's daughter arrived, the situation with them became very different."

"Has anyone thought to ask them?" Kieran said quietly.

Both William and Paris looked at him. "Not that I am aware of," William said. "De Royans and al-Kort are the senior knights in this command. If they wanted to know something, I assume they would ask."

"De Royans has been busy with a woman," Paris pointed out. "And al-Kort has been busy with all of Wrexham. I suspect he has been stepping in where de Royans has been distracted."

"What are you suggesting?"

"Let's go and ask the Irish what they're involved in," Kieran said in a low voice.

William looked at Paris, who nodded. "My sentiments exactly," Paris said.

William could see what they were driving at, and, quite frankly, this was what he'd hoped for, because he and Addax and Tristan were too close to the problem. There was too much going on. A situation like this needed the fresh eyes of outsiders, and he trusted Paris and Kieran with his life. At the moment, there was a powerful dynamic going on at Wrexham, and it had the potential to turn deadly if they didn't figure out what was happening.

After a moment, William nodded.

"Let's go," he muttered.

☙

"WELL… HERE WE are."

"Aye, here we are."

Tristan grinned at Andromeda because she'd replied to his obvious statement so casually. As if the fact that they were married meant nothing to her, but he knew that wasn't the truth.

It meant a great deal to them both.

They'd just entered her chamber in the keep, the one she'd been sleeping in since her arrival, because her room was much nicer—and cleaner—than his. Tristan hadn't wanted to consummate their marriage on linens he hadn't washed in a year, so they'd come to her chamber, which already had a fire in the hearth and wine and food on the table. Flora and Aldis must have anticipated where they'd spend their wedding night, so the chamber was clean, warm, and fragrant.

It was a perfect place for romance.

"I must say, I think this chamber is the cleanest in all of Wrexham," he said, looking around. "And all of these things came out of that storage chamber?"

Andromeda nodded. "Everything," she said. "But it all had to be repaired. There was actually quite a bit of furniture in the chamber, but it was in pieces. I put the servants and the wheelwright to repairing it all."

"Excellent work."

"If you recall, I offered you chairs and tables and other things we found, but you refused."

He shrugged. "That chamber is simply a place to lay my head," he said. "There is no comfort there. I wouldn't get any use out of chairs or tables."

Andromeda went over to the large dressing table they'd found in that treasure room, one that had been missing legs that the wheelwright had replaced. It even had a bronze mirror, polished so that the reflection was true. She began pulling the iron pins out of her hair, releasing the careful style that Flora had created for her wedding.

"Where *do* you find comfort, Pat?" she asked.

He watched her as she pulled one pin out after another. "I don't really know," he said. "Someone in my profession doesn't make a habit out of seeking creature comforts."

"Everyone should have something that brings them comfort and respite," she said, turning to look at him. "What about something to do in your leisure time? Hunting, mayhap?"

He shook his head. "I don't find any pleasure in killing a frightened animal," he said. "I do like horses, however. A good horse brings me pleasure."

"What about fishing?"

He smiled. "I used to fish with my father when I was young," he said. "I have not done it in years, mostly because I cannot stand the taste or smell of fish."

Her mouth popped open in horror. "But I served baked fish in the hall last week," she said. "A fishmonger brought his catch to the castle, and it was so fresh that I purchased it. You never said a word!"

He laughed softly. "I know," he said. "I did not want to hurt your feelings. You seemed so proud of the dish."

She sighed sharply as she pulled the last pin out. "You will never again withhold the truth from me like that," she said. "Especially now. We're married, are we not?"

"That is what the priest says."

"Then, as I am your wife, you will tell me everything," she said. "And I will tell you everything also. I think it only fair."

The smile was still on his face as he moved over to the chair next to the bed and sat down. "Agreed," he said. "But we cannot know every little thing about one another in just the few weeks we've known each other. Still, we've been acquainted longer than some married couples I've known. I cannot imagine marrying someone I've only just met."

She began unbraiding the big plait that had been coiled on the back of her head. "God's Bones, nor can I," she said. "But I am curious about something."

"What?"

"How old are you?"

"I've seen forty summers," he said. "And before you tell me what an old man I am, it is too late. We are married, and you cannot leave me for a younger man."

She started laughing. "That is not what I was going to say," she said. "Well, not much. You may be older than me, but I have no intention of leaving you for a younger man. Most men my age are still children. I cannot stand the thought of being married to someone like that."

"Fortunately, you do not have to worry over it."

"Luckily for me," she said. "But that brings about my question. With your lineage, how on earth have you not been married before now? To a wealthy princess or prestigious lord's daughter?"

He sat back in the chair and propped an ankle on his thigh as he began to unlace his boots. "Simple," he said. "I did not know of my lineage until a few years ago. Until then, I thought I was an orphan. I was adopted by Juston and his wife, so I had parents who loved me, but they never told me about my true lineage."

"How did you find out?"

He grunted. "In a most unpleasant way," he said. "There was an incident with one of John's royal assassins, a man who knew who I was, and because of an encounter, the Marshal was forced to tell me of my lineage for my own safety."

With her hair unbraided, Andromeda picked up a comb. "There are men after you?"

He shook his head. "Not now," he said. "But when John was alive, he wanted me, probably because I was his only real competition for the throne. Had I any ambition, I might have been a real threat, but I have no desire to rule England. With young Henry on the throne and the Marshal advising him, I have made it clear that I am no threat. I do not want to rule. God, what chaos that would be."

She smiled as she ran a comb through her locks. "Truer words were never spoken," she said. "There are still supporters of my grandfather who would like to use me for the same purpose, but I cannot imagine agreeing to such a thing. I do not want to rule Dublin. I would be in a knife fight every day of my life, for the rest of my life. What a terrible prospect."

He finished unlacing the boot and yanked it off. "But if you ruled Ireland and I ruled England, we would be the most powerful rulers since Alexander the Great," he said. "In fact, a marriage like this could be seen, by some, as an alliance between Ireland and England. It could be viewed as a threat to many people in both countries."

She made her way over to him, brushing the ends of her hair thoughtfully. "I suppose it could," she said. "Does it feel like an alliance to you?"

He grinned as he pulled his other boot up and began unlacing it. "It feels like a dream," he said softly. "*My* dream. I hope it will be your dream, too."

She paused in front of him, smiling at his sweet words. "It already is," she said. "I am perfectly happy to live the rest of my life as a garrison commander's wife. It's more than I ever hoped for, truly."

"Happy?"

"More than I've ever been."

"Good," he said, pulling off his other boot. "Because it is my intention to make you deliriously joyful every moment of every day, for as long as you will let me. We are going to be very happy together, you and I."

Andromeda went to him, wrapping her arms around his head as he enveloped her in his powerful embrace. He had his head between her breasts, hearing her heartbeat strong and steady in his ear, as she gently ran her finger through his hair. It was a touching moment, one of hope and joy. A moment of peace.

For just this brief and shining moment, there was just the two of them in the entire world.

They stayed like that for quite some time, silently holding one another, as the fire in the hearth crackled softly. Tristan finally patted her buttocks gently.

"I'm weary," he said. "Shall we retire?"

Andromeda nodded, releasing him from her grip and making her way back over to the dressing table. Next to it was a small alcove with a painted wooden screen in front of it, something Flora and Aldis had set up as a dressing area. Some of her clothing was behind the screen, hanging from pegs in the alcove, including a luxurious sleeping shift that had been found in the cache of clothing in the painted wardrobe. It had been too large, like everything else they found there, but Aldis had managed to alter it so it fit perfectly. Made from silk and lamb's wool, it was a divine piece of clothing. Setting her comb down on the dressing table, she slipped behind the screen and disappeared.

Tristan noticed.

"What are you doing back there?" he called to her.

"Changing to a sleeping shift," she said. "Can we eat before we go to bed? I haven't eaten since this morning."

He was already over at the table that held the food and drink. "Of course," he said. "There's quite enough here. I suppose they left enough so we would not want for more until tomorrow, at least."

There were two big pewter plates on the table, also part of the trove from the storage room, and he began putting food upon them both. There was a small iron pot filled with chunks of beef in gravy, along with bread, cheese, and dried fruit. He piled both plates up, and as he turned for the bed, Andromeda emerged from behind the painted screen.

Tristan paused, drinking in the sight of her as she approached. In the delicate shift that draped in all of the right places, she looked like an angel.

"My God," he murmured. "You are a glorious creature, Lady de Royans."

Andromeda blushed furiously. "You are supposed to say that," she said. "You are my husband."

"Indeed I am," he said. "But I say it because it is the truth. Come; sit on the bed. We'll eat on the coverlet and try not to make a mess."

She giggled softly, following him over to the bed. She climbed onto the middle of the bed, and he set a plate down in front of her carefully as he sat at the head, leaning against the pillows with the plate on his lap.

They began to eat.

"Your cook is very talented," Andromeda said as she took a bite of bread. "He looks like he should be shoveling out stalls, but he knows a great deal about the kitchen and food. Where did you find him?"

Tristan's mouth was full. "Pembroke," he said. "Having him

here was the only real comfort I had until you arrived. It was just a garrison then, Andie. You have made it a home."

She smiled modestly. "You gave me a roof over my head and a place to stay," she said. "I wanted to be worthy of your generosity."

"You are more than worthy," he said. "In fact, I fear that I may be lacking where you are concerned. You are worthy of a great man."

"I have a great man," she said. "*You* are a great man, Pat. Do you not even realize that?"

He shook his head, putting more food in his mouth. "I am nothing," he said, chewing. "A royal bastard, that is all."

"And I am the granddaughter of a murdered king," she said. "I think we must stop looking at our heritage as something terrible. We are what we are, but the future is ours to shape. That is what will define us. It will define our children as well."

He looked at her then. "Strange," he said. "I've never thought of children until now."

"Why not?"

He shrugged. "Because I never thought I would marry, I suppose."

"Now you will not jump away from me when I touch you."

He knew what she meant, and he lowered his head, terrified she was going to see that she'd embarrassed him. "Nay, I will not jump away," he said. "I am yours to touch now."

Andromeda couldn't help but notice he didn't seem overly eager about it. She swallowed the bite in her mouth and put her plate aside.

"What is wrong, Pat?" she asked.

His eyes flicked up to her. "What do you mean?"

She cocked her head. "I mean that you will kiss me ferociously, but whenever I have touched your groin, you act as if I have struck you with lightning," she said. "Is there something I should know about?"

He was shaking his head before she even finished. "Nay," he said firmly. But then he sighed heavily. "It is nothing, really."

"What is it? Please tell me."

He swallowed the bite in his mouth and pushed his plate aside also. "You want total truth between us, and I have agreed," he said. "But this… this is difficult for me. I do not speak on my emotions or personal matters easily."

"Don't you like to be touched there?"

"I do," he said quickly. "It's simply that… God, this is worse than I thought."

"I will not force you to tell me if you are not ready to."

He shook his head and stood up from the bed. He seemed to be gathering his thoughts, or courage, or both. Andromeda sat patiently, watching him unfasten the belt at his waist and toss it over the back of a chair before turning to her.

"I haven't done this in quite a while."

"Done what?"

He pointed to the bed. "What we must do to consummate the marriage."

Her eyes widened. "You have done this before?"

"Did you think I hadn't?"

"*I* haven't."

He was trying not to smile at her indignation. "You are a woman, and a young one at that," he said. "Women do not give themselves over to anyone but their husbands."

Andromeda didn't know why she felt so incensed by his confession. He was an older man, seasoned and worldly. Of course he would have had other women before her. It would have been ridiculous if he hadn't. But it still didn't sit well with her to think her sweet husband had other lovers in the past.

Faceless, nameless women touching the man she loved.

"I think that is a silly standard," she said. "A woman must keep herself pure, but a man must not."

"A man does not want a rose that is wilted because others have touched it."

She scowled. "Ridiculous," she said. "The reality is that I married the leavings of other women, and I am going to assume they were like the wenches in the tavern that I saw. Surely you did not… do *this*… with a proper lady?"

He put his hand over his mouth so she wouldn't see his grin. "Does it matter?"

"How would you feel if other men had touched me before you?"

"I wouldn't like it in the least."

She simply lifted her eyebrows at him before averting her gaze, looking over to her plate and pulling it back onto her lap. Seeing that he'd somehow hurt her feelings with his clumsy confession—which wasn't really a confession at all, because he hadn't even come to the point of it—he went over to the bed.

"Although I cannot defend my actions and I cannot erase them, I hope you will let me explain," he said softly. "Men have needs that most women do not have. Aye, I've done… *this*… before, but I was young. Women were exciting to me back then, and the world, as a man, was new. It sounds stupid to say that it is the way of the world, but it is. It does not mean I have a stable of lovers in my past, or that I bedded tavern wenches, but I was trying to make a point in all of this, and it wasn't to announce my conquests. It was to tell you that, quite simply, I am nervous."

Her head came up, and she looked at him curiously. "Why would you be nervous?"

He sighed heavily, sitting down on the edge of the bed. "Because the last woman I was with… she was older and a widow," he said, stumbling over his words. "She was rich and took a liking to me. She bought me horses and swords and anything else she thought I might like, and I finally succumbed to her advances. When it was over, she told me that I was a terrible lover and had no idea how to please a woman. That was about fifteen years ago, and I've not had a woman since, so I am looking at our wedding night with a good deal of anticipation and dread. You wanted me to be honest, so I am. I hope it does not cost me."

Andromeda hadn't been expecting that. She could see how ashamed he was, and she was seized with pity for the man. Her big, strong husband had what he considered a personal failing, and he was ashamed to admit it. So very ashamed. She began to feel bad that she'd been outraged over any past lovers he may have had.

It had been foolish of her.

Standing up, she silently put her plate back on the table and took his away from him, placing it beside hers. Moving over to the bed, she began to pull the coverlet back as he sat on the bed and watched her somewhat anxiously. When their eyes met, she smiled warmly at him.

"I think she is a terrible woman who did not deserve your attention," she said softly. "And I think we should prove her wrong."

He relaxed somewhat, breaking into a grin as he stood up so she could pull the rest of the coverlet down. "Not that you have a choice, but that is a brave declaration," he said. "I can only say that I will do my best."

"But there is a difference with me."

"What's that?"

"I am your wife," she said simply. "And I love you. That other woman did not love you at all. If she had, she would have never said such terrible things."

His features softened. "Do you, Andie?" he murmured. "Do you truly love me?"

She nodded. "Of course I do," she said. "And you love me, so that is why this will be a perfect moment. You must not worry."

He had to chuckle at her, telling him what he was feeling and being so very certain about it. But it was true—all of it was true. He did love her. He couldn't remember when he hadn't. With a smile on his lips, he peeled off the dark blue tunic he'd been wearing, revealing his gorgeous muscles and slightly freckled chest with a faint matting of red hair over it.

"I do love you," he whispered. "Until there is no more God and no more heaven will I love you."

With that, he came down on the bed, on his knees, and reached out to pull her to him. Andromeda threw her arms around his neck as their lips met, instantly seeking one another with an inherent need that was driving them harder and faster than it ever had. Andromeda wanted to be touched. She wanted Tristan's hands upon her.

It was time.

Tristan lowered her back onto the bed even as he moved to pull off her sleeping shift. She could feel his hands on her waist, pulling at the garment, as his kisses grew feverish. She could feel him quivering with anticipation. Or perhaps fear, considering the last time he did this, he'd been called a failure. But he wasn't failing now. Andromeda was breathing heavily, trying to catch her breath between heated kisses, encouraging him onward. There was something building in her body, liquid fire coming to life, and she had no control over it.

Every time Tristan kissed her, the fire grew.

This shift suddenly came over her head. There was nothing left between her and Tristan as their flesh came into contact for the very first time. Heat against heat, skin against skin. His mouth left hers, seeking her neck, her collarbone, and points farther south. Kissing the swell of her bosom, his hands began to roam. They drifted to her waist, her belly, and moved across her back. Soon enough, they moved away completely, and she could feel him fumbling with his breeches until he finally rid himself of his last bit of clothing. His mouth then moved from her bosom to her breasts, and Andromeda groaned with pleasure as he captured a tender nipple in his mouth.

That took her to an entirely different level. She writhed beneath him, unaware that he had pulled her legs apart and settled in between them. She had her hands on his head, her fingers in his hair, experiencing his mouth on her breasts with the greatest enjoyment. She began to realize what the serving wenches at the tavern in Ruabon had found so delightful. What every experienced woman throughout time had found so delightful. She felt shameless, but she didn't care. Legs open wide, she gave herself over to him completely.

Tristan's fingers moved to her private core, that warm and wet junction between her legs. It was a new sensation, something that initially startled her, but he settled her down with a few whispered words, stroking her in a way that made her entire body tremble.

She wanted more.

More kisses, more suckling on her breasts. More of everything he was doing to her. Andromeda was adrift on a sea of desire when he abruptly stopped kissing her. Disappointed, she opened her eyes to question him, only to see that he was on top of her, his arms braced on either side of her body and his legs between hers. She could feel something hard pushing at her virginal core.

Then he was thrusting into her.

But her nubile body was ready for him. His manhood pushed into her wet body, and in two thrusts, he was fully seated. There had been no pain, only a sensation of fullness that she very quickly realized she liked. She liked it very much. Tristan took her bringing her legs up as a sign that she didn't find any of this a failure on his part. Her hands went to his chest, caressing him gently, and he coiled his buttocks, thrusting into her again and again.

Andromeda couldn't have loved it more.

"Sweet Jesus," she breathed, her hands moving to his waist, his hips. "Is this… this…?"

"This is how we were always meant to be," he whispered, biting gently at her soft mouth. "This is our moment, Andie. You are my wife and I am your husband, and this is our moment."

She pulled his head down to hers, latching on to his lips as he plunged into her. He kissed her deeply, a gesture full of the power and emotion they were both feeling. A few more thrusts and Andromeda felt an explosion between her legs, the likes of which she had never experienced in her life. It was like a burst of stars that radiated outward, pleasurable in the most intimate sense, and her entire body stiffened with the thrill of it. But he continued to move within her, thrusting in and out, and twice more she felt the burst of stars. Each time, it drained her a little more until she was nothing but a mass of limp, pleasured flesh.

But Tristan wasn't finished. He continued to make love to her, and she experienced at least one more burst of stars in that time, but she couldn't do anything more than softly moan as her body twitched. Dazed, she let him have his way with her until he made one hard, final thrust and she heard him grunt with pleasure. She could feel his manhood twitch as he released his seed deep into her womb. But she continued to lie there, overcome, as he gathered her into his arms and held her tightly. He was warm and sweaty, but the comfort she derived from it was immeasurable. His steady, if not heavy, breathing in her ear was enough to lull her into a deep, exhausted sleep.

Tristan held her in his arms all night.

CHAPTER FIFTEEN

"MAC EDAN. *DERMOT!*"

Dermot awoke with a start. It was dark in the vault of Wrexham, a tiny space that contained two heavily barred cells, and as of a few hours ago, he'd found himself in one. Carr was in the other. Now, his cell door was open and someone was calling his name. He couldn't see who it was because the torch on the wall was too far away to give much light. It only made the figure a silhouette, but instead of one silhouette, there were three.

Three big figures crowding into his cell.

Dermot backed up against the wall.

"What do you want?" he demanded, holding a hand up to try to block the torchlight a little so he could see who was in the cell with him. "Who is it?"

"Who is this cousin you plan to marry Carr's daughter to?"

Dermot didn't recognize the voice. "Who *are* you?" he demanded. "What are you doing here?"

"Answer my question."

"Not until you answer mine!"

A fist flew at his face from the figure to his right, catching him in the jaw. He toppled into the iron bars, seeing stars.

"Wrong answer," the voice said. "I will ask again. Who is this cousin you plan to marry Carr's daughter to?"

Moving his jaw from side to side, Dermot didn't want to take another blow like that, but his fury had the better of him. "Tell me who you are first," he said. "I do not speak to bastards who converge on me like this. If you—"

Another fist came flying at him, hitting him in the head this time. Stars danced in front of his eyes again, but he began swinging back. Very quickly, the encounter deteriorated into a brawl, right in his tiny little cell.

And very quickly, he was losing.

In the cell next door, the commotion had awakened Carr, who was now on his feet. He rushed to the bars separating his cell from Dermot's and began yelling at whoever was attacking Dermot. He didn't recognize them in the darkness, and he was beginning to feel some panic until he looked to the small area outside of the cells, right at the base of the stairs, and saw de Wolfe standing there, watching the scene unfold.

He threw himself against his cell door.

"William!" he gasped. "Stop this at once! They will kill him!"

William didn't seem concerned in the least. His gaze moved to Carr, and he took a few steps in the man's direction.

"I will ask you the same question that has been asked of Dermot," he said. "How did the marriage to Dermot's cousin come about for your daughter?"

Carr's brow furrowed as if he'd just been asked a completely outrageous question. "Why would you ask such a thing?" he said. "It is none of your affair. Stop those men from beating Dermot this instant! That is an order!"

William lifted a dark eyebrow. "Given you have been thrown in the vault, I think it is obvious that you no longer give orders," he said. "Moreover, why would I want to take orders from a man who has treated his own daughter so poorly that he seems to have allied with some very bad men in order to remove her to Ireland? Shame on you, Carr. A knight trusted by William Marshal does not give his allegiance to rebels."

Carr's eyes were wide with confusion and perhaps a little fear. "You spout madness, de Wolfe," he said. "Who told you such lies?"

Dermot suddenly let out a howl that made the hair on the back of Carr's neck stand on end. Both William and Carr turned to see what was happening in Dermot's darkened cell, but it was difficult. All they could see was that Dermot was between two very large men, and one of them had Dermot's hand twisted behind his back.

"Now," one of the men growled. "Tell me about this cousin you plan to marry Carr's daughter to."

"I will not!" Dermot shouted. "You dirty bastard, release me!"

The man broke one of Dermot's fingers on the hand twisted behind his back, and Dermot screamed in pain. He shouted and cursed and howled as the man broke three fingers and finally his thumb. Leaving the hand snapped and useless, they started in on the other hand, but Dermot started begging for mercy.

The defiance quickly turned to terror.

And Carr was watching it all in horror.

"Have you no pity, de Wolfe?" he said, no longer demanding but now sounding as if he was begging. "This is a man you have stood side by side with in battle. Does that not count for anything?"

William was emotionless as he looked at Carr. "Tell me what I want to know and I will call them off," he said. "Refuse and they will break every bone in Dermot's body, one by one. His fate is in your hand, Carr."

Carr began to twitch. He didn't doubt William for a moment, but he couldn't understand why the man was doing this. Torturing a knight that was an ally and comrade simply wasn't done, but de Wolfe didn't seem to have any reservations about doing it.

And it occurred to him why.

Tristan had sent him.

"De Royans is behind this, isn't he?" he hissed. "*He* sent you here to do this."

William lifted a dark eyebrow. "Who is this cousin you intended to marry your daughter to?"

Carr almost refused him. Dermot was over in the other cell, gasping in pain, but they hadn't broken any additional bones. Yet. That left Carr with the decision on just how crippled Dermot was going to be. Whoever these men were with de Wolfe meant business. And that, in and of itself, was terrifying.

Carr proceeded carefully.

"He is a smithy," Carr said steadily. "I do not know his name, but Dermot does. He receives missives from his mother, and she has made the arrangements."

William's attention turned to Dermot. "Who is this smithy?" he said. "And why is your mother involved?"

Dermot was in a great deal of pain. As a knight, he was supposed to withstand such things, but he'd never been very good at it. Some men were stronger than others, and even though Dermot was English-trained, he'd never had the true gift for the knighthood. Moments like this made him realize that. He knew he couldn't stand any more of what they were doing to him because, already, his sword hand was useless. He didn't want to lose use of his remaining good hand.

God only knew what else they would take from him, the English scum.

Hatred and terror filled his chest.

"Leave my mother out of this," he said, breathing heavily. "I'll not tell you anything about her, but—"

He was cut off when a snapping sound filled the air. Another bone had been broken, this time in his wrist, and Dermot began screaming.

"You cannot stop them!" he cried. "You cannot protect her! They're coming for her, and you cannot stop them!"

William yanked the torch off the wall and brought it closer to the cell, illuminating Paris and Kieran as they stood on either side of Dermot. Kieran had Dermot's smashed left hand in his grip, twisted behind the man's back, while Paris had him around the neck.

But William wanted to hear what he had to say.

"*Who* is coming for her?" he asked. "The Irish rebels?"

Dermot was broken and bloodied. He simply wasn't that strong of a man, not like some of them. There were men who could withstand this and men who couldn't.

He was one who couldn't.

Better confess and pray for mercy.

"*Aingil Lochlainn*," he said, spittle dripping from his lips. "The Angels of Lochlainn. Do you know the name?"

William shook his head. "Nay," he said. "Who are they?"

Dermot was having difficulty concentrating because his injured hand was still being held by the enormous knight who had broken it. "Tell the knight to release me and I'll tell you everything," he pleaded. "Please. Just let me go and I'll tell you what you want to know."

William looked at Kieran and nodded his head, causing Kieran to immediately release Dermot's smashed hand. Dermot fell to his knees, cradling the limb against his chest, trying very hard not to weep.

"Well?" William said. "Who are the Angels of Lochlainn?"

Dermot took a deep breath. "Not rebels," he said. "Men dedicated to Irish rule for Irish lands. I could tell you more, but it's complicated. There are many factions in Ireland right now, and many royal families of kings who no longer have kingdoms. Lochlainn was Leinster. They are the mortal enemies of mac Ragnaill."

The light of understanding went on in William's mind. "The same group who tried to take Lady Andromeda from Rockbrook."

Dermot nodded. "Aye," he said, sounding weary and defeated. "They know she's at Wrexham, and they will take her. Mark my words."

"How?" William demanded. "Where are they?"

Dermot looked up at him. "I swear upon my oath as a knight that I do not know that," he said, his voice trembling. "I only know that they are in the town, somewhere, but they've not contacted me yet. They're here. And they are watching the castle."

That was exactly what Tristan had speculated, so William wasn't particularly surprised to hear it. And, to be truthful, he wasn't surprised that Dermot knew it. Somehow, the quiet knight who never said much was involved in something covert, and that simply didn't come as a revelation.

It was the quiet ones that usually had something to hide.

"Then you're one of them," he said. "You've been spying for them."

Dermot cradled his arm a little closer, fearful they might start up the torture again. "My mother is a Lochlainn."

William cocked his head in thought. "You and your mother communicate on a regular basis," he said. "I have seen it the entire year I've been here. Do you mean to say that she is part of the nest of rebels, too?"

Dermot sighed heavily. "That is how *Aingil Lochlainn* received their information," he said. "Through my mother. No one would suspect a mother and son sending notes to one another, would they? But the truth is that I was sent to watch Carr. The man is a mac Murda, married to Brigid Ni Ascall. It was my task to watch him, and when his daughter came to Wrexham, I sent word to them. I knew they wanted to marry her to Gavan mac Lochlainn."

"Is that the cousin you have back in Ireland?" William asked. "The man you called the smithy?"

Dermot nodded slowly. "Aye," he said. "The same. One way or the other, she would be married to him. If we could not get her at Rockbrook, then we could get her here, at Wrexham."

"You *bastard*," Carr suddenly spat. "You bloody bastard! You've been spying on me all this time?"

Dermot looked over at him, surprisingly unemotional. "You made it easy," he said. "When your daughter arrived and you told anyone who would listen that you didn't want her here, you made it very easy. She's going back to marry young Gavan, whether or not you like it. You don't want her, anyway."

Carr started slapping the iron bars. "If this cage wasn't between us, I'd snap your bloody neck!" he hissed. "I cannot believe you were spying on me!"

He seemed more angry that he'd been spied on than the fact his daughter was in peril. They could all see it. William simply shook his head in disgust and returned his attention to Dermot.

"The lady cannot marry Gavan," he said. "She married de Royans earlier tonight, so if you think you are going to get your hands on her, think again. De Royans will slay anyone who tries to get near his wife."

Dermot's momentary surprise turned to an expression of understanding fairly quickly. "I thought it might happen," he said. "We could all see how he treated her. But I was hoping to get her away from him before he could marry her."

"You're too late," William said. "She is Lady de Royans now, and Tristan brings the strength of the army of Wrexham with him. If your Irish brethren want her, they'll have to battle a thousand men and walls of stone to get to her."

Dermot shook his head. "If they want her badly enough, they'll find a way," he said. "They do not give up easily."

"Would you know them on sight?"

Dermot shrugged. "More than likely," he said. "It has been years since I last gathered with the group, but most of the faces haven't changed, I'm sure. Why?"

"Because you are coming into the town with me, and we are going to find them," William said. "That is the price for sparing your life. Refuse and I will leave you alone with Kieran to finish what he started."

Dermot turned to the massive man next to him, the one who had snapped his bones. He was young—that was clear. He had a young face, but his eyes were ageless and intense. The killer instinct was there.

Dermot didn't want to be a victim of it.

"As you wish," he said, returning his attention to William.

"But if I go into town with you, they may recognize me first. They'll see me with you. They may not be too trusting."

"That is a chance we will have to take," William said. "I want to know where they are and how many there are, and you are going to help me with that."

"And then what?"

"Then we tell de Royans, and he can decide what is to be done."

"With me?"

"With you all."

Carr, who had been listening to everything up until that point with rage and loathing building in his veins, suddenly let out a growl.

"I'm not part of that lot," he said. "They've killed my own kin. I do *not* throw in with them."

William looked at him. "That may be true, but you tried to harm your daughter today, and that is why you are here," he said. "Your daughter became Lady de Royans this afternoon, so you are here until her husband decides what to do with you. That is his privilege."

Carr kicked the iron bars in frustration, muttering to himself as he turned away. William motioned Paris and Kieran out of Dermot's cell, and they emerged, shutting the cell door behind them and using the old key to turn the bolt. Dermot was still on his knees, still cradling his broken hand against his chest, but there was no sympathy among the knights. They'd done what they had to do, and it had worked. Now, they knew what they were facing.

The Angels of Lochlainn were on their doorstep.

The stakes, for Tristan and Andromeda, had just been raised.

CHAPTER SIXTEEN

"YOU'RE UP EARLY," Addax said, eyeing Tristan. "Why on earth would you be up this early? You just got married."

Tristan couldn't stop grinning. He felt like a fool, but it couldn't be helped. "So I have," he said. "But that does not mean the world stops because of it. Life goes on."

It was just after dawn on a bright morning. Addax was at the gatehouse, organizing the soldiers for the day, because de Wolfe and his two friends seemed to have disappeared. Not only that, Dermot was gone, and Carr had given Addax an earful when he came down to the vault. Addax knew he should have told Tristan immediately, but he was trying to give him a few more blissful hours with his new wife before the realities of command came bearing down on him. But here he was, and Addax knew he had to tell him.

Something was afoot.

"Life does indeed go on," he said after a moment. "More than you know. I have a report to give you that will not bring you pleasure."

Tristan looked at him. "What is it?"

Addax grunted. “It seems that the Irish have been up to something,” he said. “I received part of the story from Carr this morning, but de Wolfe will have to give us the rest of it. Evidently, William and his two friends went down to the vault last night and tortured Dermot into a confession.”

Tristan’s eyebrows lifted. “They did?” he said, surprised. “What confession?”

“I am telling you this because you need to know,” Addax said, lowering his voice. “Your wife needs to know. Pat, it seems that the same faction who tried to wrest her from Rockbrook is here in Wrexham, preparing to do the same thing. That cousin of Dermot’s that she was supposed to marry? It’s none other than Gavan mac Lochlainn, the same lad they’ve tried to marry her to for years. As it turns out, Dermot’s mother is a Lochlainn. He’s been spying for them all along. They know she’s here because he told them.”

Tristan’s jaw dropped. “*Dermot?*” he repeated, shocked. “He’s compromised her safety?”

Addax nodded. “Carr evidently had no idea he was part of the Lochlainn rebels,” he said. “He’s enraged by the entire situation.”

“But why?” Tristan said, enraged himself. “He’s the one that conspired with Dermot about the betrothal.”

“But he didn’t realize it was to a clan who has killed some of his own family.”

Tristan shook his head firmly. “It does not matter,” he said. “If he is going to conspire behind my back, he gets what he deserves. Where is he?”

“Still in the vault.”

“He is going to remain there until I decide what’s to be done with him.”

"Agreed," Addax said. "But back to the subject of Dermot—de Wolfe and his comrades took the man into the village today because they are going on the hunt for the Irish rebels. The *Aingil Lochlainn*, they call themselves. Dermot said that he will recognize them on sight, so de Wolfe wants to find them."

Tristan was still furious and shaken, but not so much that he didn't see what de Wolfe was trying to do. "So he took the initiative," he said. "Good lad. I would expect nothing less from him."

"That is what I think also," Addax said. "He's a good lad, Pat. He just wants to help. And those friends he has… de Norville and Hage? They beat Dermot badly. Hage broke nearly every bone in the man's right hand. I think we did right by bringing them here."

He was grinning as he finished speaking, causing Tristan to crack a smile. "Thank God we did," he said. "With the Welsh activity and now Irish on our doorstep, we could be in for a barrage of unholy proportions. I'm glad for the brash young knights who have a penchant for gambling."

Addax snorted. "Agreed," he said. "But something else, Pat… You've not sent word to the Marshal since the lady arrived here. I really think you need to tell him what has happened. Especially since you married. I think—"

He was cut off when the sentries on the wall began to shout, indicating that a rider was approaching. Both Tristan and Addax made their way up to the wall, where the sentries were pointing toward the south. They moved to a vantage point, seeing the verdant countryside and then a lone rider approaching from the south. It took several long minutes, and the rider drawing quite close, before Tristan got a good look at him.

Then it occurred to him.

"That's Sherry," he said.

He was flying off the wall, with Addax right behind him. The order to lift the portcullis went up, and both Tristan and Addax went to stand on the drawbridge, waiting as the knight, on a bay warhorse, approached. He wore the colors of de Lohr, royal blue with the yellow lion, but to designate de Sherrington of Wigmore Castle, his garrison, the shield had a crown draped on one corner.

"Quickly!" Tristan suddenly yelled. "Hide the good wine before Sherry drinks it all!"

The soldiers standing back at the mouth of the gatehouse chuckled as Alexander lifted his visor, glaring at Tristan.

"Is this how you greet me?" he demanded. "By maligning my reputation as a drunkard and a thief?"

Tristan snorted. "You would do the same to me."

Alexander reined his horse to a halt. "That is true," he said. "The next time you visit Wigmore, I will make sure of it."

Both Tristan and Addax were smiling as Alexander dismounted his steed. He extended a hand to Tristan in greeting, who took it firmly.

"Welcome," Tristan said, looking him over. "I suppose I am glad to see you."

Alexander cocked an eyebrow, releasing Tristan's hand and extending it to Addax. "How do you tolerate this rude man?" he asked. "I would have thrown him in the well long ago."

Addax laughed softly. "I would if I thought no one would notice," he said. "What brings you to the wilds of Wrexham, Sherry?"

They began to head across the drawbridge, and Alexander handed his horse over to a hovering stable servant. "Good news, I hope," he said. "Good enough that Chris asked me to come personally to deliver it."

"Oh?" Tristan said. "News from de Lohr?"

Alexander shook his head. "Not really," he said. "It is from the Marshal, but Chris has been with him for the past several months in London. I've been doing double duty between Lioncross and Wigmore."

"Where is Peter?"

"At Ludlow," he said. "Peter's wife delivered a child about six months ago, and it was a difficult birth, so she's not been well. She's on the mend now, but Peter did not want to leave her to go to Lioncross or to London with his father. He has stayed close to home."

"I'm sorry to hear that," Tristan said. "Liora is a lovely woman. We all know how mad Peter is for her."

"As I said, she is much better than she was," Alexander said. "Chris' wife has been with her nearly the entire time, tending her. She will heal."

They had crossed under the gatehouse and emerged into the bailey. Behind them, the portcullis was immediately lowered, and the concussion when it hit the ground reverberated throughout the bailey.

"All good to hear," Tristan said, pausing to face Alexander. "But that is not the good news you came to deliver, is it?"

Alexander shook his head. "Nay," he said. "I come bearing a summons from William Marshal, and also a message."

"What's the summons for?"

Alexander gestured to the hall. "Can I at least sit down and wash the dust of the road from my throat?" he said. "Or will you hold the wine hostage until I have told you everything?"

"I will hold it hostage," Tristan said, a glimmer in his eye. "I do not appreciate your drawing out the news for dramatic effect."

Alexander grinned. "It is nothing dramatic, I assure you," he said. "But it is important. It seems that young Henry, our king, wishes to offer you an important post in his household."

Tristan looked at him with shock. "*Me?*" he said. "But I've never even met him."

"I know," Alexander said. "You are aware that the Marshal has been advising the young king. He's practically ruling the country, to be honest, and he has had many long conversations with Henry about you. They have decided to confer an earldom upon you and give you an important post in Henry's court. You're his uncle, after all, Pat. You should be something more than a mere knight on the Welsh marches."

Tristan wasn't sure how he felt about that, and it was reflected in his expression. Shocked, he looked around the bailey, up at the towers, before finally returning his attention to Alexander.

"I like it here," he said simply. "An important royal post… I don't know, Sherry. I do not have an appetite for such things. I've made my home at Wrexham."

Alexander put a hand on his shoulder. "But it does not belong to you," he said. "This is an honor, Pat, truly. But there's more."

"What more?"

"A bride comes with it," Alexander said with a smile. "She is the heiress to the Earldom of Eastbourne, which will become yours when you marry her. Congratulations, old man. I hear she's wildly wealthy."

Tristan backed away, throwing up his hands. "Stop right there," he said firmly. "I cannot marry an heiress or anyone else. Sherry, I was married yesterday. I already have a wife."

It was Alexander's turn to look surprised. "You *did*?" he said, looking to Addax for confirmation. When the man nodded, Alexander was rather stunned. "Christ, Pat, that makes for a rather awkward situation."

Tristan puffed out his cheeks, emitting a harsh exhale in a gesture that suggested he quite agreed. "Aye, it does," he said. "Although I am honored by the Eastbourne betrothal, it simply won't happen. I'm very happy with my wife."

"Who is it?"

Tristan looked at Addax, who shook his head at the man as if to silently reiterate that he should have told the Marshal much sooner about the situation at Wrexham. Tristan knew that, but there was nothing he could do about it now.

"Come into the hall," he said. "There is much happening here that you should be aware of. I think we may need that wine."

Curiously, Alexander followed.

ଓ

Relent, and harbor your time along the shores of my
tranquility,
Nothing is as valuable.
Turn your unfettered eyes towards infinity,
For we are no longer solitary.

It was another note, slipped under the chamber door. Andromeda had awoke to an empty bed just after dawn, naked and wrapped up in the coverlet. She was rather disappointed to have woken up without Tristan beside her, but she knew he had duties. When she finally climbed out of bed, it was to watered wine and bread and cheese on the table nearby, and the poem on the floor near the door.

She smiled as she read it.

It was awful, like the rest of them, but she didn't care. To her, it was the most beautiful poem she'd ever read. It meant that he was thinking of her and wanted to express himself in a way that meant something to him.

It was the dawn of a new life between them.

Putting the poem on her dressing table, she proceeded to wolf down the food and drink all of the watered wine, which tasted more like the weak apple juice it had been cut with. Once she was finished with that, she hurried and washed with cold water and a cake of soap that smelled of rosemary, before dressing in one of the durable garments that Aldis had made for her. This one was a light green in color, with a linen apron, and she wove her hair into a single braid and was prepared to let it hang over one shoulder before she remembered that married women turned their hair up. With a smile, she pinned the braid at the nape of her neck.

Just like a married woman would.

Ready for the day, Andromeda headed out of the chamber and down to the entry where servants were sweeping for the day. They knew about the marriage and congratulated her. In fact, the entire castle knew about the marriage, so Andromeda received congratulations until she was fairly blushing with them. Flora and Aldis greeted her, coming into the keep from the castle laundry, and she asked them to tidy up her chamber now that she and Tristan were going about their day. As the old servants headed up the stairs, Andromeda went to the kitchens.

It was all part of her usual routine, checking in with the kitchens in the morning to find out what was being prepared for the day. She usually left the menu to the cook, but today she wanted something a little special. She requested baked eggs with cheese, and the cook agreed, but he also mentioned that Tristan was in the great hall breaking his fast with Addax and a visitor who had come earlier that morning. Given that Andromeda was the chatelaine, she headed to the hall to be introduced to the visitor and see to his, or her, comfort.

The hall smelled heavily of smoke in the morning hours because the fire in the hearth had burned all night, down to ash. Entering the hall from the servants' door, the wall of smoke hit her in the face, seemingly more heavily than it had been in times past, so she grabbed the first servant she came across and asked him to open all of the doors. Better to let the smell escape than have everyone who spent time in the hall smelling like smoke before the day's end. As she entered the main part of the hall, she could see Tristan, Addax, and another man sitting over by the dais.

Quickly, she made her way in their direction.

Tristan saw her coming. He stood up and held out a hand to her as she approached, and she took it, smiling adoringly at him before turning her attention to the table. Addax was smiling at her, but the other man at the table seemed to be studying her. He was big, clearly powerful, with black eyes, black hair, and a trim black beard. He was a handsome man, but she felt a little uneasy with the way he was looking at her.

"I apologize that I was not here when your guest arrived," she said, mostly to Tristan. "I have only just been told."

"It is no trouble," Tristan said, holding her hand tightly. "This is my dear friend, Sir Alexander de Sherrington, commander of Wigmore Castle. Sherry, this is my wife, Andromeda de Courcy. She is the granddaughter of Ascall mac Ragnaill."

Alexander stood up and greeted her politely. "Lady de

Royans," he said. "We had no idea that Pat had married himself such a beauty. A well-born beauty at that."

Andromeda smiled hesitantly, turning somewhat questioningly to Tristan, who indicated for her to sit. "I have just finished telling Sherry everything that has happened since your arrival," he said. "I have told him of your grandfather, your father, and your lineage. We were just speaking on what happened last night with your father."

That explained a little about Alexander's curiosity about her. Andromeda was about to reply when Addax interrupted. "The lady may not know what has happened over night," he said to Tristan. "But there is something you should know as well. When I told you of the actions of de Wolfe and his comrades, I did not tell you what Dermot told us. Sherry arrived, and I've not yet had the chance."

"Dermot?" Alexander said. "Mac Edan?"

Addax nodded. "The same."

"He has served the Marshal a long time, in England as well as at his Irish holdings," Alexander said. "A morose man, as I recall."

Addax nodded, his gaze moving to Tristan. "It seems that Dermot has been spying for a group of Irish that calls themselves *Aingil Lochlainn*," he said. "The same group that tried to breach Rockbrook to get to Lady Andromeda."

Andromeda gasped. "Those are the same people who murdered my grandfather!"

Addax held up a hand to ease her. "I am sorry if what I am to tell you is frightening, my lady, but it is better that you know," he said. "It is better that you be cautious. Dermot is part of this group, and when you arrived at Wrexham, he sent a message through his mother and told them you had come.

Because of this, they have come to Wrexham. They are here."

Andromeda nearly bolted out of her seat, but Tristan held her fast. "Dermot said that?" he said grimly. "Where are they?"

Addax shook his head. "Dermot does not know," he said. "William and his friends interrogated him enough, and they are convinced he is telling the truth. All he knows is that they are in the village of Wrexham, and they have gone out to locate them. Carr does not seem to be part of this group, but was rather tricked into the betrothal by Dermot. As it turns out, Dermot's cousin happens to be Gavan mac Lochlainn."

Andromeda had her hand over her mouth in shock, closing her eyes tightly when Gavan was mentioned. "Then it is him," she whispered. "They could not take me from Rockbrook, so they were going to take me from Wrexham."

"And your father unknowingly facilitated it."

"But they are here? Somewhere in Wrexham?"

Addax nodded. "Do not fear," he said. "De Wolfe has gone on the hunt for them. We will find them before they find you, my lady, I promise."

She nodded and lowered her head, but the tears were starting. She was frightened, and rightfully so. As Tristan put his arm around her shoulders and hugged her gently, Alexander was digesting everything he'd been told of the entire convoluted situation playing out at Wrexham.

There was certainly a good deal happening.

"Let me see if I have this straight," he said. "The lady was sent to England for her own safety because enemies of her grandfather wanted to marry her to one of their own, a grandson of a high king named Gavan. She came to Wrexham, and her father was incensed that she had been sent here. He did not want her here, even though it was to save her life."

Tristan, trying to comfort his wife, nodded. "Exactly."

Alexander tilted his head, thinking. "You refused to send her away and instead made her your chatelaine, so Dermot realized who she was and seized the opportunity," he said. "He has been spying on Carr and on the Marshal for some time, so he tells Carr he has a cousin looking for a wife. Carr agrees, and Dermot sends word to his Irish brethren."

"He had already sent word to them when she arrived," Addax said. "They knew she was here from the start."

"Right," Alexander said, fitting all of the pieces of the complex puzzle together. "Dermot tells Carr that his cousin accepts a betrothal with the lady, and Carr thinks it's a smithy when, in fact, it's Gavan, the same man who forced her to flee Ireland in the first place."

"That is true," Tristan said. "Now, we discover the Irish rebels to be in Wrexham, waiting for the opportunity to take the lady back to Ireland."

"Were they waiting for Dermot to deliver her?" Alexander asked.

"It seems so," Addax replied. "They are here, somewhere. De Wolfe will find them."

"But we have more troubles, Sherry," Tristan said. "It's not just the Irish who are a threat. We've seen the Welsh amassing to the west, flocking to the home of one of the warlords who held Wrexham before we were able to take it back. We may be looking at another attack, so the Irish rebels could not have come at a more inconvenient time."

Alexander understood that. He poured himself a second cup of wine and took a long drink before replying. "Something is abundantly clear to me that may not have occurred to you," he said.

"What is that?" Tristan said.

Alexander looked at him. "That you must get the lady out of here," he said. "If you have Welsh amassing and Irish waiting to grab her, the Irish could very well take advantage of any chaos with a Welsh attack. As I see it, the lady is in extreme danger. You must get her out."

"And go where?"

"To London," Alexander said. "The king wants to see you, and so does William Marshal. Take your wife and go to London. She will be safe there, far from any Irish rebels or Welsh who want Wrexham back. You are sitting on something incendiary here, Pat. Do you really want her in the middle of it?"

Tristan didn't. He looked at Andromeda, who was wiping the last of the tears from around her eyes, and sighed quietly. "Nay," he said. "But I cannot simply leave, not with the Welsh possibly preparing to attack. I cannot leave Addax and de Wolfe alone in a time like this."

Alexander wasn't unsympathetic. "Addax is a competent commander," he said. "De Wolfe is a master with the sword, and—"

Tristan interrupted him. "I did not mean to sound as if they cannot get along without me," he said. "I know their strengths. But the loss of my sword would be substantial."

"I will stay with you," Andromeda said before looking to Alexander. "My lord, I realize you are saying such things to keep me safe, but he cannot leave at the moment, and I will not be separated from him. The Irish are here, the Welsh may be coming, but Wrexham is strong, and I trust the knights. I will be safe."

She said it with almost too much confidence, and Alexander

could see that there would be no separating Tristan from his wife. Not that he blamed him—he had a wife of his own and hated being separated from her—but in this case, he genuinely thought it was a good idea to take Lady de Royans from Wrexham for her own safety. More than that, however, was the summons from William Marshal hanging over everything.

That could not be ignored.

"I appreciate that, my lady, I do," he said, before shifting his attention to Tristan. "But the Marshal wants you in London, and so does the king. He has been a warlord for many years, so I do not think your reasons for not going to London at his summons would be well met. Castles on the marches are always under threat. Leaving Addax in command would be perfectly acceptable whilst you attend the king. Garrison commanders do not disobey their liege's summons unless they are in the middle of battle or dead, and you are neither."

Tristan got his meaning. "Then I do not have a choice."

"Nay, I do not believe that you do."

"When must I leave?"

"Immediately. And take your wife with you."

It was settled. Tristan looked at Andromeda, and for a moment, they simply stared at one another. She had such a trusting look in her eye, and he was coming to think that perhaps Alexander had been right in suggesting he take her away from Wrexham. It was true that it was his command, and he was loath to leave it with such chaos on the fringes, but Andromeda was far more important to him. They would leave Wrexham, the Irish rebels would be none the wiser, and hopefully he wouldn't have to worry about them trying to abduct her for the rest of his life. Perhaps he'd accept the post from the king and become an earl with a big estate and a big army, somewhere.

Big enough to protect his wife from those out to take her away from him.

Perhaps Alexander *was* right about it.

Tristan finally nodded his head.

"Very well," he said. "Mayhap you are correct. I must face the Marshal with what I've done by marrying her as it is, so we will go. We will face him together."

"I think that is wise," Alexander said.

Tristan smiled at his wife, taking her soft hand and giving it a kiss. "Can you find a satchel to pack some of your clothes in?" he said. "You do not have to bring everything, just enough comfortable clothing to get to London. If you need anything more, I will buy it for you when we are there."

Andromeda nodded. "I will find one right away," she said. "And you? May I help you?"

He smiled at her sweet offer. "Worry about yourself first, and then you may help me," he said. "Go along, now. I will see you later."

Andromeda stood up, excusing herself politely, before heading out of the hall. Tristan watched her go, waiting until she disappeared from sight before turning to Alexander.

"If she were not involved in this, I would refuse to go to London," he said flatly. "I did not want to argue the point in front of her, but I would be a poor commander, indeed, if I deserted my men on the brink of something destructive. I hope you can appreciate that, Sherry."

Alexander nodded slowly. "I do," he said. "But I think it's better that you take her out of here. She must be your priority, Pat. I realize you are new to being a husband, but your wife must take precedence over everything. Addax and de Wolfe can handle what is to come. But you would never forgive yourself if something happened to her."

That was very true. As Addax struck up a conversation about the Welsh and the warlords to the west, Tristan's thoughts lingered on his wife. Even now, she was out of his sight, and he was having some anxiety about Irish rebels making it into the castle and stealing her away from him. Knowing that they were in the town of Wrexham made him nervous. He found himself very grateful that de Wolfe had taken the initiative to locate the rebels. Very grateful, indeed.

But he still couldn't shake that edgy feeling.

Something was about to blow.

CHAPTER SEVENTEEN

The Squire and The Tart Tavern
Wrexham

"WHY ARE WE stopping here?"

"Because no one ever comes to this place."

"Why not?"

"They have the ugliest women in town."

Paris' features screwed up in confusion at William's statement. "And you are bringing us here?" he scoffed. "You are supposed to be our dearest friend."

"Shut up and go inside."

With a heaving sigh and a roll of the eyes, Paris stomped through the entry door to a low-ceilinged, small, and smelly tavern. Because of the market in Shrewsbury the following day, most of the taverns in Wrexham were full, and William had selected this one for a brief respite in their search for the Irish, banking on the fact that it wouldn't be particularly full.

He'd been right.

The moment they entered, three women rushed the knights, grabbing hold of arms and hands and pulling them over into a semi-private alcove that faced the street. Paris wasn't thrilled that he was being clawed by women who didn't seem to care what they smelled like, and he kept trying to pull away, only to be grabbed by another one. There might have only been three women, but it seemed like there were thirty. They were everywhere. Kieran wasn't paying much attention to them, but rather walking toward the alcove with Dermot in his grip.

That left William bringing up the rear.

In truth, he was having a difficult time keeping a straight face as the women pawed at Paris. He was blond and handsome, flashy and pretty for a man, so he tended to draw the women to him quickly. This was no exception. But he wanted no part of wenches who were, in fact, the daughters of the tavern keeper. They were loud and quite tall for women, big-boned, but not heavy. They were, quite simply, big women and not delicate flowers. When one tried to sit on Paris' lap, the chair collapsed and they ended up on the floor.

William laughed so hard he thought he was going to choke.

But Paris wasn't amused. He heaved the woman off him and stood up, pushing the other women back and demanding another chair. All three ran for one and then fought over who was going to bring it to him. Paris turned to William in a panic.

"Please let us leave," he demanded quietly. "I cannot take much more of this."

William glanced at Kieran, who was fighting off a grin, before answering. "We cannot leave," he said. "In fact, I want you to ask your admirers if there have been any Irish visitors."

"Must I?"

William sighed sharply. "We have been all over this town and have yet to even see a sign of them," he said. "Mayhap a place like this would be preferable to visit because they are trying to stay out of sight."

"You have gone too far this time, William."

He shot Kieran a pointed look. "Good," he said. "I'm sure they'll tell you anything you want to know, so ask when they return. That is not a request."

Several feet away, the three sisters had resorted to slapping each other, and Paris was genuinely appalled. "Please, William," he whispered. "Show pity."

"They're returning."

"Then I am a dead man."

"I will remember you well at your funeral."

As William sat down to enjoy the show, two of the sisters came up to Paris, each of them tugging on the same chair. But one sister, the brunette with hair that looked like a horse's tail, yanked hard to get it away from her red-headed sister and ended up slamming the chair into Paris' chest. He grunted with the force of the blow and stumbled back into the wall as William and Kieran burst into laughter. Paris pushed himself off the wall and pulled the chair from the brunette's grip, sitting heavily on it but kicking the redhead away when she tried to sit on his lap.

"Stop!" he boomed. "God's Bones, ladies, bring my friends and me some food and drink. I am too weary for your attentions! *Go!*"

They did, arguing and slapping all the way. William had tears streaming down his face, and Kieran was so far gone with laughter that his head was on the table, face-first. Dermot was the only one not laughing, for obvious reasons, but Paris was furious with his friends.

"I am so glad I could be entertaining," he said sarcastically. "How kind of me to give you such joy."

William couldn't stop laughing as he wiped the tears from

his cheeks, and Kieran sat up, putting his hands over his face and struggling not to burst into giggles again.

"Only you would have that effect on women," William said, taking a deep breath. "You are so beautiful and alluring."

Paris had no patience for his taunts. "You are a horrible man, and I hope you die alone," he told him. "And this place is hell. I hope the food is good, at least."

William shrugged. "It is better than most," he said. "But now you can see why it is hardly full. That trio causes men to stay away in droves."

"*I* would like to stay away in droves."

As William and Paris went back and forth, Dermot's attention was off toward the common room. He didn't care about the bickering knights. The tavern, in general, was fairly dark, with a few open windows allowing the midday sun to illuminate the common room, and beyond that room he could see another chamber.

There were people in that distant chamber, and his gaze lingered on them for a moment, but his mind was turning toward his throbbing hand, tightly wrapped and lashed to his chest. His entire right arm was completely useless, and the physic that William had taken him to at dawn, an old man who was well known in the village, had given him a poppy potion for the pain that was starting to wear off. He was looking forward to copious amounts of wine to at least help him forget the ache, but here he was, sitting in a tavern with the very bastards who broke his hand.

Life was ironic sometimes.

And then he heard it.

An Irish accent met with his ears, and his head came up, turning toward the common room again. There were people in there, just a few, but the buzz of conversation could be heard. He listened closely, trying to pick up the Irish accent again, but more than that, he was studying the figures hunched over tables or sitting against the walls, trying to see if he recognized any of them.

And then he heard it again.

Someone was laughing, and he heard "*tá do bhéal chomh láibeach le feirm mhuice.*" That meant that a man's mouth was as muddy as a pig farm, which was a saying sometimes used to accuse a man of telling a tall tale.

"*Tá do bhéal chomh láibeach le feirm mhuice.*"

That was one Irishman calling another man a liar.

Dermot had heard it before. It took him back to the days of his youth, carefree days that seemed so far away from the man he'd become. An English servant who fought for English causes. It occurred to him that the laughter, and the accent, was coming from the group on the other side of the tavern in the chamber off the common room. When one man turned to another and laughed, he swore he recognized a cousin he'd grown up with.

He turned to the table.

"I want you to listen to me carefully," he said steadily. "Do not react to what I am saying. Do not look around. Look right at me as I am speaking, for the very men we've been looking for are here. They're in the small room just off the common room, directly across from us."

William, Paris, and Kieran did as they were told. They looked straight at Dermot, very casual about the revelation.

"Are you certain?" William said.

Dermot nodded. "I am," he said. "I think I see a cousin I grew up with. They must not have seen me, because if they had, they'd be in our laps right now."

Paris yawned and sat back in his chair. "How many do you

see?"

Dermot scratched his head. "Four, at least."

"Is it possible there are so few?"

Dermot shrugged. "There could be more we simply do not see, of course," he said. "I've no way of knowing unless I ask. What do you want to do?"

William thought on that quickly. He glanced over his shoulder because he could see the three daughters bringing out trays from the kitchen, so whatever they did, they would have to do it fast. They didn't want the women involved, and they didn't want to bring attention to themselves, so he would have to move swiftly.

"Paris, Kieran," he muttered. "Quickly—out through the back now. I will follow you. Dermot, you are going to go over to the table and talk to your friends. I want to find out how many there are and what their plans are."

"Wait," Dermot said, and they all came to a halt, midway out of their chairs. "Then what?"

"Then you will tell them you will bring the lady to them," William muttered. "Set up a rendezvous. I do not care where it is, but set up a future time and place with them where you will deliver the lady."

Dermot frowned. "Why am I doing that?"

"Just do it," William said, waving Paris and Kieran on. "The chamber they are in has windows, just like this chamber. We are going outside to listen to everything you say beneath those windows, so if you think to betray us, know that I can catch you before you leave this tavern and your throat will be the first one I slit."

Dermot knew he meant it. Not that he'd planned on betraying the knights, because he knew to do such a thing would be futile, but he was an Irishman at heart. He was a rebel and a spy.

William could threaten and Dermot could comply, but if there was a chance to turn on the English, he would take it. It might cost him his life, but he simply couldn't go down without a fight. He hadn't come this far to fold, and now might be his only chance to take back the control he'd lost.

He might have the last word in all of this after all.

"You needn't worry about me," he said.

"I'd better not," William growled. "Now—give us a moment to clear the tavern, and you will go over there and speak to them. Tell them you've been looking everywhere for them. And make it good."

William slipped away, toward the rear of the tavern, and Dermot could hear the tavern keep's daughters cooing and praising Paris as he tried to push past them and out into the livery yard. Unfortunately, they wouldn't let Paris go easily, and it was apparent they might attract attention, so William and Kieran pushed all of them out into the livery yard as they went around the side of the tavern, to the small ventilation windows that lined the wall of the chamber where the Irish had been sitting. As William mentioned, they were just like the windows in the chamber facing the street. While Paris kept the tavern keep's daughters busy purely out of necessity, William and Kieran hunkered down to listen.

They heard, clearly, when Dermot introduced himself.

What they didn't see, through all of the greetings and conversation, was Dermot taking a knife and carving words into the table that was littered with bread and empty cups. When he was finished, the Irish were well informed of the situation. Six simple words said it all:

Tá a fhios ag na Sasanaigh.

The English know.

CHAPTER EIGHTEEN

HE DIDN'T BELONG here.

One of the advantages of being locked in the vault was the fact that one had a great deal of time to think about how things had gone awry. How a seasoned, dedicated knight had ended up on the other side of the coin—jailed instead of the jailor. No longer a trusted commander. There was nothing but time in the vault, and Carr was using that time to his advantage.

He had a lot to think about.

Loyalties.

He had been thinking a lot about loyalties. He thought about days long ago, in Ireland. When he'd come to England with Dermot, he was comforted by the fact that he hadn't come alone. Another Irish knight had come with him. They were a pair, he and Dermot, and as the years passed, he came to trust Dermot like a brother.

And that was where he had been wrong.

For years, he'd been wrong. He was still trying to come to grips with the fact Dermot had been sent to spy on him because of whom he'd been married to. Never, in all the time he'd known Dermot, had he suspected that the man was an enemy and not an ally. He and Dermot had shared good times as well as bad times, and in Carr's mind, they had bonded. He felt that Dermot was someone he could trust and depend on.

It was a harsh dose of reality to be told that was not the case.

Not strangely, Carr felt very alone. He was surrounded by a thousand men and fellow knights, but he still felt so very alone. Now, with Andromeda here, the very last thing he should have felt was loneliness.

But he did.

It was loneliness of his own making.

Carr's time in the vault was something of a crossroads for him. Everything he thought was truth was, in fact, a lie. The biggest lie of all was something he'd pushed to the back of his mind all those years ago, a secret he'd been hiding. He'd been perpetuating the lie to cover the secret his entire adult life. The life he'd left behind in Ireland was at the heart of the lie, and it was finally catching up to him. He thought that he would get away from the lies by coming to England, but they followed him.

She had followed him.

Carr never thought he would have reached this moment in his life, but here he was. Sitting in a dark and lonely vault and wondering if he was going to spend the rest of his life here. The lies had found him. That was why he'd been so angry, so unreasonable in a situation that should have invited his understanding. But he'd had none, at least none for his daughter, and he knew why. But he hadn't wanted to face what she really represented to him.

Perhaps it was time to reexamine everything.

And finally admit the truth.

CHAPTER NINETEEN

WILLIAM KNEW IMMEDIATELY what had happened.

They'd been betrayed.

He and Kieran were crouched beneath the windows of the tavern, beneath the very room they knew the Irish to be in, and they heard conversation. Because both William and Kieran had spent much time on the Scots border, they were fairly well versed in Scots Gaelic, but that was nothing like Irish Gaelic. Not even close. It never occurred to William that Dermot would speak to them in Irish and he wouldn't be able to understand a word. That meant listening to the conversation wasn't having the desired effect because they couldn't make anything out. No plans, no information.

Then something happened.

A brief pause in the conversation was followed by Irish jumping from the windows and landing on top of them. One man leapt out of the window over Kieran's head and ended up falling onto Kieran, who reacted as if a hornet's nest had just been dumped on him. He was all arms and legs, lashing out madly, and from a man that size, the Irishman didn't stand a chance. He went down quickly from a vicious strike to the head, but the second man who came from the window after him fared a little better. He brought a dagger with him, which forced Kieran to arm himself.

As Kieran and the second Irishman fought over the body of the Irishman's unconscious colleague, William had his hands full with two more Irish rebels. There were no weapons at this point, but plenty of kicking and punching. Because William had been caught off guard by a man literally dropping on his head, he had a cut above his left eye that was bleeding steadily. He was able to get one man in a headlock, swinging him around like a battering ram until he took the legs out from underneath the fourth Irishman, who was aiming a club at William's head.

Dermot had been wrong about the number of Irishmen in the room—there were seven, three of them back in the shadows where he couldn't see them. Therefore, three more men were bailing from the windows, going after Kieran and William as Paris, realizing what had happened, left the tavern keeper's daughters and rushed to aid his friends. Fists and feet were flying as he entered the fray.

The man on the ground between Kieran and his opponent regained consciousness fairly quickly, but as he tried to get up, Kieran kicked him in the head again to keep him down. As he went out like a candle, Paris managed to unsheathe his sword, and the fistfight became something deadlier. Until that point, they'd only been throwing fists, mostly, but the swords began to come out—first Kieran, then Paris, and finally William. Now, the English were in their element as the Irish produced weapons to match.

The fistfight became an all-out sword fight.

The Irish kept switching opponents, meaning two would fight William and then one would rush off to engage Paris, who already had two men against him. William dispatched the Irishman he was fighting against, clipping the man so that he dropped his sword and ran off, but once that man ran, all of the Irish followed except for the unconscious man on the ground, who was just starting to come around again.

Kieran kicked him in the head yet again, and out he went.

As quickly as it had started, the fight was over.

A little bloodied, and a little beaten, William, Paris, and Kieran faced each other, breathing heavily with exertion. But one word from William had them all running again.

"Dermot," he breathed.

The three of them bolted back into the tavern, rushing into the room where the Irish had been, only to see that it was vacant.

Dermot was gone.

"Damnation," William said. "He betrayed us."

Paris wiped his bloodied lip. "No tie is so strong as the one that binds a man to his brethren," he said. "He was never ours, William. He has always belonged to them, and we brought him right to them. Delivered on a silver platter."

William knew that, but he felt stupid that he'd taken the chance and failed. He'd thought his threats would be enough to keep Dermot in line. "We need to return to Wrexham immediately," he said. "Dermot knows how to get in and out of the castle, and it's possible he's taking them back there and convincing the gate guards to admit them at this very moment."

That thought sent them running for their horses, but not before Kieran returned to the man he'd kept kicking into unconsciousness. Pulling the semi-lucid man to his feet, he half carried and half dragged him back to the stable.

Now they had a hostage.

ᏣᏰ

SHE'D NEVER BEEN to London before.

In fact, Andromeda had hardly strayed out of Rockbrook Castle, but in the past year, she'd certainly had a world of travel, from Dublin across the sea to Liverpool and down along the Welsh marches. She'd discovered that she liked travel, or at least she would if it was not under such stressful circumstances, so she was looking forward to the trip to London with her husband.

Her husband.

She could still hardly believe she'd married Tristan, but in the same breath, she felt as if they had always been together. He completed something in her that she never knew was missing. Though they'd not known each other a great length of time, they knew each other enough to fall in love with what they knew.

She was looking forward to falling in love with what she *didn't* know.

Flora and Aldis joined her in her chamber, and when she told them that she needed a satchel or a case, they hurried back down to the storage room, which still wasn't completely cleaned out. Andromeda knew that she and Tristan would be traveling by horse, probably two horses, which meant the satchel couldn't be too large. A sack would probably do just as well. Something to tie to the saddle, and not too heavy.

And that brought about the question of what to bring.

She had so many lovely things now, garments from the painted wardrobe that had been altered for her, along with the four garments that Aldis had made. She had dresses and shifts and aprons to work in, but she suspected that she wouldn't be doing much work in London. She was there to meet people and present a well-dressed wife for Tristan, so that knowledge alone made the decision for her.

Only nice things should be packed.

Going over to the wardrobe, she pulled forth three well-made and expensive garments, all of them dresses that had been altered for her. There was one of red brocade, another of pale blue damask, and a third of an exquisite dark yellow that glistened in the light. She didn't know what the fabric was, but the dress was quite rich looking. But there were others she liked, so several ended up neatly strewn across her bed as she tried to make a decision.

But other things had to come, as well.

Soaps and combs and oils, things a well-dressed wife would need. Shoes and hose, ribbons and shifts. And the jewelry—the previous lady of Wrexham had left behind a goodly amount of expensive jewelry that now all belonged to Andromeda, including pearls and sapphires and gold necklaces and earrings. She didn't want to leave any of it behind because she was afraid it might disappear in her absence, so she hunted down a silk purse to store it all in.

There was one thing she wouldn't have to store, and that was her wedding ring, or at least the ring that had been used as a wedding ring. One small piece of the jewelry cache in the painted wardrobe had been a gold ring with elaborate etchings and a rock crystal center stone. She'd found it whilst dressing for their wedding mass and shown it to Tristan, who was keen on the idea of using it for a wedding band until he could buy her something else. It was a little big for her finger, but not uncomfortably so. She looked at it even now as she dug around in the wardrobe, admiring the lovely ring and remembering the look in Tristan's eye when he'd slipped it on her finger.

It was such a lovely memory.

"I told you that I'd buy you another ring," Tristan said, standing in the doorway. "You can have any ring you wish when we get to London."

He'd caught her looking at it. Andromeda turned to him, still holding her hand up as she looked at the band.

"But this one is so pretty," she said. "And it is the one we used at our wedding mass. I do not know if I want another one."

He shrugged as he came into the chamber. "That is your decision," he said. "If you wish to keep it, you'll get no argument from me."

She smiled at him, putting her hand down and turning back to the wardrobe. But she noticed that he was looking over the garments on the bed, so she left what she was doing and went over to him.

"I know we will be seeing important people in London, so I want to bring some of the nicer things," she said. "Mayhap you can help me decide. Which ones do you like best?"

He fingered the red brocade. "All of them," he said softly, smiling at her. "Anything you wear is my favorite."

She smiled in return, falling into his embrace when he opened his arms up to her. "You're supposed to say that," she said. "Now that we are married, you are obligated by the law and by God to tell me how beautiful I am."

"Is that so?"

"It is."

"I will have to ask the priest about that."

"No need. Take my word for it."

He started chuckling. "Then I shall," he said. "Confidentially, however, I will tell you a secret—even if it was not a legal requirement of marriage to tell you that you are beautiful, I would do it anyway."

She stroked his cheek affectionately, watching as he kissed her hand. "I have been thinking," she said. "I know you are a seasoned knight and have spent your life devoted to warfare, but somewhere, you must have had a good example set for you on how a man should treat a woman. What you do… it is not inherent. It must be trained and developed."

He smiled faintly. "In fact, I did have an excellent example set for me," he said. "My adoptive parents, Juston and Emera, were very much in love with one another. For a family, that kind of love radiates everywhere—to my brother and sisters, and to me. I always equated love with security. With comfort. There is nothing more satisfying than knowing you are loved and to love in return. That was the example I had set for me, and one I had always hoped to carry over into my own marriage and family."

Andromeda smiled in return. "You and I had the same sort of familial life," she said. "I, too, was raised by adoptive parents who were quite kind to each other. I had two sisters, and I was never made to feel differently. I never felt alone. Did you?"

"Never," he said. "Although I did not come to Juston and Emera's home until I was around eight years of age, up until that point, I had been well tended by a farmer and his family, and then sent to Canterbury for a time before a knight took care of me."

"Who was this knight?"

"Sir Erik de Russe," he said. "He taught me a great deal about honor and responsibility."

"Where is he now?"

"Dead," he said. "He died on crusade with Richard."

"Oh," she said, feeling some sadness because of the way he'd said it. She could tell it had affected him. "But I am certain he would be very proud of you. He taught you a good deal about how a man should conduct his life."

"Indeed, he did," he said. "I hope it is not too much to ask, but I always thought I might name a son after him, should we have one. I would like to honor a man who meant a good deal to me when I was younger."

Her smile returned. "I like that name," she said. "It would be an honor for our son to carry it."

He pulled her into his arms, hugging her tightly. "You are a gracious woman, Lady de Royans," he said. "And that's something else I have been thinking of."

Andromeda held him fiercely. "What?"

"My name," he said. "It is really not de Royans. It is Plantagenet. However, I do not want to use that surname, for obvious reasons, so I simply use de Royans."

"What was it when you lived with the farmer?"

He smiled, a quirky little smirk. "Tarr," he said. "I went by Tristan Tarr. That was the name of the farm where I lived, but I was not called that at Canterbury. I simply went by Tristan."

"I think de Royans sounds more dignified than Tarr."

"I agree," he said. "But what I was going to say is this—Sherry said that the king wishes to confer an earldom upon me, so whatever that earldom is, I think I should like to take that as my family name. That will define us and our descendants for generations to come."

Andromeda thought on that. "The kings of England and the kings of Dublin will commingle in the new name," she said. "Mayhap our standard can have a tree in it."

"Why a tree?"

She nodded. "That is the ancient symbol for Dublin kings," she said. "A tree with many branches representing life and family. Nothing is stronger than an oak tree withstanding the test of time."

He kissed her head and let her go. "Not a bad suggestion," he said. "I will think on it. Meanwhile, let us finish getting you packed, and then we shall work on me. What do you intend to pack all of this in?"

Andromeda went over to the door and peered into the stairwell. "I sent Flora and Aldis to find an appropriate satchel," she said. "They went to the storage chamber downstairs. Mayhap I should go and help them."

He shrugged. "If you wish," he said. "I will go to my chamber and begin to prepare my saddlebags while you are searching for a satchel."

Andromeda nodded and started to come away from the door when she abruptly came to a halt. "Pat," she said, her focus still on the stairwell. "I think… I see Addax down there. Wait… he's coming up the stairs. He looks as if he's in a panic."

By the time Tristan came over to the doorway, Addax was already at the top of the stairs. He was indeed breathless, not a usual state for the normally unflappable knight.

"You'd better come," he said to Tristan. "De Wolfe and his friends are back, and they've been in a fight."

"A fight?" Tristan repeated, confused.

Addax fixed him in the eye. "With some Irish."

Tristan understood the implication immediately. It was what they'd been waiting for. He was rushing down the stairs before he drew another breath, with Addax right behind him and, unbeknownst to either of them, Andromeda as well. This threat was against her, after all, and she wanted to see what had happened. The Irish were involved, and that made her both furious and terrified. Men like her husband were being put in an unnecessarily dangerous situation because of her.

Because *Aingil Lochlainn* wanted her.

She had a right to know what they had done.

Tristan and Addax were faster than she was. Andromeda tended to take the stairs of the keep slowly because they were steep, and she was in a long skirt, so she emerged from the keep well after her husband and Addax. They had already rushed into the bailey, where Alexander was standing along with William, Paris, and Kieran, who had a beaten man between them. Soldiers were crowding around and the gates were being sealed up.

There was tension in the air.

Without delay, Andromeda made her way into the bailey, seeing the knights circled around someone who seemed to be injured. Kieran had the man tightly. She couldn't see who it was until she peered around Tristan's big body, trying to catch a glimpse of the man. Undoubtedly an Irish prisoner. When Tristan shifted, the man's face came into view.

Shock bolted through her.

Before she realized what she was doing, Andromeda rushed forward, pushed between Tristan and Addax, and slapped the man across the face, so hard that his hand snapped sideways. As Tristan rushed forward to protect her, pulling her away from the prisoner, she screamed at the man with the bloodied face and black eye.

"You left me!" she yelled. "You vile bastard, you left me! You took the money and you left me to fend for myself in a country that was not my own! How could you do such a thing?"

Tristan had her by both arms. “Do you know this man, Andie?” he said, concerned. “Who is it?”

Even though he had her by the arms, it didn’t stop her from lashing out a foot and kicking the man in the hip. “One of the guards who escorted me from Rockbrook,” she said, so furious that she was verging on tears. “He took Lord de Courcy’s money and ran off, like a coward. But now he’s come back, and I want to know why!”

All eyes turned to the battered Irishman, who was looking at Andromeda with some surprise. But her anger threw Tristan over the edge, and the man was the victim of a blow to the jaw that sent him flying onto his back. It was strong enough to jerk him from Kieran’s grip. Tristan was on top of the man, pulling him up by the front of his tunic.

“So you return to the scene of your crime, you piece of filth?” he growled. “And we find you gathering with the enemy. It is my guess that you were part of *Aingil Lochlainn* all along. Weren’t you?”

The man cast him a long look with his one good eye. “If I were, she wouldn’t be here now, would she?”

“Then you joined them after returning home?”

The man snorted, blood and mucus flying. “Why should I tell you?” he said. “You’re only going to beat me again.”

“I’ll beat you if you do not speak,” Tristan said. “I would be more afraid of that.”

The Irish rebel eyed him. “If you kill me, you’ll never know what I know.”

Tristan’s eyes narrowed. “I can already guess what you’ve been involved in,” he said. “I know men like you. I know that your heart is filled with coin rather than blood.”

The man eyed him, feigning disinterest. “You think you

know everything, don't you?"

"I know enough," Tristan said. "I'm going to assume you went back to Ireland and made contact with the *Aingil Lochlainn*. You knew they wanted her because you were her escort when she fled their grasp. You knew where you left her, here in England, and you offered to return to find her. But Dermot's mother told them exactly where she was, so you came with them to identify her. Isn't that it?"

The man made a good show of not being intimidated, even though Tristan's speculation was very close to the truth. But the Irishman, a soldier with a drunkard father and a mother who took men to her bed for money, knew how to play the game. Liam de Courcy had paid him well to escort Andromeda to England, Lochlainn's rebels had paid him well to help them identify the lady, and now he saw another opportunity for money.

For him, it was all about the money.

"Pay me well and I'll go back to them and tell them I never saw her," he said, his gaze moving to Andromeda. "She looks far better than she did the last time I saw her. Had I known she was such a beauty, she would have fetched a fine price."

That was enough for Tristan. He geared up to pummel the man again, but Addax stopped him.

"Wait, Pat," he said. "We have bigger problems. De Wolfe says that Dermot seems to have gone missing."

Tristan's features twisted in confusion at the change in subject. "Missing?" he said, looking at William. "What do you mean?"

"When the Irish attacked us, Dermot fled," William answered. "He betrayed us, and in the chaos, he disappeared. We thought he might have returned here."

Tristan looked at Addax. "Is it possible that he did?"

Addax shrugged. "I asked the men at the gatehouse, but no one seemed to know," he said. "I've sent word to the gatehouse commanders for more information."

It was very possible Dermot had somehow slipped back into the castle. The soldiers would have known him as a trusted knight because no one really knew he'd been in the vault. That was something Tristan had chosen not to spread around until he could figure out what was going on with Dermot and Carr, but now he was sorry he hadn't.

The ordinary soldiers wouldn't have known he was the enemy.

With that on his mind, Tristan returned his attention to the man in his grasp. He was coming to think that Dermot wasn't missing at all, but that he had disappeared by choice. Had he returned to the castle? Possibly. But it was more probable that he'd run off with his Irish comrades, using the chaos of the fight between the knights and the Irish to his advantage.

The whole situation was becoming more and more disturbing.

"Nay, he is not missing," Tristan said after a moment. "I would wager to say that he's run off with his Irish brethren. De Wolfe?"

He boomed William's name, and the man was instantly beside him. "My lord?" he answered.

Tristan's gaze lingered on the Irishman even though he was speaking to William. "I heard you did terrible things to Dermot," he said.

"We did, my lord."

Tristan stood back, hauling the Irishman to his feet and practically throwing him in Kieran's direction.

"Take him," he said. "I want to know where his comrades are. I want to know where Dermot might be. I want to know everything you can possibly get out of him, so do your worst, and I mean that literally."

Kieran didn't have to be told twice. He grabbed the prisoner around the neck, dragging the man back to the gatehouse as Paris followed. William started to go after them, but Tristan stopped him.

"Nay," he said. "You will stay with me. Let your young and eager friends tear up Ireland. I will, however, ask Sherry to go with them."

They turned to Alexander, who had been standing by silently as the situation unfolded before him. Now, he was being called into service. His reputation as an assassin and agent was known far and wide by men who traveled in such circles. Having gained his reputation in the Holy Land during the second crusade, Alexander was one of the more cold-blooded killers that England had ever spawned. He'd done things that gave most men nightmares, so interrogating a lone Irishman was almost beneath his dignity.

But not quite.

He understood the implication. This was a job for an Executioner Knight. With a nod, Alexander turned for the gatehouse, but not before he lowered his voice to William.

"I'll teach your friends a thing or two," he muttered. "If they're bright, they'll learn something."

"They're bright, my lord."

"Then this will be an education for them."

With that, he headed off, a very big man with terrifying skills. Even William was a little concerned as he watched Alexander follow Paris and Kieran to the gatehouse. He knew

Kieran would shut his mouth and observe, but he was truthfully a little concerned about Paris. But perhaps a sharp rebuke or threat from a seasoned veteran might temper that arrogance. For a while, anyway. Long enough for him to see how the older generation did things and learn something from it.

Men like Alexander de Sherrington were legends.

Thinking on what was about to take place in the vault, William was in the process of rubbing his chin and contemplating the situation when he heard a soft voice next to him.

"You have a cut above your eye, William."

It was Andromeda. When William turned to her, she smiled and pointed to the messy gash above his left eye.

"You must let me tend the wound," she said. "I may need to put a stitch in it."

William put a finger to the area, coming away with semi-dried blood. "It is not bad," he assured her. "It will heal."

Tristan peered at the wound. "Let her clean it up," he said. "Things are calming now, at least for the moment, so let us go into the solar and she can tend it. I also want to congratulate you on a task well done, and there is some wine in the solar that is perfect for such an occasion."

William was still fingering the wound, but he looked at Tristan curiously. "Me, my lord?" he said. "What did I do?"

Tristan nodded. "You took the initiative to get what information you could from Dermot and go looking for the Irish," he said. "On a personal level, you have my gratitude. What you did was personal to me and me alone. It was not important to Wrexham or to the Marshal, but to me because I married the woman those Irish bastards are hunting for. I owe you a debt, William, and I will not forget it."

William smiled with some embarrassment. "I did not do it

so you would owe me a debt, my lord," he said. "I did it because it was the right thing to do."

"And that is why you will go far in life, de Wolfe."

"I intend to," he said. "But bear in mind I probably would not have done this for just anyone. But you… you have given me a chance. More than that, you have given my closest friends a chance, too, when most warlords had passed us on. I would say I owe you more than you owe me for giving me the opportunity to prove that the young fool I once was has matured."

Tristan smiled at the young knight, clapping him on the shoulder in a show of support. It was a bonding moment between them, one that meant a good deal to William. His year with Tristan had been an important one in his development as a man and as a warrior. As they started to move in the direction of the keep so Andromeda could tend William's cut, a shout came from the direction of the gatehouse. Everyone paused, turning to see one of the sergeants in command approaching.

"My lord!" he called.

"What is it?" Tristan replied.

The man picked up the pace, running toward them, until he came within a few feet. "I've been on the wall with the soldiers who have assumed their duty shift for the day," the sergeant said, out of breath. "I just came down and heard that you were looking for Sir Dermot."

The mention of Dermot's name had their attention. Tristan, Andromeda, Addax, and William crowded near the man.

"Aye," Tristan said. "What of it?"

The sergeant came to a halt. "I admitted him back into the castle before I went into the wall," the sergeant said. "He returned not fifteen minutes ago."

Tristan stiffened with the news as Addax and William passed concerned glances. "I see," Tristan said with as much steadiness as he could manage. "Did he say anything to you?"

The sergeant shook his head. "The gate was closed, and he asked to be admitted," he said. "But he said nothing beyond that."

"Did you see where he went?"

"Nay, my lord."

"Thank you for telling me. Now, I want you to listen very carefully."

"My lord?"

"Sir Dermot is to be considered a dangerous traitor," Tristan said evenly. "I want you to spread the word. Every man is to keep an eye open for him. I will reward whoever finds him and brings him to me alive. If he knows he has been discovered, he will fight, so the men must be advised to protect themselves. Do you understand?"

The sergeant nodded, trying not to look stricken that he'd evidently allowed an enemy into their fold. "Aye, my lord," he said. "I… I did not know. Forgive me."

"I know you didn't," Tristan said. "It was not your fault. But you will organize a search party from the men not currently on duty."

"I will, my lord. Right away."

The sergeant ran off, shouting to the men at the gatehouse who were changing shifts at this time of day. Tristan watched him go before turning to the small group standing behind him. The first person he addressed was Andromeda.

"You will not leave my side," he said quietly, but calmly so he wouldn't frighten her. "I'm not entirely sure why Dermot would return, knowing that we would know of his treachery, but that is the situation. It seems he did not go off with his Irish brethren as I assumed. However, that is of no matter—we will find him. De Wolfe, after my wife tends your eye, you will oversee the search."

"Aye, my lord."

It was a new crisis on a day that had been rife with them, but they were ready for it. This was what the knights were trained for and, in truth, knowing Dermot was somewhere in the castle perhaps made their task of containing him and his treachery a little easier. At least he wasn't out with the Irish, planning something else.

Tristan turned to Addax.

"I have something important for you," he said. "I want you to…"

He was cut off by the same sergeant, once again running in his direction. "My lord!" the man shouted. "The patrols are returning!"

"God, what now?" Addax muttered. "They should not be returning this time of day."

Tristan knew that. He was all too aware. Reaching out, he grasped Andromeda's hand tightly. Hoping they weren't about to face yet another crisis, he felt better with her in his grip. There was something about the human contact between them that settled him. Gave him peace of mind, something he was in need of, because the early return of the patrols could only mean one thing—something was on the horizon, something more critical than Irish rebels or kings in London demanding to see him.

Something terrible was coming.

He could feel it.

The first patrol returning beneath the open portcullis was

part of the same patrol that went out to the west on a daily basis. Tristan had ridden with this patrol on the day he found Andromeda in the tavern in Ruabon. There were four regular scouts, all of them dressed for travel and stealth, meaning they wore little by way of protection, mostly dirty clothing so they'd blend in with the landscape. This was also the patrol that William had ridden with when he'd seen the buildup at Lord Gryffyn's home.

Tristan, Andromeda, Addax, and William went to meet them.

"My lord." The man leading the patrol was older, and he'd grown up on the marches so he knew the land well. "I've taken the liberty of recalling all of the patrols because the castle must be secured. The Welsh that were gathering at Lord Gryffyn's home of Garth Hall have amassed overnight. They are moving towards Wrexham as we speak."

No one was particularly surprised to hear the news. In fact, Tristan felt a strange sense of relief. He'd been expecting that very thing every single day, and now that the moment was here, he was relieved. At least now he knew what was coming. The past year, living peacefully as they had, seemed unnatural given the volatility of the marches.

Nay, he wasn't surprised in the least.

"How many men?" he asked.

The old man leaned forward on his saddle, wearily. "More than we keep here at Wrexham," he said. "Enough to make ladders and scale the walls, if they can. They'll try."

"How long until they get here?"

"They'll be in our lap by dawn."

So it had come, the counterattack they'd been waiting for since the English had taken Wrexham back from the Welsh, and it sounded like a big one. But Tristan knew what they all knew—that the Welsh were going to have to fight to get it back because the English weren't going to let it go easily.

They were going to be prepared.

"Thank you," he said to the scout. "We'll be gathering in the great hall in a short while to inform the men of what is happening and to discuss our plan of defense. I want you there to answer any questions."

"Aye, my lord."

"Be on your way."

The scout and his men headed for the stable yard as Tristan turned to Addax and William.

"And it comes," he said quietly. "William, go to the vault and tell the knights what has happened. They can leave the Irish rebel alone for now because I need them up here to organize defenses. We meet in the great hall in a half-hour for this purpose. Make sure they attend."

William nodded and was gone, heading for the gatehouse amidst the bustle of the bailey and the returning patrols. Tristan then turned to Addax.

"I want everyone in the great hall," he said. "We have known this day would come and we have a plan, so we must be prepared to execute it."

Addax nodded smartly. "Aye, my lord," he said.

With that, he dashed off, rushing toward the gatehouse. Tristan finally turned to Andromeda, who was watching Addax run away. When she caught Tristan looking at her, she smiled weakly.

"I've never seen a castle preparing for war before," she said. "The last time I saw something like this, the *Aingil Lochlainn* was at the door and I was being sent away through the postern gate. I will admit that it brings back those feelings of uneasiness."

She was trying to be brave. He could see it in her face. Surely the news was shocking, terrifying, even, but she was trying hard not to show it. He took her by the arm and walked her back toward the keep, removing her from the busy bailey.

"I can imagine," he said softly. "But I have been thinking, Andie. Sherry was right. I do not want you in a compromised castle. Although this came much sooner than we anticipated, there is still time to move you to safety. I can ask Sherry to take you back with him to Wigmore."

Andromeda came to a halt and pulled her arm from his grasp. "You think I would be so cowardly that I would flee when my husband is facing danger?" she said. "You will need me, Pat. I cannot leave."

He was trying to be gentle with her. "You are not a coward," he said firmly. "You are the bravest woman I have ever known, but the Welsh can be… determined."

"So am I."

"Sweetheart, if they get over the wall, there is a chance they may capture you," he said, trying to be realistic with her. "They may even kill you. I couldn't live with that, Andie. I cannot live without you. I would, therefore, consider it a great favor if you would go with Sherry. Please, my love. I am begging you."

Andromeda was growing increasingly stubborn, though his gentle plea had her wavering. But she stood her ground.

"Nay," she said flatly. "Where you go, I go, and if you face the Welsh, then so do I. We are together in this, Pat. If you stay, I stay. I could not leave you in your time of need."

"But—"

She cut him off. "Would you leave me in mine?"

He was becoming frustrated that she was being so obstinate, but he was also immensely touched. For a man who had never had the affection of a woman, someone who belonged only to him, her loyalty to him was staggering. He tried not to let it cloud his judgment, because he knew she should leave, but damn… what a wonderful thing it was to have a woman who was so dedicated to him.

It was the most wonderful thing in the world.

"I am going to beat you soundly if you do not go," he threatened weakly.

"And I am going to kick you in the face if you try."

He frowned, holding out for about two seconds before breaking down into laughter. "Would you really?"

"Are you truly going to beat me?"

"I am."

"Then I will kick you. I will probably bite you also."

"I believe you would."

"*Try* me."

He rolled his eyes, still laughing, before opening up his big arms and pulling her into his embrace. "I love you dearly," he murmured into her hair. "I love you so much that it is making me physically ill to think of your being here when the Welsh attack. Is there anything I can say that will convince you to leave?"

She pressed against him, feeling his warmth and power filling her like blood in her veins. "Nothing," she said, muffled against his chest. "Unless you go with me, I am not leaving."

He didn't want to fight with her. Not now. Perhaps after they'd met with the men in the great hall to discuss the attack and she could see just what they were facing, he would try again, but at the moment, he didn't want an argument on his hands. For now, he'd let her have her way.

But time was passing.

Soon, it would be too late to safely remove her.

"Then if you intend to stay, you will make yourself useful," he said. "It will be important to lock down the keep. It will be important to move buckets of water to the roof in case the Welsh decide to throw flaming projectiles over the walls. It will be important to make the kitchen animals safe by bringing them into the vault. Move anything flammable away from the windows and cover them with cloth soaked in water. Make sure there is an adequate supply of food, and make sure the water supply is adequate. I know the well is in the kitchen, so we want to keep that secure. And most of all, we will need bandages for the wounded. It will be up to you to boil linens and tear them into bandages for the wounded. Will you do this?"

She was overwhelmed with all of the things he wanted her to do, but in a good way. She was ready.

"I will," she said. "But I must hurry if I am to get all of that done, so I must go."

"Not without a guard."

"A guard?" she said. "Why?"

He lifted an eyebrow. "Because Dermot is here, somewhere," he said quietly. "I cannot be with you right now, and you will not walk about alone. Not until we find him."

She understood. "Very well," she said. "Send whomever you wish to watch over me, but I will put him to work."

He gave her a half-grin. "Do as you must," he said, catching sight of someone over near the stable entry and realizing it was the scout who had brought the news of the Welsh movements. Emitting a whistle between his teeth, he caught the man's attention and waved him over. "I have the perfect man to watch out for you."

Andromeda could see him coming, the older man who was rather tall, with big arms and a big head. "The scout?" she said. "I remember him from Ruabon on the day we met."

"Indeed," Tristan said. "He was with us on that day, and I trust him."

Andromeda fell silent, thinking of everything she had to do, pleased he hadn't put up more of a fight about letting her stay. But she had a feeling that wasn't the last she was going to hear of the subject. Perhaps he'd been too distracted planning the coming defenses to make demands again, but she knew that he'd never forget about her safety. The scout coming toward them was proof enough of that.

"My lady, this is Dolan," Tristan said, introducing her to the scout. "Dolan, this is my wife, Lady de Royans. I realize that you've been out on patrol and haven't heard the latest news from the castle, but I have a most important task for you."

Dolan cocked his head curiously. "My lord?"

Tristan pointed to Andromeda. "Her safety," he said simply. "We have a rogue knight in Dermot mac Edan who is trying to harm her. With the approach of the Welsh, I have many things to attend to, and I do not want to leave her unprotected. That is why I am entrusting you with this task, Dolan. This is of the utmost importance to me. Will you do this?"

Dolan looked at Andromeda, who was shielding her eyes from the sun as she gazed up at him. "I will, my lord," he said, nodding firmly. "I have a daughter about her age. I understand your fear."

"Thank you," Tristan said sincerely. "I will gather your patrol and have them join you. If Dermot tries to get near her, you have my permission to run him through. Are you armed?"

"Always, my lord."

"Good," Tristan said. He waved his hand in the direction of the keep. "The lady has much to do, so stay by her side at all times. When the battle begins, she is to remain in the secured keep, and you will remain with her. I would prefer to have seasoned men in the castle with her in case your experience is needed."

Dolan understood the implication. *If the Welsh breach the castle, you will need to defend the keep and my wife.*

"Aye, my lord," he said quietly. "She will not be alone."

Andromeda didn't catch the nuances that were going back and forth between them, seasoned fighting men facing yet another battle. They knew the stakes. They knew the possible outcome. She lowered her hand from her eyes, looking to Tristan, oblivious to just how nervous he really was. But perhaps that was a blessing. He was calm, so she was calm.

And that was the way Tristan wanted it.

"On your way," he said, bending down to kiss her on the mouth. "Come to the hall shortly, because I will address the me. I want you to hear what I tell them."

"I will," she said.

He winked at her. "Go," he said. "You have much to do, and your husband is demanding."

With a grin, she gathered her skirts and fled toward the keep with Dolan on her heels. Tristan watched them go, the smile fading from his face. Was he doing the right thing by not forcing her to leave? Was he being too weak? But there was more to his fears, something he wouldn't admit to himself until this very moment.

Could he really lead this battle well enough to keep her, and everyone else, safe?

In all of his years as a knight, he had been the one following orders. Of course, he knew how to command men and coordinate a battle, but this would be his first time as the commander of a castle under siege. There was so much at stake, not the least of which was his wife, who would probably be here for the battle. He had to force himself to admit that he would never convince her to leave.

If you stay, I stay.

War was on the horizon.

He could only pray that he was good enough, and strong enough, to win it.

CHAPTER TWENTY

JUST AS ADDAX had predicted, the Welsh were in their laps before the sun rose. Just like that, Wrexham was a castle under siege.

Andromeda had never seen a battle on this scale before. Throughout her life in Ireland, Rockbrook Castle had seen perhaps a couple of skirmishes, but nothing serious. In spite of the reputation of the fighting Irish, her home had remained peaceful. Even those small skirmishes were certainly not on the scale of what she was witnessing at this moment.

The Welsh had come to fight.

The action had commenced before dawn. The castle had been sealed up at that point and it had been for several hours, ever since the villagers caught wind of the approaching Welsh. Those who hadn't fled sought refuge from the castle, which was normal in times of trouble. However, because of the Irish faction, Tristan refused to let any of the men into the castle. He admitted women and children, but none of the men were allowed to enter, so those from the village were forced to hide in the countryside as the Welsh contingent arrived from the west. Perhaps it had been cruel of Tristan not to admit men, but he simply couldn't take the chance that the Irish rebels were among them.

Andromeda had taken all of the women and children into the keep. Because it was so large, there was plenty of room for those who seeking shelter. There were dozens of women and children and babies, and they fit easily within the lower levels of the keep. The only problem with the additional people would be the strain on the food stores, and that was something that Andromeda would have to watch carefully. She had soldiers and wounded to feed, and they would be her priority.

Unlike at the siege commanded by William Marshal a year ago, the Welsh didn't bring siege engines or trebuchets to batter down the walls. They brought manpower and hundreds of archers, who almost immediately started firing flaming projectiles over the walls with the hopes of lighting fire to things like the stables and the great hall. Their initial strategy seemed to be to try to burn out the occupants of Wrexham Castle, but that strategy would fail. What they didn't know was that Tristan had reinforced the roof of the great hall with slate that had been left behind by the Welsh when they occupied the castle.

Unknowingly, they had stymied their own assault.

There had been stacks of the smooth, sometimes brittle slate rock in the yard near the troop house, and the Marshal had speculated that the Welsh were preparing to build something with it, or to use it to line the roof of the keep, but never got around to it. That meant Tristan had all of that beautiful slate from the Nantlle Valley near Caernarvon to do with as he pleased, and one of the first things he did was line the roof of the great hall with it when the thing was rebuilt. No more thatching, but slate instead.

The Welsh couldn't burn it.

Tristan had lined other things with the slate as well, including several of the outbuildings and part of the stable, until he ran out of it. That meant a portion of the stable was vulnerable to the flaming arrows, but they had managed to saturate the thatching with so much water that the arrows couldn't get a foothold and burn.

That had been the first day.

Infuriated that they somehow hadn't been able to burn Wrexham Castle immediately, the Welsh turned to the town and began to torch it. Since the villagers had all been evacuated, they were simply burning the shells of homes and businesses. When they became bored of that, they returned to the castle and resumed their bombardment of arrows. Welsh archers were legendary, and they used them to their advantage. Daily, bolts rained down from the sky.

While this was going on, the Welsh put another strategy into place. Hundreds of them had returned to the forests to the west and began cutting down the young trees in order to make ladders with which to mount the walls. It was going to be a difficult task because, given how fortified Wrexham was, they couldn't make ladders tall enough to get to the top of the walls. That meant they were going to have to have some sort of anchor to pull themselves up to the wall walk, and they began devising grappling hooks for this very purpose. If they couldn't burn the English out, then they were going to have to evict them by force.

With occupants oblivious to what was going on outside, life inside of Wrexham's keep wasn't entirely bad. The villagers stayed to the lower floors, in the larger rooms, but the logistics of so many people in one place needed to be managed. Andromeda had the kitchens working day and night, baking bread and making food for both the villagers and the soldiers. While feeding the villagers didn't pose many challenges, bringing sustenance to the soldiers was a little more complex. There was no such thing as the ability to sit down to a meal, so the kitchen sliced bread into chunks and melted cheese on it to distribute to the soldiers as something simple to eat with one hand. Sometimes the bread and cheese had chunks of meat on it, too, which was always welcome. Even if the food wasn't elaborate, the soldiers were well fed.

For the villagers, it was a little easier because they could make great pots of boiled beans and turnips to feed the frightened throng. A week after the battle began, the villagers had settled down and the families had their own little living areas. Children played and the mothers tried to keep them entertained as the hours and days dragged on. Andromeda would go down to visit frequently, and it was a good chance for her to get to know the people of the village. They seemed most appreciative and curious about her, and even though she spoke with a heavy Irish accent, no one seemed to be put off by it. They all came to know and respect the Lady of Wrexham.

For Andromeda, the days had been a time of baptism by fire. Some things were simple; some things weren't. Keeping the keep locked up was simple; dealing with the mass human habitation wasn't. There was feeding to think about, and keeping everything clean. There was one garderobe for everyone to use on the first level, and that quickly became overwhelmed by so much usage, so Andromeda put a few of the older women in charge of keeping it clean so the smell wouldn't drive them out of the keep and into the arms of the Welsh. But it didn't take her long to become accustomed to everything that was going on and take control of it. So far, everything had been managed quite well.

But there was one thing she wasn't managing well.

She missed her husband.

Andromeda could only see Tristan from the windows, which was torture when all she wanted to do was hold him. He began to make a habit of appearing in front of her window every morning, and she would wave to him. He would smile and wave in return, yelling his love for her, and she would call down to him in the same fashion. He would also appear every night at sunset if he could, right about the time the kitchens would send out whatever they had prepared for the evening meal. They were only issuing one meal a day, but it was a plentiful meal. The cook, who had been through sieges before, knew how to divide the food up to make it last.

So far, everything had gone smoothly.

In fact, as the days went on, it seemed as if the battle was beginning to diminish. Every day, the Welsh would shoot arrows over the walls but not much more than that. It was true that a few men had been hit by the projectiles, but there had been no life-threatening wounds. Still, Andromeda could see it all from her window, and she grew more and more concerned with the wounded that they were being kept in the great hall. The lady of the castle was expected to nurse the sick and wounded, as was customary, so she had no idea who was actually helping the soldiers. Tristan did not keep a surgeon with his army, so it was anyone's guess as to who was doing the tending.

Increasingly, that was not sitting well with her, but there wasn't anything she could do about it. She'd promised Tristan that she would remain in the keep, but that promise was becoming more difficult to keep. Andromeda knew the basics of caring for the wounded because that had been part of her education as a noblewoman. She'd never been one to remain idle when there was work to be done, and that was part of the problem. She was a producer, fond of hard work, and that was never more evident than it was now.

She didn't like to remain idle.

The days dragged on, with no real end in sight, but the second week of the siege was when things began to get interesting. The Welsh stopped the constant barrage of arrows, but they had not left the area. They still encircled the castle to the point where they'd set their encampment up very close to the moat.

They'd dug in to stay.

It was an uncertain time because no one was sure what the Welsh were doing. Andromeda could see the soldiers and knights on the wall, always watching what was going on below. She could see Tristan and Addax, and William and Paris and Kieran. She could also see Alexander, and he tended to mostly stay at the gatehouse, but there was also someone else she could see:

Her father.

That was a distinct shock. Somehow, her father had been released from the vault. She had no idea why, but she suspected it was because Tristan felt that he needed the manpower. It was also true that Tristan believed her father had nothing to do with whatever Dermot was involved in, so there was no reason not to release him. It was an odd sight for Andromeda to see Carr mac Murda back on the walls of Wrexham.

She thought the sight might even make her a little nervous, but ultimately, there was no reason for her to be concerned. Her father was of no consequence anymore because she had a husband who would fully defend her from anything the man tried to do or say. It was an entirely new world for her father now that his daughter had married his commanding officer.

For Carr, life had changed, indeed.

On a slightly misty morning on the tenth day after the siege began, Andromeda was pondering the new reality that her life had become when she began to see a frenzy of activity on the wall that included her father. It also included Alexander, who came running along the parapet from the gatehouse. Something was happening down below, something critical, but she had no idea what it was until she heard one word, shouted by the sentries:

"*Ladders!*"

As it turned out, the Welsh had been lulling the English into a false sense of security. While the English had watched the Welsh milling around the castle moat, building an encampment and hardly engaging in warfare, hundreds of them had been able to bring up the ladders that they had been building in the woods. Now, those ladders were front and center, coming right at Wrexham, and as the English scrambled on the walls to get the archers in place, the Welsh either walked across the moat or glided across in small skiffs, moving their ladders to the base of the walls. There was just enough real estate between the walls and the moat that they were able to get a foothold.

The ladders were going up.

As that was going on, the English archers let loose with everything they had. Tristan's army began firing at the Welsh who were trying to prop up the ladders. In preparation for this very moment, they had also been stockpiling oil, used to light the lamps, but it was also effective when small earthenware jugs filled with oil were lit and then poured or thrown onto the men below. That seemed to be the most effective in deterring them from climbing the walls, because the burning Welsh would fall back into the moat, many of them too injured to continue. Several of them drowned before their friends could get to them.

Very shortly, the battle for Wrexham had turned quite deadly.

In response to the English archers, the Welsh resumed firing arrows over the walls in an attempt to drive the English away from the ladders that were being propped against the walls. On the battlements and from the tower, the crimson shield of Tristan de Royans and the scarlet lion of William Marshal were being torn to shreds by the constant bombardment. The wounded began pouring into the great hall. Men with bolts sticking out of them, men who had fallen from the wall, and any number of injuries now that the battle had heated up. By noon, Andromeda could no longer remain idle.

She had to do something.

Summoning Flora and Aldis, she explained that she was going to go to the great hall through the servants' passages to tend the wounded. The servants offered to help, assistance that Andromeda gratefully accepted. Aldis had her sewing kit and Andromeda had an embroidery kit, one of the man things found in the painted wardrobe, so at least they could sew any gaping wounds.

But they needed more.

"We can use wine and ale to clean the wounds," Andromeda told the servants. "But what else do we have that can ease pain or help with healing?"

Flora shook her head. "Sir Tristan never had a physic," she said. "Men simply healed themselves."

Andromeda thought that sounded rather bleak. "The cook boiled a good deal of linen for bandages before the battle began," she said. "Wine and ale will clean the wounds. And drinking it could help with the pain."

"That may be all we have, my lady," Flora said. "We've heard from the kitchen servants, the ones who are feeding the men, and they say there are more wounded than ever and the men are simply helping one another. There is no surgeon."

Andromeda squared her shoulders. "Then we must get down there right away," she said firmly. "I want you to tell the cook that we are going to the great hall to help the wounded. Have him give you all of the wine and ale he can spare. If that is all we have to use, then we must take all we can. Aldis, I want you to find some servants to help us. Have them bring hot water into the great hall. We'll need it to clean wounds and the soiled linen bandages. Hurry, now; there is no time to lose."

Flora and Aldis went on the run. Andromeda quickly changed out of one of her nicer gowns and into one of the more durable ones that she wore when working alongside the servants. Her hair was braided and pinned to the back of her head, keeping it out of the way, and she put on one of her linen aprons.

Then she simply looked at her reflection in her dressing table mirror.

Strange how such a short time ago she was without direction, terrified and alone, and now she was the lady of a great castle, married to a man she loved with all her heart. She knew what her duties were as the Lady of Wrexham, and she knew what she was capable of. In another life and another time, her birthright would have made her a queen. She was married to the man who should have been king. Perhaps they weren't in the royal positions their heritages dictated, but they were the king and queen of their own wonderful little world. It was time for

Andromeda to become the queen she was born to be. While Tristan was out there risking his life, she was going to help the men who were fighting alongside him.

She was going to make a difference.

Grabbing the embroidery kit, she headed down to the great hall.

CHAPTER TWENTY-ONE

THE WELSH WEREN'T making it easy.

Tristan knew that the lackluster performance of the Welsh at the beginning of the battle had been deliberate. It was a smart military tactic designed to lower the defenses of the enemy. While no one's defense had been lowered enough to make a difference, the rush at the walls with ladders had been a surprise. Ten days after the battle started, the war was in full bloom.

He was on the section of wall where the Welsh were trying to put up several ladders. They were becoming smarter now and positioning archers where the ladders were going up. When the English showed their faces, the archers would let fly. Tristan had lost two men to the most recent barrage, one of them hit in the head and the other in the eye. That made the English very reluctant to look over the wall.

"Pat!"

Addax was heading toward Tristan, tucked down in a crouch position as he moved. Tristan went over to meet him, ducking low when a few bolts went over his head.

"How is the gatehouse holding?" he asked.

Addax glanced back at the enormous gatehouse partially masked in the mist. "The Welsh have managed to burn part of the drawbridge," he said. "Once they can get in through the gap, they'll go for the portcullis."

"Then make sure there is an army of archers waiting for them," Tristan said. "Have them start firing through the portcullis now to keep them at bay."

Addax nodded. "We have," he said. "Sherry is in command of the gatehouse. But he sent me to tell you that we are running low on bolts. We are collecting what we can of those that come over from the Welsh, but we may have to start restricting the use."

Tristan grunted. "That was only a matter of time," he said. "What about everyone else? Where are the knights?"

Addax motioned to the wall by the kitchen yard and the keep. "De Norville is on the back of the wall, facing the river," he said. "The ground slopes too much there, so the ladders have been unable to get a foothold. De Wolfe is at the gatehouse, but I'm sending Hage to help you and Carr."

Tristan nodded, looking over his shoulder at Carr, who was bellowing commands to the English on the wall. "He's a good knight," he said. "Given the current situation, the only logical decision was to release him from the vault so he can lend a hand."

Addax nodded, his gaze on the Irish knight. "He has not said anything about Dermot or your wife since I released him," he said. "Has he said anything to you?"

"Nay," Tristan said. "He has behaved like a loyal knight."

"He's probably afraid to misbehave," Addax said. "He's afraid that you'll have Sherry do to him what he did to the Irish rebel."

Tristan looked at him. "What did he do to the Irish rebel?"

Addax shook his head in a manner that suggested Tristan had better prepare himself for the answer. "It did not take him long," he said. "The rebel refused to speak, and spat in Sherry's eye, which is never a good thing. Sherry was not merciful."

"What did he do?"

"He used a method he'd learned on crusade," Addax said reluctantly. "We've all seen it, Pat. It was so terrible that de Norville vomited. Hage witnessed it without flinching, but Sherry did it so quickly that it was as if he'd done it a thousand times before. I know Sherry has a reputation of being a dark killer, but this… this was an impressive bit of killing."

That gave Tristan pause. "Truly?" he said. "What happened?"

"Have you heard of the *Blodörn*?"

Tristan cocked his head curiously. "I have," he said. "It's a method of execution, the blood bird or the blood angel. It's when a man's ribs are broken and… God's Bones, Addax… Did he really do *that*?"

"He did," Addax said, clearing his throat to suggest just how gruesome it really was. "I've seen it done to men in the Levant, but never here. The ribs near a man's spine are broken by a blade and his organs are pulled from the openings. A painful way to die, Pat."

Tristan's eyebrows lifted. "I would imagine so."

"Sherry did it with surprising ease."

"I take it the fool is dead."

"Verily."

"That's what a man gets for betraying my wife and then spitting in the eye of a trained assassin."

"I will never insult Sherry again after this."

Tristan chuckled, hardly disagreeing with him, as grappling hooks were thrown up the wall, anchoring on the crenellations. Soldiers were now struggling to dislodge the hooks, which were attached to rope ladders. There was about a twelve-foot gap between the top of the ladders and top of the wall, and the Welsh were trying desperately to close that gap while the English were desperately trying to stop them. It seemed as if the situation was tilting in the Welsh's favor.

But not if Tristan could help it.

Addax's story about Alexander's ghastly punishment had given him an idea. If the Welsh knew what the English were capable of doing to those that displeased them, then it might slow them down, if not discourage them altogether.

It was worth a try.

"Send Hage down for the dead Irishman," he told Addax. "Have him bring him up to the wall and throw him over, down on those men trying to mount the walls. The sight of someone who has been carved like that might give them second thoughts about trying to breach Wrexham."

Addax's eyes glimmered with approval. "Of course," he said. "Show them what will happen to them if they are able to make it over the wall."

"Exactly," Tristan said. "Tell Sherry what we are doing, because if any of the Welsh make it to the top of the wall, I will have a job for him. An unsavory one."

The implication was clear. Addax nodded swiftly and was gone, dodging men and projectiles as he went. Once Tristan lost sight of him, he made his way to the crenellation, which was the rampart built around the wall, with intermittent gaps to allow for firing arrows or fighting. Carr was there, trying to look at the men below without getting hit by an arrow, and Tristan joined him. Together, they tried to gauge what was going on with the ladders and realized that there were more men down there than they originally thought. It looked like a hive of bees, all of them swarming around the ladders as they prepared to raise them.

"They are sending one man up the ladder with the grappling hook," Carr said, using his hands to demonstrate what he was explaining. "An archer comes up behind him, and as soon as we look down, the archer lets the bolt fly. That chases us back so their man can get to the top of the ladder and launch the grappling hook."

Tristan nodded, settling against the wall. "We've been watching it down the line," he said. "Clearly, they have been planning this for days, so it is simply a matter of making sure they cannot climb the walls. Keep vigilant, Carr."

"I will, my lord," Carr said. As Tristan started to move away, he called to him. "I… I want to thank you for releasing me. I know that you did it because there was a battle going on and you need my sword, but given what's happened with Dermot, I did not expect that you would. I do not blame you, of course. But I will tell you to your face that I was never involved in whatever he is mixed in. I swear that upon my oath."

For a brief moment, Tristan's focus moved from the battle to his father-in-law. That's exactly what Carr was—his wife's father. They were now family. Since imprisoning the man, he'd had no contact with him because he was busy with other things, but now there was a moment between them. Just the two of them. No emotion, but simply rational men. In fact, this was much more like the Carr he knew. Therefore, he carefully considered his reply.

"I believe you," he said. "I would not have released you had

I thought otherwise."

Carr seemed humbled by that. "I'm grateful," he said. "Mayhap this is not the time for such a discussion, but there may not be another chance. Being in the vault… I had time to think. There were two paths I could follow, and the one I'd been on was not taking me where I wanted to go. I do not want to end up like Dermot, shunned and in the vault."

"What are you telling me?"

"That I've chosen a path to redeem my honor."

Tristan eyed him. "Given how you've treated your daughter, you can understand my reluctance to accept that," he said. "I married Andromeda, Carr. She is my wife, and I will protect her, even from you."

Carr nodded. "I know," he said. "But you needn't worry about me. Since the situation with Dermot, I've been forced to face some unpleasant things."

"Like what?"

"I should not have done what I did to Andromeda," Carr replied, though it was difficult to admit it. "I do not know why I did it, only that my emotions had the better of me. But she is your responsibility now, and I understand that."

"Exactly." Tristan paused before continuing. "Carr, what were you so angry about when she came here? You know it was not her choice. She did not come simply to annoy you."

Carr inhaled deeply, thoughtfully, as he pondered the question. "If you truly wish to know, I will tell you."

"Go on."

Carr fixed him in the eye. Those lies he was running from, something he'd never spoken of, had been heavily on his mind during his time in the vault. Now that he was released, his resolve to face them hadn't wavered.

It was time for the old lies to be exposed.

"I left Ireland some time ago," he said. "There was a reason for that. Aye, it was to serve the Marshal, because my clan had a treaty with him and I was part of the Irish contingent pledged to Pembroke, but there was more to it. I went willingly even though I had a wife and child."

"You seemed to enjoy serving the Marshal," Tristan said. "But I've been around you for some time, and I know you have female companions. We all know it. Is that why you did not want her here? Because she reminded you that you had a wife in Ireland?"

Carr shook his head. "She reminded me of my wife, but not in the way you think," he said. "I came to Ireland to get away from Brigid."

"Why?"

"Because Andromeda is not my child, Tristan."

Tristan looked at him in shock. That wasn't the answer he'd been expecting, so it hit him rather hard. "Oh, God…" he muttered, suddenly understanding why Carr should be so bitter toward her. "And… and you know this for certain?"

Carr ducked when another projectile flew overhead, waiting until it cleared the wall and didn't hit anyone before continuing. "Because my wife did not wish to marry me," he said. "We were forced together by two clans who wanted the bloodlines merged. The hope was that Brigid would bear a son to continue the cause. But she loved another. She was pregnant when I married her."

Tristan was caught up in the story. "And you knew this before you married her?"

Carr nodded. "I did," he said. "But, like me, she had little choice."

"Then who is her father?"

"My brother, Muir."

Tristan had to make a conscious effort to keep his jaw from dropping. "He and your wife were in love?"

Carr nodded. "My brother was already married, you see, so my father insisted that I wed Brigid," he said. "When the opportunity presented itself to come to England with the Marshal, I took it. My wife loved my brother, her daughter was being raised by English lords, and there was nothing left for me. So I came to England to forget. I nearly had until Andromeda showed up at Wrexham."

Tristan felt genuine pity for the man. "It makes sense now," he said. "Your behavior makes complete sense. Truthfully, I had no idea who you were anymore. You turned into someone I did not recognize with your vicious behavior toward Andie, which made little sense because you'd spoken of her before and you seemed… proud. That is what was so odd about this. I always thought you were proud of her."

Carr shrugged. "I *am* proud of her bloodlines," he said. "But they are not mine. I've spent nineteen years pretending my niece is really my daughter, Pat. That is a hard way to live."

Tristan could only imagine the depth of truth to that statement. "Andie must not know," he said. "She has never said anything about it."

Carr shook his head. "She does not know," he said. "I doubt it would do any good to tell her. Let her think what she will. Let her hate me, because it is better than her knowing the truth."

Just as he said that, a hook landed on the top of the crenellation directly above them. Tristan and Carr leapt up to dislodge it, sending it crashing back the way it had come. Tristan dared to take a peek over the end, only to see that the grappling hook, the man who had tossed it, and the archer behind him had tumbled back down to the ground.

Tristan slapped Carr on the shoulder in a gesture of victory, but more hooks were flying over the wall further down the line, so he had to pull himself away from the conversation with Carr and make his way back down the wall, urging the men to throw the anchors back where they came from. Off to his right, he could see Kieran coming out of one of the towers with a body over his enormous shoulders. Tristan could see, even at a distance, that Alexander had used considerable skill in gutting the Irishman.

Even the soldiers drew back at the sight.

Alexander, in fact, was right behind Kieran, and when there was a break in the flying arrows, he helped Kieran throw the body over the side. When Alexander and Kieran started yelling at the horrified Welsh below, the soldiers on the wall picked up the cry, and a booming sound of terror lifted to the sky. It was a cry of madness, momentarily stunning the Welsh. The English clapped each other in encouragement, feeling as if they'd somehow accomplished something by tossing that sad body over the side and frightening their opponent.

But the Welsh came back with a vengeance.

Tristan happened to be looking at Carr when the man was hit by two bolts in quick succession. One hit him in the shoulder and one in the chest, and he toppled backward, flipping over the side of the wall and crashing down about twenty feet below.

Tristan went on the run.

He had to run past Kieran and Alexander in order to get to the stairs that led to the bailey. Alexander, seeing that Tristan was running in a panic, ordered Kieran to stay on the wall as he followed Tristan down the stairs and across the bailey, where Carr was lying on his side. The man was unconscious but alive, so between Tristan and Alexander, they picked him up and carried him into the great hall, which was slowly filling up with the wounded. There was a male servant at the hall entrance, and he directed Tristan to set Carr down near the smoking hearth.

Carr was starting to come around.

"Easy, lad," Tristan said. "You're in the great hall. We'll find help for you."

Carr was only half-conscious, struggling to open his eyes, as Tristan looked to the hovering male servant.

"Who do you have to tend these men?" he asked.

"Me. I am tending them," a female voice answered.

Tristan heard the words before he saw his wife, but the moment he laid eyes on her, he felt a surge of shock run through him. He bolted to his feet just as Andromeda walked up to him, wiping her hands on her apron, which was bloodied.

His eyes bulged.

"*What* are you doing here?" he demanded, trying not to shout. "You're supposed to be in the keep, safely locked up."

Andromeda didn't rise to his anger. She had known this moment would inevitably come, so she was prepared. She simply smiled at him, disarming him as she knew it would, and stood on her toes to kiss him.

"Is that the greeting I am given after not having seen you in several days?" she said, her pale eyes glimmering warmly at him. "I thought it would have been kinder than that."

Tristan didn't know what to do. He wanted to spank her, hug her, or yell at her—or possibly all three—but he ended up putting his arms around her and pulling her against him. After having not touched her for ten days, it was something of a spiritual experience. In fact, tears stung his eyes as he wallowed in the feel of her, the smell of her. For a brief moment, his control slipped and he allowed himself to feel his exhaustion and his fear. Exhaustion in the situation, fear for his wife.

But that moment was over quickly.

"You are not supposed to be here," he said, releasing her and standing back. "You promised to stay to the keep."

She nodded patiently. "That was before the hall started filling up with wounded," she said, looking at the bodies lying around. "I had to come. The men needed help."

"But you—"

She cut him off. "Pat, you have no surgeon," she said, more firmly. "The servants were down here doing what they could, but these men needed care and attention. That is what I have been doing—stitching holes, cleaning wounds, and giving comfort where I can."

His jaw twitched, indicative of his level of emotion. "But I want you in the keep."

She shook her head. "And I must help your men," she said. "It is my duty. This is war, and we must all be brave in times like this. Would you really send me back to the keep like a precious princess, protected from the ills of the world and as fragile as a lamb? Or do you want a wife who stands alongside you and helps you when it matters the most? Make your choice now so I know how you intend to diminish my dedication."

He stared at her, preparing for a verbal lashing, but he simply couldn't do it. She was brave and strong, and he honestly couldn't berate her for it. In fact, he probably would have been disappointed had she been any less. With a heavy—if not ironic—sigh, he shook his head in defeat.

"Where are the men I sent to guard you?" he asked. "Did

you at least bring them? Or did you lock them in a room somewhere while you are down here, cavorting about?"

Andromeda fought off a grin. "They are all around the hall, helping as well," she said, pointing to Dolan on the far end of the room. "Do not be so smug next time you ask me a question like that. I know you want me to be safe, so naturally, I brought them with me. And I do not cavort."

Tristan was very nearly sneering at her by the time she was finished. That confident, bold, and sometimes bossy woman that he loved with all his heart. He had absolutely nothing to say to her after that, because she had an answer for everything, and his frustration knew no limits. Behind her, he caught sight of Alexander, who was trying very hard not to laugh. When their eyes met, Alexander threw up his hands in surrender.

"Do not ask me anything about the control of women," he said. "You know whom I married. My wife was a spy before I married her, and a more determined, headstrong woman you will never meet. Therefore, I cannot help you, Pat. You are going to have to figure this out on your own."

Andromeda smiled at Alexander. "I am looking forward to meeting your wife someday," she said. "I think that we could be friends."

Alexander chuckled. "Lady de Royans, I *know* it," he said. "Christin will love you. Now, if you will excuse me, I must return to the wall. Are you coming, Pat?"

Tristan waved him off. "I will be there in a moment," he said. As Alexander headed out of the hall, Tristan's gaze was soft on Andromeda. "If you are going to help the wounded, then please stay in the hall. Do not go out into the bailey, because the Welsh are shooting bolts over the walls. And if the command comes to seal up the hall, you will do so without question. Am I clear on this?"

She nodded as she went to him, her fingers looping into his. "Of course," she said. "But why would it need to be sealed?"

"If the Welsh make it over the wall."

"But the walls are very tall. How can they do this?"

He didn't want to tell her about the ladders or the bombardment on the gatehouse. He simply bent down to kiss her and took strength from it.

"Strange things happen at a moment's notice," he said vaguely. "Just keep everyone in here—and you stay in here, please. There is too much happening out there that could kill you."

"I understand."

"Good," he said, giving her a wink. "I must return."

Andromeda force a smile, blowing him a kiss as he turned for the door. She turned for her patient at the same time, suddenly realizing it was her father as he lay there and bled on the floor.

Tristan was halfway to the hall entry when he heard her gasp. Concerned, he turned to see that she was backing away from Carr. Tristan returned to her, grasping her by the arms because she nearly backed into him.

"What is wrong?" he asked.

Andromeda had a strange look on her face. "*Him,*" she breathed. "I… I do not think I can help him."

Tristan recalled the conversation he had with Carr not a half-hour before, a conversation where many revelations were brought into the light. He was quite aware that Andromeda knew none of them and was, in fact, still in the mindset that her father was her enemy. The last time she saw him, he had been rough with her. Though Tristan understood Carr's perspective now, it didn't absolve him from being brutal with Andromeda.

But he couldn't tell her what Carr had told him.

That was a secret he would never reveal.

"Listen to me," he said, turning her to face him. "Carr has been working hard to keep the Welsh from taking possession of Wrexham. I would consider it a personal favor if you would tend his wounds. He also fell from the wall walk, so he may have more injuries than those you see. He needs help."

She looked at him sharply. "How can you ask me that?" she hissed. "You know what happened the last time I saw him!"

He nodded patiently. He wasn't without sympathy. "I know," he said. "But he is injured. Time in the vault… it has changed him. He is sorry for what he did. He told me so. Mayhap if you tend his wound, you will give him the time he needs to apologize to you, too."

"But—"

"Will you ruin a chance to make peace with him?" Tristan interrupted softly. "Please do not disappoint me, Andie. I know you are made of better stuff than that."

She was still frowning, but at least she wasn't refusing any longer. She was simply standing there, eyeing her father, and Tristan kissed her on the cheek.

"I must go," he said gently. "Please, Andie… do the right thing. Sometimes bravery is not about facing your fears. Sometimes it is about facing things we simply do not want to face. It is about being the bigger person and showing that you are a woman of honor."

She sighed and looked at him. "When you put it like that, how can I resist?"

He smiled. "You cannot," he said. He tilted his head in Carr's direction. "Do what you can, my lady. I know he is in good hands."

With that, he headed out of the hall, for good this time, leaving Andromeda to take a deep breath and focus. Tristan had asked her to forget and forgive, so she would try. He was so fiercely protective that she knew he wouldn't ask her unless he had a good reason to do so.

She was going to have to trust him.

She called to Flora, who was walking among the wounded, carrying a bowl of very watered wine with a cup for those who were thirsty. When Flora came near, she asked the woman to find a couple of strong male servants, because her father had two arrows sticking out of him, and Andromeda had learned the hard way that they were difficult to remove. When she first came down to the hall, she'd caused a man unnecessary pain trying to remove one. Flora handed over the bowl of watered wine and cup to Andromeda before going in search of male servants. When she was gone, Andromeda knelt down beside her father.

"Carr?" she said softly. "Can you hear me?"

Carr's eyes fluttered open and moved in her direction. When he finally saw that she was kneeling down beside him, he sighed faintly and closed his eyes again.

"Andie," he muttered thickly. "What are you doing here, lass?"

Andromeda waved over a female servant, who came bearing rags and hot water and a flask of wine. As the woman crouched on the other side of Carr, Andromeda began peeling back his layers of protection to get a look at the damage.

"I am the wife of the garrison commander," she said. "It is my duty to tend the wounded. Even you. Are you in much pain?"

He grunted. "Enough."

"Can you breathe?"

"I've been better."

Andromeda had to call for a knife so she could cut away his tunic, but he had a mail coat underneath it that was providing a substantial barrier.

"I'm going to have to have someone help me with your mail," she finally told him. "I must remove it so I can see how badly you're injured. Mayhap you'd better take some wine. It might help with the pain."

She poured some of the wine into the cup and helped him lift his head. He drained the entire cup, though some of it ran down his chin as he smacked his lips. When he laid his head back down, it was wearily, as if it had taken everything out of him simply to lift his head.

"Thank you," he said, his eyes opening again as he fixed on her. "You are kind. I do not deserve it."

Andromeda could feel her emotions starting to rise again, but she fought them. "Nay, you do not," she said. "But I promised Pat that I would help you, so I am. I will do my best."

Carr didn't say anything, but he continued to look at her. Andromeda gazed back at him, waiting for him to say something more, but he didn't. He simply looked at her.

"What is it?" she asked, lifting her eyebrows. "Why are you looking at me?"

Carr shook his head weakly before closing his eyes. As a couple of male servants came over to help her get the mail off and remove the bolts, Carr suddenly spoke up.

"I do not expect forgiveness," he said. "I will not ask for it. But know that I am… regretful for the things I've done. What I've said to you. I wasn't angry at you, lass. It was something quite different."

He turned his head away from her, and Andromeda sat there for a moment, feeling a stab of... something. Sadness? Forgiveness? Anger? She wasn't sure, to be honest. All she knew was that Carr's words made her feel something. She wasn't sure she liked it, but there was nothing she could do about it at the moment. He needed help, and she'd promised to give it, so she was prepared.

The male servants were on either side of Carr. One was standing immediately to her left, the other one directly across. She explained what needed to be done, removing the mail coat and then removing the bolts, but the servant directly across from her pointed out that they needed to remove the bolts before they could remove the mail. The bolts were literally pinning the mail to Carr's body. Andromeda saw the logic of it and agreed, so the plan was to remove both bolts quickly, pull Carr into a sitting position, and then pull the mail coat over his head.

Everyone took their positions.

The servant across from her had his hands on the bolt sticking out of Carr's shoulder. That was to be the first one. She instructed the servant standing next to her to hold Carr still so he wouldn't move around and hurt himself. But the servant didn't move, nor did he obey her instructions. Puzzled, she looked up to see why he hadn't obeyed, only to be confronted with something she hoped she would never see again.

Dermot was looking down at her.

And he had a dagger.

CHAPTER TWENTY-TWO

HIDING HADN'T BEEN the difficult part.

The difficult part had been getting close to Andromeda.

Dermot had been working covertly since he'd been a boy because that was what his family demanded. The *Aingil Lochlainn* took all of their young men, at a very young age, and trained them to be spies and more. That was all he knew.

That was why he knew what to do when he managed to shake the English knights.

De Wolfe and his friend had been young, arrogant, and too trusting. Dermot was counting on that. He had been able to fool them in the end and escape, rushing back to Wrexham Castle and gaining admittance before the three duped knights could return and spread the news that Dermot was a traitor. He'd made it back and gone straight into hiding.

Someplace they would never find.

He'd been able to remain there for ten long days.

Of course, he'd been stealing food. He'd had to. Scraps were all he'd been able to find as he hid in the rafters of the pigsty. No one would think of looking for him there, and he had access to the food and water for the animals, so although his diet had been limited, it had afforded him a place to hide and plan.

Plan for what was coming next.

The Welsh had attacked, as far as he could tell, the day he went into hiding. Dermot had been around enough battles in his lifetime to know the sounds of them. The pigsty was in part of the stable, a corner of it reserved for the pigs that fed the castle. The most anyone did was come to feed them and make sure they had water, and since he was in the rafters overhead, no one bothered to look up.

For a time, he was safe.

But he knew he couldn't spend all of his time hiding in those rafters. At some point, he was going to have to come out and reveal himself. At the very least, he intended to escape, but not without insurance.

Andromeda was that insurance.

It was going to be tricky leaving the castle with her, especially with Tristan providing a very large barrier between him and freedom. He knew Tristan well enough to know that the man would not give up at all, which meant Dermot was going to have to establish some rules for Tristan when it came to Andromeda. He knew Tristan would not want her to be harmed in any way, which meant he would be willing to negotiate.

That was going to be Dermot's only saving grace.

Of course, there was the question as to why he had returned to the castle in the first place. He could have simply kept running, and by now, he would have already been in Ireland. But he had been sent to follow Carr mac Murda for a reason those years ago, and to simply flee would have been to shirk his duties. At least, that was how his kin would look at it. He had spent a very long time in the service of William Marshal, not something to be given up on so swiftly.

He still had work to do.

That work revolved around Andromeda. On his ninth day of hiding, he dared to emerge from the rafters after the pigs had been fed. He removed nearly every scrap of clothing he was wearing, his expensive protection and tunics bearing the scarlet lion of William Marshal. All of that was buried underneath one of the pig troughs, with the exception of a thin linen tunic, his boots and breeches, and a very long and very sharp dagger.

Since the castle was under siege, there weren't people milling about in the stable yard as there would normally be. There were bolts flying over the castle wall, so most people had taken cover. Dermot was able to stand at the stable door and watch the activity without being seen, and it helped him understand what was going on. It also helped him plan what he needed to do.

While in the stable, he noticed some clothing hanging on a peg near the door. He was able to steal it, nothing more than a long and dirty tunic and an oil cloak. His beard had grown in somewhat, which helped in disguising him, but he knew he would still be recognized in his current state. Therefore, using the water barrel as a mirror of sorts, he soaked his hair in the water and used his dagger to shave his head. Chunks of brown hair fell into the water and sank to the bottom. In short order, he was completely bald.

It changed his appearance dramatically.

The tenth day was when he decided to move. The battle seemed to be diminishing, which meant the Welsh would soon be leaving, and the castle, at some point, would be open. It would be his opportunity to depart with his hostage. Based on his extensive experience with sieges, the lady of the castle could only be in one of two places—either she was locked up in the keep or she was helping the wounded. Since there were some wounded in the hall, because Dermot had seen a few being moved in that direction, he decided to check there first. If she wasn't there, he'd have to figure out a way to get into the keep.

With his bald head and his worn tunic, and partial growth of beard, Dermot tossed on the oil cloak and headed out into the yard. He stuck close to the buildings and away from the open space where the bolts were landing. They seemed to be coming in waves, so he waited until another barrage died down before running from the yard and into the main bailey. Once there, he pressed himself against the western side of the great hall and made his way toward the servants' entrance.

It was dark and smoky in the hall. It smelled of dirty bodies and festering wounds. There were a few servants around, but they were busy tending the wounded. In fact, he was able to stay back in the entrance alcove, concealed from the room, as he searched for the lady in question. He didn't see her at first, but the day was still young. He wasn't going to head to the keep until he was sure the lady wasn't tending the wounded. At this point, something told him to simply wait, and he did. Things were quiet at the moment, so there was no need for him to do anything other than wait.

In the end, it had been the right thing to do.

As he lingered in the servants' alcove, he began to hear voices approaching the door. Startled, he slipped out into the hall and concealed himself under one of the three heavy feasting tables. He was shielded from the room by benches and table legs, and it was with some glee that he realized Andromeda and two female servants had been the voices he'd heard. As he watched, Andromeda and her servants entered the hall, carrying supplies with them.

Finally… she was here.

From his vantage point, Dermot could watch her as she worked on the wounded in the hall. More men were brought in, almost all with some kind of arrow wound, and she tended them calmly and kindly. She had a smile for the men who were in pain or frightened. She was kind to them, even sweet when she smoothed the brow of a very young man who had broken his leg in a fall.

In that action, Dermot saw the queen before him. Regal and gentle, a woman descended from the last King of Dublin who would have made a magnificent queen. The *Aingil Lochlainn* wanted her to breed with one of their own, and, truthfully, she would bear magnificent sons. Then all of Ireland would be one step closer to home rule, without the English trying to invade their shores and take lands and power that didn't belong to them. William Marshal, the very man that Dermot served, was one of those men.

But a woman like Lady Andromeda… she could help the Irish cause immensely.

If he could only get her back to Ireland.

Dermot was counting on the fact that the battle was waning. He knew there would be no chance to take her from the gatehouse, so he would have to plan on the postern gate between the stable yard and the kitchen yard. It was heavily fortified, with a small wooden bridge that spanned the moat, but Dermot was certain that bridge had long since been burned away. That simply meant that he and his captive would have to swim the moat.

Swim or die.

Was it foolish? Absolutely. But his precarious situation was forcing him into a risky decision. If he could only use the battle as a distraction, he could remove the lady while Tristan was fighting the Welsh. He was tired, and hungry, and he had to salvage what this situation had become. He couldn't let so many years of watching Carr or William Marshal go to waste. He thought he'd been able to wrest the lady away when Carr agreed to a betrothal, but that had fallen apart. But now… now was his chance to take her once and for all.

He couldn't go back to Ireland empty-handed.

More men were being brought into the great hall. Because of Dermot's position beneath a table, away from the doors, he couldn't see that the Welsh had surged. He couldn't see the dozens of bolts hitting the bailey, though he could hear it faintly on the slate roof overhead. At least, he could hear the noise, but because he was tucked underneath a heavy table, he wasn't sure what, exactly, he was hearing.

As the day progressed, Carr was brought in by Tristan and Alexander. They carried the man between him, and Dermot could see that he had two bolts sticking out of him. They dropped him gently near the hearth, and Andromeda came away from the men she'd been tending when she saw Tristan, who didn't seem entirely delighted to see her. She and Tristan had a few words, but in the end, Tristan hugged her tightly and all seemed right with the world again. When Tristan left, Dermot came out from underneath the table.

It was time.

Hood of the cloak over his shaved head, Dermot went to stand next to the lady as another male servant hovered over Carr. There were a few servants standing around them, so Dermot simply blended in with the group. Andromeda was completely oblivious to his presence, and with great stealth, he pulled out the dagger he'd brought with him. She was discussing the need to remove the bolts from Carr's chest and his mail, and it was decided, by necessity, that the bolts needed to go first. Andromeda asked for assistance with it, but when Dermot didn't respond to her request, she turned to look at him in puzzlement, and he put the dagger against her left armpit.

"Scream out and I shall push this blade into your body," he said in a low, steady voice. "Do you understand me?"

Andromeda's eyes widened. "Der—"

He jabbed her with the dagger, and she yelped softly. "I told you not to speak," he growled. Grabbing her by the left arm, he pulled her to her feet. "Stand up, my lady. Be a good lass."

Andromeda was stiff in his arms. "What are you doing?" she said. "You cannot take me anywhere there are not a dozen soldiers. You cannot even get into the keep."

Dermot snorted softly. "I can go anywhere I wish," he said. "You are my key."

He was trying to pull her away, but she was reluctant to go. "Look around," she whispered loudly. "These men are injured and I must help them. I cannot go anywhere with you."

"You'll go or I'll cut you to pieces."

He meant every word of it.

ᴄᴕ

DERMOT DIDN'T LOOK like the man she'd known.

Truthfully, the only way Andromeda knew it was Dermot was because of his eyes—he had very distinctive eyes that were green with a brown ring, so that was how she identified him. He looked filthy and desperate, and she knew he'd been hiding for almost two weeks, so his mental, and physical, state couldn't be very solid.

She could see madness in the depths of those bloodshot eyes.

But he was carrying a weapon, something that put him at an advantage, but only for a moment. Andromeda knew she couldn't go anywhere with him because she most likely would never make it out alive, so her sense of survival kicked in as she faced the edgy knight. She was surrounded by wounded men and servants who would cower in a fight, but over at the other side of the hall, Dolan and his men were helping feed some of the wounded. That meant she had to fight Dermot long enough for Dolan to come to her aid.

She had to get away from that knife.

She had to survive.

Rapidly, she assessed her surroundings. The male servant was still next to her father, who was more than likely unconscious at this point. She couldn't be sure. There was a small but sturdy bowl of watered wine at her feet, but that was about all. Nothing much to defend herself with except what she had on her body, which was clothing.

But she had her hands.

And feet.

… and knees.

Dermot had her by the arm with the dagger pointed at her left breast at this point. She put her hands up in surrender.

"Very well," she said quietly. "I'll go. But may I at least help my father?"

Dermot didn't like that answer. He looked to Carr as Andromeda moved so she was essentially facing Dermot. He still had the dagger pointed at her, but because she had moved, the dagger was now pointed at her arm. Her question had given Dermot enough pause that she could get into position.

She'd had to do this very same thing once or twice when she was working at the tavern in Ruabon.

No fear.

Without another word, Andromeda brought her right knee up, straight into Dermot's crotch. It was hard and swift, and he dropped the dagger and doubled over as Andromeda jumped back, grabbed the wooden bowl of watered wine, and smashed it over his head. Dermot started to go down as she tried to bolt out of the way, but he took hold of her skirt, and she ended up slipping on the watered wine that had splashed all over the floor.

Andromeda started screaming as both she and Dermot went down in a heap.

The man assisting her with Carr leapt to his feet and rushed to help, but Dermot saw him coming. The dagger hadn't fallen far—in fact, it had fallen under Andromeda's skirt, and he saw it, grabbed it, and stabbed the servant in the thigh with it. As the man yelped and toppled over, nearly falling onto Carr, the commotion roused Dolan and his comrades across the hall.

They came running.

Meanwhile, Dermot had the dagger. He slashed at Andromeda's leg, stabbing at her, and managed to catch her in the ankle. She screamed and kicked him, as hard as she could, in the head, which stunned him enough to release his grip on her. But the floor was wet, and she was trying to get up, slipping, trying to get away from him, as Dermot launched himself at her. He landed on her legs and her back, and Andromeda went forehead-first into the stone floor.

She went out in an instant.

Now with an unconscious lady underneath him, Dermot lifted the dagger again, but Dolan and his men were on him.

Dermot was a trained knight and knew how to fight in hand-to-hand combat, but he couldn't do that and keep his prize of the lady. He tried to grab her, to put the dagger against her throat so the others would back off, but Dolan grabbed his wrist, and Dermot ended up dragging the blade across her neck. As Andromeda fell back to the floor, bleeding streams of bright red blood from the gash on her neck, Dolan and his scouts struggled to restrain Dermot.

But Dermot was in a panic.

He punched and kicked and fought, trying to shake four men who were restraining him. Someone went running for Tristan as Flora, who had been watching the fight with horror, rushed over to Andromeda on the floor. Seeing the bloody neck, she began calling for bandages. Servants were scrambling to find some.

"Here." A raspy voice came from behind Flora. A hand was holding out boiled bandages. "Use these. She left them beside me."

Flora looked up to see Carr beside her. The man was ghostly pale, still with two big bolts sticking out of him, and there was blood around his mouth. Shocked, she took the bandages from his outstretched hand.

"My lord, you should not be up," Flora said. "Please lie down!"

Carr didn't listen. He couldn't move very well, but he also couldn't lie there while Andromeda bled. He'd heard the fight, too dazed to do anything about it, and it had taken an extreme effort to sit up and gather the bandages that Andromeda had left beside him. He'd never done much for her in her entire life, but he figured that he could do this.

He could help her when she truly needed it.

When he'd fallen from the wall, he'd landed on his right side. He knew he had broken ribs and a broken arm, and probably greater damage than that because he felt so weak, but his left arm still worked. He helped Flora roll Andromeda onto her back, carefully, to assess the damage on her neck. Dermot had sliced her fairly good, so he had Flora put the bandage over the wound and apply gentle pressure. Anything more and it might choke her, so Flora was very careful. Blood still ran down Andromeda's neck and into her hair, but Carr didn't think anything vital had been severed. If it had been, she would have been dead by now.

On the other hand, he was feeling quite terrible himself. Perhaps getting up from his sickbed hadn't been the smartest thing to do, but he didn't regret it. It was becoming more difficult to breathe now, and his entire right side was screaming in pain. With Flora tending Andromeda, Carr attempted to make it back to his pallet but ended up collapsing on the floor just short of it. As he lay there on his side, he could see Dermot several feet away being restrained by Dolan and his men.

But the dagger Dermot had used on Andromeda was lying between them.

Slowly, Carr crawled toward it. Someone was begging him to lie back down so his wounds could be tended, but he wasn't listening. He was crawling to that dagger as the servant who had been stabbed in the thigh stood beside him, begging him to go back to his bed. Carr ignored the man, crawling far enough that he was able to collect the dagger. Then he pushed himself to his knees. He covered the rest of the distance between himself and Dermot in a kneeling position, as if he was doing penitence. For what he was about to do, he'd be begging forgiveness from God for the rest of his life.

But this had to end now.

Dermot didn't see him. He was on his back as Dolan and his men practically sat on him to control him. Carr rose up beside Dermot's supine body, dagger raised, and Dermot finally caught a glimpse of it as it was lifted right above his chest. He hardly had time to scream before Carr was bringing the blade down, straight into his heart. As quickly as the battle in the hall started, it was over, as Dermot fell dead.

And Carr fell down right beside him.

Also dead.

It was finished.

When Tristan finally rushed into the hall just a minute or two later, he came onto quite a scene. Dermot was dead on the floor with a dagger in his heart, Carr was lying next to him with two enormous bolts sticking out of him, and Andromeda was about ten feet away, unconscious with a bloody rag over her neck.

Tristan couldn't help the gasp of horror from his lips when he saw her. Alexander, Addax, and William were behind him, and when Tristan ran to Andromeda with Addax at his side, Alexander looked over the scene with horror.

"What in the hell happened?" he demanded of anyone who could answer.

It was Dolan who stood up from his crouched position over Dermot. "I am not entirely sure, my lord," he said. "We were tending soldiers on the other end of the hall and the lady started screaming. She was fighting Sir Dermot, and by the time we got here, the fighting had rendered her unconscious. Sir Dermot tried to cut her throat, but we were able to prevent him from killing her. But Sir Carr… with his great wounds, he was still concerned for his daughter. He tried to help her before using Sir

Dermot's own dagger to kill him."

Alexander's concerned gaze moved over to Tristan, who was weeping as he and Addax inspected the injury to her neck. He could see Addax patting Tristan on the shoulder, trying to give him some comfort, telling him that the gash wasn't too bad. The lady would live. But the news that Carr had killed Dermot, for his daughter, no less, was shocking, indeed.

Perhaps the man had finally found his honor in the end.

The fact remained, however, that they were still dealing with ladders against the walls. The Welsh were still trying to get in, even though the body of the Irishman had slowed them somewhat. The news of the horrific torture injuries must have spread, because the Welsh had cleared away from the gatehouse entirely. But they were still at the wall, and they were still a threat.

And that gave Alexander an idea.

He looked over at Tristan and Addax, knowing that Tristan would be occupied while he tended his wife. He didn't blame him in the least. But Alexander was the veteran of countless battles and sieges, and he knew how to end this one fairly quickly. But he needed the help of two dead Irishmen. He didn't think Carr would mind if it spared his daughter's life, and Dermot… well, Alexander didn't care what he thought.

It was of little consequence now.

"De Wolfe," he said to William. "Take Carr and Dermot outside. And get that knife out of Dermot's chest. I will have need of it."

William looked at him curiously. "What are you going to do?"

Alexander looked at the young knight. "We've been given a gift," he said. "Carr and Dermot have sacrificed themselves so the rest of us may live, and we will honor them. This is what military tactics are all about, my son. Carr and Dermot are going to end this siege."

William still had no idea what Alexander was talking about, but he soon found out.

About a half-hour later, one body, carved in the *Blodörn* fashion, was tossed over the wall, specifically on top of the Welsh who were still trying to gain a foothold. The second body, carved in the same fashion, was posted at the damaged section of the drawbridge as a warning to all who would try to breach the gatehouse of Wrexham. It made the entire castle look like a house of horrors.

To many of the Welsh, it was too much of a bad omen.

It was indicative of what waited inside for them.

Not strangely, they were gone by morning. When word got around as to what the men inside of Wrexham were doing to the bodies of their enemies, the *Aingil Lochlainn* discovered that all three of those gruesome bodies had been Irish. It was enough to send them back to Ireland, never to return again.

In death, Carr did what he could never do in life—he saved Andromeda.

And that was how he would be remembered.

EPILOGUE

Nine months later
Westminster Palace
London

"AND WITH THIS honor, I bestow upon you the Earldom of Wrexham." The young boy of twelve years was quite solemn. "May you serve with distinction, Lord Wrexham. Lord Pembroke? You have more to say?"

He turned to William Marshal, who had been standing beside him in the fine throne room of Westminster Palace. It smelled of incense and wood and smoke, of all things timeless that were the very cornerstone of English tradition. Tristan was on his knees in front of the young king, looking rather uncomfortable at all of the accolades hurled in his direction. His head was lowered, but off to his right, he could see Andromeda standing there, resplendent in a gown of blue velvet, a fabric new to England that had come all the way from Genoa. She was smiling proudly as Alexander, Addax, Bric, and Peter de Lohr stood near her in their best regalia.

Also present at the ceremony were Christopher de Lohr, Earl of Hereford, and Julian de Velt, brother of Cole de Velt, lord of the de Velt empire. Julian and Tristan were old friends, and Julian had made the trek down from the Scottish borders to be present at this momentous occasion. Last but not least were Tristan's father and brother, Juston and Ashton.

Juston, perhaps, looked the proudest of all.

With all of these very special people witnessing the ceremony that took Tristan de Royans from a mere knight to a powerful earl, and acknowledged him as the uncle to the reigning king, the Marshal came forward with a piece of vellum in his hand. He opened it, reading the words in his deep and steady voice.

It was the voice of England.

"Your uncle, Philip of France, has granted you the title Duc de Lorraine," he said. "He has sent a missive, for you personally, that details your lands and holdings. As the nephew of the King of France, you are entitled to these holdings, and they are prestigious ones. But let us continue to discuss your English honors—you shall also be given the title Guardian of the Realm and the Earl of Dublin. Because of your wife's Irish lineage, this makes her the Countess of Dublin, something that is her right and her due. Congratulations, my lord. You are now richer and more powerful than I am."

The chamber, which was full of courtiers, advisors, and fighting men, broke out in applause as Tristan looked up at the Marshal, an embarrassed smile across his lips. He hated being the center of attention.

"Thank you, my lord," he said. "I think."

The Marshal chuckled, motioning for the man to rise. Tristan stood up, taking the missive that the Marshal offered him before looking over to his wife, who was nearly bursting with joy. But she looked as if she was fairly bursting these days as it was, with her visibly pregnant belly encased in the lovely blue dress.

Tristan had never seen her more beautiful.

"You and I will have a long conversation about your new titles and lands, Pat," the Marshal said. "As Guardian of the Realm, that is a title tantamount to my own. I think that, between you and I, we can make England stronger than ever. You've proven yourself time and time again. It is time you reaped the reward and take your place amongst the great titled lords of England."

Tristan nodded, but it was with reluctance. "That is what my father said," he said. "In fact, I should go speak with him before he grows impatient. We will speak soon, my lord, I promise."

The Marshal's gaze lingered on him a moment. "I do not give many people permission to do this, but I shall give it to you," he said. "You may address me by my name. There is no need for formalities between us any longer, Pat."

Tristan smiled faintly, genuinely touched by the gesture. Of all of the tributes he'd received since his arrival in London a short time ago, this was perhaps one of the most significant. He put his hand over his heart in gratitude.

"Thank you, William," he said. "I am honored."

As William snorted softly and turned away, back to a young king who was eager to be told he had performed Tristan's ceremony flawlessly, Tristan crossed the room to where his father, brother, and wife were standing. The first person that greeted him was Ashton, who threw him a big hug and nearly squeezed the life from him.

"My brother, the earl," Ashton said with delight. "I'm very happy for you."

Tristan was rubbing his chest where Ashton had nearly crushed him. "I can tell," he said. "I may never be able to breathe again."

Ashton opened his mouth to reply, but Julian stopped him, embracing Tristan as strongly as Ashton had. "My father would have been so proud of you," Julian said, grinning at Tristan. "He knew what he had in you. He always said that if you were unleashed, it would have been a mighty thing to witness. Mayhap this is the start of that."

Tristan's expression grew soft with the memory of the great Jax de Velt. "I miss him, every day," he said. "Serving at Pelinom was a great privilege, Julian. I hope I reflect your father's training in everything I do."

Julian patted him on the cheek. "Of course you do," he said. "Cole and I will come to visit you at Wrexham once you've returned. We have much drinking and conversation to catch up on."

Before Tristan could answer, Juston stepped in and pushed Julian aside. He was tired of waiting. An enormous man who still kept his hair past his shoulders, tied back behind his head these days because his wife didn't like him looking like a barbarian, Juston de Royans had just celebrated his seventieth year on the earth. He was still very healthy and strong, and nothing short of an act of God would keep him from witnessing Tristan's ceremony. For a moment, he cupped Tristan's face and simply looked at him.

It was a poignant moment.

"I remember a very little boy coming to Bowes Castle and being eager to work," he said, his voice full of emotion. "Do you remember that moment? The first time we met?"

Tristan smiled at the man he loved deeply. "I do," he said. "I was so frightened. I'd spent my life quietly until I ended up at Bowes with fearsome knights, so I was absolutely petrified."

Juston smiled at the memory. "I know," he said. "But I also knew you had come with a purpose, and that was to learn to be the man you are today. Henry's seed may have given you life, Tristan, but you were my son. You will always be my son."

That made Tristan feel quite emotional. He put his hand over Juston's as the man still held his face. "Thank you, Papa," he murmured. "I would not be who I am without you."

Juston kissed him on the cheek before letting him go. "And now, you will soon have your own son," he said, turning to look at Andromeda. "A son who is the product of both English and Irish royal lines. He will be the finest knight the world has ever seen, and I cannot wait to train him myself."

Tristan snorted softly. "He should only be so fortunate," he said. "My children will grow up with something I lacked in my early childhood, and that is stability. The first time I ever had that was with you. But they also will grow up as the sons and daughters of the Earl of Wrexham and Dublin, and the grandchildren of the great Juston de Royans. That is a grand lot in life for any man."

"But they are also the bearers of royal blood," Juston said. "Irish kings and English kings. That is a rare and unique gift. It is too bad one of them will not rule."

"Rule where?" Tristan said. "Ireland? England? Even France? Pick your country, for I have a claim to all three now. But I suspect that royal blood is not the great blessing people think it is. Look at Henry and Richard and John."

Juston couldn't disagree. "True," he said. "But I still think *you* would have made a marvelous king. You are the monarch England needs but will never know."

"Do not say that too loudly. Henry is already nervous enough around me."

Juston laughed softly, patting Tristan's cheek as Andromeda came toward him. She had stayed away long enough and wanted to embrace her husband. Juston, Ashton, and Julian moved away, allowing the couple some time to be alone, which would be a rare moment on this day. A great feast was planned for this evening, and it promised to be a well-attended affair. All of the nobles in London had received invitations, and preparations were already in the works. Tristan had to admit that he was rather looking forward to it.

"The Earl of Wrexham and Dublin," Andromeda said, hugging him tightly. "I am so terribly proud of you, my love. How does it feel to finally be recognized as one of the great men in England?"

He loosened his grip on her, looking her in the eye. "Nothing feels different," he said. "I am the same man, only now I have a bit more power and money."

Andromeda rolled her eyes. "A *bit* more?" she said. "I would say a good deal more. I still think they should not have told you any of this before the ceremony. Think of the surprise it would have been!"

She grinned at him, that adorable gap-toothed smile that he cherished, and he was forced to laugh at her enthusiasm. "That is true," he said. "It would have been quite a surprise. But knowing it was coming gave me a chance to speak with the royal scholars about the town of Wrexham and learn something about it. In ancient times, it used to be called *Caer Fantell.* Remember I told you that I wanted to take the name of the earldom I was granted?"

"I do. We will be called Wrexham?"

He shook his head. “Nay,” he said. “I would like to use the ancient name. We will be known as de Royans-Fantell.”

Andromeda’s eyes lit up. “I like that,” she said. “And our standard?”

“A golden oak set within a crimson shield.”

She hugged him tightly. “Thank you, my love,” she said. “It will be the most prestigious standard in all of England. But what about the French property? You will use the same standard?”

“Of course,” he said. “In truth, I did not know about the Duc de Lorraine title. The Marshal kept that one from me. He must have written to Philip about me and the fact that I was to finally take my place among the great warlords. It seems my uncle in France wishes for me to take my place there as well.”

“And you should,” she said. “Your uncle is the king. Does it feel strange to acknowledge that openly?”

He grinned. “A little,” he said. “For most of my life, I was hidden because of my royal blood. But now, it only seems to bring me earldoms and admiration.”

With a laugh, Andromeda kissed him on the cheek, thrilled for her modest, noble husband who was truly humbled by all of the attention. In fact, she noticed that his friends were standing several feet away in conversation, but they kept glancing over at Tristan. She knew they wanted to congratulate him, but they also didn’t want to interrupt this special moment with his wife. They were all men she’d come to know and love, men who had risked themselves for her. In a small way, she, too, felt as if she was part of the Executioner Knights.

She owed them a debt she could never repay.

“You already had the admiration of your friends, you know,” she said after a moment. “I’m just sorry that William and Paris and Kieran could not join us.”

Tristan acknowledged that. "As am I," he said. "But someone had to remain in command of Wrexham when we came to London, and they volunteered."

"Are you sure they're not turning it into a notorious gambling establishment while we are away?"

He cocked an eyebrow. "They'd better not, or my first act as the Earl of Wrexham will be to strip them of their dignity and publicly humiliate them."

Andromeda laughed softly. "I was only jesting," she said. "They admire you too much to do such a thing. Hopefully the Welsh have remained quiet while we are in London."

Tristan shrugged. "They have been quiet since the battle that claimed your father's life."

She looked at him, her smile fading. "If they think you are going to do such terrible things to their dead, then they should stay away… shouldn't they?"

He met her gaze. She knew what they had done to the Irish rebel and ultimately to Carr and Dermot in order to weaken the Welsh resolve. She understood that, under the circumstances, it had been necessary to end a battle, and her father, in that regard, had given the ultimate sacrifice. She still didn't know what Carr had told Tristan—that he was not her real father—and Tristan had decided that was something he would never tell her, because her opinion of Carr had improved since his death. She understood her father's sacrifice at the end, and she respected him for it.

In Tristan's opinion, that was all she ever need know.

He thought Carr would have wanted it that way.

"They should," he said. "They think a madman is in command of Wrexham Castle, so let them think that. If it keeps them away, then I am happy to let them believe that I am quite mad."

Andromeda agreed. As they smiled at one another and Tristan kissed her cheek, Alexander and Addax and Peter finally joined them, crowding around Tristan and offering their felicitations. When others joined in—Christopher, Bric, Julian, and Ashton again—Andromeda wandered away, letting her husband have his moment with his friends, who were all so happy for his good fortune. She was standing near the throne that young Henry had sat upon when she heard someone clear their throat.

"Lady de Royans?"

She turned to see Henry standing behind her. He smiled timidly when their eyes met, and Andromeda dropped into a practiced curtsy.

"Your Grace," she said. "May I say that you did very well today? The ceremony was flawless."

Henry brightened. He was a short lad for his age, with blond hair that looked like straw and one droopy eye that was the trait of some of the Plantagenet males. But he was a good boy, trying to do good things, and part of those good things was embracing a bastard uncle who was greatly respected by the fighting men in England.

Young Henry, so far, was trying to make a difference.

"I have been practicing things like this," he admitted. "I do not do ceremonies often, but my tutors and my advisors have me practice so I do not fail."

"You did very well."

Henry nodded, but he seemed a little ill at ease. As if he wanted to say something more. He eyed Andromeda for a moment before finally summoning the courage to speak.

"I… I know that your grandfather was the King of Dublin,"

he said. "Did you know him?"

Andromeda shook her head. "I did not, Your Grace," she said. "He died before I was born."

"I see," Henry said. "Do you hope to go back to Ireland someday? Now that you're the Countess of Dublin, there is a castle that belongs to you. Lands, too, I think. Would you like to visit it?"

She nodded. "I would," she said, putting her hand on her swollen belly. "I would like my children to see where I was born. It is their heritage, too."

"Do you ever wish that you were queen?"

She laughed softly. "Nay, Your Grace," she said. "I will leave ruling countries to men like you. You are much better suited for it than I. Tristan feels the same way."

Henry looked over at Tristan standing with his friends, laughing and enjoying their company. "I hope he will spend time here in London with me," he said. "He is my uncle. I do not have any more uncles, at least not on my father's side."

"He will be a very good uncle, Your Grace," Andromeda said. "Do you know why?"

The boy shook his head. "Why?"

"Because he will love you for who you are, and he will always want the best for you."

That seemed to be a foreign concept to Henry, who had grown up with King John as his father. Even at his very young age, he understood politics. He understood the nature of men, or at least he tried to. An uncle who wanted the best for him was an odd thought, indeed.

But a good one.

As Andromeda watched the young king's expression as he tried to rationalize an uncle who wasn't out for his blood, a woman entered the throne room through the painted entry doors. Andromeda watched as the Marshal crossed the floor in the woman's direction, carrying on a brief conversation with her. She was an older woman, dressed in fine clothing, with a delicate wimple over her head.

As Andromeda watched the woman at a distance, Henry left her side and went over to the knights standing in a circle with Tristan. He seemed to want to be part of the group, and she smiled when she saw Tristan put his hand on the boy's shoulder in a show of kindly affection It was something Henry probably didn't know much of. As the knights were distracted with the young king, the Marshal caught Andromeda's attention and waved her over.

Politely, she complied.

"Lady de Royans," the Marshal said as she came near. "I should like to introduce you to someone. This is the Countess of Ponthieu. You may know her as Princess Alys."

Princess Alys.

Andromeda knew the name, and a bolt of shock ran through her. Eyes widening, she looked at the woman who was quite lovely and fragile-looking. Blonde hair peeked out from beneath her wimple, and she had eyes of the deepest blue. Fascinated, Andromeda studied her face for a moment, thinking that she saw a little of Tristan in the shape of her eyes.

"My lady," she said, dipping into a respectful curtsy. "It is a great honor to meet you. I did not know you were coming today."

The Marshal's dark eyes twinkled. "Give me the privilege of one more surprise for Pat," he said. "When I wrote to Philip about the titles to be conferred upon his nephew, he told Lady Ponthieu, who wrote and asked if she could attend. I took the liberty of welcoming her."

"Of course you did," Andromeda said. She couldn't help herself from reaching out and taking Alys' hand. "You are most welcome, my lady. I am so happy you are here."

Alys smiled timidly. "Thank you, my lady," she said. "I know it is irregular for me to ask to attend, but anyone who tried to keep me from my son is dead now, and I thought… I had hoped… that he would be agreeable to finally meeting me."

"He will be very happy to," Andromeda said, holding the woman's hand tightly. "I'm so sorry… sorry that you were kept from him. I know it was not your fault."

Alys' lips were trembling. "That is an old sorrow now," she said. "I will admit I thought of seeing him when John died, but time passed, and I thought that, mayhap, he would not want to see me after all. There is no reason to."

"There is every reason to," Andromeda insisted. "Will you come with me? I would like to introduce you."

Alys seemed nervous, and rightfully so. She could see a group of strong, tall men standing about, but she had no idea what her son might look like.

"Is he over there?" she asked.

Andromeda nodded, pointing to Tristan, who was standing next to Henry still. "He is wearing the dark blue tunic," she said. "The king is by his side. Do you see him there?"

Alys strained a little to get a good look at him, and when she did, her eyes grew moist. "I do," she whispered tightly. "Oh, I do. My God, he looks like Henry. But he also looks like my father. And he is so big!"

Andromeda smiled. "He's very strong," she said. "He's a warrior, something he has trained for all his life."

Alys watched Tristan as he said something humorous to a

man standing next to him. She watched him laugh. "I feared so for his life when he was born," she said. "But the Marshal has told me the path his life took. He is a knight, something quite noble and shining. Something far away from the world of his father and brothers. He escaped the curse."

Andromeda looked at her. "What curse, my lady?"

Alys shrugged weakly. "The curse of a battling family," she said. "Tristan does not hate his brothers. He does not hate his family. He has been trained and nurtured by people who taught him what I could not. Mayhap I did not wish to send him away from me, but in the end, it was best. What a fortunate man he has grown to be."

"I agree," Andromeda said softly. "Will you come with me? Please meet him. He will be very happy to know you."

Hesitantly, Alys allowed Andromeda to lead her over to where Tristan was standing with his friends. The Marshal, knowing it would be an emotional moment for all involved, motioned to Alexander, who moved the group away from Tristan. When they cleared away, Andromeda gently introduced Tristan to his mother, watching the man's features ripple with emotion—first shock, then disbelief, and finally awe.

So much awe.

And that was where Andromeda left them. She, too, wandered away so Tristan could be alone with the woman who had given birth to him. It was only right that they have that time together, she felt. Given the fact that she was due to give birth in a couple of months herself, she could hardly imagine being separated from a child she had grown in her belly, a child that was part of her and part of the man she loved. A child she was forced to surrender the moment he was born, only to see him again thirty-eight years later.

Perhaps that understanding gave Andromeda a little more insight than most when it came to a mother and her child, but she knew how important it must have been to Alys—and to Tristan—to finally see each other once again. When Andromeda saw Tristan kiss his mother's hand and finally embrace her, it was one of the most emotional things she had ever witnessed. It was the stuff dreams were made of.

And legends.

The joy on Tristan's face when he looked at his mother said it all. The next morning, when Alys awoke, there was a slip of vellum under her door with a poem written on it. At least, she thought it was a poem. She wasn't sure who had sent it until she mentioned it to Andromeda, and the woman told her that those little poems were the way Tristan expressed his emotion.

The poem he had written for his mother was about their reunion.

At dawn, the day awakes. Light touches the earth.
She came to me in the crystalline light,
Ere, she made such softly murmured words,
Joy in my heart but grew from an unholy night.

Alys slept with that yellowed piece of vellum under her pillow for the rest of her days. That awful little poem was the way Tristan showed his love, and it took a mother's love to see such beauty in the words.

And a wife's.

The man who should have been king loved, and was loved, more deeply than he could have ever imagined.

ꝏ THE END ꝏ

Children of Tristan and Andromeda
Keir
Daira
Kellan
Brendan
Erik
Devin
Riana
Morrigan
Kevin
Alys
Brigid

Kathryn Le Veque Novels

Medieval Romance:

De Wolfe Pack Series:
Warwolfe
The Wolfe
Nighthawk
ShadowWolfe
DarkWolfe
A Joyous de Wolfe Christmas
BlackWolfe
Serpent
A Wolfe Among Dragons
Scorpion
StormWolfe
Dark Destroyer
The Lion of the North
Walls of Babylon
The Best Is Yet To Be
BattleWolfe
Castle of Bones

De Wolfe Pack Generations:
WolfeHeart
WolfeStrike
WolfeSword
WolfeBlade
WolfeLord
WolfeShield
Nevermore
WolfeAx
WolfeBorn

The Executioner Knights:
By the Unholy Hand
The Mountain Dark
Starless
A Time of End
Winter of Solace
Lord of the Sky
The Splendid Hour
The Whispering Night
Netherworld
Lord of the Shadows
Of Mortal Fury
'Twas the Executioner Knight
Before Christmas
Crimson Shield

The de Russe Legacy:
The Falls of Erith
Lord of War: Black Angel
The Iron Knight
Beast
The Dark One: Dark Knight
The White Lord of Wellesbourne
Dark Moon
Dark Steel
A de Russe Christmas Miracle
Dark Warrior

The de Lohr Dynasty:
While Angels Slept
Rise of the Defender
Steelheart
Shadowmoor
Silversword
Spectre of the Sword

Unending Love
Archangel
A Blessed de Lohr Christmas
Lion of Twilight

The Brothers de Lohr:
The Earl in Winter

Lords of East Anglia:
While Angels Slept
Godspeed
Age of Gods and Mortals

Great Lords of le Bec:
Great Protector

House of de Royans:
Lord of Winter
To the Lady Born
The Centurion

Lords of Eire:
Echoes of Ancient Dreams
Blacksword
The Darkland

Ancient Kings of Anglecynn:
The Whispering Night
Netherworld

Battle Lords of de Velt:
The Dark Lord
Devil's Dominion
Bay of Fear
The Dark Lord's First Christmas
The Dark Spawn
The Dark Conqueror
The Dark Angel

Reign of the House of de Winter:
Lespada
Swords and Shields

De Reyne Domination:
Guardian of Darkness
The Black Storm
A Cold Wynter's Knight
With Dreams
Master of the Dawn

House of d'Vant:
Tender is the Knight (House of d'Vant)
The Red Fury (House of d'Vant)

The Dragonblade Series:
Fragments of Grace
Dragonblade
Island of Glass
The Savage Curtain
The Fallen One
The Phantom Bride

Great Marcher Lords of de Lara
Dragonblade

House of St. Hever
Fragments of Grace
Island of Glass
Queen of Lost Stars

Lords of Pembury:
The Savage Curtain

Lords of Thunder: The de Shera Brotherhood Trilogy
The Thunder Lord
The Thunder Warrior
The Thunder Knight

The Great Knights of de Moray:
Shield of Kronos

The Gorgon

The House of De Nerra:
The Promise
The Falls of Erith
Vestiges of Valor
Realm of Angels

Highland Warriors of Munro:
The Red Lion
Deep Into Darkness

The House of de Garr:
Lord of Light
Realm of Angels

Saxon Lords of Hage:
The Crusader
Kingdom Come

High Warriors of Rohan:
High Warrior
High King

The House of Ashbourne:
Upon a Midnight Dream

The House of D'Aurilliac:
Valiant Chaos

The House of De Dere:
Of Love and Legend

St. John and de Gare Clans:
The Warrior Poet

The House of de Bretagne:
The Questing

The House of Summerlin:
The Legend

The Kingdom of Hendocia:
Kingdom by the Sea

The BlackChurch Guild: Shadow Knights:
The Leviathan

Regency Historical Romance:
Sin Like Flynn: A Regency Historical Romance Duet
The Sin Commandments
Georgina and the Red Charger

Gothic Regency Romance:
Emma

Contemporary Romance:

Kathlyn Trent/Marcus Burton Series:
Valley of the Shadow
The Eden Factor
Canyon of the Sphinx

The American Heroes Anthology Series:
The Lucius Robe
Fires of Autumn
Evenshade
Sea of Dreams
Purgatory

Other non-connected Contemporary Romance:
Lady of Heaven
Darkling, I Listen
In the Dreaming Hour
River's End
The Fountain

Sons of Poseidon:

The Immortal Sea

Pirates of Britannia Series (with Eliza Knight):
Savage of the Sea by Eliza Knight
Leader of Titans by Kathryn Le Veque
The Sea Devil by Eliza Knight
Sea Wolfe by Kathryn Le Veque

Note: All Kathryn's novels are designed to be read as stand-alones, although many have cross-over characters or cross-over family groups. Novels that are grouped together have related characters or family groups. You will notice that some series have the same books; that is because they are cross-overs. A hero in one book may be the secondary character in another.

There is NO reading order except by chronology, but even in that case, you can still read the books as stand-alones. No novel is connected to another by a cliff hanger, and every book has an HEA.

Series are clearly marked. All series contain the same characters or family groups except the American Heroes Series, which is an anthology with unrelated characters.

For more information, find it in **A Reader's Guide to the Medieval World of Le Veque**.

About Kathryn Le Veque

Bringing the Medieval to Romance

KATHRYN LE VEQUE is a critically acclaimed, multiple USA TODAY Bestselling author, an Indie Reader bestseller, a charter Amazon All-Star author, and a #1 bestselling, award-winning, multi-published author in Medieval Historical Romance with over 100 published novels.

Kathryn is a multiple award nominee and winner, including the winner of Uncaged Book Reviews Magazine 2017 and 2018 "Raven Award" for Favorite Medieval Romance. Kathryn is also a multiple RONE nominee (InD'Tale Magazine), holding a record for the number of nominations. In 2018, her novel WARWOLFE was the winner in the Romance category of the Book Excellence Award and in 2019, her novel A WOLFE AMONG DRAGONS won the prestigious RONE award for best pre-16th century romance.

Kathryn is considered one of the top Indie authors in the world with over 2M copies in circulation, and her novels have been translated into several languages. Kathryn recently signed with Sourcebooks Casablanca for a Medieval Fight Club series, first published in 2020.

In addition to her own published works, Kathryn is also the President/CEO of Dragonblade Publishing, a boutique publishing house specializing in Historical Romance. Dragonblade's success has seen it rise in the ranks to become Amazon's #1 e-book publisher of Historical Romance (K-Lytics report July 2020).

Kathryn loves to hear from her readers. Please find Kathryn on Facebook at Kathryn Le Veque, Author, or join her on Twitter @kathrynleveque. Sign up for Kathryn's blog at www.kathrynleveque.com for the latest news and sales.

Ingram Content Group UK Ltd.
Milton Keynes UK
UKHW021052140723
425136UK00014BA/389